"So what? You staged [...] myself in your arms and [...]" Mia demanded.

"Not a bad idea, actually." Nick's smile was slow, its intensity making her shiver. "But no, this isn't a trick. I was called off the assignment. Technically I'm on my way back to Washington."

"But you're not." She chewed the side of her lip, trying to determine where the truth lay.

"No." He shook his head.

Their gazes met and held, and she struggled with herself, one side arguing that he was the enemy, the other desperately wanting to accept that he could be an ally. She sure could use one.

"So what happens now?" she finally asked.

"We get you out of here. And then we try to find some answers."

Their eyes met again, and she could almost feel him probing, trying to read her in the way she'd tried to read him. The only difference was that she had nothing to hide...

DEE DAVIS

CHAIN REACTION

HQN™

ISBN-13: 978-0-373-77206-3
ISBN-10:   0-373-77206-8

CHAIN REACTION

www.HQNBooks.com

Printed in U.S.A.

In memory of my grandfather,
George R. Bailey

S. AMDT.1020 to H.R. 2316: To provide continuing funding in the State of Idaho for environmental impact studies of nuclear testing sites on the Snake River Plain aquifer and the adjacent Caribou National Forest.

PROLOGUE

"HERE YOU GO." Nancy Wilcox placed the paper bag in front of Mia Kearney, studying the younger woman with a maternal eye. "I put a Danish in there with the coffee. You don't eat enough."

"Patrick's pastries play havoc with my waistline," Mia laughed, patting her stomach for effect. "One a week is the limit."

"Well, it's only Monday," Patrick called through the window between the café and the kitchen. Nancy shot an indulgent look at her husband. Still handsome at fifty-eight, he was happier than she'd ever seen him. Cedar Branch had done right by them.

Which was saying a lot, considering she'd dragged her heels every inch of the way four years ago when Patrick had announced he'd had enough of corporate life and was buying a restaurant. And matters had only gotten worse when she'd realized said restaurant was out in the boon-docks of southeastern Idaho.

But in truth, Cuppa Joe had been the best thing that had ever happened to them.

"Go on, take it, Mia," Patrick said. "Nancy's right, you need to eat." His paternal tone made Nancy smile.

It was Mia who'd sold them Cuppa Joe. Or rather, her grandfather's lawyers had done so. Patrick and Nancy hadn't actually met Mia until after they'd moved lock, stock and barrel to the tiny hamlet nestled at the foot of the mountains.

Leo Kearney had been the biggest rancher in the area. And as such, he'd accumulated a large amount of property, most of it in Cedar Branch. In its day the town had rivaled any outpost on the northwestern frontier. Boasting two stockyards, sixteen saloons, five hotels and some of the best brothels in a four-state area, Cedar Branch had had it all.

But nothing was forever, and when trucking replaced the railroads, Cedar Branch died, the Northern Pacific shutting down the rail line, the new interstate passing the town by. A post office, the café and a gas station were all that remained of the once booming main street. Added together with Buster's Bar and Sly's Feed Store, you had the sum total of what was left.

Still, the fact that the town had seen its heyday didn't seem to faze the locals. The ranchers and farmers in the area depended on Cedar Branch. It was their lifeline. And thanks to Patrick's cooking, Cuppa Joe had become the heart of the community.

Nancy pushed the bag toward the younger woman. "You know better than to argue with Patrick."

Mia still owned her grandfather's house, which abutted the café. Referred to by most everyone as the Town House, the structure had seen better days, but Mia didn't seem to care. The building, she swore, was perfect for her studio. And because it was literally only a few steps from the café, she took most of her meals there—when she remembered to eat.

"All right," she said, holding up her hands in mock surrender. "I'll eat it. But you have to let me pay for it."

"No way," Patrick hollered through the pass-through. "You're practically family."

"What about me?" Joe Biagio asked, waving a hand at his fully loaded plate of bacon and eggs. "I eat here all the time."

Patrick laughed. "Yeah, but you didn't sell us Cuppa Joe."

"I would have," he grumbled, "but you didn't give me the chance."

A third generation rancher, Joe, too, had property in town. Only it was so run-down the only way to use it would have been to tear down the existing structure and start from scratch. The café, however, had only needed a little elbow grease and TLC.

"Ain't no one going to buy that piece of crap, Joe," Wilson McCullough quipped from the stool beside him. "Better to just bulldoze it."

"Well, someone ought to use it," Joe grumbled.

"Maybe you should give up ranching and move into town," Wilson said, laughter coloring his voice. "You could open a knitting shop. I hear that's popular with the ladies these days."

Joe Biagio was an outdoorsman to his core, and the idea of him doing anything that involved the word *town* resulted in chuckles from several of the other morning patrons.

"How about a nursery, Joe?" Carson Greer goaded. "You were always good with kids."

"Hell," Joe said, "I'll just pay for the meal."

"Me, too," Mia said, resolutely pulling out her wallet. "It's not like I'm destitute."

In fact, just the opposite. To hear talk around town,

Mia's gallery in West Yellowstone was doing really well. And Nancy knew for a fact that she'd sold a couple of her own paintings recently. To be honest, Nancy wasn't sure exactly what to make of Mia's newer work. Called mixed media, her pieces often resembled a train wreck more than anything else, with bits of trash and bric-a-brac protruding from a wildly spray-painted and lacquered canvas. Patrick called it a combustion of art.

Nancy just tried to be supportive, although in truth she preferred Mia's earlier style. Portraits in charcoal, landscapes in watercolor. Traditional, yes, but still hauntingly original. At least as far as she was concerned. But then, heck, what did she know?

"Fine. We'll take your money." Nancy smiled. "But I want you to eat the Danish, all right?"

Mia nodded solemnly, her seeming acquiescence negated by the mischievous curve of her grin. Nancy handed over the sack and shook her head. "I'll call you around dinnertime if I haven't seen you before."

"If I've hit my groove, I'm not stopping, Nancy," she said, pushing off of the counter stool. "This piece is commissioned, which means I have to finish it on time."

Mia's latest work involved etching, and she'd taken to working in the old house's basement, trying to duplicate some kind of ancient technique. In plain truth, it made Nancy nervous as hell. All those chemicals and solvents. It was a wonder Mia hadn't addled her brains. But it wasn't Nancy's place to protest.

"You just be careful down there," she said, handing her a napkin. "Patrick and I worry about you."

"And I love you for it." Mia smiled over her shoulder, heading out the back door toward her studio.

"That girl needs a husband," Nancy said, reaching out to pick up an order of pancakes.

"That *young lady*," Patrick corrected, eyes twinkling, "needs a little less mothering, if you ask me. You're going to drive her crazy with your nagging."

"Me?" Nancy scoffed, setting the pancakes in front of Carson. "You're the one who bakes apricot Danishes even out of season just because she loves them. If I didn't know better, I'd say you were sweet on the girl."

"I've only got eyes for one woman, Nancy Wilcox, and she's standing right in front of me." Her husband reached through the opening to cup her cheek.

"Aw, come on," Joe said, ever the confirmed bachelor. "Give us a break, it isn't even ten o'clock yet."

"I think it's sweet," Betty Freeman said, holding out her cup for more coffee.

"You would." Joe tucked into his eggs, blatantly ignoring the wistful look on Betty's face.

The two of them had been an item a few years back, Joe escaping by the breadth of his John Deere cap. Betty still kept the torch burning, but Nancy figured it was a lost cause.

Outside, a loud noise broke through the shimmering August heat, the reverberation rattling the glass in the front window. Betty frowned at the clear blue sky outside. "Was that thunder?"

"Don't think so. Look at the sky." Joe said, swiveling the stool so that he could see out the window.

"Could be a car backfiring," Wilson suggested.

"Nah." Joe shook his head. "Too loud for a car."

"Maybe one of the tractor trailers from over on the highway?"

Since the interstate was almost twelve miles away, that

didn't make much sense. Nancy looked over at Patrick, trying to figure out why the sound bothered her so much.

"Could have been an explosion," Patrick said.

"Here?" Betty's eyes widened as an idea took hold.

"I don't see any smoke or anything." Carson had crossed over to look out the window. "Could it be the tree-huggers?"

There was some kind of ecological facility located close to Cedar Branch. It was all very hush-hush. Electrified fences and scientific types coming and going. They'd been told it was something to do with nuclear plant fallout. Some twenty years back, the area had been home to a nuclear plant. But the political tide had turned and the plant was long gone.

Residents had sent thankful prayers heavenward and gone on about their business. But apparently there were still worries.

"Don't think they're likely to be doing anything that'd cause an explosion. Probably was something up on the highway, like Wilson said."

"Didn't come from the right direction for it to be the highway," Joe said, turning back to his eggs. "Can't be anything too important or we'd be able to see it."

"The sky looks a little hazy," Carson observed to no one in particular. But he was right. The air outside had taken on a misty cast, even though the sun was still shining. Almost as if there were tiny raindrops filling the air.

Nancy blinked, and the illusion disappeared. Obviously her imagination working overtime.

Patrick had come out of the kitchen to join the others at the window. "Well, something's going on." He pointed up the street to a white Buick that had stopped in the middle of the road, its driver leaning drunkenly against the open door.

"There's another one," Betty said, pointing in the opposite direction.

Nancy followed her line of sight. Sure enough, a blue pickup was sprawled across both lanes of traffic, the driver on his knees on the pavement outside the truck.

"It feel hot in here to you?" Betty asked, the front of her dress soaked in perspiration, her cheeks bright red as she struggled to draw in a breath.

"Not just hot," Carson choked out, his face also burning with color. "On fire. I'm on fire."

Nancy felt her own throat tighten, as if something was obstructing her airway. She tried to pull in a breath, but nothing seemed to be reaching her lungs. The raindrops were back, dancing across her vision like a gray curtain. Panicked, she reached out for Patrick, but he wasn't there.

Forcing herself to focus, she turned in a circle, trying to find her husband, and almost tripped over him lying at her feet. "Call for help," she managed to say, as she dropped to her knees beside him. He was gasping for breath, his skin ashen, his lips turning blue.

Behind her she heard someone drop the phone, the clatter of the receiver punctuated by the clanging of one of the metal counter stools hitting the floor. Glancing over her shoulder, she saw Joe beside the fallen stool on his hands and knees, fighting for breath, trying to reach the telephone.

"Patrick, can you hear me?" Nancy gasped, returning her attention to her husband. "Open your eyes, sweetheart." She fought against a wave of nausea and dizziness, her lungs feeling as if a vacuum were sucking out all of the air she was fighting so hard to pull in. Her heart was pounding, the muscles in her chest contracting so fiercely she thought they might explode.

"Can't breathe," Patrick whispered, his blue eyes fluttering open. "What's happening?"

Nancy opened her mouth to respond, but couldn't find the power to get the words out. She shook her head, her body starting to feel like jelly, the mist in front of her eyes thickening with each passing second.

Another thud behind her signaled someone else down. She twisted her head, forcing her vision to clear. Betty. Betty was on the floor by the window, Carson facedown just beyond her. Neither of them moving.

A couple in the back were passed out across the table. Nancy could see them, still holding their forks.

"Patrick?" she whispered, curling up beside her husband, the cold tile floor comforting against her burning skin.

Slowly he turned his head, his hand tightening on hers, his eyes cloudy. "I love you, Nancy." His voice cracked with the words, and his fingers loosened.

"Patrick?" she called again, even though she knew he was gone. She struggled for a breath, knowing it was pointless. Her last cognizant thought was that at least she wouldn't have to live without Patrick.

CHAPTER ONE

"WHAT THE HELL AM I doing here?" Mia Kearney paced around the hospital room, talking to herself, the monitor behind her beeping in agitation as she moved too far away, stretching the leads that connected it to her body.

Despite all the testing and probing, as best she could tell there was nothing wrong with her. Nothing, at least, that she could identify. She hadn't seen anyone except medical personnel since she'd woken up a couple days ago. At least she figured it was about two days. There wasn't a clock, and no one would give her straight answers. Only that there had been a nuclear accident of some kind, the resulting radiation affecting the people of Cedar Branch.

She'd asked to see someone else. To talk to Nancy or Patrick, even Joe. But so far they'd insisted she was better off in isolation.

Her mother had always hated the idea of all the nuclear reactors in Idaho, predicting dire consequences if the plants weren't closed. Well, time had proven her mother right—if not in Idaho per se, then with incidents like Three Mile Island and Chernobyl. All of which meant that most of the reactors in Idaho were gone. There was still a test facility, but it was miles from Cedar Branch.

Which left Mia with a load of unanswered questions. Maybe a silo? The remains of cold war posturing were scattered throughout the Northwest, but she'd always been told the nearest live missiles were in Montana. Seemed a little far away to cause a local accident. Maybe it was an attack of some kind? But why would terrorists focus on Cedar Branch? There weren't more than fifty people in the whole county, and only a handful in town at any point in time.

Not that Idaho was devoid of crazies. There were extremist groups all over the state. People who believed that violence was the only way to solve problems. But as far as she knew none of them lived nearby. And even if they did, Cedar Branch wasn't the kind of place one chose as a target.

New York or L.A., or even Boise, would be a better place to garner the kind of attention terrorists wanted. It just didn't make any kind of sense. And to top it all off, Mia didn't feel the least bit sick.

She'd racked her brain trying to remember the symptoms of radiation poisoning, but hadn't come up with anything concrete. Still, she was pretty damn certain that by now she'd be a lot sicker if she had in fact been exposed. All of which begged the question she'd voiced earlier.

What the hell was she doing here?

She'd stopped taking the sedatives they were giving her, pretending to ingest them and then flushing them down the toilet. She just acted dazed whenever hospital personnel were in the room. But it was getting harder to be cooperative, everything inside her signaling that something was very wrong.

And it didn't help that her memory seemed to have gone wonky. The last clear thing she remembered before waking up here was buying coffee from Nancy. They'd talked about Danishes and eating and free meals. And then she'd gone to her studio and, after a couple of bites of food, had begun to work. Just thinking about her latest project ratcheted up her agitation.

The piece had been commissioned by a collector in Sante Fe. He'd seen some of her work at the gallery and requested a piece for his wife. It wasn't an exhibition in SoHo, but it was a step in the right direction. And opportunities like that didn't come along every day. All the more reason to get out of here and back to her own life. She'd tried leaving once, but hadn't made it three feet down the hall before an orderly with arms like steel girders had intercepted her and escorted her back to her room.

From then on the door had been kept locked. As if she were a threat or something.

And to make it all the more confusing, the brief glimpse she'd had of the hallway hadn't looked like any hospital she'd ever seen.

Crossing her arms, she fought to contain a shiver. Now she knew what Alice had felt like at the bottom of the rabbit hole. Only Mia didn't have a little bottle to help her get out the door.

As if on cue, said door swung open, sending her scrambling for the bed.

"You're up." The man in the doorway was a stranger—and unlike the rest of the staff attending her, not dressed in scrubs. It was almost absurd, the relief she felt at the sight of someone so seemingly normal.

"I was just testing my legs." She sat down on the bed,

her feet swinging above the floor making her feel all of about two. Resisting the urge to stand up again, she tucked her legs underneath her instead, careful to keep the blue cotton gown strategically covering all the requisite places.

The man smiled, the expression easing the harsh cast of his features. Not handsome by any kind of standards, his face was still interesting, and her fingers itched for pencil and paper. The sharp angle of his jaw was bisected by the faint white line of a scar. Dark hair curled around his ears and temples, a silky wash of blue on black. His mouth hinted at a sensuous side, the sardonic twist of his lips almost making her want to reach out and touch them.

Touch him.

She fisted her hands. This was a dangerous man, his stance predatory, his veiled green gaze cautious and knowing all at the same time. Whoever this was, he was not her friend.

"So how'd it go?"

For a moment she had no idea what he was talking about, then realized he was looking pointedly at her legs. "Better than yesterday. But I think all the drugs are playing havoc with my coordination." Of course, she wasn't actually taking all of them, but he didn't know that.

"They have a way of doing that." He shrugged, his eyes probing hers as he held out his hand. "My name is Nicholas Price."

Mia hesitated, not sure exactly why she still had reservations about touching him. Maybe just because he was the first person who'd been anything but perfunctory with her since she'd woken up to find reality altered. "Mia Kearney," she said, shaking his hand for only the briefest of moments before retreating farther back onto the bed. "But then I suspect you already know that."

"Yes, I do." His voice was mild, almost soothing, the sound puzzling. Nicholas Price didn't look like a gentle man. "I understand you've been through quite an ordeal."

"So I've been told. But I don't remember anything traumatic. Except maybe being in here." She hadn't meant for the last to slip out. And an ugly idea occurred to her. "Are you a shrink?"

Nicholas laughed, the sound genuine, buoying her heart even as she questioned his sincerity. "If you only knew how ridiculous the idea is. No. I'm not even a doctor. I work for the government."

Her mother had always made that word seem dirty, but Nicholas Price used it as though it would explain everything. "Who exactly is it you work for, Mr. Price?"

"Most people call me Nick." There was a false note of congeniality in his voice. As if he wanted her to believe he was her friend.

But he wasn't.

"I'm not most people." She pitched her voice to match his tone, and offered a smile.

Amusement crested in his eyes. "I can see that. Mind if I sit down?" He tilted his head toward the lone chair in the room. A dilapidated ladder-back that looked as though it had seen better days.

"It's your prison."

"Now why would you say that?" His expression was back to guarded, and she wondered what she'd said to put him on alert.

"Because the door's locked?" She waved at the door as if looking at it would prove her point.

"Maybe they just want to be sure you stay put."

"Now there's a blinding glimpse of the obvious. Look,

why don't we just skip the social niceties. I'm a captive audience, Mr. Price. So just get on with it."

She might have been mistaken, but she thought she saw the slightest hint of admiration in his gaze. Not that she gave a damn.

"I want to know what happened out there, Mia." His use of her first name grated on her nerves. She wasn't a kid and she didn't know him from Adam. But she held her tongue. There wasn't much point in arguing.

"I already told you, I don't remember anything."

"Well, I'm not sure I believe you. Your doctors say there isn't any physical reason why you can't remember."

"So maybe I wasn't conscious when it happened."

"It?"

"The nuclear meltdown or whatever it was. They haven't really been all that forthcoming."

"It was an explosion. At least that's what the briefing papers call it."

"Papers?" She couldn't help the question.

"That's all we've got to work with at the moment. The site's too hot. No one's going in there right now."

"The site. You mean Cedar Branch?" She frowned, trying to assimilate the information. "So is everyone else here, too?"

"As far as I know you're the only survivor."

"I'm sorry?" Panic rose, bitter in her throat, threatening to cut off her air supply.

"I said you're the only one who survived."

"People were killed?" The surprise in her voice must have alarmed him, and he looked away, clearly realizing he'd said too much. "Come on, Mr. Price—Nick—you can't just drop something like that on me and then clam up." The back of her eyes tightened with tears. "How many people are dead?"

He paused, still staring down at his hands, then looked up. "Everyone was killed, Mia. Everyone living in Cedar Branch is dead."

Her brain reeled as she tried to understand what he was telling her. Nancy, Patrick—Joe. All of them gone. "You're lying."

"Why would I do that?"

Bile filled her throat, the edges of her vision fading to black. She fought against her terror, trying to stay focused—to stay in control. "I don't know. But it can't be true. They can't all be dead."

He was beside her suddenly, holding a trash can as she lost her battle with her stomach, his big hand stroking back her hair as she expelled everything inside her.

"I'm sorry," he whispered, "I thought you knew."

"I want to see the bodies," she demanded, fighting against the continuing waves of nausea.

"I'm afraid that's not possible," Nick said. "They were incinerated in the blast."

She struggled to find her composure, to stop the roiling in her gut, but it was simply more than she could handle. A commotion at the door indicated the cavalry had arrived, except that Mia felt certain they weren't there for her.

A nurse pushed Nick aside, and for a befuddled moment Mia had the urge to reach for him. Fortunately, her hand wasn't up to responding. The nurse ordered him from the room, drawing a syringe as she spoke.

Mia fell back against the sheets, mind still reeling, and held out her arm, for the first time since she'd awoken into this nightmare grateful for the sedative.

"WHY THE HELL DIDN'T YOU tell me she didn't know?" Nick stood in the corridor outside Mia's room, trying to control the rage that was surging through him. He wasn't against manipulating a suspect to get an admission, but he also wasn't in the habit of torturing people just for the hell of it.

"I didn't think it was necessary." James Waters shrugged, clearly unperturbed by the pain his omission had caused. Waters was the doctor assigned to Mia's case, a government flunky who wouldn't have lasted a day in private practice. "I was told to give you access to Miss Kearney. No one said anything about briefing you. I just assumed you were aware of the situation."

It was clear from his tone that the man resented the fact that he was here at all, but Nick didn't give a damn. If he'd needed people to like him, he'd have found a different line of work. "I was briefed. But no one told me she didn't know about her friends."

"How do you know they were friends?" Waters asked, his tone bland, but his eyes sparking with interest.

"I'd say it's pretty damn obvious. She's lived and worked in the area for most of her life. And if that wasn't proof enough, one look at Mia's face after I told her certainly convinced me."

He was mildly surprised that he'd used her first name. After all, he'd just met the woman. But then holding someone's hair while they puked had a way of cutting through all the bullshit.

The doctor shrugged. "Davies didn't want her to know." Charles Davies was heading the investigation. Director of the CIA's Security and Containment division, Davies was

a snake of a man. Nick had dealt with him in the p᠁
wasn't relishing a repeat performance.

"Does he suspect her?"

"You'd have to ask him. As far as I know, it's all pretty straightforward. A rig transporting a nuclear weapon lost control on the Old Dam Road. It broke through a guardrail, tumbled down the side of the mountain near Cedar Branch and slammed into a stand of pines. The result was a hell of an explosion that took out the town."

"Except for Mia Kearney."

"Exactly. She was found unconscious in the rubble of a house just off Main Street." Waters paused, his eyes narrowing. "So we brought her here. Obviously, we're trying to understand why she's still alive."

"A medical miracle." Nick didn't bother to keep the sarcasm from his voice.

Waters frowned. "I don't believe in miracles, Mr. Price. They'd put me out of business. But I do believe in anomalies, and I intend to find out why Miss Kearney is one."

"Then we're working on the same side." They were banal words, offered more in dismissal than anything else. Talking to underlings was a waste of time.

"Hardly." Waters's words were clipped. "We're assuming it was an accident. You're assuming it wasn't."

"I'm not assuming anything. I'm simply looking at the facts." Nick's bosses at Homeland Security had sent him here for answers, and he intended to get them. If not from Mia Kearney, then from the staff attending her.

"She was found at the edge of the destruction zone," Waters said, his fingers tightening on the clipboard he was holding. "So while she could have been in the truck, the odds are against it. Even if you assume delayed detonation, the radiation zone stretched something like half a mile beyond the physical destruction. She wouldn't have been able to escape."

"But the point is that she did. Which all by itself is suspicious. But when you add it to the facts that everyone else in the area was obliterated and that the woman was found in a nuclear shelter, I'd say that should be enough to raise a few red flags."

"Except for the fact that it was a fifty-year-old, homemade shelter that probably wouldn't have held up when it was new. Certainly after all this time it's doubtful that it would have been part of any terrorist scheme. Although it may have played a role in her survival."

"I thought you didn't believe in miracles."

"I don't. But I do believe in dumb luck. Sometimes a person is just in the right place at the right time." Again Waters shrugged dismissively. "Anyway, the point is that until proved otherwise, I'm treating Ms. Kearney as a victim. Like the rest of the people in Cedar Branch."

"Except that they're all dead, and she's not." Which set Nick's internal alarm bells ringing no matter what Waters had to say on the subject.

"But I'm telling you, all the evidence indicates that it was a tragic accident."

"And that's why Langley's S&C is involved?"

The doctor hesitated just a moment too long, and Nick wondered if he'd hit a nerve. "I don't know why any of the specific personnel on this project were called in. I only know that the orders originated in Washington."

That much was definitely true, and Gordon Armstrong, Nick's boss, wasn't happy about it. Turf wars were old hat between the CIA and Homeland Security, but this incident had uncharacteristically been passed off to the CIA's little known S&C division without so much as a by-your-leave to any other agencies. Considering the ramifications should it come to light that the so-called accident had been intentional, it was understandable that Gordon was pissed. And he'd pulled strings to make certain that Nick was allowed on site.

"Gentlemen, I think this discussion needs to be held somewhere more private." Charles Davies strode down the hall, his expression thunderous. Davies was short and square, his everyman looks helping him blend into the crowd. He was the kind of man most people misjudged, missing the steel that glinted behind his bland expression. But then, Nick wasn't most people. "If you'll follow me." Davies turned and walked back the way he had come, leaving Nick and the doctor to follow in his wake.

Nick had first dealt with Davies years ago in Lebanon, the bastard showing his true colors. Although they'd never been forced to work together, from time to time they'd connected tangentially as assignments had crossed agency lines. And Nick's opinion never changed. Bottom line— Charles Davies was a snake and Nick didn't trust him any farther than he could throw him.

Davies sat down behind the desk, motioning for Waters to close the door. Nick perched on the arm of the side chair, not wanting to give Davies the height advantage. Not a subtle move, but Nick didn't give a shit.

"Thanks to your blunder," Davies began without preface, "you've shut her down completely."

"She didn't seem exactly forthcoming before I told her, Charles."

"What did you think she was going to do?" Waters asked. "Shrug and say the losses were all for the greater good?"

"No. But unless she's one hell of an actress, she had no idea those people were dead, which means at least part of what she's been saying is true."

"Which would support what *we've* been saying all along." Davies leaned back in his chair, steepling his fingers. "This was an accident, Nick. Nothing more."

"I don't see it that way." Nick shifted on the arm of the chair, careful to keep both men in his line of sight. "The rig belonged to Kresky International, and they're not the type to skimp on security. If they were transporting something as volatile as a nuclear warhead, I guarantee you they would have made damn sure something like this couldn't happen. And what's even more interesting to me is the fact that *you* believe they could have made this kind of mistake."

Charles's expression gave away nothing, but his fingers tensed, a sure tell that Nick's comments had hit home. "We certainly haven't ruled out the possibility of sabotage. But there's not much left to examine. Just a hell of a crater and the clutter of debris at the edge of what was once Cedar Branch. But the little bit we have managed to work out indicates an accident. Add to that the fact that no one has stepped up to claim responsibility, and I think you're trying to build a conspiracy where there isn't one."

"It's not like I want it to be a terrorist attack," Nick said. "It's just that the pieces don't fit. You've got a survivor where there shouldn't be one. You've got one of the biggest contractors in the country moving materials that were probably classified, and definitely dangerous, across state lines. There should have been memos on the memo. Add in the fact that you're here, and it feels like something more than a tragic accident."

"Look, I just go where I'm told, and do what has to be done. The rest of the crap I let the suits take care of." Davies leaned forward, his expression grim.

"Then you'll understand why I have to follow through with this. Orders are orders. And mine are to debrief the girl."

"But she told you," Waters said, "she doesn't know anything. You just said her reaction was genuine."

"And I believe it was. But that doesn't mean she wasn't involved somehow. Her mother, Angela Kearney, was a political activist with connections to some pretty questionable people. And her grandfather was a staunch opponent to nuclear fission in all its incarnations. Particularly the danger of nuclear facilities to local populations."

"But this had nothing to do with a reactor." Waters frowned in obvious frustration.

"Yes, but the damage is comparable and definitely plays better on the news."

"Then why choose an out of the way place like Cedar Branch?" Davies asked, the question clearly rhetorical. "Besides, both the mother and the grandfather are dead. In fact, Miss Kearney has no living kin."

"That doesn't mean she doesn't share her family's radical tendencies."

"Fine." Davies stood, a sure indication that the meeting was over. "Talk to her, there's nothing I can do to stop you. Just try not to upset her any more than you already have."

"Like you give a flying fuck."

"I don't." Davies shrugged. "But I do want to know how she managed to survive an explosion that killed everyone else in the area, and your goading her into agitation isn't going to help me achieve my goal."

"Well, I sure wouldn't want to do anything to get in your way," he said, studying the other man, certain that Davies was hiding something. And accident or not, Nick wasn't leaving until he figured out what the hell it was.

CHAPTER TWO

"GET OUT OF HERE. I don't want to talk to you."

Nick ducked, just missing the pillow Mia threw at him. "You know I can't do that."

"I don't have anything to say to you." She sat cross-legged on her bed, her eyes shooting fire. She was no longer attached to the monitor, which he assumed signaled improvement. At least his pronouncement hadn't caused her any physical damage.

"I'm sorry about before. If I'd known you didn't know…"

She glared at him, then shrugged. "Someone would have told me eventually." She might be pretending not to care, but he could see the tension in her shoulders, the grief in her face.

"You lived in Cedar Branch most of your life, right?"

"Technically, I lived about fifteen miles away, at Thornyhold."

"Your grandfather's ranch," he prodded, knowing that sometimes the best way to gain someone's trust was to talk about comfortable things.

"Yeah." She eyed him suspiciously. "Although some of the time I lived with my dad's family in South America or with both parents when my dad's schedule allowed."

"Renaldo Vasquez. He was a jazz musician, right?"

"He played the sax. In a quartet called Mercury. But you already know that, Mr. Price."

"Nick," he corrected, "and I'd like to hear it from you."

She considered the idea as she leaned back on the bed, stretching out her legs, the blue gown she wore riding high on her thighs. In any other woman, he'd have thought it was meant as a distraction. But from what he'd seen, Mia Kearney was without artifice.

"Why didn't you take your father's name?"

"I was born out of wedlock." Her eyes flashed, daring him to make something of the statement, but he wasn't about to bite.

"But your parents were together, right?"

"Yeah. They just didn't believe in following the dictates of society."

"Like getting married."

She nodded still scowling. He'd hit a nerve, although he wasn't sure why.

"So, tell me about your father."

"I don't see what he has to do with what happened in town, but you're the boss." The defiant tone from earlier was still present, but it was tempered with resignation. As if she'd finally accepted that she had no choice but to cooperate.

Or maybe she was just exhausted.

"My father's gigs were primarily overseas. In England and Germany and other spots throughout Europe. He traveled too much for me to go to school, so while school was in session I lived with my grandfather while he and my mother went on tour. Then in the summers, some of the time, I'd get to go along for the ride. And if that didn't work, I'd stay with my *abuela*."

"In Colombia."

"You have done your research." Her voice held a note of censure. Probably an effort to get him to back off. But he'd tangled with suspects a hell of a lot more evasive than Mia Kearney. "My *abuela*'s been dead for almost twelve years."

"In my world, everything is relevant, Mia." He paused purposefully, the silence intended to intimidate. She lifted her hand to smother a yawn. So much for tactics. "According to your file," he continued, "you also spent a lot of time in Africa, Asia and the Middle East."

"When my dad wasn't playing, my mom put in time at some of the organizations she supported. Hunger relief, land mine removal, immunization efforts, anything that made the world a better place."

"Your mother was quite an activist."

"Is this what this is all about? My mother? I don't see what… My God, you think that what happened in Cedar Branch was an act of terrorism?" Mia swung her legs around so that she was sitting on the end of the bed, her fingers clutching the sheets.

"We think it's a possibility."

"Who? Who thinks that?"

"Homeland Security."

"That's where you work?" She was frowning now.

"Yes. Since its inception, actually."

"But the people, the doctors and that man, Charles Davies, they're not with Homeland Security."

"No." Nick frowned, trying to figure out what was going on in her head.

"So you aren't part of this." She waved at the room in general. Then hopped off the bed, surprisingly nimble.

"I'm not sure what you mean, exactly, but I don't work for Davies." Thank God.

"Can you get me out of here?" The question came out of left field.

"I haven't any control over that, Mia. I'm just here to ask you a few questions."

"And pin a terrorist attack on a dead woman." There was a new note of bitterness in her voice as she sank back on the bed. "My mother has been dead for five years. I don't see how you can think she had anything to do with the deaths in Cedar Branch." She stumbled a little on the word *deaths,* but otherwise held on to her composure.

"It's not your mother I'm interested in." He waited for the thought to sink in, and was rewarded by a scowl.

"Me? You think that I was involved?"

He shrugged. "It's an obvious conclusion. You were on site. You're still alive. And you have been seen meeting with some of your mother's associates."

"Her *friends.* I have been to see her friends. They worried about me when she and Daddy died."

"And that's what you were doing in Turkey and North Africa?"

"Grieving? Yes. That's exactly what I was doing. I needed to get away. To remember her. And she loved Turkey. And had lots of friends there. If your research was a little more thorough you'd know that I was in Africa working with a relief organization. It was a commitment my mother made and I felt honor-bound to fulfill it."

If he were a normal man he'd have been humbled by her words, but he'd met a hell of a lot of liars in his time and wasn't about to be suckered in by Mia Kearney. "Ammon Akkad has been on U.S. watch lists for almost fifteen years."

"Ammon cares deeply about his country. But I know nothing of his politics. Only that he was my mother's friend, and reached out to me when I was hurting and had no one else."

"Your grandfather was already dead?"

"He died the year before my parents."

"So you're all alone."

"Does that fit the profile for a terrorist?" She was back to being angry, and he found he almost preferred it that way. "How about being bright? Or being artistic? Does that fit the pattern, too?" She was standing again, her fists clenched. "I have a birthmark on my shoulder. Does that show a propensity for acts of treason?"

"Mia, I—"

"Or is this only about my parents," she continued, her anger energizing her. "Activism in the genes?"

"I'm just trying to connect the dots."

"How lucky that I have so many. Don't forget my grandfather. He was as conservative as my mother was liberal, but they were in agreement on one issue. They wanted the reactors out of Idaho. He fought as hard as anyone to close the facilities. And for the most part he was successful." She laughed, but there was no humor in the sound. "How ironic is it that when the unthinkable finally does happen, it's in his own backyard? So tell me, Mr. Price, is that what it boils down to—pedigree? Civil disobedience in the genes?"

"Causing a nuclear explosion isn't civil disobedience."

"No." She deflated as quickly as she'd become angry, her shoulders drooping at the reminder of what had happened. "It's a stupid correlation. But then so is the idea that the only explanation for my survival is that I was somehow involved." She sat on the bed again, staring down at her hands. "They were my friends, Nick."

He didn't ask who she was talking about. He knew. Nor did he comment on her use of his given name. Despite his thick layer of cynicism, even he could hear the note of anguish in her voice. Whatever else Mia Kearney was or wasn't, she had truly cared about the people in Cedar Branch.

"So tell me what you do remember."

"Not much. Images more than anything. I remember walking into Cuppa Joe—that's the café in front of my studio. I was in a hurry. Which isn't all that unusual. I'm a bit driven. Especially when I'm working on a piece." She blew out a long breath, still staring at her hands. "Anyway, I stopped in for some coffee. And Nancy insisted on giving me a pastry. Patrick always makes apricot ones. They're my favorite." She swallowed tears and lifted her head.

"Nancy was worried that I didn't eat enough, and we argued over whether or not I'd pay for the stupid Danish. They wanted me to come in for supper, and I told them I was too busy. It was the last time I was ever going to see them, and all we talked about was eating." She wrapped her arms around her middle and Nick fought the urge to offer comfort.

"After that you went to your studio?"

"Yes. I'm working on..." She stopped, correcting herself. "I was working on a commissioned piece. My first, actually. And I was behind deadline. So I was burning the candle at both ends to get it finished."

"Do you remember hearing or seeing anything unusual?"

She shook her head. "Nothing at all. I get kind of wrapped up in the work. Sometimes I lose all track of time. I remember feeling a little light-headed, and thinking

Nancy was right, that I should eat more, and then the next thing I recall is waking up here at Hotel Hell."

He smiled at her reference to the facility. "It's not that bad, surely."

"As prisons go." She sighed. "I just want to get out of here and get on with my life. Whatever's left of it. Surely you can understand that."

"And you can understand that until we get a handle on what happened out there, and why you skated through it all unscathed, you have to stay here."

"I don't think I'd use the word *unscathed*. I may not be physically injured, but believe me, there are going to be scars."

"I didn't mean to be flip." He wasn't certain why he was apologizing. Maybe it was the look on her face. He'd seen it in the aftermath of war, the survivors trying to make sense out of the incomprehensible, to pick up the pieces and go on. "Have you had any contact with any of your mother's *friends* recently? Are any of them here in the States?"

"No. I haven't seen anyone since I came back. I get a letter now and then."

"Did you keep the letters?"

"No." She shook her head. "I'm not big into stuff. Another hand-me-down from my mother."

"I take it you were living in your studio?"

"Only when I'm obsessed with my work. The rest of the time I live at the ranch."

"Your grandfather's house."

She looked down at her hands once more and blew out a long breath. "No. It's too painful. He was a crusty son of a bitch, my grandfather. But I loved him. Walking around his house, with all the memories—it's just too hard. So I've been living in an old line shack."

"*Line* shack?" Nick shook his head, trying to make sense of the word.

"It's a ranching term. A place where hands can stay when they're checking fence lines. On a spread as big as my grandfather's, that can take several days. I take it you're not a country boy."

"Born and raised in the city. Never saw farm animals up close until I joined the army." There'd been plenty in Bosnia. More often than not slaughtered, but he didn't share that fact.

"I should have known you were military. Something intense and dark, right? Like the SEALs."

"That's the navy. I was with Special Forces."

"It fits."

It was his turn to frown. "How so?"

"You're so still. It's like you barely even breathe. And yet there's energy all around you. Kinetic, almost frenetic. I can feel it when you walk into a room."

"Sounds a little too New Age for me."

"No. I didn't mean it like that. It's just that I see the world differently from other people. More clearly, you might say. It's part of being an artist, I think. " She offered a timid smile and he realized it was the first civil conversation they'd had. Although why the hell that mattered was beyond him.

"Have you always been into art?"

"Yes. In some form or another. Like every kid, I started with finger painting. But I've always been fascinated with texture. That's why I work in mixed media. I like working in three dimensions."

"So why not sculpt?"

"Because I don't have the patience. Or the talent."

"Well, I can't even draw a straight line, so you're one up on me."

"What time is it?"

The question was a total non sequitur, but he glanced at his watch, anyway. "It's almost five. Why?"

"I've lost all sense of time. That's all. And no one else will answer my questions."

"Sometimes doctors forget there's a person inside the patient."

"Particularly miracle ones, right?" She tipped back her head, the fluorescent light creating rivers of red in her long blond hair. "Did you know that there's no radiation in my system at all?"

"How do you know that?"

"I got a look at my chart. They didn't see me. Anyway, there was nothing about radiation. Funny, isn't it? Everyone I care about is wiped out in a nuclear accident, and not only do I survive, I show no traces of having ever been there at all."

CHAPTER THREE

"I DON'T KNOW WHAT to think, Gordon," Nick said into his cell phone as he poked his head out the office door to check the corridor again. Everything was quiet, no one about, but there were ears everywhere. "On the surface she appears to genuinely not have anything to do with this. But the pieces just don't add up. She hasn't been exposed to radiation. At least there's nothing in her charts."

He'd managed to check them himself. Which, considering how closely Waters guarded them, had been no small feat. But it was exactly as she'd told him. There was no mention of radiation at all.

"So unless she was wearing some kind of protective suit, I just don't see how the hell she could have been where they say they found her."

"It definitely sounds like there are discrepancies," his boss said, sounding as if he were in the next room rather than D.C. "But I'm afraid it isn't your puzzle to solve anymore."

"Come again?" Nick frowned into the phone. "I'm not sure I heard you right."

"There's nothing wrong with your hearing. I got a phone call about an hour ago from the Oval Office. The President wants to turn the investigation over to S&C."

"What the hell for?" He tried but couldn't contain his anger. "They're always pissing in our pond."

"Well, the crassness of the analogy aside, it's the President's pond, and he can choose whomever he likes to piss in it."

"So you just want me to pack it in? Despite all the inconsistencies?"

"Look, Nick, I don't like it any better than you do. But the truth is this President has a decided bias toward the CIA. And in point of fact we are playing for the same team. They're as capable as we are of figuring out what the hell really happened out there."

"Except that they've already bought into the idea that it was an accident."

"For all we know it *was* an accident. There still hasn't been anyone trying to take credit. Not even the crazies. Which supports the idea of it being exactly what it appears to be."

"Then how do you explain Mia?"

"The girl? I can't explain it. And frankly, now that we've been pulled off the case, we don't have to. Leave that to S&C. Let them be the ones to come up empty-handed for a change."

Nick had to admit there was a certain temptation in the idea. "Fine. It's out of my hands. When am I supposed to clear out?"

"I've got you booked on a flight first thing in the morning. There's no reason to stick around. There's nothing more for us to do."

"I still think we're better suited to the task than S&C."

"I'm not arguing," Gordon said. "But it's not our call."

"Right." Nick closed the phone, relief warring with agitation. On the one hand, he was more than happy to get the hell out of here, but a part of him couldn't help but feel that he was leaving things half-done.

Nothing here made sense. At least not in a rational, logical kind of way. But given enough time, he was certain he could have figured it all out.

An image of Mia hunched over on the side of her bed presented itself front and center. Why the hell was he feeling guilty about leaving her? He didn't even know the woman, and if there was any logic present at all, he was pretty damn certain she was at the center of it.

"Heard you're leaving us." Davies stood in the doorway, the hint of a smirk at the corners of his mouth.

"News travels fast. I only just found out myself."

"I got a fax from my bosses saying that we'd assumed principal authority for the situation. Figured that meant you were out."

"Yeah. Seems the President's changed his mind." Which in and of itself was annoying. First he called them in and then he yanked them out. Nick hated political leadership; it was so nonlinear. Give him the military anyday.

"Well, I'm sure there are real terrorists out there that need your attention." Davies was goading him.

But it didn't work. "You might want to consider the possibility a little more seriously yourself."

"We have considered it, Nick. And rejected the idea. And clearly the president agrees."

Which didn't make either of them right, just of one accord.

"So when you taking off?" Davies asked.

"Later tonight. I've got a flight out of Jackson early in the morning. Figured I'd catch a few hours of sleep here, then hit the road."

"Sounds like a plan. They're still serving in the cafeteria, if you're hungry." Davies made it sound like a damn hotel. "Oh, and Nick, I don't have to tell you that everything you've seen here is eyes only. As I said before, the president wants to keep this contained."

He nodded, not willing to dignify the request with a verbal answer. "And Mia Kearney?" he asked, unable to help himself. "What's going to happen to her?"

"We'll keep her here until we figure out why she wasn't affected like the others."

"But that could take months."

"It sucks." Davies shrugged, clearly not giving a shit.

Nick resisted the urge to punch the guy's lights out. There was too much history, and he couldn't trust his instincts. The truth was there was no sin in being a prick. Sometimes that's exactly what it took to get the job done. Without some kind of defense mechanism, there'd be no way to deal with the kinds of things they faced on a daily basis. The fact that this was Davies shouldn't have made a difference. But it did. There was no denying it.

"If I don't see you again, have a nice trip."

Nick sighed and wondered when it had all gotten so fucking political, turf wars and jurisdiction taking precedence over more substantive issues—like protecting the citizenry. Hell, maybe he was as big a bastard as Davies. After all, he was about to walk away at the whim of a President, without ever looking back.

But then that was the way of the world.

THE DOOR WAS UNLOCKED. It called to Mia as if it had a physical voice, and she paced the space at the end of the bed, trying to figure out what the hell she should do. The nurse had dropped a tray on the way out, meds rolling all over the floor. In her haste to clean up and get out of there, she'd forgotten to lock the door behind her.

Freedom beckoned, but Mia was frozen by indecision.

At least in here she knew what to expect. There was something to be said for routine. And in an odd sort of way she was protected against the horror of what had happened to her world. If she left, she'd have to face it. All of it.

But if she stayed, she'd be at the mercy of Homeland Security and the CIA and whoever else was involved in her incarceration. And despite her instincts to trust Nick Price, she knew that it would be a mistake. Nick, Davies, all of them. Their goals were completely at odds with her own desire to pick up the pieces and find a way to move on.

If such a thing was even possible. Everything she loved was gone. Dead. For a moment she faltered, her courage failing. Who was she kidding? There was nothing left to build on. Nothing at all.

She closed her eyes, her grandfather's voice echoing in her ears. *"Life is hard, girl. But you're a Kearney. And we come from strong stock. When all else fails, that'll see you through."*

Mia pushed away from the bed, forcing herself into action. Her grandfather was right. Grabbing her pillows, she placed them under the blankets, plumping and adjusting until the bedding took on the form of what she hoped could be mistaken for a sleeping human.

Next she edged closer to the door, her heart pounding. Even with her decision made, she realized there might not be a choice. There could easily be someone standing watch on the other side. Maybe that's why it was unlocked. She looked around the room, searching for a weapon. Something that could give her the upper hand.

The last time she'd escaped, she been manhandled into

returning. If she wanted to succeed this time, she needed to even the odds.

With minutes ticking by, she grabbed the ladder-back and flipped it on its side. Grasping one of the rickety legs, she twisted, satisfied when she felt it wobble. Using all of her strength, she jerked the leg free. Not the most lethal of weapons, but certainly better than nothing at all.

Returning to the room's entrance, she flipped off the lights, sucked in a breath and cracked the door open. The hallway outside was quiet, and blessedly empty. The nurse had brought Mia's bedtime meds, which meant that it was late. Or at least she assumed so. If there was ever going to be an opportunity, this was it.

She stepped out into the hall, the cement floor cold against her bare feet. Wherever she was, the building hadn't originally been intended as an infirmary. It was too austere even for a hospital.

The hall was a short one, and she made it to the end without any company. The perpendicular hallway extended to the right and to the left, the sound of voices emanating from a door about halfway along the passage on the right.

Left it was, then.

Waiting a minute to make certain the coast was clear, she turned left, heading toward the far end and hopefully the way out. She'd gone maybe a hundred feet when she heard the sound of footsteps from an intersecting corridor off to the right.

Scanning the doors around her, she picked one marked Storage and slipped inside, the dark surrounding her like an old friend. Holding her breath, she waited until the voices crescendoed and then receded.

She opened the door a tiny bit to check for signs of life,

the light from the hallway illuminating the cramped space. The closet was filled with cleaning supplies. Brooms, mops, detergents, and in the far corner, hanging from a hook, a pair of coveralls.

Clothes.

In seconds Mia had stripped off the hospital gown and pulled on the coveralls. They were huge, and she had to roll the arms and legs up several times to make them wearable. She still didn't have shoes, but at least her attire no longer sent neon signals that she was out of place.

Grabbing a baseball cap with a cleaning company logo, she jammed it on her head, tucking her hair underneath. Maybe it wasn't the best of disguises, but at the moment it was all she had. She thought about swapping her chair leg for a broom—the latter more unwieldy, but also less conspicuous, considering the getup—but rejected the idea. The chair leg was heavier and easier to swing. Better to choose weapon over cover. She'd just have to keep it out of view.

Checking again to be certain the corridor was free, she stepped back into the hallway, taking the passageway leading off to the right. At the far end she could see the tantalizing red lettering of an exit sign.

If only she could make it that far.

The hallway was still, the incessant hum of the overhead lighting the only noise. She moved as quickly as she dared, fighting the urge to break into a run. Better to keep calm. Blend in. The thought almost made her laugh, the idea of herself barefoot in oversize coveralls more in line with Ringling, Barnum and Bailey than some top secret government facility.

Still, you had to work with what you were given.

Another swell of voices, this time behind her, sent her

into an office of some kind. It was tempting to have a look around, but she knew there wasn't time. Besides, the idea of gaining her freedom meant more to her at the moment then trying to figure out what the hell was going on.

Leaning against the door, Mia searched for windows, disappointed to see that there were none. The office, in fact, was empty. Nothing on the desk except a phone. Instinct demanded she call someone, and she was halfway across the room when it hit her that there was no one to call.

Choking on tears, she forced herself to focus. She wasn't going to get out of here if she allowed her emotions to hold sway.

Cracking open the door, she checked the hall, relieved to find it empty again. The exit door still beckoned with its glowing sign, and she started to breathe easier as she got nearer.

This part of the hallway was darker, two of the overhead lights burned out, the third flickering ominously. But the darkness was her friend. All she had to do was traverse this last bit of corridor and she would be outside. Of course, she had no idea where the hell that would turn out to be, but anything was better than here.

As she neared the exit, a door to her right swung open, the door itself blocking access to the person emerging. It also kept them from seeing her, and using that advantage, she raised the chair leg, baseball bat style, and swung hard as a man stepped around the door into the hallway.

The chair leg connected to his midsection with a sickening *thwack,* and she swung again, this time connecting with the back of the man's neck as he bent over in pain.

Swinging a third time, she hit his head, relieved when he dropped to the floor.

Thank God for her grandfather and all those afternoons playing baseball. He'd always said she hit like a boy. Not that this was exactly what he'd had in mind.

Stepping over the man, she got her first good look at his face. Remorse flooded through her, but she pushed it aside. It wasn't as if she'd killed him. Adrenaline pumping now, she ran for the exit door and pushed it open, praying there wouldn't be an alarm.

After all the subterfuge, the starlit landscape seemed amazingly normal, an owl calling from somewhere high on the mountain. The air was crystalline, the first hints of fall already descending into the valley.

She recognized the topography. She wasn't all that far from home.

Running now, she headed away from the compound, the only remaining obstacle a barbed wire fence. But barbed wire wasn't much of a deterrent for a rancher's kid. Especially one with a will to survive.

As she shimmied beneath the wire, she heard noises behind her, light spilling out into the enclosure. Safe on the other side of the fence, she sprinted into the night, mindless of the rocks cutting into her feet, her only objective now to put distance between herself and her captors.

She stopped at the top of a rise to take a quick look behind her. The enclosure was still lit, the figure of a man silhouetted in the doorway. A part of her was relieved that he was all right. In his own way, he'd been kind to her. But it wouldn't be long now until he called for reinforcements.

Best she get a move on.

Turning away from the compound, she began to make her way up the ravine leading deeper into mountains, knowing that if she ever saw Nicholas Price again there'd be hell to pay.

CHAPTER FOUR

"DIDN'T THINK I'D LIVE to see the day when you were bested by a girl." Davies's amusement was tempered by his anger. "So what the hell happened?"

"She caught me by surprise. From behind." Nick frowned, gingerly rubbing the knot on the back of his head. "Thought it was a baseball bat, but it was a chair leg." He motioned to the object propped in the corner.

"From her room. Resourceful bitch."

"Surely that's a bit harsh. Under the circumstances you can't blame her for making a run for it."

"No thanks to you." Davies looked haggard. "At the very least she's a wild card. And at the worst—" he stretched out his hands "—well, you said it yourself, she could be a terrorist. You get anything conclusive out of her?"

"Nothing that confirmed anything."

"But nothing to deny it?"

"Look, I'm out of this investigation, remember? And if I had to guess, I'd say you had a hand in that. So why don't I just get out of your hair and leave it to you to round up Mia Kearney." He had absolutely no intention of letting her get away, but he also wasn't about to throw in with Davies and his lot.

"There's no sign of her, sir." A lackey stood in the doorway, a sniper rifle in his hand.

"Pretty serious method of subduing." Nick eyed the gun with interest. "I thought you wanted her alive."

"We do," Davies was quick to assure. "But it's best to be prepared for all eventualities." He turned his attention to the man at the door. "You've secured the entire compound?"

The man nodded. "And the outlying areas within about a hundred-yard circumference. We found where she went through the barbed wire, but after that there's no sign of her. And without a moon it's hard as hell to see anything out there."

"It's all right. She can't get far. We've got the whole area cordoned off. I've alerted all the outposts. My guess is she'll turn up by morning."

"Sounds like you've got it all figured out," Nick said, standing up and reaching for the duffel at his feet. "Which is my cue to exit."

"I hate to admit it, but we could use the extra man." Davies's scowl belied the request, and had the situation been less serious, Nick would have laughed.

"Not happening. My orders were to head out, and that's exactly what I'm going to do. I'll brief my superiors, but other than that you can count me out of this little fiasco. Kinda glad I don't have to stick around and clean up the mess, actually."

"Yeah, well, I can't say that I'll be sorry to see the backside of you." For a moment Davies held his gaze, his expression bordering on smug.

"Right, then." Nick turned for the door. Davies might think he'd gotten one over on him, but as usual, Nick was one step ahead of the game. "I'm outta here. Good hunting." He touched the tips of his fingers to his forehead and walked past the flunky with the gun. Two minutes later he was inside his rental car heading for the main gate.

Time was limited, and he knew that Davies and his team would eventually work out where Mia was. But at least for the moment he had an advantage. She'd mentioned the line shack. Now all he had to do was find it before someone else did.

According to his notes, Mia's grandfather's ranch was about fifteen miles due east of Cedar Branch, well out of the radiation zone. Using the GPS on his computer, Nick had managed to come up with a couple of likely spots for the line shack. But he couldn't take a direct route. Davies was too shorthanded to have him followed, but if by chance one of his flunkies saw Nick on the road to the ranch, he'd quickly put two and two together.

So Nick needed an alternative route. One that kept him away from S&C's checkpoints, away from Cedar Branch and its contamination, but still cut a short course to Mia and the line shack.

The guard at the gate waved for him to stop, and Nick tried to curb his irritation. No use creating suspicion.

"I just need to search your things, please." The man was polite, but there was a note of authority in his voice.

Fucking Davies. There was no question that this was his doing. The man got his rocks off making Nick's life difficult. "Fine," he said, handing over his duffel bag.

"I'll need to see your computer, too." The man nodded at the laptop lying on the passenger seat.

"What the hell for? It's password protected," he snapped. Davies was pushing his luck.

"It's just routine, sir. We check everyone going out."

"Think I've got Mia Kearney hidden in cyberspace?" He'd meant it as a joke, but the guard didn't seem to have a sense of humor. "Here. Take it."

He sat back against the car seat, drumming the steering wheel with his thumbs, imagining various ways to stick it to Davies. The bastard had been a thorn in his side from day one. Truth was he'd be happy to see the last of this place. And just for a moment he considered ignoring his gut and heading for the airport. Let Davies deal with Mia Kearney. The woman had a hell of a swing.

He rubbed the knot on the back of his head and grimaced. There wasn't any way he was letting this go. If for no other reason than the pleasure he got thinking about trumping Davies.

"Here you go," the guard said, handing him the duffel and computer. "Sorry for the inconvenience."

"No problem." Nick threw the bag in back and returned the computer to the seat next to him. Then, with a mocking salute, he drove through the gate. From there he purposely headed for the road to Jackson, following it about two miles before pulling off to the shoulder. The cedar trees lining the pavement raked the side of the rental, but Nick barely registered the noise.

Turning off the engine, he opened his computer, hoping that the built-in GPS would still be able to triangulate. It took a few minutes, but technology won the day and a map appeared on the screen, a dark blip indicating the stand of trees and his car. He studied the map. The area was practically a wilderness, Cedar Branch the only bit of civilization for miles, a hub for all the farmers and ranchers in the area. And now it was gone.

Along with most of the people who had lived there.

Nick wasn't easily moved. He'd seen too damn much in his life, but the death of Cedar Branch marked more than just the end of a town. It marked an attack on something

intrinsic to all Americans. A way of life. A simplicity that
deserved something better than annihilation. The transport
route had been chosen for a reason. No highways. Not even
main roads. The deserted back roads assuring that should
the worst occur, the costs would be minimal.

Tell that to the dead.

If it was an accident, it was reprehensible. If it was an
act of terrorism, the bastards deserved to fry. And either
way, Mia Kearney was the best chance Nick had at finding
answers. He snapped the computer closed and turned the
key in the ignition.

There was a spur road about a half mile ahead. Another
half mile or so on foot and he'd be at the ranch's property
line. From there he'd be able to find the line shack and,
with a little luck, the girl.

MIA SECURED THE BANDAGE on her foot. It was the last of
several, but considering the amount of ground she'd
covered, it could have been worse. After pulling on a pair
of thick socks, she gingerly slid her feet into her boots.

One step, then another and then one more. There was
pain, but nothing she couldn't handle. At least now she was
dressed for battle. Or whatever the hell came next.

The journey had been a rough one, the moonless night
acting as both friend and enemy. The dark sky had hidden
her from hunters, but also camouflaged the terrain, making
shadowy holes where there were none, and concealing
rocks and debris that tore at her feet. Still, all in all, she
was in remarkably good shape.

Considering what she'd been through.

The ranch was in the opposite direction from Cedar
Branch. A blessing, certainly. But a part of her wanted to

see the town firsthand. To see with her own eyes what had happened. But radiation was a dangerous thing, and even with the passage of time, it wouldn't be safe to go there. Not without the proper equipment. And while she considered the line shack well stocked, it didn't run to hazmat suits.

Crossing to the stone fireplace, she felt along the base of the mantel until she found the notch. Leo Kearney hadn't been a trusting man. Ranch hands were drifters by nature, and even in the line shack her grandfather had wanted a safe place.

She pushed the hidden latch and waited as a portion of the rough planked wall swung open. The cabinet behind the wall was only about three feet wide, but it ran from floor to ceiling. There was a strongbox and a half-dozen guns—mostly rifles—along with an assortment of medications meant for cattle.

Mia took the strongbox first, placing it on the table. The box was old, and rusting a bit at one corner, but the lock was still solid. She'd already retrieved the key, and with a twist of her wrist the box was open.

Inside were three stacks of bills. Small denominations, meant for the foreman. Money for whatever need might arise this far away from the ranch house. She'd meant to put it in the bank, but somehow she'd never gotten around to it, comforted somehow that her grandfather's idiosyncrasies had survived him.

And now—well, now she was just grateful she'd left it all alone. Pocketing one stack of bills, she took another and split it in two, stuffing half into her backpack and the rest in her boot. Probably a bit melodramatic, but in all honesty she had no idea what she was up against, and she figured it was better to be overprepared.

On that thought she walked back to the cupboard and pulled down a rifle. A Winchester, it was old but in perfect condition. She'd used it since she was a kid, her grandfather teaching her to shoot almost before she was big enough to hold the thing. Laying the gun on the table, she replaced the strongbox and, after taking a couple of boxes of ammo, closed the cabinet.

She turned back toward the table with a sigh. She might not have shared her mother's passion for lost causes, and she certainly didn't have her grandfather's innate suspicion of everyone he came in contact with, but she'd grown up with them both, and learned a lot in the process. Things that, hopefully, would keep her from being recaptured.

If nothing else, clubbing a Homeland Security agent with a chair leg was probably a federal offense. And she doubted that Nicholas Price was a forgiving sort of man. She loaded the rifle, put the remaining ammunition in the backpack and then, with a sigh, dropped down onto a chair by the table.

Adrenaline had seen her safely home and kept her moving, packing food and money and firepower, but now that she was finished, it seemed to have deserted her. She closed her eyes and massaged the bridge of her nose in an attempt to ease a pounding headache.

How in the world had it all come to this?

Just a few days ago she'd been laughing with Nancy in the café. Tears filled her eyes as she thought about her friend. *Friends*.

Patrick had been there, too, along with Joe and Carson, Betty and Wilson. Their faces flashed through her mind. If Nick Price was to be believed, they were all dead. Killed in an instant. A single flash of light.

The clock in the corner rang the hour. It was almost morning.

Tick-tock, seven o'clock…

The phrase sang through her head. An old story she'd loved as a kid. *There Will Come Soft Rains.* Everyone in the story had died. Even the house hadn't been able to withstand the nuclear blast.

She shook her head, banishing her thoughts. It served no one to get maudlin. What she needed was a plan. She could grieve later. After she understood exactly what had happened. When she was safe.

Safe. Now there was a word. When had she ever felt safe? Bounced around from one relative to another, she'd never really felt as if she belonged anywhere. Her father's world was made up of musicians and groupies, an unending stream of people intent on hanging on to Renaldo Vasquez's coattails.

Her mother, the original free spirit, had flitted from cause to cause. Whales, nukes, hunger, AIDs. She'd studied with philosophers and guerillas. Self-appointed prophets and militants. There'd even been a stint with the Dalai Lama.

And in between her father and her mother, there'd been her grandfather and the ranch. The mountains the one constant in her life. And yet, in the end, they'd betrayed her, as well, sucking her into a life she'd cherished. A real home. Real friends.

And now they were gone.

Anger replaced her melancholy and she grabbed the backpack, swinging it over her shoulder. The sooner she got out of here, the better. Her car was in Cedar Branch. Or at least it had been. But there was an old Scout in the shed outside. The truck had seen better days, but it was serviceable, its jeeplike traction making it ideal for off-roading across the ranch.

And it would serve her purposes now.

She knew she needed a plan, but the best she could figure was to get as far away as possible. Once she'd done that, she could better assess the situation and decide what to do for the long run.

She picked up the rifle and headed for the front door. Most likely she still had a lead on them. But every minute she lingered closed the gap. Stupidly, she'd told Nick Price about the line shack. And as much as she wanted to think he wouldn't remember, she knew that he would. Which meant she was wasting serious time.

The night sky was still star-filled, although they were beginning to dim, morning just around the corner. She stood on the porch, searching for signs of life. The rutted road was hard to spot, overgrown with grass and wildflowers. In the dim light everything was black and gray, but in her mind's eye, Mia could see the colors of the paintbrushes and lupines.

She'd miss this place.

But surely everything could be made right. After all, no matter what they suspected, her only real crime was surviving. She shivered against the predawn chill and turned to pull the door shut behind her.

As her hand closed around the knob, the still air exploded, the wood of the door frame splintering.

She froze for an instant, her mind scrambling for an explanation, but a second bullet answered the question, smashing into the door only inches from her hand. Shoving it open, she leaped inside and slammed it shut behind her, panting as if she'd just run a marathon.

Obviously, they'd found her, and any question she'd had about their motives was now painfully clear. They wanted her dead.

The image of Nick Price flashed through her brain. She'd actually been sorry she'd hurt him, but now she wished she'd hit him harder. He was the one who'd led them here.

If only she'd kept her mouth shut.

Keeping low and out of range of the windows, she moved to the door, dropped the heavy bar in place and killed the lights. She'd often kidded her grandfather about the antique locking device, but he'd only laughed. In his mind, older meant better. And just at the moment she was inclined to agree. It wouldn't be easy to break down the door.

Of course, there were always the windows, a helpful little voice in her brain reminded.

As if to underscore the fact, the right front window shattered, the spray of glass just missing the corner where Mia was crouched. Adrenaline surged again and she swung up into the opening, her eyes scanning the area for signs of movement.

Another bullet whizzed past her ear and she ducked, but not before she saw the flash emanating from the fence line about fifteen yards dead ahead. Her heart pounded in time with the clock as she struggled to think—hell, to breathe.

Counting to five, she forcibly slowed her breathing. And then, with determination forged from fear and anger, she swung up into the window, leveled the rifle and shot toward the fence line.

Two could play at this game.

Ducking back beneath the windowsill, she searched the room, trying to figure out how best to proceed. The shack was a one-room affair with an upstairs loft serving as her bedroom. There was no back door and only three windows. Two of them facing the front and the third in the back wall up in the loft.

The front windows were obviously of no use to her. The shooter's position was directly between them, giving him an easy shot should she emerge from either. The loft window was her best bet. The drop from there wasn't exactly her idea of a good time, but she was fairly certain she could manage it without serious injury.

The trick was going to be climbing the ladder. She could crawl over to it without being seen, but once she started up she'd risk being spotted, even in the dark. Still, it was better than sitting here waiting for him to come inside to get her.

She popped up and fired a round just to the right of where she'd seen the flash. If he had shifted that direction, he'd shift back. And if he hadn't, he'd hold his position, waiting for her to make the next move. It was a gamble, surely, but if it worked, he'd be out of alignment for a good shot at the ladder, which would buy her a few precious seconds.

Drawing a breath for fortification, she fired again, then ducked down and scuttled across the floor to the ladder. Without giving herself a chance for second thoughts, she began to climb, the rifle in her hand slowing her progress slightly.

A bullet shattered the second window, the glass successfully deflecting the shot. Three more rungs and she was out of range. A second shot rang out, the bullet lodging in the rung she'd just vacated.

Pushing herself up and over the last bit of ladder, she landed on the hard pine floor, heart pounding as she pushed forward until she could see over the edge. Everything was quiet. Which meant she only had seconds before the shooter realized what she was doing.

Securing her rifle in the side loop of her backpack, she moved to the window and pulled it open, the sash groaning with the effort, the sound seeming to echo through the air. She waited two beats and then, encouraged by the returning quiet, threw her leg over the sill.

Another shot ripped through the night, this one coming from somewhere in front of her. Either the shooter had anticipated her movements and shifted location or, worse still, there were two of them.

Whoever was out there, the shot had gone wild. But that didn't mean it wouldn't be closer the next time. She retreated back into the loft, cursing her luck. If only she'd moved faster. But there was no sense beating herself up over something she couldn't change. Better to stay in the moment and figure out another option.

If there were only one shooter, then maybe the front was clear. It was an idea, anyway, and just at the moment she preferred action to inaction. Still toting the backpack she shimmied down the ladder, jumping the last few feet to the ground.

So far, so good.

Scooting across the floor to the front door, she inched it open and, leading with the rifle, stepped out onto the porch. Gunfire flashed off to her left and a bullet embedded itself in the porch at her feet. Diving back inside, she ran toward the ladder again. If he was shifting positions, maybe she could fake him into moving.

All she needed was a decoy.

She eyed the room without inspiration, finally settling

on a cushion from the sofa. It wasn't exactly a stand-in for a human, but the color matched her sweater, and even with night vision glasses it would be hard to make out much more than movement inside the cabin from the fence line.

Tossing the pillow up into the loft, she was rewarded with another shot fired through the window. This one nicking the corner of the cushion.

Silence followed, and she resisted the urge to cut and run. She needed to give the man some time. Finally, her patience was rewarded. Another shot rang out, this one clearly coming from the back of the house.

Her ruse had worked.

She sprang forward, and was almost to the door when she heard a second shot. This one from the front of the house. Closer than before.

Her heart sank. There *were* two of them.

"Son of a bitch." The expletive came out of its own accord, the phrase a favorite of her grandfather's.

This was it, then. Mia released the rifle, squaring it on her shoulder, gripping it with both hands.

Whatever happened next, she sure as hell wasn't going down without a fight.

CHAPTER FIVE

FOR A MOMENT THERE WAS nothing but silence and the staccato beating of her heart. Then all hell seemed to break loose, both shooters opening fire at once. Bullets strafed the porch outside the door, and a couple sang through the broken panes of glass in the front windows.

Mia huddled behind the sofa, rifle ready, trying to keep her focus on both windows at once. The shooting grew closer, then stopped again, the silence almost more nerve-racking than the sound of gunfire.

Keeping to a crouch, she rounded the end of the sofa and crawled across the room until she was under the window. If either of the men showed himself, she'd be ready.

"He's gone."

The words reverberated through the room like a cannon shot and Mia whipped around as the lights came on, the rifle trained on the man standing at the top of the ladder. He was holding a gun in his right hand, but it was pointed at the floor.

"How the hell did you get up there?" she asked, her mind spinning as she struggled to assess the situation.

"Rope and a grappling hook," he said, lifting an arm to show the coil of rope wound around his shoulder.

She lifted the rifle, pointing the barrel directly at his chest. "So who's gone?"

"The guy from S&C."

"Left the dirty work to you?" She tightened her finger on the trigger.

"No. Figured two against one weren't exactly winning odds."

She digested the statement and rejected it. Nicholas Price wasn't on her side. "You're lying. This is just a trap." She glanced over her shoulder, relieved to see that the second shooter hadn't materialized.

"If this were a trap, it would already have been sprung." He shrugged as if this kind of thing were an everyday occurrence. For him, maybe it was.

"Throw down your gun."

"Now why would I want to do that?" His smile was disarming, but she wasn't buying.

"Because if you don't, I'll shoot." She leveled the rifle, the gesture meant to underscore the point.

His smile broadened, his gun arm still relaxed at his side. "Somehow I don't believe that."

She shot on instinct, anger and confusion spurring her on. The bullet whipped by his right shoulder, missing by a fraction of an inch. At least she'd wiped the smile from his face.

Her victory, however, was momentary. He jumped from the loft and in one swift move managed not only to disarm her, but to pin her against him, arms behind her back. She fought to break his hold, but he was too strong.

"I should have killed you," she said, struggling to contain her fear.

"You're not a killer, Mia." His breath was hot against

her cheek, an implied intimacy in his tone. It grated on her, and she kicked back with one foot, connecting satisfyingly with his shin.

"I might not have been one two days ago, but considering you've just spent the last half hour trying to kill me, I think I'm up to the task."

He twisted her around so that she was facing him. "Believe me, if I'd wanted you dead, you'd be dead."

It was an arrogant statement, but she had no doubt it was the truth.

"And your friend outside? The man from S&C?" She repeated his acronym, not knowing what, exactly, it stood for, but more than certain it meant enemy.

"I told you, he's not my friend. And for the record, he's not out there anymore. I scared him away."

"You?" She sounded like a monosyllabic idiot, but it was hard to think with him only inches away.

"Yes. Me." He was back to looking amused again.

"You were shooting at me, Mr. Price. I saw the flash of your gun from the loft window." She drew a breath, trying to calm herself, to think. Her rifle was on the floor by the chair, if she could just find a way to break free. He was clearly better at this sort of game than she was, but once reinforcements arrived she didn't stand a chance.

"I was shooting at the man out front. If I'd been shooting at you, you'd be dead."

"So you said." She glared up at him, twisting her wrists to try and break free.

"Look." He spoke slowly, as if she were three. "Whoever it was out there, he wasn't trying to kill you, either. He was trying to keep you penned inside. I shot at him when he rounded the corner of the cabin. If I hadn't, he'd have nabbed you when you dropped from the window."

"The hell he would have." The words came out of their own volition, and he smiled again, the sentiment not quite reaching his eyes.

"Look, sunshine, I'm sure you're more than a match for most men. But I seriously doubt you're up to evading S&C. At least not on your own."

"You might be surprised at what I'm capable of." The minute the words were out, she regretted them. But there was no taking them back.

His eyes narrowed, and she struggled again to break free. "I can always leave you here on your own. The guy's gone for now, but he'll certainly be back—with reinforcements."

A rock and a hard place if ever there was one. She needed help, but she didn't trust Nick Price. She stared up at him, trying to read his expression. "What the hell *is* S&C?"

The question seemed to catch him by surprise, and he loosened his grip. Taking advantage of the situation, she broke free, diving for the rifle, but he was faster, tackling her with the full force of his body.

Dazed, she struggled to breathe under his weight, thrashing against him, trying to make him move. "Can't breathe." The words were hardly more than a whisper, but he heard her, the pressure easing immediately.

She rolled to a sitting position, her breath still coming in gasps.

He sat unfazed on the floor across from her, casually holding her rifle. "I'll say one thing, Mia, you don't go down easily."

"Can't say the same for you."

He rubbed the back of his head, his green eyes glittering. She knew better than to poke a wildcat, but truth be told, she'd never been good at keeping her mouth shut. Sticking her chin out in defiance, she held her ground.

A minute passed, and then suddenly he smiled, his eyes crinkling with laughter. "I see you don't mince words, either. Your grandfather would be proud."

She scowled at him, frustrated by his seemingly effortless ability to keep her off balance. "Don't pretend you know me or my grandfather."

His expression darkened as he studied her for a moment, eyes narrowed, and then he shrugged. "S&C means Security and Containment." The non sequitur confused her for a moment, but her head finally cleared and she realized he was answering her question. "It's an elite corps within the CIA. They handle things that no one else wants to deal with."

"Like Cedar Branch." She hadn't meant to respond, but her need to understand what had happened overcame all other sentiment.

"Exactly." He nodded, as if he sympathized.

"But you're not S&C. You're Homeland Security." He'd told her that earlier, but suddenly she wondered if it had been a lie, something meant to get her to open up to him, confess that she'd been involved in the explosion somehow.

Well, it hadn't worked then and it wasn't going to work now.

"That's right. I was called in after the fact. After S&C was already in place."

"The right hand checking up on the left?"

"Something like that." He nodded again, his expression carefully guarded, but she could tell that she'd hit a nerve. Nicholas Price wasn't as cool a customer as he'd have her believe.

"So, what? You staged this little ruse so that I'd throw myself in your arms and tell you everything?"

"Not a bad idea, actually." He smiled. "But no, this isn't a trick. I was called off the assignment. Apparently the powers that be aren't all that keen to have extra scrutiny. S&C is in charge, and technically, I'm on my way back to Washington."

"But you're not." She chewed her lip, studying him, trying to determine where the truth lay.

"No." He shook his head.

Their gazes met and held and she struggled with herself, one side arguing that he was the enemy, the other desperately wanting to accept that he could be an ally. She could sure use one.

"So we're back to you trying to gain my trust to get at the truth."

"Only I'm not working with S&C." He shrugged, his lack of denial comforting in an odd sort of way. It was the first time she actually believed he was telling the truth. Of course, all it meant was that she had two enemies. But if she were perfectly honest, she'd have to admit she preferred Nick to the CIA.

"So what happens now?" It had probably been a foregone conclusion, considering that he held both the guns, but she was still surprised at how easy it had been to acquiesce.

"We get you out of here. And then we try to find some answers."

"You mean I spill my guts."

"If there's something to spill." Their eyes met again, and she could almost feel him probing, trying to read her in the way she'd tried to read him. Only difference was that she had nothing to hide.

"Except for what you've told me, I don't know anything at all."

"I almost believe you." It would have been a triumph, except for the cynicism that lurked in his eyes. Whatever he was, Nicholas Price was not a man who gave his trust easily.

"You said they'd be coming back."

"Right." He nodded, pulling away from his thoughts. "I need to get you out of here, but I can't do that if you're going to fight me the whole way."

"Well, you can't expect me to follow you around like a little lamb. I'm not the docile type." The tension between them was back, radiating through the room like a living, breathing thing.

"I never said you were. How about we settle for something between docile and spitfire."

"How about you give me back my rifle." She held out her hand, holding his gaze, waiting for him to make a move.

The seconds seemed to drag on forever, and then, with what sounded like a laugh, he handed it to her. "Spitfire it is."

She resisted the urge to shoot him on the spot, and instead motioned toward the far wall. He'd made the first move, now it was up to her to counter. "There are more guns in there. Do you want an upgrade?"

He frowned and then looked at the weapon in his hand. It was a lethal-looking handgun, but it didn't offer the luxury of distance. "I'm fine with what I have. Although on second thought, maybe we'd better have backup."

She noticed his use of the word *we*. Maybe it was all a trap, but for the moment she needed to give him the benefit of the doubt. And better that he thought she was buying into his act. The more compliant she was, the more likely he'd let down his guard.

It was win-win as far as she could tell. If he was telling the truth, then she had help. And right now she needed it. And if he was lying—well, then she'd just have to figure out a way to turn the game to her advantage.

LEO KEARNEY HAD A SMALL arsenal stored in the hidden cabinet in the line shack. Nick wasn't really surprised. If Mia was any kind of reflection of the old man, he'd been one tough hombre. He selected a rifle with a scope. Once Davies realized Mia had help, he'd double his efforts. And Nick had learned a long time ago that it was better to be prepared.

"That was Grandfather's gun. I used to wonder what he thought he was going to hunt with it." Mia was standing by the table, a backpack slung over one shoulder. "You should get some ammo, too."

She seemed to have accepted the situation with remarkable ease, but Nick wasn't fooled. She'd merely accepted the status quo—for now. Which worked to his advantage, actually. He wasn't ready to throw himself into her camp. At least not yet. Time would tell, and in the meantime, they'd just continue the dance.

He grabbed a couple of boxes of ammo for the rifle and tossed them to her. She caught them one-handed and then stuffed them into the backpack.

"What else you have in there?"

She stared at him for a moment, her look assessing, then she shrugged. "More ammo, some money, a change of clothes and some peanut butter." He raised an eyebrow and her lips lifted slightly at one corner. "A girl's got to eat."

Under different circumstances, he'd probably have been intrigued by her. She was an odd combination of innocence and bravado. A fighter with soft brown eyes and a fierce loyalty to the people she loved. She was the kind of woman who slid into a man's heart before he had the time to strengthen his defenses. But Nick's walls were solid. And the truth was that had the situation been different, he'd never have met her at all.

Attaching a strap to the gun, he swung it onto his shoulder. "Let's go."

She started for the door, but he reached out to stop her. "What is it?" she asked with a frown.

"Someone could be watching. We're better off going out the back."

Without arguing the point, she nodded and began to climb the ladder. He followed behind and when they were in the loft, he moved to the open window.

"You really think he's still out there?" She scanned the shadowy tree line, concern etched across her face.

"Yeah. But he'll have pulled back to call for reinforcements. He knows you've got help now, and he'll want to even the playing field."

"So why exactly are you on my side?" She shot the question over her shoulder as she straddled the windowsill, waiting for him to uncoil the rope.

"Because I saw your file," he said, willing to admit at least that much. "And you were right. There was nothing about radiation."

"But you're forgetting, I was found in a bomb shelter." She was baiting him now, testing him.

"A really old one. Look, Mia, even if it did protect you from the worst of the blast, you ought to show at least a little radiation in your system. And there's nothing."

She waited, her fingers tightening on the sill.

"And yet when I talked to Davies he didn't even mention it. In fact, he insisted the explosion was an accident."

"I don't understand." She frowned at him, her eyes troubled.

"If I'd found a woman alive in the aftermath of that kind of an explosion with no sign of exposure to radiation, I'd interrogate her until I had some answers."

"But no one interrogated me," she said, shaking her head. "They just stuck me with all kinds of needles and kept me in isolation."

"Exactly."

"So you think there's something more to this."

"I think it's possible, and until I figure out what it is, I've no intention of letting you out of my sight."

"Keep your friends close, and your enemies closer?" Again the side of her mouth lifted. "Should have thought of that before you let me go first."

The sentence hung in the air as she dropped over the sill, the soft sound of her landing mocking him. Cursing his stupidity, he abandoned the rope, vaulted over the sill and hit the ground running. Damn woman. She'd played him like a fiddle.

"Going somewhere?" Her voice was filled with laughter. He spun around, still fighting his anger.

"What the hell are you playing at?"

"Nothing." She shook her head, her hair glinting silver in the moonlight. "Just reminding you that I'm not as malleable as you seem to think."

He opened his mouth to retort and then snapped it closed. He'd be damned if he'd let her sucker him into a war of words. After mentally counting to five, he met her gaze. "My car is hidden a couple of miles from here. I need my gear."

"And then what?" she asked.

"We leave my rental at the airport and disappear. If we're lucky, it'll take them awhile before they put it all together."

"And if we're not lucky?" There was a note of vulnerability in her voice. The first he'd heard from her, actually. And his response to it made him answer more sharply than he'd intended.

"Then we're in deep shit." Her eyes widened, and he swore under his breath. "Look, we'll be fine. It's not like I haven't dealt with this kind of thing before."

"Good for you. Not so much for me. We're not exactly on the same side, you know." At least she called it like she saw it. He had to admire her for that.

"Maybe not." The least he could do was reward her honesty with his own. "But for the moment our interests intersect, and that makes us at least grudging allies. Besides, I'm the only thing you've got."

"For the moment." She adjusted her backpack. "So, shall we get on with it?"

They stood for a heartbeat, and then he turned, starting for the woods, his mind moving to the journey ahead. But she reached out to stop him, her hand hot against his skin.

"What?"

"We can take my Scout. It's not much to look at, but it beats running cross-country."

He nodded and changed direction, following her into a

small shed. The truck had definitely seen better days, but the engine turned over smoothly when she turned the key.

"Which way?" she asked, her profile showing determination. Whatever else Mia was, she wasn't a pushover.

"We need to head southeast." He pointed toward the pink-fingered sky. "I'm parked just off the spur road."

"Any chance they could have found the car?" It was a reasonable question, but he bristled just the same.

"None. It's hidden in a cave I found. More of a tunnel, really."

"Probably an abandoned mine shaft. The place is riddled with them. You said it was off of the spur?"

"Yeah, a couple hundred yards or so."

"I think I know the place." She nodded, flooring the Scout. "Won't take too long to get there."

"Except that we can't go there directly. They'll follow our trail. Better we cut back and forth. Confuse them. We can use the river to our advantage."

She shot him a look, her eyes narrowed in speculation. "You *have* done this before."

"Once or twice." It was an understatement and they both knew it. But he wasn't a share-his-life kind of guy, and nothing was going to change that fact—not even Mia Kearney.

CHAPTER SIX

SUNLIGHT STREAMED through the window, pulling Mia from sleep. For a moment she wondered where the hell she was, but then reality came crashing in. The explosion, her escape—Nick Price.

"How long have I been out?" She sat up, pushing the hair out of her face. He was sitting in the chair across from the bed, his feet propped up on the motel room's air-conditioning unit.

"Three hours."

"Shit," she said, swinging her legs over the edge of the bed. "Why didn't you wake me?"

"Because you needed the sleep. And because, at least until nightfall, we're better off here." His expression remained neutral, but there was something in his eyes that made her glad he was on her side—at least for the moment.

"But what about S&C? They might have bought into the idea of your leaving the state, but they're still going to be looking for me."

"They are. But at the moment, they're looking in the wrong place."

"What do you mean?" She frowned, shaking off the last dregs of sleep.

"While you were sleeping I took the Scout and left it

about twenty miles from here. Abandoned on the side of the road leading up into Caribou National Forest. They'll think you decided to disappear into the mountains."

"How did you get back? That's a long walk."

"I managed to liberate a ride."

"Resourceful. What makes you think Davies and his men will believe I went into the mountains? Seems like a lot to conclude just from finding my truck." She tried, but couldn't keep the note of skepticism out of her voice.

"There's a little more than that." His smile was wicked, its heat reaching her even from across the room.

"Like what?" she asked, intrigued despite herself.

"A piece of cloth hanging on a tree branch. From your shirt." He nodded toward her duffel.

"You took my shirt?"

"Just a bit of the hem. I needed something that smelled like you. In case they use dogs."

"So you left them my truck and my shirt. What else?"

"Just a bad attempt to cover up tracks, and some strategically broken twigs. It won't work forever, but I figure it's enough to buy us a little time."

"So we should be making the most of it." She stood up, heading for the duffel in the corner.

"Not so fast."

His words grated on her, but she stopped anyway, turning around to face him. "Look, I understand that you know what you're doing. But this is my life we're talking about and I don't like being left out of the loop."

"Sorry, princess," Nick said, holding up a hand, "next time I'll be sure to ask for permission." It might have mollified her, except that his eyes were filled with contained laughter.

"That's not what I meant and you know it."

"I know." He sighed, running a hand through his hair. "I just thought it was better to let you get some sleep. You've been through a lot."

She sank down on the end of the bed, her anger evaporating. "I'm sorry. I didn't mean to sound harsh. It's just that everything is happening so fast. Just a few days ago the biggest threat to my life was whether I remembered to wear my mask while I worked."

"Your mask?" He leaned forward with a frown.

"Yeah. I've been trying to reproduce an old etching technique. Unfortunately, the chemicals involved are toxic, so I'm supposed to wear a mask when I'm working with them. Only half the time I forget."

"Were you wearing it before the explosion?"

She blew out a long breath. "I don't know. I had it with me, of course, but I don't remember if I had it on. And even if I did, I don't know that it would have protected me against the radiation."

"It's definitely a possibility. Did you mention the mask to Waters?"

"The doctor? No way. He wasn't exactly opening up to me, so I figured what was good for the goose…"

Nick smiled. "I like the way you think."

"There's no way to prove it, anyway. I mean, the mask is gone, right? Along with the rest of Cedar Branch." She fought against tears, the image of Nancy and Patrick standing in Cuppa Joe burned into her retinas.

"We don't know that for sure."

"But you said everyone was dead. Surely that means the town was destroyed."

"Most of it, yes. The explosion was caused by an

enhanced radiation weapon—an ERW. Or at least the payload of one."

"Bunker busters." The minutes the name was out, she regretted it. He already suspected her, and here she was helping him with his allegations.

His fierce scowl indicated that he was following the same train of thought. "What do you know about them?"

"Just what I hear on TV." She held up her hands in mock surrender. "They're meant to dig into the ground, to penetrate hidden caverns. Like in Afghanistan. Right?"

He nodded, the speculation rising in his eyes. "The bunker busters used in Afghanistan didn't contain nuclear material. But the weapon exists."

"I thought we had a ban on nuclear weapons development. My mother and grandfather both campaigned for it."

Nick shrugged. "The work on B61-11 is couched in rhetoric. But the basic idea is that it's just a new use for an old weapon. Ergo not breaking the ban."

"So it's all about semantics."

"No. It's about politics." And really, the word said it all.

"So we're talking about an explosion similar to the one in Hiroshima, only smaller?" It was almost impossible to get her mind around the fact that Cedar Branch was gone. And her only real frame of reference was the horror of WWII Japan.

"No." He shook his head, his eyes narrowing as he watched her. "You really don't know anything about ERWs?"

"Nothing more than what I read in the papers."

He waited a moment, still studying her, then sighed. "Well, an enhanced radiation weapon is an entirely different animal. The bombs used in Japan were atom bombs. Twenty kilotons of payload detonated at around nineteen thousand feet. Maximum damage because of the height of burst. In contrast, a thermonuclear warhead like the one in Cedar Branch was probably no more than one kiloton. And on top of that, it was detonated from the bed of a tractor-trailer rig, which means the height of burst couldn't have been more than about ten feet."

"Meaning it was less damaging?"

"Exactly."

"Then how did it kill everyone in Cedar Branch?"

"Depending on the variables, a warhead like that could take out an area with a diameter of something like three hundred yards. That's three football fields. And from what I gather Cedar Branch wasn't very big."

Mia shook her head, her eyes welling with tears. "So the blast killed them?"

"Most likely. Although if it didn't they were doomed, anyway." He stopped, frowning as he realized what he'd said. "I didn't mean it like that."

His eyes met hers, regret reflected in his gaze as he reached out to squeeze her hand. But she pulled away, shaking her head, certain that if he touched her, she'd lose it. To say she was hanging by a thread was an understatement. He accepted her withdrawal without comment, which left her strangely conflicted, but she concentrated instead on understanding what had happened to her friends.

"A thermonuclear bomb," Nick continued, his expression purposefully blank, "emits about thirteen times the lethal amount of radiation. That's why it's called an ERW. It's designed to release the neutron spray created by fusion, instead of absorbing it upon detonation. Less physical damage with maximum bang for the buck. The radius for contamination is much larger than the actual blast range. In this case, death would be instantaneous for up to a half mile."

"So you're saying if the blast didn't get them, the radiation would have." Mia choked on a sob. "Then why wasn't I...I mean, if the radiation is designed for maximum penetration, I can't believe for a minute that my grandfather's bomb shelter could have protected me. Or my mask, for that matter."

"I think that's the whole point, Mia." This time when he reached for her, she didn't pull away, his strong fingers feeling as if they were the only thing keeping her from collapse. "You shouldn't be alive. But you are. And there has to be an explanation."

Through the waves of emotion the impact of his words hit hard, and she jerked her hand free. "And you still think it's because I had something to do with all of this?"

"Nothing's been ruled out." All signs of sympathy had vanished as his face hardened with what was no doubt seasoned indifference.

"Including the fact that it could just have been a terrible accident."

"As I said, nothing has been ruled out."

"But you intend to get to the bottom of it."

He shrugged. "It's what I do."

"I thought you said that your bosses had called you off the investigation."

"They did." The words hung in the air and Mia frowned, trying to understand.

"But you're here."

"Let's just say I don't deal with authority all that well."

There was something more. Some underlying motivation she wasn't following, but asking him outright would be a mistake. At least for the time being, she needed his help. "So where does that leave us?"

"Well, to start, I've got a few questions." He looked out the window and then down at his watch. "And I figure we've got a couple of hours to kill."

"Shoot." It wasn't the best choice of words, but it felt apropos somehow. She braced herself with her hands, her fingers curling into the cotton of the bedspread.

"Tell me more about your mother."

"Tell me about yours," she snapped, losing her hard-won control. After everything that had happened, they were still at square one.

He paused for a moment, his eyes narrowing, and she sucked in a breath, certain that he was about to blast her. Then just as quickly he relaxed, the mocking smile back in place. "Not much to tell. She lives in Connecticut, on the coast. We haven't spoken in eleven years."

"I see." Of course she didn't, but she was so surprised he'd answered, she couldn't find a coherent thought.

"So turnabout's fair play. And besides, my mother's political proclivity ends with who's elected president of her garden club. Not exactly incendiary stuff."

"And by extrapolation I take it you believe my mother's is?" It was stating the obvious, but she was still having trouble gathering her thoughts. Nick Price had a way of throwing her off guard when she least expected it.

"I think it's worth examining."

"Same song, old record. My mom is dead. And unless you know something about the afterlife I don't, she can't have been involved in any of this. Did she care about the dangers of nuclear proclivity? Yes. Would she have been involved in something as catastrophic as blowing up a town of innocent people? No fucking way. She believed in the peaceful resolution of conflict. And so do I."

"Sometimes passive resistance isn't enough." His eyebrows rose with the unasked question.

"Look, even if I tended toward radical causes—which I don't—I loved Cedar Branch. It was home. And the people who lived there were my family. There's no way I would ever have done anything that would put them in harm's way."

"All right. For the moment, let's put aside the idea that you were directly involved—"

"That's easy," she fumed. "I wasn't."

"I'm not trying to fight with you, Mia. I'm trying to cover all the bases. I've read the file on what happened, but I need to fill in the gaps and figure out what, if anything, was missed. The plain facts are that there was a nuclear explosion in Cedar Branch and the entire town was obliterated. Not as a casualty of war, but because of a seemingly senseless accident."

She sighed, thoughts of her friends filling her mind. She owed it to them to explore every option—even distasteful ones. "So what do you want to know?"

"Let's start with the people your mother knew," he said, his emerald eyes probing. Mia felt like a butterfly pinned to corkboard. "I realize it's a long shot, but at the moment it's the most direct line we have. You said there were letters. Was there ever mention of someone coming to the States— or more specifically, to Cedar Branch?"

"Nothing at all like that. Mostly they were just notes to check in and see if I was okay. Nothing subversive."

"How about the people in the area? Anyone there with questionable connections?"

"To a terrorist group?" She tried but couldn't keep the surprise from her voice. "These people were salt of the earth types. You know, third and fourth generation ranchers."

"There are all kinds of terrorists, Mia. And Idaho is full of questionable groups. Right-wing extremists topping the list." He sat back, waiting.

"No one I knew was involved with that sort of thing. And I think I'd have known, if for no other reason than the fact that my grandfather had his own rather extreme views. He hated outsiders. All of them. But none so much as government types. To hear him tell it, they ruined the West with their rules and regulations. And then they systematically stripped the land. First with mining and then with missile silos and nuclear testing. Never once stopping to think about their impact on the livelihood of the people who live here. All they ever do is spout about the greater good. So if there are extremists here, maybe there's a reason."

"Surely you're not defending some of the more militant groups."

"I'm not defending their methodology. I'm just saying that where there's smoke, there's usually fire. Things don't develop in a vacuum, Nick. And I truly do believe the government would be better off taking a long hard look at themselves before they start throwing stones at others."

"I thought you believed in a passive stance?"

"I do. But that doesn't mean burying my head in the sand and pretending I don't understand what's happening." She sucked in a breath, her hands shaking with anger and frustration.

"Did you know that four out of five U.S. nuclear testing

sites are, or were, located in the West? And that half of the active Strategic Air Command units are located in this part of the country? And that's just military. Idaho alone was once the site of the largest concentration of nuclear plants in the world. The Idaho National Laboratory, the biggest nuclear research facility in the country, is still located here. And why? Because we have low population density. So theoretically, there's less danger in case of an accident. The needs of the many outweigh the needs of the few. Unless you're one of the few."

"So much for only knowing what you read in the paper." His eyebrows rose with the comment, but there was no humor reflected in his eyes.

"We were talking about the specifics of nuclear bombs," she said. "Not politics. I wouldn't know a missile from a cluster bomb if it walked up and introduced itself. But I do know about the risk involved in living in an area where you're surrounded by potential disaster. If it hadn't been for some government flunky trying to transport the nuclear payload of a missile, I'd be fielding a worried call from Nancy about whether or not I'd remembered to eat the lunch she'd left me."

"Who is Nancy?" he asked, his gaze solemn.

"A friend." Mia swallowed, trying to contain the pain that rose inside her. "She and her husband, Patrick, owned the café in town. I sold them the place."

"In front of your studio, right?" She nodded, surprised that he remembered. "How long ago did they buy the café?"

"Four years. They took the building and turned it into something really special. Up until then the only meeting place was Buster's Bar, and since most of his customers are there to blow off a little steam, it wasn't quite the same ambiance. Patrick and Nancy really pulled us together as a community." Tears welled again and she angrily brushed them away. "Anyway, they deserved better than this. At the very least someone should have warned us the truck was coming our way."

"That's not the way it's done."

"I know. But maybe it should be. If we'd known…" She trailed off, words deserting her.

"If you'd known, you'd probably have ignored the fact."

"Maybe. I don't know. It's all easier with hindsight, isn't it?"

"Look, I know this is hard for you," he said, the hard lines of his face softening with the words. "It's difficult to lose people you love. To try and make sense of it all…"

Hot tears spilled onto her cheeks, and she held up a hand to cut him off. "Please don't be nice to me. I can't take it. Being angry is the only thing keeping me from falling apart."

"I think you're a hell of a lot stronger than you give yourself credit for."

She fought against her surging emotions, digging her fingernails into her palms, the resulting pain instantly quelling her tears. A trick she'd learned from her mother. Crying women were seldom taken seriously, and Mia had learned a long time ago the importance of keeping tears at bay.

"Maybe we're looking at this the wrong way round," she said, her voice steady again. "If the principal anomaly of the situation is that I'm still alive, and if the people at S&C weren't interested in the fact that I had no radiation in my system, then maybe the answer lies there."

"With Davies?" Nick asked with a frown.

"Well, with the CIA. You said it yourself—they should have been questioning me. And they weren't. Instead they were prodding and poking me like I was some kind of mutant survivor from a mission to Mars. Believe me, I'm happy for the miracle, but even I have questions. And you walked in, took one look at the file and branded me part of the problem. So what's with S&C?"

"I'll admit it felt off to me. The whole setup just seemed wrong. But I don't have anything to support the hunch. And the truth is Davies had access to more information than I did."

"But isn't that weird in and of itself? I mean, aren't the CIA and Homeland Security supposed to be playing for the same team?"

"Yeah. But like anything else, issues arise. Particularly territorial ones. Folks at Langley see us as interlopers, a redundant organization tasked with doing what the CIA was already supposed to be doing."

"Well, considering what happened with the Twin Towers, I'd say maybe the redundancy was necessary."

"I agree with you, and I've worked for both organizations. But there are still kinks to be worked out. The point being here that I was only given information on a need-to-know basis. And even that was too much for the powers that be. I was called off the case, remember?"

"So you're saying the odd behavior by Davies and his team could be explained by information we're missing."

"Possibly."

"Then we need to find the information. The reality here is that someone was trying to kill me last night. And I, for one, would like to know why."

"I already told you. He wasn't trying to kill you. If he had been—"

"I know." She held up her hands. "I know, I'd be dead."

"It's the truth."

"Okay. Well, if they don't want me dead, they certainly don't want me out there in the general population running my mouth. And there's got to be a reason for that. The logical one being yours—that I was somehow involved in all of this. But they weren't questioning me at all. Which leads me to believe that there's something else. Something *they* want to cover up."

"So we go to the source."

"Langley?"

"No." He shook his head. "Kresky."

"I'm sorry, I'm not following." She leaned forward, waiting for clarification.

"Jameson Kresky." He got up to walk to the window, his attention momentarily on the parking lot outside. "He's the contractor who was moving the nuclear material. It was headed for Malmstrom Air Force Base. In Montana."

"From where?"

"Nevada," he said, turning back to face her, his expression impossible to read. "According to the briefing I had, he was contracted to modify an existing missile by adding a nuclear device. The truck was carrying the modified payload."

"But shouldn't there have been safety precautions of some kind? There have got to be regulations."

"Of course there are protocols. But that doesn't mean that accidents are impossible."

"So now you're agreeing with Davies?"

"No. Although on the surface it seems as if Davies is telling the truth. But the very fact that Davies is present doesn't fit the scenario. If there was really an accident, then I don't see the need for S&C to be on the scene at all.

They're tasked with cleaning up messes that need to stay buried. But in this case there's nothing to cover up. The explosion is headline news."

"Headlines, maybe," Mia said, "but there's not much substantive text here. I mean, they mention the accident— but there's no real detail, and nothing at all about the people who died."

"It's standard op to wait to release the names. Next of kin—that sort of thing. And Davies mentioned they were trying to delay even that."

"Until they could explain me?"

"It follows, but it doesn't make sense."

"None of this makes sense, Nick. None of it." She crossed her arms, fighting her emotions again. She needed to keep control, to stay on her toes. She didn't have the luxury of falling apart. "So what do we do next?"

"We head for Nevada—and Kresky International." He stood up and pulled out his cell phone. "But first I need to check in."

"But you're supposed to be on your way home." A niggle of anxiety wormed its way into her newfound confidence. "What if they want you to bring me in?"

"Don't worry," he said. "That's not going to happen."

She searched his face, looking for reassurance, but his expression remained guarded. She wanted to believe him, wanted to know that someone, at least, was on her side. But he worked for the government. The same one that had blown up her town and kept her a prisoner. CIA, Homeland Security—they were all the same.

Bottom line, she'd be a fool to let herself trust Nick Price. And suffice it to say, her grandfather hadn't raised a fool.

CHAPTER SEVEN

THE PARKING LOT WAS EMPTY. Which wasn't all that surprising: the Twin Pines had certainly seen better days. It was one of those places that time had ignored, the rusting chairs outside each motel room a testament to a bygone era. Nick flipped open his phone and walked toward the far end of the lot. Even though there was no one around, it didn't hurt to be cautious.

He hit speed dial and waited for the phone to connect, watching as a cattle truck on the highway maneuvered around a Suburban.

"Young."

"Hey, Matt. It's Nick."

Matt Young was one of a handful of people Nick called friend. An intel and research specialist for Homeland Security, Matt was a go-to man when it came to information. Hell, he was a lot more than that.

Their paths had first crossed on a mission in Budapest. They hadn't been playing for the same team at the time, but their interests had coincided. A grudging trust had been established, and from there, true friendship. The world of espionage was a small one, and everyone had their network of people they could count on. For Nick, Matt topped the list.

"Where the hell are you?" Nothing like cutting right to the chase.

"What, no niceties? Don't you want to know how I am?"

"I can guess." There was a note of amused tolerance in Matt's voice.

"So how much trouble am I in?" Nick might call his own shots, but that didn't mean there weren't going to be repercussions.

"To hear Ricks tell it, he's looking at hanging you out to dry, which means not even Gordon can save your ass." Amos Ricks was a political appointee, and as such his reign at Homeland Security was subject to the whims of the politicos above him. "I've even been getting calls. Whatever you're playing at, Nick, it's time to stop. Things around here are pretty damn intense."

"Believe me, it's not a picnic at this end, either. The more I learn, the murkier everything gets."

"Yeah, well, it's not your mess to straighten out. You were supposed to get on a plane and get your ass back to Washington."

"I'll admit it was a good idea in theory, Matt, but you know I've always been easily distracted. Especially when Charles Davies is part of the package."

"Look, Nick, I know you've got a personal beef with Davies. Hell, with good reason. But things are tough around here. And the flack is coming from the top. Which means unless you want your career to land in the crapper you've got to get back here ASAP. And if you've got Mia Kearney, you need to turn her over to S&C."

"What makes you think I've got the girl?" He frowned into the phone.

"Word travels fast. According to Davies, she had to have had help getting away. Apparently, they had her cornered?"

"Yeah, with an assault rifle. You actually talked to Davies?"

"No. I wouldn't give that cocksucker an umbrella in a monsoon. But his bosses called our bosses, and the resulting scuttle is that you've gone rogue. Bottom line is that the powers that be want Homeland Security out of this."

"All right, so there's some pressure. That doesn't mean I have to cave."

"Maybe not if you were on your own. But with the girl…" Matt trailed off.

"There's nothing I can do, Matt. She's not here." Technically, he was telling the truth. Mia wasn't in the parking lot. "Davies will just have to run her down on his own."

"Why don't I believe that?"

"Because Davies is an inept son of a bitch?"

"That's not what I meant and you know it."

"Look, Matt, I'm not going to let this go. I can't. Something about this whole affair is off. Just the fact that they want us out of it sets off all kinds of alarm bells. Surely you're not buying into all this S&C over Homeland Security shit."

"No one gives a damn what I think, Nick. Just play it safe and come back to Washington. The key players are heavy hitters."

"I hear what you're saying." This was the part of his job he hated the most. Political interests always outweighed things like truth and justice.

"But you're not coming back."

"I don't think you want an answer to that. Better for deniability."

Silence bounced from tower to tower, stretching from Idaho to D.C. "I know better than to argue with you," Matt said finally. "But if I were you I'd stay off the grid. There are people who would like nothing better than to see you take a fall."

More than he could count, actually. Nick had pissed off some pretty powerful people eleven years ago, and politicos had long memories.

"Nick, you still there?" Matt's voice interrupted his thoughts.

"Yeah, I'm here."

"I'll cover for you as much as I can."

"I appreciate the support, Matt. But I don't want to drag you into my mess."

"Hey," Matt answered, "it's not like we haven't had our share of shit to deal with." Matt had pulled Nick's ass from the fire more times than either of them could count.

"Yeah, but you said yourself, this time there's a target on my back."

"Hell, Nick, there's always a target on your back." Matt laughed, and then sobered. "Seriously, though, if you need me, use my cell. Or e-mail. The private one. And most of all watch your back. I've got a bad feeling about all of this."

"Yeah." Nick frowned into the phone. "Me, too." He flipped his phone closed, and stood for a moment watching the soft purple haze of the mountains on the horizon. He was stepping off a cliff with this one. Matt was right. There were powerful forces at work here. The problem was separating the good guys from the bad guys.

Common sense pointed to Mia Kearney playing a major role in the destruction of Cedar Branch, but his gut wasn't buying the idea. She just didn't come across as an operative. Even an untrained one. Which left him back at square one.

Nick's gaze dropped back to the highway. A tractor-trailer rig whizzed by, the contents of its container safely locked away from prying eyes. The truck that had destroyed Cedar Branch had probably looked much the same. Deceptive in its normalcy.

It was time for action. Time to figure out how best to access the information they needed from Kresky International. Kresky dealt in protected technology, which meant there'd be top-notch security. Not an insurmountable problem, but definitely one that demanded a little prep work.

At least for the moment he and Mia were off the radar. But if Matt was right, there'd be no holds barred in trying to find them—which meant they had to act quickly.

MIA SKIMMED AGAIN THROUGH the directories listed on Nick's computer. Most of them were password protected, and although she'd tried several obvious word combinations, nothing had worked. The files that *were* available told her absolutely nothing, except that Nick wasn't keen on filing his paperwork. Six e-mails from someone in accounting asking for his expense reports said it all.

There was something humanizing about the idea of a superagent having to file an expense report. But it was cold comfort. What she wanted was insight into Nick Price—and his abhorrence of minutia aside, there wasn't anything there to give her a clue as to whether he could be trusted or not.

The computer was high-end and carried enough gadgets to please even James Bond. Mia had figured the machine was her best bet—even knowing that it carried protection.

She'd studied computers in college. Her grandfather's idea of a practical fallback should her attempts to make it as an artist prove less than lucrative.

He'd wanted her to skip the idea of art altogether, but she could be just as stubborn as he was. Eventually, after she'd threatened to blow off college, they'd reached a compromise. Mia had wound up with a double major, in art and computer sciences. It would have been a victory for them both, except a heart attack had robbed them of any chance for celebration. And ironically, his death had left her with enough money to avoid the very financial pit he'd been trying to protect her from.

Mia sighed and moved the cursor to the last item, a file titled KAP. Inside, the documents all had .jpg tags. She clicked the first one and the smiling face of a beautiful young woman filled the screen. She was laughing at the photographer. Something he'd said just before snapping the picture.

The next image was also a photograph. Same woman, this time in a bikini, standing ankle-deep in the surf. Somewhere tropical, judging by the cerulean cast of the breaking waves behind her. She was smiling again, motioning toward the cameraman, as if she were trying to coax him into the water.

Mia clicked on the remaining files, her browser screen filling with images—all the same woman. Time was marked in the changing hairstyles and seasonal backgrounds, but in every one she smiled impishly, her grin compelling even when confined to the small screen of the laptop.

Mia searched the file again for some sign of who the woman might be. Another operative, maybe? A friend? A wife? There was no name and no further information. But obviously there was some significance. There were seventeen photos.

Mia sorted through them again, the images lining up like dominoes across the computer monitor. She right-clicked on the first one and selected properties from the list that appeared on the screen. Lots of detail about location and size, but nothing that gave away the subject of the photographs.

Following suit with the rest of the pictures, she wound up with only one useful bit of information. The pictures varied in the time taken, but the most recent, the one at the ocean, was over eleven years old.

She enlarged the photo so that it filled the screen, and frowned at the image reflected there, as if willing the woman to say something. Give her some insight into the man who held Mia's life in his hands. But of course the screen remained silent. Ghosts of the past preserved forever in bytes and bits.

"What the hell are you doing?"

It took all of her willpower not to slam the laptop shut and dive for cover under the bed. But if she was going to hold her own with Nicholas Price, now was a good time to begin.

"You know everything about me." She jutted out her chin, meeting his angry gaze. "And I know nothing about you. Seemed a bit unfair. So I figured this might help me even the odds." If looks could kill she'd be six feet under, but they couldn't, and so she held her ground, waiting.

He reached across to shut the laptop. "My computer is private. You had no right."

"Look, I'm trusting you. And for that I think I deserve to know something beyond the fact that your mother doesn't talk to you."

His eyes narrowed. "Well, there's nothing on my computer that'd help you. It's just business. Most of it's security protected, anyway."

"Given enough time I could probably find a way to circumvent that. But for now I just want to know who this is." She opened the laptop again and turned it toward him. For a moment his face softened, as if just seeing the mystery woman's picture gave him joy. But before Mia could react, his brows drew together, his expression hardening again.

"Close it."

"Who is it?" She frowned up at him, absorbing his tightly controlled anger, for the first time feeling a flicker of fear. "Your wife?"

"It's my sister," he said, wrenching the computer from her hands. "She's dead."

"What happened?" The words were out before she could stop them.

"None of your goddamned business."

Mia flinched, all thoughts of holding her own evaporating. There would be no leveling of the playing field. Nick held all the cards. "I'm sorry."

"No. You're not," he said, setting the laptop on the bed. "Except maybe that you got caught. Next time you decide to snoop, maybe you'd be better off sitting by the window. That way you can make sure that I don't sneak up on you."

"I wasn't trying to hide anything. I just saw the computer and figured it was a chance to see what I could find out. Which was a big fat nothing, basically. Except that you're late with your expense reports."

With that pronouncement his scowl relaxed slightly. "I hate paperwork."

"I surmised as much." She knew better than to push any further. In some ways Nick reminded her of her grandfather. When goaded, he'd always rise to the bait, but with proper care he was also fairly easy to subdue. "What did your boss have to say?"

"I didn't talk to him."

"But I thought—"

"I called the office," he said, waving her silent. "Just not my boss. I figured it was better to get the lay of the land first."

"And I take it it wasn't good?"

"Predictable heat. When the powers that be want you to jump, they're not happy to see you disobey."

"Did you tell them I was with you?" She sucked in a breath, knowing his answer was important.

His smile was slow and a little crooked, and she thought for the first time that had they met in some other way, she might actually have been drawn to him. But this was not that kind of situation, and she wasn't in the habit of falling for interesting smiles. "Actually, I told Matt you weren't with me," he said. "Which, at that exact moment, was the absolute truth."

"Matt?" she asked, allowing herself to breathe again.

"Young. Good people. He's had my back more times than I can count."

"And I assume you've had his?"

"Not so much. But then Matt doesn't have a tendency to get himself into trouble."

"Like you." An understatement, surely.

His smile broadened to a grin. "Something like that." Just as quickly he sobered, his fingers circling her wrist, his eyes locking on hers. "If I catch you going through my things again, I'll turn you over to Davies personally. Am I making myself clear?"

"Perfectly." She kept her eyes steady, stiffening her backbone. "But just so you know, I'm not the type to be cowed easily."

"I wouldn't expect any less." He released her arm and the side of his mouth quirked upward again, just slightly. "So what do you say we work on a plan."

"For getting into Kresky's offices?"

"Yeah. But it won't be easy. They're not likely to hold the door while we waltz in and go through their files."

"Unless we're auditors." She sat back, waiting to see what he thought of the idea.

He shook his head. "That would take too long to set up. There'd have to be letters and all kinds of verification. The IRS moves slower than the M15 in the rain."

"M15?" she asked, trying to follow his train of thought.

"A bus. In Manhattan. It's not important. The point is that it won't work. At least not in the timeframe we've got available. If something is off with what happened, you can bet your ass that, given enough time, Kresky will bury it so deep no one can find it. Our only chance is to hit before he's had the chance to regroup."

"You're assuming there's something to find." She tried but couldn't keep the note of hope from her voice. Maybe he was starting to believe her.

"I'm not assuming anything. But I'm willing to be proven wrong."

"All right, so what other options do we have?"

"We could break in directly, but that'd take a bigger team, and right now I hesitate to bring in anyone we don't have to."

"What about Matt?"

"No way. Two isn't enough to make a team."

"I think you're miscounting. With Matt there'd be three."

He eyed her for a moment and then shrugged dismissively. "You're not used to this kind of thing."

"Maybe not. But it *is* my life that seems to be on the line. Which means I'm already invested. Not to mention that I'm hardly a moron. I think I can figure out whatever it is you want me to do." She paused to draw a breath, anger coloring her judgment. "Unless there's some other reason why you don't want to break in. Like maybe you think I'm up to my neck in this and this whole conversation is just a ploy to see what I'll spill?" He stared at her for a moment, and her heart fluttered. "I'm right. This is all some kind of test."

"No. It's not. I just don't want to involve any more personnel than I have to. We need to do this on our own."

"I know you said Matt was on your side, but what about your bosses? If you don't show up, won't they figure you'll head for Kresky's?"

"No. Matt made it pretty clear that the CIA is calling the shots here. Homeland Security's off the case."

"Okay, so we've just got Davies—but he's not a stupid man."

"Far from it. But he's scrambling. He can't know for certain that you're with me. Which gives us a slight advantage, as long as we move quickly."

"So where does that leave us?" She started to bite the cuticle of her index finger and stopped midway, catching Nick's eye. "Bad habit." She dropped her hand into her lap, searching for a solution. "How about we try a disguise of some kind. Get in without using cloak-and-dagger. Maybe we could pretend to be the cleaning crew. They do that all the time in the movies."

"Yeah, but since it's all pretend there really isn't much of a risk. Anyway, it's too obvious. And even if it wasn't, they'd have to clear any changes in personnel."

She frowned. He wasn't making it easy. Her gaze dropped to the computer. "Maybe I could hack in."

"Excuse me?" If the situation hadn't been so serious she'd have laughed at his obvious surprise.

"Hack. You know, break into their computer?"

"I know what the word means." His voice was terse, his tone dismissive. "But I'm not sure I understand how you think you might be able to break into Kresky's system."

She sighed and swallowed a retort. They were going nowhere fast. "I'm not sure that I can. But I do have a certain knack. When I was in college I managed to get into the university's main server—in particular into student transcript records."

"I'll bet that made you popular."

"It would have if I'd gone on to change people's grades. In all truth, I could have made a fortune. But I didn't. I just wanted to see if I could get in."

"Well, breaking into Kresky's computers will be a little bit more difficult than some coed college prank."

"I went to Stanford," she said, narrowing her eyes. "Hardly 'some' college. But that isn't the point. What's important here is that people are less likely to clean their computers than their filing cabinets. Or if they do clean them, they don't realize that in all actuality the information is probably still on their hard drive somewhere."

"So how many other computers have you hacked into? I thought you weren't part of your mother's shenanigans."

"Now there's a word that will date you," she said, his wince making her smile. "But my hacking was limited to college. I did it for the challenge. You'll find it's sort of a driving force among computer geeks."

"But you're an artist."

"I am. But my grandfather insisted I have something to fall back on. So I've got a double major. Art and computer sciences. Wasn't that in my dossier?" She had the distinct delight of catching him off guard. Only for a minute, but still it was a moment to hang on to.

"Obviously not."

"It doesn't matter. I'm telling you now. I know my way around computers, and given enough time I think I can get into Kresky's."

"But we've already established that we don't have time."

"Right." Her confidence in the idea evaporated. His laptop was no doubt state of the art, but there was no question it would take time for her to feel her way into the back door of Kresky's system.

Silence descended, the late afternoon sun streaking the motel room with gold.

"Could you do it if I get you inside?"

"It'd be a lot easier." She studied him, trying to follow the logic of his thoughts. "But haven't we already rejected direct access? That's why I mentioned hacking in the first place."

"Maybe there is a way." He frowned, and she could almost see the wheels spinning. "You mentioned an audit."

"And you shot me down. Too much verification required. Remember?"

"Yeah, but I was thinking of the IRS. What if we go in as federal auditors?"

"Like from the Department of Defense?"

He shrugged. "With all that's happened, it might not be that big a stretch. Especially if we don't hit the plant itself.

There's a separate office complex. But the computer system would be the same, right?"

"Yes." She allowed herself a moment of self-congratulation. Unless she was missing something, Nick was actually asking her opinion. "But like you said, getting in will still be difficult. I mean, most likely, both physical and virtual records would be kept there. Which I'd think would make it almost more important protectionwise than the physical plant."

"There's truth in that. But the reality is that it's smaller than the plant, which means less personnel and possibly less security. The entire complex is in the middle of the desert. So they're not likely to have a lot of traffic. If we pick the right time, I think it's possible we might be able to skate right past security. If S&C is to be believed, Kresky's people ought to be spooked enough to buy that we're from the feds. So if I can arrange to get us inside, you think you can get into the computer?"

"Yeah. I think I can make it happen. But only if you promise not to add hacking to my negative column."

"Okay, you've lost me," he said with a frown.

"Well, you're obviously keeping some sort of tally. Mia is good. Mia is bad. And I don't want this to go to the bad side. I'm really not the enemy. And for that matter, you'd have liked my mother."

"I like a lot of people, but that doesn't mean I trust them. And that certainly doesn't mean we're playing for the same team."

"You use a lot of baseball metaphors. Did you play?"

"Hey, you're the one who has a way with a bat." He rubbed the back of his head for emphasis.

"It was a chair leg. And we weren't talking about me. We were talking about you. I'm guessing first baseman?"

His eyes widened for an instant, then narrowed in denial, but she knew she'd scored a point. Not to put too much emphasis on the metaphor.

"It doesn't matter," she said, waving away the question. "The point is, do you trust me enough to let me give it a try?"

The only sound in the room was the traffic whizzing down the highway outside. Mia sat back, waiting, knowing that to catch a fish you had to bait the hook. It was a lesson she'd learned right after managing to snag her grandfather's ear with a particularly expensive fly. He'd never let her live it down. And she'd never made the mistake again.

"All right. If you really think you can do this, I can provide what you need to make it happen." It wasn't a glowing endorsement, but considering that less than twenty-four hours ago Nicholas Price had thought her an adversary, it was a start.

CHAPTER EIGHT

KRESKY INTERNATIONAL WAS basically located in the middle of the Nevada desert, near the remnants of a town called Wildwood. The road, a state spur, was old and rutted, the asphalt shimmering in the late summer heat. All the better to keep the curious away. The property itself was unpretentious, the main building sitting just off the road, the factory a couple hundred yards behind that.

The latter was surrounded by barbed-wire-topped chain link—the only sign that this was not just an out-of-the-way plant of some kind. There was an entrance gate, complete with guard station, but fortunately, it was empty. Nick doubted the place had that many outside visitors. Especially unplanned ones.

He drove past the front entrance and continued for a couple hundred yards until a curve in the road yielded a small stand of desert willow. He pulled off the pavement and drove behind the willows, the gray Nissan blending nicely with the trees.

It had taken most of the night and the better part of the morning to get things lined up, but his work in black ops had created a network of netherworld contacts. The kind who, for the right amount of money or information, could produce pretty much anything an operative might need—

no questions asked. In short order, he'd managed to obtain not only information on Kresky's computer system, but passable IDs identifying them as DOD inspectors.

A quick stop at an area mall for the proper clothes and they were all set—Mia's dark skirt and white blouse accentuated by a pair of heavy frame glasses, Nick's newly grayed hair and pinstripe suit a perfect imitation of a middle-aged bureaucrat. All that was left was a good dose of pretension and boredom.

They'd already cased the place—in a different vehicle—so all that remained now was to time their entrance to allow for least resistance. Assuming Kresky's employees hadn't suddenly developed a penchant for overtime, the two of them shouldn't have to wait long. With a little luck, they'd be in and out before anyone had the chance to raise an alarm.

He still wasn't completely convinced that Mia was up to the task. Or maybe worse, he was concerned that if she *was* able to access Kresky's secrets, it meant she had more than a passing connection with her mother's so-called friends. Either way, they were committed to action.

As if on cue, Mia lowered the field glasses she'd been looking through. "The exodus has begun."

He took the binoculars, turning the lens to focus. A slow stream of employees was indeed emerging from the front doors. A few stopped to talk, but most of them headed straight for their cars.

Twenty minutes later the parking lot was almost empty.

"It's time to move," Nick said, shooting a glance at Mia. "You want to go over it one more time?"

"I think I've got it down. We tell whoever's manning the front desk that we're with DOD, here for anything referencing the accident in Cedar Branch. You flash your badge and they take us to the files and hopefully a PC. Then I'm going to work my magic. And if there isn't a PC, you'll do your espionage thing and find one for me."

"I'm not in espionage anymore, Mia."

"Well, you know the drill and that's all that matters."

He started the car and pulled back onto the highway. The drive back to Kresky's was uneventful. The gate was open and the parking lot almost empty.

"So far so good," Mia said as they pulled to a stop in front of the building.

"Yeah." Nick killed the engine and clipped the DOD badge on his lapel. It was a copy, but there was no way anyone but an expert could tell. Mia was waiting on the sidewalk, her own badge hanging from a lanyard. "Ready?"

She nodded, with a little half smile that was more about nerves than pleasure. "As I'll ever be."

For a moment, he questioned his decision to involve her in this. There were any number of reasons why it was a bad idea. But none of them held sway over the fact that they needed answers and this was the best way to get them. And so far, at least, Mia seemed to be adapting to his way of life with unusual ease. Which in and of itself probably should be cause for alarm.

The reception area of the office complex was sterile. Chrome furniture and industrial-grade carpet. Obviously Kresky wasn't interested in impressing visitors. The front desk was empty, no doubt owing to the hour, but a man emerged from the door behind the desk before they'd actually reached it.

"I'm sorry, we're closed. I'm only here to catch up on some paperwork," he said in the harried tone of someone with too much overtime.

"Federal inspectors," Mia said, holding up her badge. Nick held back a smile. If he hadn't known better, he'd have thought she was actually enjoying herself. "We're here to examine all the files and documentation you have on the hazardous shipment that caused the incident in Cedar Branch."

"I wasn't expecting you until next week." The man frowned, reaching out to have a closer look at Mia's badge.

"Sorry to catch you off guard," Nick improvised, careful to keep his tone laced with the right balance of authority and deference. The fact that the man was expecting someone seemed odd. DOD wasn't known for it's speed even in a crisis. But never look a gift horse in the mouth…

He fingered the hard outline of the gun in his pocket, senses on red-alert. "Considering the magnitude of what happened, our bosses figured sooner was better than later. We'd have been here earlier, but we had a little trouble finding the place."

"Well, I can understand that," the man said, relaxing slightly. "We're pretty much in the middle of nowhere out here."

"So I gather things have been difficult around here since the accident?" Nick probed, trying to gain the man's confidence.

"No shit. We've been barraged with e-mails and calls for the last couple of days. I think every environmental group in the nation has contacted us. It's been an endless stream of questions. Most of which I can't even answer."

"Why not?" Mia asked, her voice steady. Nick breathed a sigh of relief. At least she was following his lead.

"Not sure that I should be saying anything. How do I know you're really who you say you are? Besides the badges?"

Nick reached into the briefcase he was carrying and produced an official-looking document complete with three-colored stamp. It was a forgery, but as with the badge, only an expert would be able to tell. "This should do the trick."

The man studied the letter for a moment. Then, seemingly satisfied, he smiled. "Paul Brennon. Plant manager. In truth I'm damn glad to hand this mess off to someone else. The senator said you'd help take care of things."

"The senator?" Mia blurted the question, and Brennon's look changed to concern.

"I thought you were part of the team Senator Tucker put together. I got the memo from Kresky himself."

"We work for DOD, not the senator," Nick explained. "But he did in fact instigate our involvement. We kept his role need-to-know. I'm afraid my colleague wasn't in the loop." He lifted his eyebrows in a manner to suggest that Mia wasn't as senior as he, and Brennon nodded in understanding. "I'm Agent Dray and this is Agent Ferrell." He held out his hand.

"Nice to meet you." He shook first Nick's hand and then Mia's. "What exactly do you want from me?"

"Well, to start with," Nick said, "I'd like to see any documentation you might have for the transported warhead. And I'll need the transportation authorization forms, along with the application for permits to transport. And anything else you might have that connects the dots to show that Kresky International followed proper procedure for conveying the warhead to Malmstrom."

"We've got most of what you need here." Brennon hesitated, his frown returning. "But I'm not sure I'm comfortable with you going through the files on your own. Our transportation coordinator was going to put a package together for you. But she's gone for the day, and as I said, we weren't expecting you so soon."

"Are you saying you've got something to hide?" Mia asked, her tone glacial. Again, Nick was impressed with her acuity.

Brennon swallowed convulsively. "No, of course not. It's just that I don't actually deal with the transportation paperwork. And so I'm not sure what exactly you're going to find."

"Maybe I didn't make myself clear," Nick said, trying a different tack. "We're here to help you, Mr. Brennon. Kresky International has a long and valued partnership with DOD. And we'd hate to see anything sabotage that relationship. Which is why we're here to make certain that your documentation is unimpeachable. " He waited for the meaning of his words to sink in, gratified when the little man relaxed.

"Well, I guess when you put it like that…" Brennon shrugged, his frown dissipating.

"Great," Mia said. "Then if you'll just show us to the file room?" Her smile was warm as she reached out to touch the older man's arm. "Oh, and we'll also need access to your computer system." She looked to Nick for confirmation, just the right amount of subservience in her voice.

Nick nodded. "Best to double-check against the files. You want everything to jibe."

"I suppose you have a point," Brennon said, handing him back the letter and gesturing for them to follow. "The file rooms are in the back. And there's a computer in there, as well. There's even a table where you can spread things out if you want to."

"Thank you," Mia said as they followed him through a maze of cubicles.

Nick checked each cube as they walked by. So far they'd all been empty. The room was quiet, their footsteps echoing as they crossed the cavernous space. There were full-fledged offices lining the window wall, but despite their privacy they weren't much bigger than the cubicles. Not a place Nick would want to spend eight hours a day.

"This way." Paul turned into a hallway connecting to the main room, and stopped in front of an open door. "The files are in there." He gestured to a wall lined with gray metal filing cabinets. "The first cabinet has most of what you'll need. The PC's over there on the desk. It's networked into the system."

"Will I need passwords?" Mia asked, her face reflecting nothing more than mild curiosity.

His gaze lingered on her for a moment, his eyes narrowed in speculation. Then abruptly, he shrugged. "Current passwords should be listed on a file card in the left-hand drawer of the desk. They'll give you access to most areas of the computer."

"Thanks. We should be good to go then," Nick said.

"All right," Brennon said, clearly debating whether he should leave them alone.

Nick smiled. "We'll call you if we need you."

"Okay. Good. My extension is 426." Brennan shot them a halfhearted smile and headed for the door.

Nick turned to face the room. Filing cabinets lined three walls, the PC sitting on a desk on the same wall as a copy machine and fax.

"That was touch and go," Mia said with a sigh. "I thought we were toast when he said we were expected."

"Well, you sure didn't show it." Nick shot her a smile.

"I just followed your lead, and prayed the guy couldn't

see that my hands were shaking." She held them up in support of her words.

He reached over to take them in his own, ignoring the accompanying warning bells in his head. "You did fine."

They stood for a moment, eyes locked, and then with a quivering smile she broke free, turning to boot up the computer. "Best to get this started before Brennon comes back."

He surveyed the room, pulling his mind back to the task at hand. "At least for the moment, he seems to believe we're here to help."

"So what happens when he finds out we're not?" she asked.

"We'll be long gone. And hopefully in possession of more answers than questions." He walked over to the file cabinet Brennon had indicated.

"Well, so far all I have are more questions. Like why would a senator be involved in helping Kresky clean up his mess?"

"Well, we don't know for certain that he actually was planning to help," he said. "But either way it's no surprise that he's involved. Lloyd Tucker is a legend in Nevada politics and a huge player on the national scene."

"Didn't he serve as secretary of defense once upon a time?"

"Good memory," Nick said, again impressed with the breadth of her knowledge. "He risked his career, actually, resigning his senate seat to be a second term appointee. There were all kinds of pundits who said he couldn't get reelected. Especially when the other party was carrying most of the country. But they weren't counting on the good people of Nevada. "

"I take it you're not a fan?"

"I don't have time for politicians. They live in a make-believe world where real people are cardboard cutouts—expendable if the right idealized objective is accomplished."

"You sound like my grandfather."

"No. Your grandfather believed in something. Me—I don't believe in anything. Not anymore." He closed his eyes, uncomfortable with his inner revelation. He normally wasn't a spew-his-guts kind of guy. But she did something to him. Made him forget caution. He'd felt it the moment he'd walked into her hospital room, and had been fighting it ever since.

"We were talking about Kresky and Tucker," she prompted, wisely steering the conversation back to safer ground. "Their mutual interests."

"Right. Well, money for the state is the obvious one. If Kresky profits, Nevada does as well."

"And if he fails…"

"Exactly." he nodded to underscore his agreement, his mind sifting through additional alternatives. "But there's more than that. They've both got an interest in the military-industrial complex, too. Kresky through his contracts and Tucker because of his longtime military service. In addition to his stint as secretary of defense, he's a decorated war veteran and an unabashed hawk. And if rumors are right, he's got his eye on the White House."

"I think I remember reading about that. Does he have a chance?"

"I have no idea. He's a cagey son of a bitch, but he's amassed a world of connections over the years. He's got a deep war chest and some of his party's most powerful movers and shakers on his side."

"He's on the appropriations committee now, right? With Senator Hatcher."

Nick shook his head, trying to place the name.

"Walter Hatcher is Idaho's senior senator and chairman of the appropriations committee. My grandfather knew him pretty well. They didn't always see eye to eye on things, but I think Grandfather believed that Hatcher had Idaho's best interests at heart." She sighed, remembering. "Anyway, Tucker's military record isn't enough to prove he's in bed with Kresky or had anything to do with what happened to Cedar Branch. He could just be looking out for the state."

"Or covering his ass."

"Except that so far we've got nothing to support that."

"Aw, come on, Mia. It wouldn't be any fun if it was easy." The sentence came out before he had time to think about how it sounded. For her this wasn't a game. Hell, on some level, it wasn't for him, either. But that didn't change the fact that he was an admitted adrenaline junkie. "You going to be able to access the entire computer?"

"Not sure yet," she said, turning her attention to the screen. "But I should be able to. And I'm betting if there's anything worthwhile, it'll be in Kresky's files."

"Won't they know you've accessed areas they haven't authorized?"

"No. If I can tap into the server, it'll be like I was never there."

Nick nodded and focused on the files. The first drawer contained DOD rules and regulations, as well as routine inspection reports and certificates. Nothing about specific production or shipping.

"You finding anything?" he called over his shoulder, at the same time checking the hallway for any sign of Paul Brennon.

"Not so far." Her fingers flew over the keyboard, the screen obediently opening new dialogue boxes with each inquiry. "I'm in, though. Figure I'll have a look around before I try and break into Kresky's stuff. How about you?"

"Nothing so far but bureaucratic bullshit." He opened the next drawer. "And this looks like blueprints. Interesting in their own right, but not anything that will shed light on Cedar Branch."

Three file drawers later, he hit pay dirt. Transportation authorizations from DOD and from the various air force bases receiving the reconfigured weapons Kresky was producing. "I think I've got something."

Mia quit typing and swiveled her chair so that she could see him. "The shipment for Malmstrom?"

"I haven't gotten there yet. But everything is filed chronologically, including authorizations in progress. So it should be here." He thumbed through the files until he got to August. Or what should have been August. "There are no files for August."

"Maybe the transportation person pulled the documents," Mia suggested.

"No. I think Brennon would have known that."

"Well, maybe it's been misfiled?"

Nick nodded and thumbed backward, looking for something that might relate to the transport to Cedar Branch. Files were color-coded, blue for hazardous materials. There weren't many. He pulled one from December and opened it. Inside there was a hazardous materials transportation form. But the warhead didn't contain nuclear material and it was bound for Texas.

He thumbed forward further, finding nothing targeted for Montana. Finally, in the last of the January files, he found a reconfigured B61-11. "I've got a transport request here. A B61 to Malmstrom. But it's scheduled for next

January." He flipped to a separate page in the file. "Wait a minute." He plucked a memo from the file, skimming the contents. "I've got a handwritten note here. Says the documentation needs to be revised."

"For what purpose?" Mia asked, looking up from the computer with a frown.

"Apparently the transport was moved up—to August."

"So this could be the one?"

He nodded, still skimming the document.

"Is there a signature?"

"Just initials. J.K. Looks like Kresky's."

"Well, at least it confirms that Kresky knew about the change. Is there any kind of route mentioned?"

"No. But there's a reference number—maybe that means something. I'll see if I can find a correlation in another file." He turned back to the filing cabinets, the click of her fingers on the keyboard resuming behind him.

"I'm not finding anything at all here. Just blank forms and so forth. Whoever monitors the IT system keeps it pretty clean. I'm going to try to get into Kresky's files. Maybe there'll be something more telling there. Since he's got his own password, my guess is he'll think it's safe."

"Seems possible. You really think you can get in?"

"Piece of cake." Her smile was a little wicked, and his body responded without so much as a by-your-leave.

Angry at himself, he jerked open a file drawer, quashing his pheromones, concentrating instead on the drawer's contents. But nothing there corresponded with the reference number for the B61-11 file. The next four drawers yielded nothing as well. He was just thinking that maybe they were on a wild goose chase when Mia interrupted his search with a whoop.

"I'm in." She swiveled to face him again, her eyes flashing with excitement. "Told you I could do it."

"I never doubted you," he said, containing a smile.

"Like hell." She grinned. And for the first time he actually felt like they were working on the same side. "Now we'll see what Kresky's been hiding."

He turned back to the cabinets, opening the top drawer of the last one. Again there was nothing of interest. At least not as far as the incident at Cedar Branch. He closed the last drawer and headed for the copy machine.

"You find the route?" Mia asked.

"No. Nothing to correspond to the reference number at all."

"So what are you copying?"

"The original file. I'd prefer to keep the original, but as soon as the real DOD people show up, or whoever it is that Tucker and Kresky are bringing in, they'll know we were fakes. This way if they do a cursory search to see what we took, it'll look as if we found nothing."

"Makes sense."

He took the original pages and placed them back in the file, then put the file back in its drawer. Finally, he dropped the copies into his briefcase.

"I think I've got something." Mia squinted at the screen in front of her. Still holding the briefcase, he moved over to stand behind her, more aware than he should be of the soft fall of her hair.

"This is one of Kresky's e-mails." She enlarged the text box so that the message filled the screen.

"There's nothing there but the word *fine*. Not even a recipient's name."

"That's because it was sent blind. Obviously Kresky

thought he was safeguarding his answer, but fortunately for us, when he replied, he forgot to delete the original message. And it's clearly from Tucker." She scrolled down the page to the second message. "It's not a lot clearer, but it definitely puts the senator right in the middle of this." She leaned back so Nick could see.

J. Need to call in my marker. Must change delivery date for 975221. Will make needed adjustments and make sure you're taken care of. No worries. I've got your back. L.T.

"That's the reference number I have for the B61-11 shipment. Looks like the change in schedule was initiated by Tucker."

"Yeah," Mia said, "but there has to be more than that. Why else would Tucker be promising to watch Kresky's back?"

"There could be any number of reasons." He frowned. "Is there any way you can check Kresky's documents for the reference number? Maybe there's something stored on the computer."

"Sure," she said. "I can do that." She pulled up a search window and entered the six-digit number. "I'm running it through the whole system, not just Kresky's files."

The computer whirred into action. At first it looked as if Kresky's e-mail was the only document containing the number. Then a second file appeared on the screen, this one actually called 975221.

"Can you open that one?" Nick asked, frowning at the flashing number.

"Yeah." She clicked on the link and the computer obediently popped up a DOD form. This one approving the

B61-11's transport. It was signed by a department head and countersigned by someone with the EPA. "You want me to print it?"

"Yes. What's on the next page?"

She clicked the mouse on the right-hand corner of the document and a new page filled the screen. This one with a detailed map and description of the exact route to be used for the transport. The modified nuclear weapon had definitely been cleared for movement from Wildwood to Malmstrom.

But the interesting thing was that the DOD-approved route for the B61-11 was nowhere near Cedar Branch. In fact, if these documents were valid, the transport shouldn't have been in southeast Idaho at all.

CHAPTER NINE

"SO YOU'RE SURE THAT we're safe here?" Mia pulled the curtains of the hotel room open a crack and stared down at the parking lot below them.

They were staying at a luxury hotel off I-15 near Provo, Utah. They'd actually switched vehicles three times, not to mention making decoy reservations at a hotel in Idaho and another in Nevada. The former in their real names, the latter using the aliases they'd used at Kresky's.

"Believe me, our trail is so convoluted not even Davies will be able to find us. You just need to relax."

"It's hard to do that with a great big target on your back." In just a few days she'd jumped from *It's a Wonderful Life* to *24* without benefit of transition. To say that she was seriously out of her element was true on so many levels she couldn't even begin to comprehend them all.

She turned from the window and sat down on the arm of an overstuffed chair. The suite was nice—a bedroom and a sitting area. There was even a small kitchen complete with refrigerator and microwave. Certainly a step up from the Twin Pines.

"At least for the moment we've still got the advantage. There's still nothing about you on television or in the papers." He waved a hand at the newest stack of newspapers they'd acquired from a convenience store at the Nevada state line. She swallowed, remembering the headlines, the spare prose and stark pronouncements adding a grim reality to what had until now seemed more like a bad dream.

"Which tells us," Nick continued, "that S&C still believes they can find you without outside help."

"But if they really believe it's an accident, then why do they need to keep me a secret at all?"

"I've been asking that from the get-go," Nick said, tipping a can to drain the last of his Coke. They'd stopped for hamburgers, the remnants of their meal on the table in front of him. "As far I'm concerned, the fact that they haven't gone public is one hell of a red flag."

"Meaning that if you'd been in charge, my face would have been plastered all over the place." She crossed her arms, insecurity flooding through her as she was reminded that she was putting her faith in a man who still suspected she might have been responsible for murdering her friends.

He shrugged and tossed the can into the trash. "I believe in using any tool at hand. That said, I'd only use the media if I was ready for the spotlight myself. I'm guessing S&C, or whoever is pulling their strings, doesn't want that kind of scrutiny. Otherwise admitting there was a survivor— AWOL or not—would only play to their advantage. Focus the story on you rather than Kresky. It would give the public someone to blame. Or at the very least, considering your background, perfect fodder for conspiracy theories."

"And if they happen to believe I'm innocent?"

"Then the world is taken with the miracle rather than the disaster. Either way it's a win for Kresky and DOD."

"Only they haven't released my name."

"Which leaves us wondering why. And it's got to be more than just moving up the shipment or changing routes. That sort of thing is done all the time."

"Well, it's not me. You already said they don't suspect me."

"I never said they didn't suspect you. All I said was that they *told* me they didn't."

"Isn't that the same thing?" she snapped, her stomach roiling.

"Not by a long shot. It could just be a strategic move on their part. Meant to keep me off the real trail."

"Of what?" Anger flashed, which was just as well, as the alternative was tears. "This isn't some kind of game. Homeland Security vs. the CIA. This is my *life*. My friends were killed in Cedar Branch. And whether any of you believe it or not, that matters to me. They were real people with real lives and they didn't deserve to die. Any more than I deserve to be some kind of medical curiosity for some government researcher who was to get his rocks off finding the answer to the question 'why did she live and they die?'"

She stood up, struggling for breath, her tangled emotions threatening to cut off the words. "I don't give a rat's ass what any of you have to say about it. All I care about is finding out what really happened in Cedar Branch. And if someone is at fault, then I goddamned well want him to pay."

"Hey." Nick moved to stand beside her, his brow furrowed with concern. "I know they were your friends. I was there when you found out they were dead, remember? No one can fake that kind of grief."

"But you still think I might have had something to do with this."

"I don't think anything. Except that, for the moment, we're in this together. And we're going to find out what happened. That much I can promise you."

"Well, it's not enough." She fisted her hands, fighting fatigue and tears, the adrenaline that had been carrying her forward suddenly gone. "This is an impossible situation. I can't survive out there without you. Not with Davies and his men hunting me. But I can't stand the idea that you're just waiting for me to trip up. To admit being involved in something so heinous there aren't even words."

"Then let's have a truce."

"How do we do that?" she whispered. "You don't believe me."

"I don't believe anyone, Mia." He lifted his hand as if to comfort her, but then dropped it, his expression hardening. "It's my nature. I just figure that everyone has something to hide. And for the most part, I'm usually right."

"Seems like a depressing way to live."

He shrugged. "It's kept me alive."

She turned away from him to look out the window again. Below, in the parking lot, two kids emerged from a minivan, fighting over a DVD or game or book or something. Their mother climbed out of the passenger seat, her face reflecting the rebuke in her tone. The kids stopped, staring at her defiantly, and then suddenly they all three laughed, their father joining them as they walked toward the hotel.

"We were just like those people," she whispered, tears filling her eyes. "We fought and we argued, but at the end of the day, we all loved each other. And now they're dead. And I'm not. So you tell me, how am I supposed to live with that?"

"You just do it." He was standing behind her, his breath

stirring her hair. "Day by day. One foot in front of the other." He spoke as if he knew her pain. She turned around, searching his face, recognizing the raw emotion reflected in his eyes. His anguish mixing with hers.

"And does it work?" she asked, thinking of his sister. "Do you ever forget?"

"No." The word hung in the air, taking on a life of its own. "But it gets easier."

"Then I'm ready for that part."

For a moment they just stood there, communicating on a level that had nothing whatsoever to do with Cedar Branch or the deaths of her friends. But it was too much, too soon. And most definitely the wrong person.

She took a step back, sucking in a breath for fortification. "So where are we?" she asked, her tight smile meant to guard against further emotional onslaught.

There was a flash of confusion and then a look of what might actually have been admiration, if it had been coming from anyone but Nick Price. "Well, we know that the shipment wasn't originally intended to go through Cedar Branch." He perched on the arm of the sofa, and she breathed a sigh of relief that he'd accept her transition away from anything personal.

"And we know that Senator Tucker was the one to request the change. What did he say? Something about calling in a marker?" She took a seat at the table, increasing the distance between them. All the better for her powers of concentration. "You intimated that Kresky probably had Tucker in his back pocket. Was that based on any real evidence? Or just a guess?"

"A guess," Nick said. "A fairly educated one. But still just conjecture."

"What if it's the other way around? What if Tucker is the one who has something on Kresky. If he's calling in a marker, that means Kresky owed him. Right?"

"Yeah. But it doesn't make Tucker culpable for what happened. It's still Kresky's warhead that exploded."

"Actually, you could argue that it was the government's bomb. Kresky was just transporting it."

"Still leaves him with liability."

"But Tucker would share in that liability if his involvement came to light." She frowned, trying to order her thoughts. "Even if it was just an accident, it's his fault the route was changed at the last minute. If that proves to have any bearing on the explosion, then he'd be culpable. Right?"

"Yes. But we don't have solid proof. What we need is to figure out why he had the shipment moved up, and why the route was changed." Nick tipped back his head and rubbed his neck, the tension in his shoulders radiating into the room.

"So do you have an in with Tucker?" she asked. "Someone on his staff, maybe?"

"No." He said shaking his head. "As I said, I've never been one for politicos. But Matt might know someone we can talk to. I'll send him an e-mail." He crossed over to the table, sitting across from her, and reached for the computer.

"Are you sure it's safe?"

"I told you before, I trust Matt with my life."

"I didn't mean Matt. I meant e-mail." She frowned at the computer. "It wouldn't be that hard for someone to use it to find us."

"Matt is even more savvy than you are when it comes to computers." He was typing while he talked, the one-fingered chicken pecking almost laughable in a man so seemingly accomplished. "He's got an encrypted address. To hear him tell it, the message bounces all over the world before it lands in his box. It's safe."

"But what if someone in Homeland Security is part of this?"

"I'm way ahead of you. It's his private account." He hit Send, and then sat back. "So now we wait."

"Yeah." She stood up, heading for the window again. "Except I'm not so good at that. Never have been, actually. I'm the kind of person who opens presents the minute they arrive. No matter how far off Christmas is."

"Instant gratification has its benefits." He smiled, and for a moment at least, the tension between them lessened.

"Yeah, but Christmas can be kind of empty without presents."

"Didn't you have your family?"

"To varying degrees, depending on the year. My father tended to have engagements over the holidays, so he was usually traveling. And if possible my mom liked to go with him."

"I take it you weren't included."

"Sometimes I was. But no, mainly I stayed home. Jazz bars aren't exactly a good place for a kid to hang out. Especially the ones my father played."

"But you had your grandfather."

"Yeah, but he wasn't exactly a celebration kind of guy. Cattle don't take time off. Which means that ranchers don't, either."

"I'm sorry. Christmas should be about families." He actually sounded as if he cared, which only muddied her perception of him. One minute he seemed so remote and the next almost—well, human.

"Before you drag out the violins, I can assure you that my Christmases were just fine. My grandfather loved me. And so did my parents. I never doubted that. And I had the whole family Christmas thing a couple of times, when I'd spend the holiday at my *abuela*'s. My father comes from a huge family, so it was quite the celebration."

"But you don't have contact with them anymore?"

"No. My father wasn't all that close with his family. He left home as soon as he was old enough to get a job. And I don't think he ever really looked back."

"But he sent you to stay with his mother."

"More for convenience than anything else. My mom and dad needed to travel, and my grandfather wasn't into small children. So the fact that my grandmother lived in comparative poverty in the backwoods of Colombia was less of an issue than it might otherwise have been."

"But you liked it."

"Yes. I did. A fact my father could never really understand. Look, my family was what it was, Nick. I'm not apologizing for them. And I'm not complaining. I was loved. And in the end, that's all that really matters. What were your Christmases like?"

He looked surprised for a moment, as if no one had ever asked him the question. Which, considering his scowl, was probably understandable. "They were pretty much like everyone else's. You know—decorations, presents, lots of hot chocolate and cookies. My mom made really good chocolate chip cookies."

"But you don't speak to her anymore?"

"No." The one-word answer should have warned her, but she persisted anyway.

"Why?"

"Because she can't stand the sight of me. Can we just leave it at that?" There was an underlying note of pain in his voice. His mother's defection had hurt him. Deeply. Nick Price might talk a good game, but he had feelings just like anyone else. He was simply better than most at keeping them buried.

"I hit a nerve. I'm sorry. I shouldn't have asked. It's just that we were talking about families and Christmas and I—"

He held up a hand, effectively cutting her off. "You were interested. I know. And considering the fact that I've been grilling you about your family background for the last couple of days, I guess it's your turn. Suffice it to say that my mother has good cause for not speaking to me. And I've accepted the fact. The rest of the story isn't worth telling."

She started to push for more, but quelled the urge. There was no point. Nick wasn't the kind of man to idly answer questions about someone he so clearly cared about. Instead, she walked back over to the window, pushing the drapes aside.

The red minivan was still parked under the window, right next to their blue Oldsmobile. The car was the very definition of nondescript. The kind of vehicle that one saw without recording any details. All the better to slip under the radar.

Across the way, a Denny's sign flickered to life as the evening shadows deepened into night. Next door, the McDonald's was doing brisk business, the line of cars extending around the building a testament to America's devotion to everything fast.

Mia sighed, thinking of Cedar Branch and Cuppa Joe. Patrick would have turned the sign on by now, the little café filling the darkness with a comforting beacon of neon and chrome. Joe and Carson would be sitting at the counter arguing about the price of beef. And Betty Freeman would pop in with the excuse that she'd forgotten to buy coffee again. Everyone in town knew she was still sweet on Joe.

Everyone, that is, except Joe.

"I'm sorry about your friends." Nick had moved to stand behind her, his hands warm on her shoulders. His words comforting in an odd sort of way.

"Thanks." She shifted slightly, breaking contact. It probably seemed rude, but she just wasn't certain she could keep her composure in the face of his sudden concern. "I was just watching the lights come on." She nodded toward a 7-11, the red-and-green logo shining against the dark blue of the sky. "They're the same everywhere. We've become a homogenous society."

"Except in backwater towns like Cedar Branch." He seemed determined to make her cry.

She bit her lip and nodded, Nancy Wilcox's kindly face swimming before her eyes. "I guess there's something to be said for the heartland." She started to drop the drapery back into place, but he stopped her, his hand closing around her wrist.

There was something in his stance, maybe even in his breathing, that signaled high alert.

"What is it?" she whispered, scanning the hotel lot below. "What do you see?"

"There." He motioned with his chin, and she followed his line of sight to a car moving slowly along the parking lot aisle closest to the building. "The black Lincoln."

She nodded as the car came to a stop in front of the Olds. A man stepped out of the passenger side of the sedan and bent over to peer into the rear of the car. He straightened after a moment, and lifted his head toward the window. Almost as if he could see them standing there. The streetlight illuminated his face as if it were daylight.

"It's Charles Davies," Mia gasped, heart pounding. "What are we going to do?"

"We're going to get the hell out of here," Nick said, his fingers tightening on her arm.

"I thought you said we were safe," she whispered, searching his face, not really certain what she was hoping to find. Reassurance, maybe. But the time for that had passed.

He held her gaze for a moment. Then with an angry grimace, he released her arm and reached back for his gun. "Looks like I was wrong."

CHAPTER TEN

"GRAB EVERYTHING YOU CAN," Nick instructed. "I'll watch the door."

Mia scrambled to gather the most important of their belongings. The computer, the documents from Kresky's office and the backpack with her money and ammo. Stuffing the laptop and papers into the backpack, she slung it over her shoulder and headed across the room for the duffel with their clothes.

"Leave it," Nick said, never taking his eyes from the hallway. "We can buy more, and there's nothing in the luggage that we need to keep from Davies."

She nodded and switched directions, coming to a stop just behind him. Her fingers itched for a gun, but the rifles were in the car with the fake badges and other accoutrements of their foray into Kresky International.

Relying on Nick for protection didn't sit well at all. If her grandfather had taught her one thing, it was the importance of self-reliance. But there was also a time for teamwork, the key being to recognize the difference between the two.

At least for the moment, she didn't have to debate the situation. She needed Nick's help. And she might as well accept the fact without fighting it. "Should we take the elevator or the stairs?"

"Stairs. At least it gives us two options for escape. With the elevator, the odds are that we're just heading into a trap."

"All right. I'll follow you."

"No." He shook his head. "You go first. I'll be right behind you. I want to arrange a little present for Davies."

She frowned up at him, trying to follow his train of thought.

"Just call it my MacGyver moment." He grinned briefly and handed her the gun. "Be careful."

She nodded, then sprinted down the hall toward the stairwell. They'd cased the exit routes when they arrived. *Just to be safe,* Nick had said. Wise words. The hall behind her remained empty except for Nick, who was doing something to the door. As far as Mia was concerned, whatever he left for Davies, it wasn't enough.

She pulled open the door to the stairs and walked onto the landing, gun at the ready. The walls were painted a dull ochre, the yellow hue making the space seem smaller than it actually was. Unlike the rest of the hotel, there was no semblance of luxury. Just utilitarian steps heading both up and down.

The hotel was fifteen stories and they were exactly halfway, on the eighth. Down was, of course, the optimal choice for travel. But she waited a moment, listening to the tinny silence of the stairwell. There was no sound at all, and with a last glance behind her, she started down, resisting the urge to run. Better to keep her wits about her.

She'd made it two flights when she heard a door open. The acoustics made it impossible to tell if the sound emanated from above or below her, so she froze on the stairs, straining for a clue to direction. Nick should be coming just behind her, so if the noise was from above it had to be him. It was tempting to call out his name, but if she was wrong she'd be alerting Davies and his goons to her presence.

Better to keep quiet.

Pressing back against the wall, she counted to ten, forcing herself to slow her breathing. The silence stretched and then was broken by the sound of feet on the stairs. Definitely coming from below. She turned and dashed back up to the landing on the sixth floor, thinking to run back into the hotel.

Safety in numbers.

She grabbed the handle and pulled, then twisted and pulled, then pushed, throwing her entire body into it. Unfortunately, the door didn't budge. One-way entry—she should have thought of that. At least she could have left the eighth floor door propped open.

Cursing her own stupidity, she headed up again. Surely by now Nick would be coming. He'd know what to do. The sounds from below were growing closer. And from the tenor she'd have to say it was more than one person.

Leading with the gun, she moved slowly toward the railing. Taking a quick peek over the top, she could see the shadows of men moving upward. Somewhere around the third floor, if she had to guess. She couldn't see them clearly enough to know if it was Davies, but she couldn't afford to wait any longer.

She needed to get back upstairs, hopefully to Nick.

Running full out now, mindless of the noise, she made it to the eighth floor in record time. Unfortunately, the door here was locked as well, and there was no sign of Nick. For one moment she considered that maybe he'd sent her into a trap, but then dismissed the notion. If Nick wanted to turn her over to Davies he could have done it back at the ranch. He might not trust her, but he wasn't turning traitor.

As if to prove the point, the door opened and he moved into the stairwell.

"What the hell are you doing here? I thought you'd be out of here by now."

She shook her head, holding a finger to her lips. "They're just behind me." He took a step forward, and she lunged for the closing door. "It's going to lock."

"Doesn't matter," he said, taking the gun from her. "We can't go back out there. Davies was coming off the elevator just as I slipped in here."

"Then he can't be below us." She frowned, realizing that the noises had stopped. "Thank God." She started for the staircase, but Nick reached out to pull her back, shaking his head.

"I think they split up," he said, his voice pitched to a whisper. "Davies doesn't miss a trick."

"So we go up?" The idea didn't hold much appeal.

"Now." He shoved her up the steps as a bullet zinged past her head, embedding in the wall by the door.

At least they didn't have to worry about being quiet anymore. Mia sprinted up the stairs, taking them two at a time, Nick right behind her. They rounded the landing on the tenth floor, stopping only long enough to check the door, but like the others, it was locked securely from this side.

Five flights later they reached the top of the building, the whine of bullets alerting them to the fact that they still had company. The door to the fifteenth floor was locked, but the one leading to the roof pulled open at Mia's insistent tug. A final set of stairs opened out onto the roof itself. The flat surface was broken up by outcroppings of pipes and vents, with the rest of the elevator shaft extending up behind them.

In the distance Mia could see the silver serpentine that marked I-15, motorists wending their way north or south, blissfully unaware of the drama playing out above them.

"This way," Nick said, motioning her around the brick elevator shaft. "There's a fire escape."

Manna from heaven.

They sprinted across the rooftop, the sound of the door slamming open indication that Davies's henchmen were right behind them. Mia drew up short at the edge of the rooftop. There was no retaining wall. Just the metal arches of the ladder's railing, and a sheer drop over the side.

"Go on, I'll keep you covered." Nick turned and fired toward the figures of three men racing across the roof.

Mia sucked in a breath and stepped over the edge, trying not to look at the ground below. This wasn't the time for hesitation. The ladder dropped down about twenty feet and then ended with a small platform. Presumably at that point, her weight would extend the next section of the fire escape.

Presumably being the key word.

She moved down the ladder as quickly as possible, eyes locked on a window washer's platform located just below and to the left. Not a job she had an aptitude for. The rickety-looking contraption was empty except for a tarp and a couple of barrel-size buckets.

At least there weren't witnesses.

Below the platform, the hard reality of asphalt glimmered like mica in a cave under the artificial lights of the parking lot. One slip and…

Swallowing her fear, Mia forced her gaze upward, grateful to see Nick on the ladder above her. The star-strewn sky yawned above his head, meaning that Davies's goons hadn't reached the edge yet.

The metal of the platform creaked as she dropped off the ladder, still holding the railing as she waited for her weight to carry the fire escape downward.

Nothing happened. A shot from above signaled the arrival of Davies's men. Mia hugged the side of the building as Nick leapt off the ladder in front of her.

"Damn thing isn't moving," she said. "I think it's stuck."

He stamped on the platform and then tossed her the gun as he knelt to examine the rusty structure. "Cover me."

Nodding, Mia twisted so that she could clearly see the ladder above her. A head extended over the edge of the roof. She hesitated for a moment, then fired, the resulting expletive indicative of her marksmanship.

"Good job," Nick said without looking up, the structure still refusing to move.

"We need to go now." Mia said, taking another shot. She'd been shooting her whole life, and while her targets hadn't been human, Davies and his lot barely qualified as members of the species. If there was emotional fallout, she'd deal with it later. "I can hold them off up there, but my guess is Davies and the rest of the team will be trying to head us off at the bottom."

"I'm thinking you're right. My little diversion will have bought us some time, but I doubt it'll slow them down for long. Unfortunately, the ladder isn't cooperating. I think it's rusted shut."

"So what the hell do we do?"

"We jump," he said, standing up and taking the gun from her.

"Are you kidding? It's still ten stories or more." She tried but couldn't keep the note of sheer terror from her voice. She'd rather be shot.

Which was certainly a valid alternative, considering the circumstances.

"Not to the ground," he said. "Over there." He nodded down at the window washer's platform, its ropes swaying lazily in the night breeze.

"While people are shooting at us?" There really wasn't time to argue the point, but clearly her brain hadn't gotten the memo.

"If you've got another option, let me know."

She stomped on the fire escape one final time, as Nick kept the gun sighted toward the roof. "Fine," she said with a sigh. "We'll jump."

"Beauty before brains." His smile lacked any humor, but she appreciated the effort just the same.

Crossing herself for the first time since her confirmation, she sent a silent prayer heavenward and leapt. For a moment the feeling of weightlessness was exhilarating, and then she crashed into the wooden platform and the side of the building with enough force to send the floor's slats shimmying beneath her.

Two seconds later Nick was beside her, the platform jerking drunkenly as it tipped to the right and then to the left. One of the buckets slid off the end, spiraling downward to splinter on the pavement below. Mia tightened her hands on the railing, heart pounding while Nick manipulated the pulley system, starting their descent.

And not a moment too soon. Davies's man was already scrambling over the side of the building onto the ladder, trying to get a clear shot.

From her vantage point she could see the parking lot on the adjacent side of the building. Like their side, it was sparsely populated with cars, and no people. The lack of activity was sort of odd, actually. She'd have thought there would be more reaction from the people at the hotel. Surely someone had called the police.

As if in answer, the wail of a siren split the night air, the flashing red lights no more than pinpricks in the distance on the highway.

"The cavalry's coming," she said, her eyes still on the horizon.

"Not for us. But with a little luck we'll be leaving Davies behind to explain the situation. The last thing we need is to be detained by locals. More than likely they'd just hand us over to S&C."

Mia nodded, turning her attention to the man on the ladder above them. "Give me the gun." She reached for it and fired a warning shot. Despite her need to stop the bastard from shooting her, she couldn't really stomach the idea of killing someone. Better to just keep him out of range.

The man stopped in his tracks, and Mia kept the gun on him as they moved even lower. Below her a couple of men emerged from the front of the hotel on the run.

"Company at three o'clock," she said, shifting so that she could cover both threats at once, her thoughts running riot as she considered the enormity of their situation.

The platform jerked, throwing Mia against Nick as it lurched to a halt about ten feet from the ground. The man on the ladder above seized the opportunity and fired, his bullet just missing the mark as it splintered the wood at her feet.

"You all right?" Nick demanded, helping her regain her balance.

She nodded, aiming at the ladder to answer fire. "I'm fine. What's with the platform?"

"I think this is as far as it goes. We're going to have to jump again."

"Right behind you," she said, firing one last time at the goon on the fire escape. At this rate, she was at least going to be cured of any problem she had with heights.

Nick hit the ground on a roll and popped back to his feet, reaching up for the gun. She threw it to him and scrambled over the edge of the platform, to dangle a moment before releasing the railing and dropping to the ground.

"This way." Nick motioned, heading in the opposite direction from the men rounding the far corner of the building. *Davies.* She could recognize him even from this distance.

She and Nick sprinted past the red minivan to their car, only to find it still blocked in by the Lincoln. The shooting was coming from two directions now, the asphalt spitting rocks as it was hit repeatedly with bullets.

Nick crouched behind the Olds, scanning the parking lot for a way out. The sirens were getting louder as their assailants moved closer. Endgame if ever there was one.

"So what do we do now?" she asked, lifting up for a quick view. "They're closing fast."

"We move on to plan B," Nick said, grabbing her hand.

Actually she hadn't known there was a plan A, which clearly meant she was in the dark about plan B. But at the moment she was pretty much game for anything that got them the hell out of here.

"What about the stuff in the car?" she asked. "The rifles are in there."

"Leave them," he said, as a bullet penetrated the Olds with a sickening thunk. "There's no time. We'll go on my count." He popped up to fire at Davies and crew, then dropped back down behind the car. "Ready?"

She nodded.

"One…two… three…*go*." He grabbed her hand and together they ran for the far side of the lot, swerving to avoid the hail of bullets.

A yellow delivery truck was parked next to the chain-link fence that surrounded the property. Nick yanked open the driver's side and Mia slid through to the passenger seat. He fired once more, then climbed into the van.

"What now?" she asked, her heart threatening to break free of her rib cage.

"We get the hell out of here." Nick flipped down the visor and grabbed the set of keys that fell with the movement. Two seconds later the van's engine leaped to life and they were on their way.

"How the hell did you know that the keys would be there?"

"I saw the guy heading for the lobby when we were on the roof," he said, flooring the gas pedal, the van shaking as the odometer climbed beyond its comfort level. "I knew from the way he was parked he wasn't staying long, so I figured the keys would be in the van."

She turned to watch behind them, grateful to see that there were no following headlights. "But why would he leave the keys?"

"Standard operating procedure. Keeps the keys from

getting lost in the rush of a delivery. I worked for a florist once upon a time." The idea would have been laughable if it hadn't just saved their asses.

He turned away from the interstate, heading instead toward a county road that led back toward Nevada.

He must have noticed her confusion because he smiled, his teeth white against the shadows of his face. "Always best to do what they least expect. Davies will assume we'll want to keep putting distance between us and Kresky International. So we'll do the opposite."

"All the way back to Wildwood?"

"No. Just until we can find another car. This one is a little too high-profile for me."

"It's certainly apropos," she countered, breathing easily for the first time since they'd left the hotel room. Leaning back against the seat, she smiled, thinking of the slogan painted on the delivery truck's side.

Accepting Impossible Missions Daily.

No shit.

CHAPTER ELEVEN

TWO HOURS LATER there was still no sign of Davies. They'd managed to ditch the van and liberate a car from a used lot in one of the towns they'd passed through on Highway 6. Fortunately there'd also been a discount store, which meant they'd been able to replace the clothing and essentials they'd left behind. Now on the outskirts of the Wasatch-Cache National Forest, Nick thought they were safe enough to stop for a bit. If only to catch their breath and figure out what they wanted to do next.

He pulled off onto a service road and then into a copse of pine trees fronting a rocky incline studded with boulders. Despite the approaching dawn, the sky was growing darker, lit only by intermittent starlight breaking through the gathering clouds. So far the weather was holding, but he didn't expect it to last long.

Before the storm hit they needed a plan, hopefully something that included a place to stay, somewhere where they could figure out what to do next. Mia slept beside him in the passenger seat. He knew he should wake her. But just for the moment, he was content to savor the soft curve of her breasts moving with each breath.

She was strikingly beautiful. All the more so because she was totally unaware of the fact. And to top it off, she was an amazingly resourceful woman, a fascinating combination of strength and vulnerability. One minute mourning her friends and the next keeping Davies's men corralled on the hotel roof.

Something about her pulled at him in a way he hadn't expected, emotions surfacing that he'd thought long buried. When Katie had died, he'd sworn never to let anyone else in; the risk was simply too great. His life wasn't the kind he could share with someone.

Too damn many shadows.

"Everything okay?" Mia's eyes fluttered open, her gaze scanning the horizon for signs of danger. "Why have we stopped?"

"We're fine," he said, reaching over to cover her hand with his. "I just thought we needed to talk, and this seemed like a safe enough place."

"For now maybe." She sat up with a frown, pulling her hand away in the process. He resisted the urge to reach for it again. Obviously he was losing it big time. Mia was no different from any other woman. And despite his instincts to the contrary, there was still a possibility that she was tangled up in all of this somehow. His hormones were just working overtime. "But those men back there were shooting to kill. Which means they've clearly lost interest in capturing me alive."

"I think the stakes have shifted." He shook his head, clearing his thoughts. "Maybe they know about our foray into Kresky's offices, or maybe it's just because Davies knows my involvement changes the game. If there is a cover-up, they can't afford to have us digging for the truth. So the more we find out, the more likely they're going to go for the permanent solution."

"So you're agreeing that he wants me dead."

"Worst case scenario. Yes. But I also think that if capturing you alive is possible, that remains the preference."

"Small distinction, since I'm not likely to come willingly."

"Not if I have any say in the matter." The words came out before he had the chance to think them through, but he realized he'd crossed a line. If it was in his power, he wasn't going to let Charles Davies get his hands on Mia.

"Thanks for that." Her smile was faint but very real, and he felt his pulse quicken. She held his gaze for a moment, and then with an audible sigh, turned to look out the passenger window. "Where are we?"

"Northwest Utah. About ninety miles from the Nevada border."

She nodded and tilted her head, stretching her neck. "Are we actually going back into Nevada? Seems to me we'd be better off heading to Idaho and familiar territory."

"Makes sense. I just want to make sure we don't walk into a trap."

She released her seat belt, twisting so that she was facing him. "If you want to do that, then we've got to figure out how they found us so easily. You said yourself our tracks were too convoluted to follow. Yet Davies didn't seem to have any problem at all. Which begs the question why?"

"I take it you have an answer?" He frowned, not certain he wanted to hear where she was leading.

"Not an answer per se, but definitely a suspicion. I haven't talked to anyone except Paul Brennon. And even if we somehow tipped our hand, he still wouldn't have known for certain who we were or where we were going. So that leaves one of two options. Either you talked to someone you haven't told me about, or Matt Young isn't as good a friend as you thought he was."

"It isn't Matt. There's no fucking way."

She held up a hand in protest. "I'm not trying to attack your friend, I'm just trying to rule out alternatives."

Which was exactly what he should have been doing instead of contemplating Mia's assets. This was exactly why he never allowed himself to become entangled with a woman. It compromised everything—certain parts of his anatomy superseding his brain.

"All right. I see your point. But I'm still certain it isn't Matt. I've only contacted him twice. Once by phone after we escaped Davies the first time. And then I e-mailed him from the hotel."

"So maybe someone was tapping your phone?"

"That'd be pretty damn unlikely. It's a secure phone, and even if it was compromised, I didn't tell Matt where I was. Hell, I didn't even admit you were with me. So if he's trying to locate me, he wouldn't have enough information to do so."

"What about the e-mail?"

"I don't know." He flipped open his computer and turned on the GPS, studying the resulting map for ideas as to where they might find a safe place to stay.

"Maybe it was tagged somehow? It's possible to track a computer through e-mail."

"Yeah, maybe to a general area, but not to a specific address. And even if it could give exact information, it wouldn't tell them what hotel we were in or what kind of car we were driving."

"That could have just come from surveillance. Or maybe the guy we got the badges from has an ax to grind?"

"Not a chance. He compromises me, he knows his days

are numbered. There are rules even in my world. You're grasping at straws." He moved the cursor over a section of southern Idaho and enlarged the screen.

"You're right," she said, throwing up her hands. "Davies is just better than you are."

He whipped around, anger flashing, then forced himself to take a breath. "Davies isn't better than I am."

"And this isn't a pissing contest. If they are using something to track us, then we need to figure out what it is."

He closed the computer. "I'm not discounting what you're saying. I just don't think it's all that likely. Despite what you've seen in the movies, blind luck is half the equation when it comes to my line of work. Davies just got lucky."

"And we almost got killed—or worse."

He opened his mouth to say that there was nothing worse, but closed it when he saw the expression on her face. "Look, we've already cleared Matt. Which doesn't leave many options. You're not wearing anything you had with you at the S&C facility, right?"

"Not even the same underwear." She frowned, her mind clearly not satisfied with his rebuff. "But you were there, too. Remember?"

"Davies wouldn't have had any reason to want to track me."

"Except that you defected with his prize captive."

"I didn't help you escape…." He stopped, his mind suddenly pulling up the image of the guard at the S&C facility gate. "They searched my things."

"What?" Mia asked, clearly not following the non sequitur.

"When I left the S&C facility, Davies had the guard at

the gate search my things. I thought it was just to piss me off—"

"But what if it was to plant a bug?" Mia finished for him, looking just a little too self-satisfied for his liking.

"It's a definite possibility. But if he did do it, then we're in the clear."

"How do you figure that?" she asked.

"The duffel is still in the hotel room. With the rest of our things." Even if Davies had gotten the best of him, at least Nick had managed to pull the fat out of the fire.

"What about the computer?" Mia sure had a way of bursting the bubble.

"To plant something in my computer, the guy would have needed more time. Besides, I could see him."

"From your car, right?"

"Yeah. And I'm certain he didn't turn it on. Even if somehow he could have managed it without my seeing, I would have heard. The damn thing could wake the dead when it boots up."

"He wouldn't have had to turn it on." She grabbed the laptop and flipped it upside down, pushing the battery release button. She lifted the battery out, the computer chiming in protest at being deprived of its power source.

"See? I would have heard it." He frowned as she stuck her fingers into the cavity where the battery had been, and felt around inside.

"There's nothing here," she said on a sigh, replacing first the battery and then the cover.

"Not to say I told you so, but…" He trailed off, restraining a grin. It wasn't that he wanted to prove her wrong; it was more that he couldn't stomach the idea that Davies had gotten one over on him.

She bit her lip, staring at the computer as if it were going to open up and confess. Then, with decided determination, she turned it on its side, hitting the button to release the CD drive unit. After popping it out, she turned it over and, with a little smile of triumph, removed a dime-size disk from the bottom.

"Son of a bitch." There really wasn't anything else to say.

"It's not your fault. You wouldn't have noticed. He could have slipped it in place in a matter of seconds. Besides, why would you have expected something like this? You guys are all supposed to be playing on the same team."

"Apparently not." He took the disk from her, lifting it to the dash light for closer inspection. "I should have known better."

"Even you can't know everything." She reached over to put a hand on his knee, the gesture meant to be comforting, but in fact, anything but.

"Davies is a snake. I knew he was jacking with me, but I should have figured he'd be covering all his bases."

"He couldn't have known you'd come after me."

"But it was a reasonable possibility. And if I hadn't gone after you, no harm, no foul. Better to cover all his bases."

"Again with the baseball metaphors."

Her words had the intended effect and he smiled, despite himself. "So what do you say we put that batter's swing of yours to good work? Knock this sucker into the outfield before they have a chance to zero in on us again."

"I've got a better idea." She waggled her eyebrows, her smile full of mischief. "Take me to the nearest truck stop."

MIA WATCHED THROUGH the back window of their latest vehicle as the red lights of the tractor-trailer rig—and the tracking device nestled cozily against the truck's rear axle—disappeared into the horizon.

"Not bad for an amateur," Nick said, checking the rearview mirror. "Not bad at all."

"With any luck, the driver won't stop until he reaches the East Coast. Hope Davies enjoys the trip." She turned to face the road ahead. "So where are we going?"

"According to the clerk at the truck stop, there's a motel a few miles up the road. I figure we can hole up there for a couple hours. Get some sleep and figure out our next move. Hopefully, Matt will have turned something up."

"I'm sorry I blamed him before. I just didn't know what to think." Still didn't, actually, but at least she was certain of one thing: Charles Davies was a common enemy. Especially now. Nick wasn't the kind of man to take being duped easily. And she had to admit it felt better than it ought to to think that just maybe he really was on her side.

"Hey, you're the one who found the bug. I think that absolves you of any need to apologize."

"Well, the important thing is that we've gotten Davies off our backs."

"At least for the time being." His grimace didn't lend a lot of support to the notion.

"Maybe it wasn't that great an idea."

"No." He shook his head. "It was brilliant. I'm just not going to underestimate Davies again."

"Hey, don't beat yourself up about it. You really were supposed to be on the same side. There's no way you could have anticipated what he did."

"The hell I couldn't have. I knew he was a slippery

bastard from the get-go. And if I hadn't been so pissed off about him getting me pulled off the operation I'd have realized that the search had to be a cover for something."

"What's done is done. Better that we take advantage of being a step ahead of him—for however long it lasts."

"So what made you think the bug was attached to the drive?"

"My mother."

"I thought you weren't part of all that." He frowned, his eyes still on the road.

"I was part of her life, Nick. Some things you just can't avoid."

"So she had a working knowledge of tracking devices?" The question was a little too casual, and she felt her defenses rising. One step forward, ten steps back.

"Yeah, but not for the reason you're thinking. She didn't bug people. They bugged her. Probably some of the guys you work with. She had one in her computer once. Courtesy of U.S. Customs. It was a sting."

"And did it yield information?"

"No. It led to a lawsuit. My mother found it. But even if she hadn't, nothing would have come of it. You overestimate my mother's connections."

"We've just had a valuable lesson in *under*estimation, Mia. Besides, whoever was behind the bug—it was just their job. Your mother opened the door by associating with people with questionable interests."

"Last time I checked, this was a free country and the Constitution protected us from guilt by association."

"Yeah, well, the founding fathers hadn't counted on 9/11. It's a new world."

"And this was an *old* bug. Besides, not five minutes ago

you were cursing Davies and his attempt to entrap you." She waited a beat for her words to sink in, and then turned away from him to look out the window.

Telephone poles raced past, the only sound in the car the whine of the engine and the squeak of the windshield wipers as they pushed away the beginning fall of rain. The storm was almost upon them.

"I didn't mean to attack your mother. I just can't help coming back to the fact that you're amazingly resilient and world-wise for someone who spent most of her life in a place like Cedar Branch."

"Just because I live in a small town doesn't make me some kind of backwoods yahoo. I traveled with my parents, I spent time in the rainforests of Colombia and I lived in California for four years when I was in college. Besides, the people I knew in Cedar Branch—the people who died there—they weren't yahoos, either. I suspect if you'd had the chance to get to know them, you'd have been surprised at just how fabulous they really were." Tears threatened but she wiped them away, not willing to let Nick see just how much he'd hurt her.

Yellow neon flashed ahead, cutting through the now driving rain, the sign signaling that they'd reached the motel. Nick pulled the car into the empty lot and coasted to a stop. She kept her face turned toward the window, hoping that he'd just get out and leave her alone.

But he didn't.

Silence stretched between them and then he reached for her, pulling her around to face him. "I'm sorry, Mia. I was out of line. But it's like I said before—everyone has something to hide. And more times than not it's my job to expose whatever it is. For what it's worth, I want to believe you.

I know that's not much. But it's all I've got. I didn't mean to belittle your friends. I'm sure they were wonderful people."

She nodded, not trusting herself with words. So much had been lost.

He reached out to brush away the tears that were trembling on her eyelashes. She shivered, her pain morphing into something more primitive, the emotion surprising her with its intensity. He leaned forward, his breath mixing with hers, and without giving herself time for second thoughts, she closed the distance between them.

There was nothing tentative in the kiss. Their pent-up anger exploded into passion, raging through her like an out of control fire. She parted her lips, opening for him, her tongue circling his as she reveled in the feel of his mouth against hers.

She pulled him closer, knowing she was treading on dangerous ground. Nicholas Price wasn't the kind of man to start something he wasn't prepared to finish.

She knew she should stop him, but here in the warmth of the car, with the rain beating a rhythm against the roof, she didn't want to pull away. The toll of the past few days was beyond measure, and just for a moment, she wanted to forget. To escape into the silent seduction of the kiss.

Thunder rolled in the distance, the vibration running through them like an electric current. She pressed closer, not sure what it was she needed, but absolutely certain that he was the only one who could give it to her.

She twined her fingers through his hair, delighting in the soft silky curls, a stark contrast to the hard-bitten strength of the man himself.

His lips moved to her cheeks, then to her eyes, his

callused fingers framing her face. Shivers of pleasure raced through her, building with each touch, each caress. Then he moved again, taking possession of her lips, his kiss demanding now—possessive.

A hint of worry rippled through her, but was gone before she had time to think about it. Her hands were trapped between them, his heart beating wildly against her fingers, the syncopated rhythm matching her own. She traced the line of his lips with her tongue, smiling against his mouth when he groaned with pleasure.

There was power in knowing that she aroused him— that the seduction was mutual, her strength matching his. And on that thought, she let go of any doubt, intent instead upon riding the wave.

Thunder crashed overhead, followed by the discordant ringing of a cell phone. Reality broke through the pheromone-charged haze that had engulfed them. She struggled to an upright position, the heat of a flush burning her cheeks—passion fleeing in the wake of embarrassment.

Nick pulled out his phone, flipping it open, his eyes meeting hers across the distance of the front seat. "Price."

There was a moment of silence as he listened to whatever the caller had to say, his scowl banishing any last vestiges of passion.

"It's Matt," he said, the words perfunctory, his mind already focused on his friend's call. As if to underscore the point, he opened the car door and dashed through the rain to the comparative cover of the porch outside the motel's office. The resulting distance seeming almost unbreachable.

For a moment, she sat frozen in the car, confused, disappointment mixing with a healthy dose of relief. She felt as though she'd managed to sidestep an emotional minefield. There was so much at stake, and she'd been about to surrender everything to a man who openly admitted that he still doubted her.

She was savvy enough to know that a door had been opened. One that wouldn't easily be shut again. Sooner or later they would have to face the attraction that lay between them. But not now.

Without realizing it, Matt Young had done her a favor.

The only problem was, she didn't feel the slightest bit grateful.

CHAPTER TWELVE

"SO I'M ASSUMING THIS is something important or you wouldn't be risking contact," Nick said, frowning as Mia emerged from the car, a newspaper tented over her head. She ran for the porch, bypassing him to go into the office without even a second glance.

"I'm on a secure line. I know there's still a risk, but the shit's hitting the fan and I figured you'd appreciate the heads-up." The tenor of his friend's voice snapped his thoughts away from Mia.

"I'm not going to like this, am I?"

"I guess it depends on whether or not you're helping Mia Kearney." It was a statement, not a question. But then Matt knew him better than pretty much anyone.

"I'm with her, but I'm assuming you worked that out on your own. As to helping her—let's just say that for the moment our interests coincide."

"Just be sure you're backing the right team. I know you like playing rogue operative, but this is getting serious."

"It's always serious, Matt. And at least for the moment, I'm inclined to believe that Mia had nothing to do with this. Which means that there's something else going on. And I intend to find out what it is."

"It may cost you your career."

"Since when has that been an issue for me?" He tried to curb his frustration. Matt was only trying to help.

"Well, the game has changed. S&C isn't just looking for a victim."

"Come again?" Nick frowned, turning so that he could see Mia through the office window. She was talking to the clerk, her hands waving to emphasize whatever it was she was saying.

"According to the scuttle I'm hearing, Davies has proof that Mia was connected to the explosion. And more importantly, he's claiming your involvement goes deeper than just an interest in the truth. He's branding you a traitor."

"That's bullshit."

"I know that. And I think Gordon's still behind you. But Ricks is buying into it. Apparently he and the director of the CIA had a little confab, and the bottom line is that Harry Norton says he has evidence."

"How many people know?" Nick watched as the *L* in the Lazy Daze's sign blinked on and off, the motion making the motel moniker seem tackier than it already was.

"So far it's been pretty contained," Matt said, pulling Nick's attention back to the conversation. "Besides Norton and Davies, I think Gordon and Ricks are the only ones. I only know about it because I happened to overhear the conversation between Gordon and Ricks."

"Happened to overhear?" Despite the gravity of the situation, Nick smiled.

"Well, let's just say there was computer technology involved." Matt laughed, and then sobered. "But this isn't a joke, Nick. Whatever's going on, there are some powerful players involved. And that means you've got big trouble. It isn't too late to get the hell out of there. To bring Mia Kearney in. We can keep her safe until all this is sorted out."

"From what you're telling me, bringing her in would only play into S&C's hands. Which means it's too late to play this by the book." Nick watched as Mia signed the register, the soft silk of her hair screening her face. "Hell, it was too late the minute she slammed me in the head with a chair leg."

"You always were a sucker for lost causes."

"If you're talking about Katie, I didn't have any choice. I had to do what I did. The only way to have any kind of closure was to find the truth about her death."

"Maybe some things we're better off not knowing."

"You don't believe that any more than I do. But I appreciate your concern."

"Hey, what can I say, I'm used to having you around. Anyway, there's more bad news."

Nick tightened his hand on the phone. "Figures."

"When I said it was some serious shit, I wasn't kidding. Davies put a trace in your computer."

"I know. We found it."

"We?"

"Mia, actually. Seems she knows her way around a computer."

"I thought she was an artist."

"She is. But apparently she's got a few more skills." He closed his eyes, his blood pressure rising with the memory of her body pressed against his. Dangerous waters. He shook his head, clearing his thoughts. "Anyway, we managed to attach it to an eastbound truck. Hopefully, that'll buy us a little time. You got my e-mail?"

"Yeah," Matt said, accepting the change of subject

without protest. "And I did a little checking. Unfortunately, folks at Tucker's office are closemouthed as hell. I pulled all the stops and nada. My guess is that I hit a nerve."

"Great. So we've got nothing."

"I didn't say that." Nick could hear the smile in his friend's voice.

"When I struck out with Tucker's folks, I went around him. Tried some of his cohorts on the appropriations committee. And I think I hit pay dirt with an aide in Walter Hatcher's office. He was fairly open about the relationship between Hatcher and Tucker, but then he shut down completely. I figured someone walked in or he got an attack of conscience. Either way I thought we were dead in the water."

"But something else happened," Nick prompted.

"Yeah. He called me back. At three in the fucking morning."

"Sounds promising."

"Actually, it was cryptic as hell. He mentioned the house appropriations bill and then mumbled something about things being hidden in plain sight."

"That's it?" Nick fought against frustration.

"Yeah, he hung up before I could ask questions."

"Have you tried to reach him again?"

"Apparently he's on vacation. Probably the permanent kind," Matt said.

"Which points to the fact that Hatcher's involved in this somehow."

"Makes sense, considering the nuke was routed through Idaho. But I'll be damned if I know what the appropriations bill has to do with any of this."

"I'll just have to figure it out."

"Let me know if I can help."

"You already have," Nick said, nodding even though Matt couldn't see. "But I don't want you to risk anything more for me."

"Hell, it's the most fun I've had in ages. You know I like the cloak-and-dagger stuff. Anyway, since your best bet seems to be the appropriations bill, I set you up with a link to the document. It's all public information, but it can be a little tricky getting the complete bill. This is the real deal."

"You get it through normal channels?" Nick already knew the answer, but Matt deserved credit where it was due.

"Guess that depends on what you call normal. Anyway, I transferred the whole thing to one of my aliases. So your access should be secure."

"Thanks, Matt."

"Not a problem." His friend clicked off, the dead air a reminder that essentially Nick was in this alone.

Sort of.

Mia walked out the door, stopping at the far edge of the porch, the distance between them telling him a hell of a lot more than any words could have. Her back was turned, her attention seemingly on the rain. Then with a sigh, she pivoted to face him, leaning back against the railing.

"I got us rooms. Fortunately, the clerk was so happy to have customers, he didn't ask questions. Just took the cash and gave me a couple of keys." She held them up, lifting her eyes to meet his, her expression guarded. Not that he blamed her, really. "What did Matt have to say?"

"A lot. But it'll wait until we're somewhere a little more private."

She nodded and started for the car, but he cut her off, stopping her with his hand.

"I'm sorry. I shouldn't have—"

"Forget it," she interrupted, shaking her head. "It was just the heat of the moment. It won't happen again."

She pulled free and sprinted down the steps toward a room at the far end of the complex. He watched her running, his head and his heart having different reactions. He knew she was right. It shouldn't happen again. There were any number of very sound reasons why getting involved with her was a bad idea.

He knew what he ought to do—but well, he'd never been one to follow the rules.

And, truth be told, he wasn't inclined to do so now.

MIA LEANED AGAINST the closed door of the motel room, fighting for breath. It had taken every ounce of her strength not to throw herself into his arms and beg him to tell her that the moment in the car had meant something more than fear morphing into passion.

But she already knew the answer and wasn't going to let herself in for the embarrassment of hearing him state the obvious. All she had to do was put the kiss behind her. Everyone had moments of weakness, and hers was understandable given the circumstances. Except that the stakes were so high, she couldn't afford a misstep.

It was perfectly clear that Davies's men wanted her dead. And it was equally clear that they'd used Nick to get to her. But what wasn't clear was whether she could trust him. One minute he was admitting that he didn't believe her, and the next he was kissing her. Definitely mixed signals.

None of which really mattered. The point was that it was over. And she wasn't going to let it happen again. A part of her knew that it would be best to put as much distance between them as possible. But she was also aware that she needed him. Despite being able to think on her feet, she hadn't had experience with people like Davies. Nick knew how a man like that operated.

Hell, if the situation had played out differently, he might have been the one hunting her.

But he wasn't.

And for now, she just needed to keep sight of that fact— and keep her emotions in check. Which of course was easier said than done.

The wooden planks of the porch outside the room squeaked, and Mia moved away from the door just in time to avoid being hit as it opened.

"We need to talk." Nick filled the doorway, his presence seeming almost larger than life.

"Yeah, I know." She sank down on the end of the bed.

"Matt confirmed the fact that Davies planted the bug. I told him you'd already found it."

She smiled, wondering why such a little thing seemed like a victory. "It was a logical conclusion."

"Maybe. But I didn't figure it out. Anyway, apparently Davies is claiming that he's got evidence proving you had something to do with the explosion."

"You guys just won't let it go."

Nick held up a hand in protest. "There's more. Davies— or his bosses, anyway—are also asserting that I'm helping you. They're calling me a traitor."

"That's ridiculous."

"Thanks for the vote of confidence." His smile was

fleeting. "The important thing here is that it changes the game. Harry Norton, Davies's boss, has convinced the head of Homeland Security that it's all true. Which means we can't expect any help from that quarter."

"But Matt called."

"On his own dime. He wanted to make sure I knew which way the wind was blowing."

"Okay, so we're on our own. I'm not sure how that changes the status quo."

"On the surface, it doesn't. But the very idea that they've manufactured evidence is indicative of the fact that there *is* something to cover up. Otherwise it wouldn't matter. S&C not questioning your involvement in the explosion raised a red flag for me—" She opened her mouth to argue, but he waved her quiet. "Doesn't matter if it's true. It still should have been the first thing they asked."

"But they didn't."

"Right. Next up, after your escape, they did two things that don't really make sense. They didn't call in backup to try and find you. And they bugged me in the hopes that I'd lead them to you."

"More red flags," she said, watching his face, trying to gauge his sincerity. "So you're saying the fact that they're making up lies about you—and, for that matter, about me—is tantamount to admitting that there's something else going on. A smoke screen to hide the fact that something happened in Cedar Branch that needs to be kept secret."

"And your survival is tied into it all somehow."

For a moment she thought he was doubting her again, but then she realized he was actually saying just the opposite. Relief mixed with sheer happiness. "You believe me."

"As much as I can ever really believe in anyone—yes, I do."

It didn't really change anything. But it was nice to hear the words. To know that at least for the moment, they were truly on the same side. She pushed the thoughts away before they could extend to areas she wasn't ready to consider. Better to focus on the situation at hand.

"So was there any good news?" she asked.

"A little bit. Matt managed to spook one of Hatcher's aides into a revelation of sorts."

"Hatcher? I thought we were shooting for Tucker."

"Tucker's staff was a little more secure. But we already talked about the connection between Hatcher and Tucker, and since Cedar Branch is part of Hatcher's constituency, it seemed a reasonable jump."

"So what did he find out?"

"It's pretty vague. But it came in the form of a late night phone call, so I think there's something to it." He leaned back against the table by the window. "Basically, he indicated that there was some kind of clue hidden in the appropriations bill. Actually his exact words were 'hidden in plain sight.'"

"I'd say that's pretty nebulous. Do you have any idea how many pages there are in an appropriations bill?"

"No, but we're about to find out. Matt e-mailed me a link to the text."

"Seems a bit dicey to be accessing a congressional Web site. Won't they be expecting something like that?"

"There's no reason to believe that they know we have the information—whatever the hell it turns out to be. And even if they did, Matt copied the document to a secure site. So I think we'll be okay."

"*Think* being the operative word."

"All right. So what do you propose we do?"

"Download it. Even if the site is secure, we're better off limiting our time online. I noticed a printer in the motel office. If we offer the manager enough money I'm sure he'll let us use it."

"Might work, but we'll have to figure out a way to distract him. The last thing we need is for him to start wondering why we're printing off a copy of the appropriations bill."

"I kind of doubt he even knows what *appropriation* means, but either way, I can handle him."

"All right, let's do it."

For the moment, at least, the rain had stopped, a fine mist obscuring the mountains in the distance. They made their way across the puddle-filled parking lot, up the steps and into the office. A bell attached to the door jangled as it closed, the noise blending into the sounds emanating from a battered black-and-white TV in the corner.

A stand with brochures flanked the oak counter, their headlines enticing tourists to come visit Humboldt National Forest, Bonneville Salt flats, a place called Fish Springs and the Pony Express Route. Unfortunately, it didn't look like there'd been too many takers.

"Whatcha need? No fresh towels until tomorrow." The manager's scowl wasn't conducive to asking favors, but Mia pasted on her best seductive smile, anyway.

"The towels are fine," she said, moving up to the counter. "What I'm hoping is that you can help me with a little problem."

The man shot a look toward Nick, who had moved over by the television, feigning interest in a rerun of *Alias*. It seemed oddly appropriate, somehow. At least he wasn't watching the news.

"Don't know what I could do..." He trailed off with a frown, his attention returning to her.

"Well, here's the thing, Roy," Mia said with a quick glance at his name tag. "I'm working on a big real estate deal. Some property around Ely. And I've got a huge presentation to put together. My boss—" she inclined her head toward Nick and lowered her voice "—thinks I've already got it in the bag. But the truth is I don't have everything I need."

"So how can I help?" The man frowned commiseratively in Nick's direction.

"Well, I do have everything on my computer." She patted the laptop for effect. "So if I could just use your printer, I'd be able to print out the data I need. Which in turn, I can hand out to the clients at our meeting tomorrow."

"But won't he know what you're up to?" Roy asked.

"It's doubtful," she said, lowering her voice. "He sort of sees what he wants to see, if you know what I mean."

"Know just the type." He nodded, patting her hand. "But as much as I'd like to help you, *my* boss won't be too happy if he finds me letting guests use the equipment. There's got to be a line—you know?"

"Of course." Mia tried to keep her tone sincere. "I wouldn't want you to get in any trouble. But I could make it worth your while." She produced a twenty from her pocket and laid it on the counter. "Would this be enough?"

Roy eyed the money with obvious interest, but shook his head. "I don't know. It's a mighty big risk. I could lose my job if anyone found out."

"Tell you what," Mia said, producing another twenty. "You just go in the back, and if by chance your boss does show up, you can pretend you had no idea. Just tell him you were called away from the desk to deal with something else. That way I'm the only one in trouble." She considered batting her eyes, but decided it was overkill. Besides, Roy's interest in her had dimmed considerably in view of the dead presidents lined up on the counter.

He slid his hand forward, his gaze darting over to Nick, who was still doing a great imitation of bored, and then he backed away from the desk, pocketing the money. "If you'll excuse me," he said. "I've got a few things to take care of." With a wink and a gap-toothed grin he spun around and damn near sprinted from the room.

"You really are good at this." Nick's voice mirrored the laughter she was feeling.

"He wasn't that difficult to deal with. But I suggest we get started before he changes his mind and comes back for more money." She was already behind the counter, attaching the computer to the printer. After making sure the laptop recognized the other machine, she connected to the Internet and, using Matt's directions, opened the file.

Two keystrokes later, the printer was happily spewing out paper.

"So how long do you think it will take?" Nick asked, his attention on the parking lot outside.

"Longer than I'd like," she said. "This printer isn't exactly cutting edge. But it's almost finished."

"Good." He was still staring out the window, something in the line of his shoulders making her nervous.

"You seeing something?"

"It's probably nothing, but there's a black Lexus that's driven past the motel twice."

"You're sure it's the same car?" She pulled part of the appropriations bill from the printer tray and stacked it on the counter.

"Yeah. It slowed down on the first pass. I got part of the license. OBD-7 something."

A shiver made its way down her spine. "You think Davies has found us again?"

"I wouldn't have thought so, but we can't be too careful. How much longer?"

"We're on the last page now." She disconnected the laptop and pulled the final sheet from the printer almost before it had finished. "What do you want to do?"

"Get the hell out of here. We're probably fine, but I think it's best if we don't take any chances."

"Well, I paid cash when I arrived, so Roy's not likely to sic the cops on us. Just let me clear the printer memory so that there's no chance of Davies figuring out what we copied. And we're gone."

"I'll pull the car up to office."

"Go." She nodded, scanning through the printer's menu until she reached memory. Two more clicks and the machine bore no trace of their ever having used it. And Roy wouldn't be able to tell Davies anything more than that they were headed for Ely. So far so good.

Grabbing the copy of the appropriations bill and the computer, she ran out onto the front porch just as Nick pulled up in the car. In seconds, she'd slipped into the passenger seat, twisting to stow the laptop and stack of paper in the back.

Nick spun the car around and hit the highway with a spray of gravel. Mia watched as Roy came running out the front door, his eyes wide with surprise. It would have been comical, except that as they picked up speed, a Lexus crested the hill behind them.

License plate OBD-7Y2.

CHAPTER THIRTEEN

"THEY'RE STILL BEHIND US." Mia was twisted around in the front seat, watching the approaching car out the rear window.

"The driver's trying to close the distance, but the wet highway is playing in our favor." Nick frowned into the rearview mirror, his gaze alternating between the black sedan and the road ahead.

"Maybe it isn't Davies's men?"

"Anything's possible, but I'd say the odds are against it."

The rain had let up, but there was still a fine mist, the clouds hugging the horizon. It wasn't full-fledged fog, but it was thick enough that the car behind them occasionally disappeared into a bank of clouds.

"Check the map. Try and find a turnoff. Something small. Preferably near a bend in the road."

"What are you thinking?" Mia said over her shoulder, her attention still locked on the Lexus.

"I don't know if it'll work, but if we time it right, there's a possibility we can use the fog against them."

"But if we disappear, won't they figure it out? It wouldn't take that much to work out where we turned."

"Not if we time it right."

She dropped back into the seat, reaching into the pocket

on the door beside her for the map. "Want to give me a little bit more to go on?"

"Thanks to the road conditions, we've got a little maneuvering room. Especially if we factor in the mist."

"So we use the cover of clouds to pull off the road. Makes sense, except that he'll know what we've done as soon as he drives out of it."

"Eventually, yes. But if we combine a curve with the fog, then we might have enough time to reverse direction and be gone by the time he figures out for certain what we've done. It's not perfect, but it's the best I can come up with."

"Not bad," she said, her hair falling forward as she bent to study the map. "If there's a creek it'll be even better."

"A creek?" he asked, shooting her a sideways glance.

"Yeah. In this part of the country, they're usually a lot lower than the roadbed."

"Which means there'll be more fog." He was, as usual, astounded at the speed with which her mind worked.

"Exactly." She smoothed the map, still looking.

The car's headlights glittered through the mist, closer than they'd been a few minutes before. It was tempting to try and increase speed, but like the other driver, Nick couldn't take a chance on losing traction.

"I think maybe I've got it," Mia said, her index finger marking a point on the map. "It's about a quarter mile ahead. There's a creek, a fairly sharp right curve and, just a little bit beyond that, a side road. And the best part is that with a couple of turns we'll wind up about half a mile back from where we started."

"Just what the doctor ordered." He gunned the car, the road already sloping downward toward the creek. A sign flashed out of the mist, the name of the creek too long to read in the seconds it took them to pass it.

As predicted, the fog thickened as the car bottomed out on the small bridge, the creek water as cloaked as the surrounding countryside.

"So where's the road?"

"Should be just ahead on the left. Maybe another hundred feet."

Almost before she finished speaking he saw the turn. Checking the rearview mirror, he was satisfied to see nothing reflected there. They were hidden in the fog. The tires screeched as he skidded into the turn, careful not to push the car hard enough to leave tread marks.

Thankfully, the road was paved, removing the possibility that they'd left tracks. Even better, it wasn't marked at all. Without the map, he doubted they'd even have seen it.

"You think they'll fall for it?" Mia asked, turning to look behind her.

"I think there's a good possibility." The turnoff had already been swallowed in the mist, which meant that they remained invisible to anyone passing by. He slowed the car and pulled off the road to stop behind a ramshackle barn that loomed up out of the mist.

"What are you doing?"

"Playing chicken," he said with a grin.

"But we need to get away. Even if we managed to fool them, it's still possible they'll double back and find this road."

"But we'll rest easier if we know they've at least fallen for the ruse."

"And how will we know that? We can't see them any more than they can see us."

He glanced down at his watch. "I'd say they were about five minutes behind us. If they don't materialize out of the fog, we're good to go."

"And if they do?" Her brows were drawn together in a ferocious frown, her glare reminding him of a particularly difficult teacher he'd had in the seventh grade.

"Then it's time they understand that we mean business." He reached for his gun, releasing the seat belt.

"One gun? You think we can take them with one gun?" Her voice rose on each word, her eyes locked on the rear window.

"I think you're underestimating my abilities, but you can stop worrying. Your plan's going to work like a charm. But to be totally certain, I'm going to add a little touch of my own."

If possible her frown intensified. "What are you going to do?"

"Change cars."

"Here?" She looked out at the mist-shrouded fields. "We're in the middle of nowhere."

"Maybe not as much as you think." He opened the door, gesturing toward the dilapidated barn.

She reached behind her for the appropriations bill and the laptop, tucking the map into her pocket. "You're certifiable, you know that?" she whispered, slinging her backpack over her shoulder.

He held a finger to his lips with another grin and stepped out into the rain-drenched field. He waited until she was behind him and then moved forward through the sparse brush until he reached the side of the road.

Pausing there, he stared into the gray mist for some sign that they were being followed. There was nothing.

"They're not coming." He could hear the relief in her voice and resisted the desire to pull her close.

"Come on," he said, pointing to the other side of the road. The fog was lighter on the road itself, but as soon as they were safely across it thickened again, swallowing them, cloaking any sound of their movement.

For a moment, he thought he'd made a mistake, but then the pale blue fender of a pickup took form as they moved closer. It was an old one. Probably kept here for driving in the fields, the spattered mud on the rear bumper lending credence to the idea.

"Get in," he said, already climbing up into the cab.

"There's no way you're going to find keys in this one." She set the computer on the seat between them, stowing the backpack at her feet.

"It's a universal habit," he said, flipping down the visor. There was nothing there, and for just a second, Mia's eyes flashed with amusement.

"Now what?" She rolled down the window, leaning out, listening for company.

"Glove compartment." Nick reached across her, enjoying the contact despite the gravity of the situation. Unfortunately, the compartment was empty. He straightened up with a sheepish shrug.

"City boys," she said with an exasperated sigh. Before he could think of a comeback, she'd leaned across his lap, twisting so that she could access the steering column. He fought against the primitive urges her position elicited, but it wasn't easy, her squirming almost undoing him on the spot.

"Hang on," she said, twisting onto her back. "Almost got it."

Suddenly the starter turned and the truck sparked to life.

She straightened up with a know-it-all grin. They were inches apart, electricity arcing between them. Nick could feel the warmth of her breath, see the rise and fall of her breasts beneath the T-shirt she wore.

For a moment there was nothing in the world but the two of them. He leaned forward, rational thought giving way to raw desire, but before he could engage, Mia sucked in a ragged breath and pulled back, her gaze moving to the fog-shrouded road. "What do you say we get out of here."

Totally bereft of words, he put the truck in gear and pulled out onto the road, satisfied to see that the rearview mirror was still empty.

"Pretty impressive," he said, his heart still pounding.

"One good idea deserves another."

"So let's see, to date you've managed to hack into a computer, hot-wire a truck and find a tracking device inside my disk drive. Not bad for an artist."

"Hey—" she shrugged "—I was raised to be resourceful. You really think we've managed to lose them?" She twisted around to look behind her once more.

"Yeah. And even if they do figure out what we did, they have no way of knowing what we're driving or where we're going."

"So we're safe."

"For the moment."

"Any idea where we're going to hole up? We need time to go over the bill." She patted the stack of paper on the seat next to her.

"Nope. But I'll know it when I see it. In the meantime, why don't you try and get some sleep."

"I can't possibly sleep," she protested, her eyes already at half-mast.

"Look, I don't know how long we'll be in the clear. So you'd better grab the opportunity while you can."

She nodded, settling back against the seat with a sigh. "What about you? You haven't slept at all."

"I'll be fine. I figured out a long time ago that sleep was overrated." He glanced over to find that she was already asleep, her lashes dark against her cheeks.

Containing a smile, he drove on through the mist, the rain beginning to fall again. There was still no sign of anyone behind him. But just for good measure, he kept the truck moving as fast as he dared, considering the conditions.

The interesting thing was that he'd never really worried about things like driving carefully, his life worth no more to him than anything else. But with Mia it was different. As if he'd been entrusted with precious cargo. Even when they were at odds, he wanted to protect her. To keep her safe.

In truth, he'd forgotten how it felt to care about someone. Hell, he'd forgotten what it felt like to care, period.

AFTER THE OFFBEAT CHARM of their last motel, the cookie-cutter sterility of their latest motor inn left something to be desired. But it was clean, and the very uniformity of it made Mia feel safer. That and the fact that they were back in Idaho. Home turf, more or less. Interstate 15 cut right through the southeastern part of the state. At the moment they were only about fifty miles from home.

Which probably should have been worrisome. But since Davies had managed to follow them through three states, it seemed better somehow to keep the home court advantage. They'd made it through Utah without further incident, and for the past hour or so had been poring over what had to be the most boring reading material on the planet.

It was a wonder congressmen had managed to stay awake long enough to pass the thing.

Nick was sprawled across the bed, papers strewn all around him. She was curled up in a chair, her rejected pages all stacked neatly on the table beside her. Despite the difference in their reading styles, they had both managed to get through something like two-thirds of the document.

Unfortunately, nothing seemed to be related to Cedar Branch, Kresky International or Senators Hatcher and Tucker.

"I feel like I'm looking for the proverbial needle," Nick said, throwing the paper he was reading onto the bedspread. "There could be something right in front of me and I'm not certain I'd be able to figure it out. I should have asked Matt to read it. He's definitely better at seeing the implied."

"Well, surely it'll appear to have some kind of relevance. Even if it's vague. Although so far nothing I've read seems to be connected at all."

"Same here. But I *can* tell you that the state of Ohio is getting a disproportionate share of the money earmarked for higher education."

"I can top that," she said with a smile. "There's a line item here that gives California money to research the impact of gangs on L.A.'s highway infrastructure."

"Probably just a fancy way to pay for cleaning up graffiti."

"Pork barreling at its very best." She picked up another sheet, this one an amendment. It wasn't enough that they'd read the whole bill; they also had to read through the various adopted amendments.

She studied the first one. Something to do with preserving wetlands in Florida. At least this one she supported. Much more so than urban renewal money for small towns in Missouri. It seemed an exorbitant amount for a relatively small number of beneficiaries. But she wasn't a politician, so what did she know?

She put down the page she was reading and with a sigh reached up to massage her temples.

"Headache?" Nick asked, his quiet observation startling her.

"Yeah. But it's nothing serious."

"Maybe you should take a break. We've been at it for a while now."

Although the idea was appealing, she shook her head. "No. I want to keep at it. It's got to be here somewhere. I just wish we had a better idea of what it is we're looking for."

"Well, Matt's source said it was hidden in plain sight, which could mean that what looks innocent is actually a cover for something more nefarious."

"Great. That probably narrows it down to half the allocations here."

"Beats all of them." He shrugged, returning to his reading.

Mia reached for another page and began skimming the contents. It was just more of the same, and she was about to toss it aside when some part of her brain registered a senate amendment mentioning Idaho.

She frowned, focusing on the words. "Hey, I might have something here."

Nick put down the page he was reading, his expression skeptical.

"Let me read it to you," she said. "Senate Amendment 1020. To provide continuing funding in the State of Idaho for environmental impact studies of nuclear testing sites on the Snake River Plain aquifer and the adjacent Caribou National Forest."

"Except for the Idaho part, I'm not sure what any of that has to do with Cedar Branch or Kresky International. I'm assuming they're referring to nuclear plant testing as opposed to nuclear weapons testing. As far as I know there are no weapons testing sites in Idaho."

"They're all around us though," Mia said. "In Nevada and Utah and the Dakotas. Of course, there were missile silos here originally, but they've all been abandoned. I think Malmstrom is the closest site with live missiles. And we know from Kresky's files that at least some of them contain nuclear warheads."

"But none of that should have anything to do with an environmental impact study." He was frowning at her now, clearly trying to follow her train of thought.

"Only I don't think that's what is." She stood up, rolling her shoulders as she framed her words. "The only remaining nuclear testing in Idaho is at the Idaho National Laboratory, which is northwest of Idaho Falls. Caribou National Forest is in the opposite direction—southeast of Idaho Falls. The most obvious choices for environmental studies would be in the forest land that actually abuts the laboratory testing facilities at Scoville. Challis National Forest or Salmon or maybe even Craters of the Moon. But not Caribou."

She walked over to the window, relieved to see nothing outside except a couple unloading their car in the parking lot. Turning back to face Nick, she crossed her arms, her mind still working over the possibilities. "The aquifer is a stronger candidate, simply because of runoff into streams and rivers that eventually drain into it, but even with that

I'd have expected to see it combined with one of the adjacent national forests."

"Okay, so maybe the study is a cover for something else? Although I'm still not sure I see the connection to Cedar Branch."

"Cedar Branch sits—sat—" she swallowed as tears filled her eyes "—on the western edge of the Caribou Forest. And there was talk around town of some kind of ecology group setting up shop in the area. I didn't really pay that much attention at the time. We get a lot of that kind of thing."

"But you think it's possible that the study alluded to in the amendment is tied somehow to the group near Cedar Branch?"

"What if there wasn't a transport? What if the warhead was in Cedar Branch all along? If Kresky or someone was using the money from the amendment to modify weapons there, an accident would be catastrophic for everyone involved. Especially the politicians who lied to their constituents."

"So the transport was only moved up on paper. To provide an acceptable explanation for what happened."

"If there is such a thing as an acceptable explanation." She rubbed her arms, feeling suddenly cold. "But it does make sense."

"Except that we don't have a shred of proof."

"We've got the amendment."

"Which could be exactly what it says it is."

"All right. Then we'll just have to find something to give my theory credence." She crossed over to the laptop sitting on the bureau.

"What are you doing?" He walked over to stand behind her, looking at the screen on the computer.

"Trying to find out who authored the amendment."

"I'm guessing Hatcher."

"That would be my guess, as well." She waited while the search engine churned out its results.

"So how does that prove your point?"

She clicked on a link and waited for the document to fill the window. "Because Hatcher wasn't acting alone." She waved toward the screen, her heart pounding against her ribs. "The amendment was sponsored by Lloyd Tucker, too. Why would he be involved in an environmental study in Idaho?"

"It doesn't track, I'll grant you that. But it still isn't conclusive proof."

"No. But I think it gives us somewhere to start. We find out who set up shop in Cedar Branch under the auspices of an environmental study—and I'm guessing we'll have our proof."

"Even if you're right, finding the name of the company that received the funding isn't going to be enough. If this is a cover-up, they're going to have buried it as deep as possible, which means that on the surface everything's going to look just as it's supposed to."

"I get that. Believe me, I do. But we're onto something here. I can feel it. Besides, we didn't find anything else in the bill that even remotely seems to be connected. This amendment was authored by Hatcher and Tucker. On its face it seems harmless, but geographically it doesn't make sense. And to top it off, I know there was some kind of environmental organization doing research in the area. When you add it all together…"

"You get something. I'll grant you that. And since for the moment it's all we've got, I think we should follow it up. But not now. It's late, and we need to get some sleep."

"Are you kidding?" She jerked out of her chair and turned to face him, trying to contain the emotions rattling through her. "After everything we've been through, we finally make some progress and you want to go to sleep?"

"So what do you want to do? Fly to Washington? Make a midnight visit to Senator Tucker? Tell him we have reason to believe he's involved in what could be the biggest cover-up in American history?" Nick stepped closer, anger coming off him in waves. "If he's guilty you're as good as dead. And if he's not, he'll turn you over to the authorities, which is a short track straight back to Davies. This isn't a game, Mia. These people are playing for keeps. We have to plan our moves carefully. And the simple fact is that there's nothing else we can do tonight."

"I wasn't suggesting we head for D.C." She said, her breathing labored. "Although my grandfather always taught me to confront my enemies head-on."

"Your grandfather was never involved in something like this."

They stared at each other, the only sound in the room the soft hiss of the air-conditioning unit. Then, suddenly, she deflated, the giddy energy draining from her as quickly as it had come. "I know that. And I know we have to be careful. It's just that—"

"I know this is hard." He cut her off, cupping a hand under her chin. "And you've been amazing. But we have to move cautiously from here."

There was a subtext she wasn't certain she wanted to acknowledge. So she nodded, unable to trust her voice.

"We'll work out a plan in the morning." He stroked her cheek with his thumb, his gaze almost hungry. She reached up to cover his hand with hers, but before she could complete the gesture, he stepped back, his expression suddenly shuttered. "Get some sleep." He spun around and walked into the adjoining bedroom, closing the door behind him.

She stood for a moment staring at the door, heart pounding, then sequestered her emotions. To hell with Nick. She didn't need him. At least not to start digging around for something to connect Kresky to Tucker's amendment. If Kresky had illicitly set up shop in Cedar Branch, she intended to find proof. And now was as good a time as any.

She sat down in front of the computer, turning her back on the closed door, determined to block out all thoughts of the man on the other side.

If only it were that easy.

CHAPTER FOURTEEN

MIA STOOD STRETCHING her muscles, the clock radio showing that it was moving on toward morning. Unfortunately, she had nothing to show for it except a stiff back. She'd allowed herself to stay online only for short bursts, routing and rerouting so that it would be difficult if not impossible to trace her activity. Just because they'd found one bug didn't mean there weren't others.

According to the congressional record, the amendment had passed without debate. Which meant that whatever had motivated it remained buried in committee. And despite gaining access to committee records, she hadn't found any further mention of the amendment. It was almost as if it had just appeared fully articulated in the bill.

Which meant, of course, that whatever had prompted the amendment was not something to be discussed in places with public access. And she'd run out of ideas on how to access anything more private.

She'd also hit a brick wall when it came to finding out what organization had been contracted to receive the appropriation. There wasn't a record of any ecological concern located, even temporarily, in the area of Cedar Branch. And yet she distinctly remembered a conversation between Patrick and Joe about that very thing. But try as she might, she couldn't pull out a name.

All of which left her exhausted and feeling as if she'd failed her friends somehow. She walked over to the window, risking a quick look out into the parking lot. The rain had followed them from Utah, the accompanying mist distorting the light from the streetlamps.

It was eerie and comforting all at the same time, the blanket of fog protecting them—or at least giving the semblance of doing so.

Mia turned back to the empty room, restless energy keeping her from sleep. She needed distraction. And so, reaching for a pad of paper and a pencil, she dropped into a chair and did what she'd done since she was old enough to hold a crayon—she drew.

At first the marks on the page seemed almost random, but gradually the familiar shapes of the café began to emerge. The padded stools, the chrome counter. Every little detail a symbol of comfort, of home. She sketched the booths and the pass-through, even the brass bell that Patrick hit to signal Nancy an order was up.

She'd always joked that he could have just told her, but he liked the sound of the bell—said that it made the place authentic.

Mia drew the broad lines of Patrick's shoulders, and then switched to sketch Joe's hat thrown on the counter. He might not have been a man of many words or any great sophistication, but he was the kind of man who always took his hat off indoors and always held the door for a lady.

People said that manners were limited to the South, but those people had clearly never been to Cedar Branch.

She finished the rough outlines of most all the people who

filled Cuppa Joe on a regular day. Wilson perched backward on his stool, pointing to something out the window. Carson next to him, arms crossed over his massive chest.

Her hand flew, the tears in her eyes not hindering her progress. Betty and her niece SueAnn at a booth, laughing at something Joe had just said. A couple of strangers who'd just wandered in for a cup of coffee.

It was only when she tried to fill in the details that her hand hesitated, her mind refusing to pull forth clear images of her friends' faces. She struggled, trying to capture the sparkle in Nancy's eyes, the bushy abundance of Patrick's brows, but she couldn't get it right, the people looking more like strangers than friends she'd known for most of her life.

Patrick and Nancy hadn't been around as long, but Joe had carried her on his shoulders when she was only about five. And Carson had always kept a Tootsie Pop in his jeans jacket pocket, making her guess where it was, even though it always in the same place. The silly kinds of things that made up a life, their everyday existence taken for granted—until now.

She stared at the drawing, willing their faces to form in her mind. Staring at each of them in turn, letting her pencil find its way. But the results weren't good enough, the lines and shading not rendering likenesses that reflected the individual character of the people she was trying to portray.

Anger mixed with frustration and sorrow as she erased and tried again, the second attempt no better than the first. Over and over she tried to make it right, to bring her friends to life again. But nothing worked. The drawings were empty—hollow renditions of their living, breathing counterparts. Still she kept at it, working until places on the drawing were torn and frayed from constant erasure.

Finally, in a burst of rage, she threw the pad across the room, the wheeling paper hitting the ice bucket and glasses on top of the TV. The bucket fell on its side, the glasses crashing onto the floor, shattering with impact, but Mia hardly noticed.

Instead, she sat in the chair, knees pulled to her chest, trying to protect herself from the grief and guilt that slammed through her. It wasn't as if she was a stranger to the feelings. In a very short period of time she'd lost her grandfather and then her mom and dad. But this was different. Before, when it had happened, it had been out of her control. She hadn't even been present when her mother and father had died.

But she had been in Cedar Branch. And logic said that she should have been killed as well, but she hadn't been. She'd lived. As if somehow she hadn't belonged. An outsider who was left behind. It was a ridiculous notion. Her brain was certain of it, but her heart couldn't let go of the idea that somehow this was her fault. That just the fact of her living meant that she should have been able to stop it, to do something. To save her friends.

"Mia, are you all right?"

She lifted her head to find Nick, gun in hand, standing in the connecting doorway. "I heard a noise. I thought…" He trailed off, his gaze questioning.

"I'm fine," she said, her voice raspy from the tears. "I just couldn't get it right." She waved her hand in the direction of the fallen notebook, surrounded now by splintered glass. "I couldn't see their faces."

After laying the gun on top of the television, he bent to retrieve the notebook, taking a moment to study the mutilated drawing. Then he crossed the room and lifted her into his arms, moving to sit on the end of the bed, still cradling her.

"You haven't forgotten," he said, his voice strong and somehow reassuring. "It's just your self-defense mechanisms. They're trying to protect you."

"But I want to remember," she said, fisting her hands, fighting against her tears. "I don't want to lose them."

"You won't. I promise. It's just too early for those kinds of memories. The pain is too great."

She pushed back, lifting her head to meet his gaze. "You sound like you know. Like you've been here before?"

"I have. With Katie."

"Your sister." She saw his wince, understood now the pain that accompanied it.

"Yes." His nod was curt, as if he resented the need to share with her. "And although it's always going to hurt, you'll learn to compartmentalize it. Which means the pain of remembering isn't quite as bad. Time may not heal wounds, but it does temper them."

"And that's what I'm doing now? Forgetting because it's too painful?"

"You're not forgetting. Your brain just isn't letting you have access to the memories. But it will—in time."

He still had his arms around her, and she let her head sink back onto his chest, the smooth rhythm of his breathing soothing her. She wasn't sure that anyone had ever really held her like this. For comfort and reassurance.

Her mother and grandfather had been more the shake-it-off-and-get-on-with-it types. And her father simply hadn't been around enough to fill that kind of need, his devotion to his music supplanting any real obligation he felt to his family.

She loved them all, but she'd always known something was missing. Maybe that's why she'd fallen in love with

Patrick and Nancy. They'd always been there. Cheering on her successes, ready with a hug if she stumbled along the way.

The tears surfaced again, but this time without the anger. Nick stroked her back, rocking her gently, whispering nonsensical words against her hair, and she let herself cry, let it come out, not giving herself time to feel ashamed of the outburst. It was as if she'd opened the dam, the rush of emotions flooding out of her, leaving her spent from the release.

She lifted her head, opening her mouth to thank him, but the words stopped in her throat as she met the heat of his gaze, registering for the first time that he was wearing only a pair of blue jeans. Suddenly she wanted nothing more than to feel his powerful chest against hers. To seek a completely different kind of comfort.

Her lips parted, inviting his kiss. Heart pounding, she prayed that he'd understand—that he wouldn't reject what she was offering. And then he was there, his mouth against hers.

At first it was a gentle kiss. Tender almost. But Mia wanted more. She opened her mouth, drinking him in with the desperation of a woman who'd been without water too long. Her body burned for him, the fire licking at her, building deep inside until she thought it might incinerate her. His tongue traced the line of her teeth, sending tiny shivers of desire coursing through her, chasing away the shadows that threatened to consume her.

She twined her fingers into his hair, drawing him closer, meeting his tongue, tasting the essence that was Nick. The kiss deepened and sensations exploded inside her, his mouth branding her, making her his with nothing more than a kiss.

But she knew there was more, and she wanted it with every fiber of her being. She shifted, meeting his gaze again, his eyes dark with passion, little flecks of gold twirling in their murky depths.

"Make no mistake, Mia." His voice was hoarse, sliding across her skin as if it were a tangible thing. "I want you. But I don't want to take advantage. You're hurting. Which means you're not thinking clearly."

"Please don't play nice guy with me now," she said, reaching down to pull her T-shirt over her head, her eyes never leaving his. "I know exactly what I'm doing."

His intake of breath was audible and he reached out, skimming a palm along the contours of her breasts, his touch so light she almost couldn't feel it. With a sigh, she closed her eyes and leaned forward, forcing the pressure. His fingers fluttered slightly and then he tightened his hold, teasing each of her nipples until they were hard, the sweet pain pooling between her legs.

And then they were kissing again, their bodies pressed together, moving slowly, the skin-to-skin friction deliciously unbearable. With trembling fingers, she traced the rugged planes of his back and chest, reveling in the contrast between the hard muscle and velvety skin.

He growled with pleasure as she caressed him, the sound rippling through her, increasing her desire. His hands found her nipples again, and she bit back a moan when he rubbed them between thumbs and forefingers.

"Come on, Mia, let it go. Show me how good it feels." His whisper tickled her neck, his warm breath teasing her with its touch.

For a moment their eyes met and held, and then he lowered his head, taking her breast into his mouth. His tongue moved in lazy circles, the gentle suction sending sparks dancing along her synapses. It felt so good. Yet innately, she knew there could be more.

Impatiently, she pushed against him. But the pressure was the same, wet and slow and amazingly wonderful. He cupped her other breast in his hand, the motion of his palm mimicking the rhythm of his mouth.

"Please," she whispered. "Please, Nick, please."

She felt him smile and then his teeth closed around her nipple, the exquisite friction threatening to send her over the edge. His fingers tightened on the other breast, the combined intensity almost more than she could bear. He stroked and sucked, driving her higher and higher, each nip and pull ratcheting up the heat building inside her.

And just when she thought it couldn't possibly get any better, his fingers moved downward, teasing as they slipped inside the elastic of her panties. Something deep inside her tightened, the ache spreading through her, demanding release.

His fingers circled the soft skin of her inner thighs, his lips still caressing her breast. Then he pushed a finger inside, unerringly finding the part of her that most needed his touch. At first he teased her with his finger, flicking against her lightly, until she lifted her hips, silently begging for more.

His mouth found hers, his tongue plunging deep, just as his fingers finally found their way home. She cried out against his lips, her breath coming in gasps, but he swallowed the sound, increasing the pressure, giving no quarter.

His fingers and tongue began moving in tandem. In and out, in and out, caressing, withdrawing, caressing, withdrawing, until she was balanced on a precipice of raw physical desire.

She flung back her head, eyes open wide, body tensed as she waited to fall. Wanting nothing but to be pushed over the edge. But he stopped, withdrawing both his fingers and his mouth, leaving her stranded, alone.

She reached for him blindly, pheromones on overdrive, her need overriding rationality. "Nick?"

"Patience, princess."

She shivered at the passion in his voice as he lifted her into his arms, turning to lay her on the bed. With a minimum of effort, he removed her panties and shed his jeans. His arousal reassuring her that she was far from alone.

He straddled her, then slowly slid down, spreading her legs, sliding his hands beneath her to cup her bottom. Lifting slightly, his eyes met hers, his lids low, heavy with passion, and with a heated smile he bent his head and blew softly on the tender skin between her legs. She arched against him, but he held his grip, keeping her in place.

"Now, Mia," he said, dipping his head. "Let me take you home."

She nodded, not sure exactly what it was she was agreeing to, but certain that now, in this moment, she'd die without it.

His breath caressed her an instant before his tongue found her. She bucked against him, unable to control her body's reaction. His dark hair fanned out against her skin, teasing her with its feathery touch as his mouth coaxed her frenzied body even higher.

His tongue flicked lightly across her, and she shivered with the deliciousness of his touch. Then his tongue tightened and drove into her, a prelude of things she knew would follow.

Again and again he stroked her, driving her higher and higher. Her hands tangled into his hair, pushing him deeper and deeper, until the world spun out of control, light splintering into fragments.

Closer and closer she came to the heat, certain it would consume her, destroy her, but then, suddenly, through the blinding light, she felt his heat surround her, his arms holding her, and she knew that as long as he was there, she'd be all right.

IT WAS ALMOST ENOUGH to taste her, to know she'd been fulfilled.

Almost.

Hell, who was he kidding? He wanted her now, the pounding ache in his groin spreading fire throughout his body. He'd accomplished what he'd set out to do. He'd taken her away, reminded her that there were some things that transcended even grief. But now he needed more.

He needed to possess her, needed it with every fiber of his being, the power of his desire taking him by surprise.

A part of him—the only part still thinking rationally—cautioned that there would be repercussions, that the connection between them was driven by circumstance and wouldn't survive the light of day. But the heat of her body burned against him and he pushed away his doubts. Tomorrow they'd deal with the fallout.

Shifting onto his elbows, he raised himself above her, sliding up so that he could see her eyes. The passion there almost unmanned him, and his body tightened with anticipation. She slid her hand down his stomach, her fingers closing around him. He bit back a groan as she slowly stroked his foreskin.

"What do you want, Mia?" he asked, his gaze still holding hers.

"I want you inside me, Nick," she whispered. "I want you inside me now."

He lifted her into his arms again, twisting around so that they were sitting on the edge of the bed, her legs wrapped around his middle, his penis hard against the moist juncture of her thighs.

She frowned for a moment, rocking against him, and then understanding dawned. With a smile, she lifted up and in one slow motion slid around him, her movement pushing him deep inside her. He fought for control, not ready to concede the battle yet.

Pulling her close, he kissed her neck. Then he found her mouth, reveling in the feel of her surrounding him, stroking him. And then suddenly she was moving with a steady motion that set his soul on fire, the slow sliding building to an almost unbearable pleasure.

Groaning, he moved his hands to her hips, guiding her, urging her on, the pace growing frenzied as they moved faster and faster — each thrust deeper and harder. He reached for release, knowing it was there just beyond his grasp.

Flipping them both without breaking contact, he moved on top of her, taking control. Deeper, deeper, faster, faster, until he exploded on a wave of pleasure so intense he thought he might shatter into pieces. From far away he heard her call his name. And he reached for her hand, wanting to share the journey—to maintain connection on every level.

Some part of his brain rebelled at the thought. He wasn't the kind of man who needed connection with a woman.

But then again, Mia Kearney wasn't just any woman.

CHAPTER FIFTEEN

MIA SAT UP WITH A START, sleep dissipating in a cloud of doubt and self-recrimination. The bed was empty, Nick gone, but her aching muscles lent credence to the reality of last night's foray. In the heat of passion, it had seemed like a good idea. A way to lose herself, to forget—if only for a moment—the horror of everything that had happened.

But now, in the cold harsh light of day, she wasn't as certain. She'd never been the type to fall into bed with a man on a whim. In fact, she could still count on one hand the number of men she'd slept with. Not that any of that mattered.

She'd thrown herself at Nick. It was as simple as that. And whatever the resulting fallout, she'd just have to deal with it. She climbed out of bed and shimmied into a pair of jeans and a T-shirt, then walked to the connecting doorway.

He was sitting with his back turned, his attention on the computer screen in front of him. For a moment she allowed herself the luxury of just looking at him, her body tightening at the memory of his lovemaking. Maybe if things were different—

She cut off the thought before it even had the chance to form. If things were different she would never even have met Nick, let alone slept with him. Last night she'd had a moment of weakness. But she wouldn't make the same mistake again—she couldn't.

Nick Price was the kind of man it would be easy to fall in love with, and she was smart enough to recognize that if she went that route, she'd be doing so alone. Their connection was intense and definitely passionate, but it was born out of grief and fear. Not exactly the best foundation for a relationship.

"You're awake." He'd turned around, his emerald gaze holding her captive in the doorway.

"Yeah. Just. You finding anything?" She nodded at the computer, striving for a calm she didn't feel.

"Nope. And I've been at it a couple hours now. There are hardly any references to the amendment at all. And nothing in any of the articles covering Tucker or Hatcher that points to anything significant."

"I couldn't find anything, either. But if we're right and the amendment was meant as a way to divert funding to some kind of project with Kresky, then they're not exactly going to advertise it."

"I know," he said, running a hand through his hair. "I just thought maybe if I kept digging, something would turn up. There's coffee over there if you want it. It's not very good, but it's better than instant."

Clearly, he wasn't going to mention the previous night's activities. Mia couldn't decide if she was relieved or disappointed. A little bit of both, probably.

"What did Matt have to say? I assume you contacted him?" She walked over to the counter and poured a cup of coffee, liberally dosing it with the powder-filled packets that passed for cream.

"He's not answering his e-mails."

"Is that unusual? Maybe he's just away from his computer."

"That's like saying he left his arm behind," Nick said with a frown. "Matt's always connected."

"Did you try calling him?" She started to perch on the arm of his chair but thought better of it, moving instead to sit on the other side of the room. If he noticed the distance, he didn't acknowledge it.

"Yeah, I tried calling. On his secure line. He didn't answer."

"He's probably just working on a case or operation or whatever you guys call it." She studied his face, trying to decipher his expression. "Are you worried?"

"A little. He usually gets back to me pretty fast, and considering the circumstances, I'd think he'd make certain he was reachable."

"Maybe it isn't safe. You did say that Davies has convinced key players at Homeland Security to doubt your loyalty. I'd think something like that would spill over onto anyone you considered a friend. Which means they're probably watching every move he makes."

"I suspect you're right on target. But even if Matt is taking heat, he'd figure out a way to get word to me."

"So what are you saying? You think something happened to him?" She hated the idea that someone else had been pulled into the nightmare.

"I'm not saying anything. I'd just feel better if he'd check in."

"Is there anything else you can do from your end?"

"I've set up a computer trace. As long as I keep it updated, it should help him locate us if he's really in trouble."

"What if someone else finds the program?" she asked. "We just got rid of one bug."

"This is a little more sophisticated than that. Something Matt devised, actually. We've used it more often than I care to admit."

"Testament to the fact that you're always walking the line?"

"More to the fact that Matt always has my back." His brows drew together with worry.

"He's all right, Nick. There's no reason to believe anything happened to him. It doesn't make any sense."

"Unless he was asking the wrong questions." He frowned, running a hand through his hair.

"If he's half as good as you are, he's not going to make that kind of mistake."

"He's very good at what he does, but he's also the kind to risk everything for a friend."

"Which is why you're worried."

"Yeah. Whatever is going on here, it's serious shit, with big-time players like Tucker securing inside help from Davies's group. So far they've managed to pull Homeland Security off the investigation, snow the press and ship in operatives to cover their asses. All while still hunting for us. "

"For me."

"You're definitely the prize," he said. "But I think if Davies could manage to take me out along the way it'd be icing on the cake. Anyway, the point is that if they've figured out Matt's been helping us, it's to their advantage to remove him from the equation."

"But Matt knows all of that. So he'll take precautions. You said yourself that he's good at intel. If that's true, then he's probably already covering his tracks. And creating a little distance could just be part of the plan."

"Makes sense. And that's probably exactly what he's doing. I just don't like the idea of him having to take the fallout from my decision to defy orders and stay with you."

"I'm sorry. I know I've put you in a difficult situation." On more levels than she was ready to admit, actually. "But I'm glad I'm not dealing with this on my own."

There was a beat as the two of them communicated on levels purely chemical, the tension in the room ratcheting up to an almost intolerable state.

"So what do we do now?" She was aware that the question had a double meaning, but couldn't seem to stop herself from asking.

"Depends on what we're talking about?" His expression was difficult to read. Silence stretched uncomfortably between them, Mia staring into her cup, pretending to contemplate her coffee. Finally she lifted her head to meet his gaze, determined to keep the focus on the issues at hand.

"The amendment," she said, ignoring the flash of disappointment in his eyes. "We've got to figure out what, if any, significance it has with relation to what happened in Cedar Branch. And the best way to do that is to figure out who actually received the allocated funds. Even if it turns out that it really is an environmental study, at least we'll have an answer."

"Well, I don't think we're going to find it on the Web. Which means we're going to have to find a more direct approach."

"I'm not following."

"If your friends knew about the environmental group,

then other people were probably aware of it, too. So we should go to the source."

"But we can't," she said, working to hold her emotions in check. "Cedar Branch is gone."

"Yes, but there are farms and ranches in the area. Places beyond ground zero. They'll have avoided the worst of the blast, but there'll still be repercussions. And those repercussions will lead to questions. So maybe they'll welcome the opportunity to tell us what they know."

"It could work. As long as we don't tip Davies off to our whereabouts."

"Is there anyone you can think of who we could talk to? A friend of your grandfather's, maybe? He must have known most of the ranchers in the area."

"He had a passing acquaintance with most everyone. But he wasn't the kind who fostered friendship. Thought it was a waste of time. I think my grandmother kind of softened the edges, but she was gone long before I was born, and he'd more than reverted to old habits."

"It must have been lonely."

"Not really. I've always been pretty self-contained. And in his own way, he loved me. He just wasn't very good at showing it." She swallowed the last of her coffee. "It was what it was."

"As usual, you're very pragmatic. I suspect your grand-father would be proud."

"There's no way to know for sure. And besides, it shouldn't matter anyway." She shrugged, pushing away emotion, focusing instead on the idea of finding someone they could talk to. "There was a guy that used to go hunting with him. Ellis Brewster. They went every year like clock-work until my grandfather had his stroke. I don't know if

Ellis is even still alive. But if he is, he'll keep our confidence. He never had much use for government types, and no rancher alive can tolerate tree-huggers."

"Where's he live?"

"His ranch is up in the mountains. Kind of off the beaten path. Certainly far enough away to have avoided the brunt of the fallout."

"Will he talk to you?"

"I think so. It's not like we were close or anything, but I did go hunting with them once or twice. And he came to the house a couple of times after the stroke. The last time I saw him was at my grandfather's funeral. Anyway, even if he doesn't remember me, he'll talk to me. My grandfather might not have had a lot of friends, but the ones he did have were loyal."

"All right, then, I say we pack up here and head for Ellis Brewster's ranch."

She nodded and pushed to her feet, leaving the empty cup on the table. But before she could make her escape, his hand closed on her arm.

"Mia, at some point we need to talk about last night."

She considered pretending not to understand, but discarded the idea. Nick would see right through her. "There's nothing to discuss."

"You know that's not true. What happened between us—"

"Was a one-time thing," she told him, saying the words before he had the chance. "Maybe it would be better if we just write it off to overwrought emotions."

"That's not going to happen." He'd closed the distance between them, his fingers burning into her skin.

"It's not?"

"No." He reached over to tuck a strand of hair behind her ear, the resulting shiver making her go hot and cold all at the same time. "When something's this good, Mia, you don't ignore it."

"You don't?" She shook her head, her brain clearly incapable of operating at full capacity—subjugated, no doubt, by the flood of hormones to the lower half of her body.

"No." He leaned closer as she struggled for breath, tracing the line of her lips with his finger, the simple touch more sensual than a kiss. "You don't."

"But I…" She trailed off, the heat in his eyes making her forget what it was she'd been going to say.

"I don't know what you think last night was about, Mia," he said. "But it sure as hell wasn't a one-night stand."

She nodded, licking her lips, still trying to form a coherent sentence, but the effort was wasted as his mouth slanted over hers, the kiss hard and demanding. With a sigh, she melted against him, relishing the contact. Some part of her was screaming for retreat, but she ignored the warning, choosing instead to answer the fire of his kiss with some heat of her own.

Time seemed suspended, the only reality the feel of his lips against hers and the steady hammering of her heart against his. A truck horn blared outside the window, reality crashing in again. With a groan he pulled away, regret clouding his expression.

"We need to talk to your grandfather's friend. And with Davies breathing down our neck, we can't afford to wait. But make no mistake, princess, last night wasn't a one-off. It was fucking amazing. And I, for one, intend to make certain you don't forget *that*."

CHAPTER SIXTEEN

"YOU'RE SURE THIS IS the right place?" Nick stepped out of their latest car, a Toyota, with a frown. Despite the neon *Open* sign in the window, the place wasn't exactly inviting. A couple of pickup trucks sat in the parking lot, along with a beat up Chevy that had obviously seen better days. The afternoon was gray, the smell of rain heavy in the air, and the temperature cold enough to hint at the coming fall.

The building itself was weathered clapboard, the wood a faded gray with worn splotches of what had once been green paint. A variety of license plates decorated the area surrounding the front door. And thanks to some strategically burned-out lightbulbs, the sign out front cheerfully flashed the words *ass Bar,* the *M* and *y*'s in *Massy's Bar* missing in action.

Colorful was the word that came to mind. Although *dump* was probably a better description.

"Ellis definitely said Massy's," Mia said, emerging from the passenger side without giving the dive a second look.

"I take it you know the place?"

"I've been here a couple times. Bill Massy and I went to high school together. His dad owns the place."

"So we'll get the royal treatment." He couldn't explain it, but the idea of meeting some guy from Mia's past didn't sit that well.

"Not likely. I was kind of an outsider. I doubt Bill would remember me. Anyway, we're not here for old home week."

"Right." He pulled open the door and held it for Mia, trying to ignore the tight curve of her ass in her jeans. There was a reason people weren't supposed to mix business with pleasure.

The inside of the bar was no better maintained than the outside. Although if there were a prize for most neon, Massy's would be a contender. Every square inch of wall space sported a beer sign of some kind, the rainbow colors reflected in the mirror behind the bar.

A group of men huddled solemnly around a color TV mounted above the bar. Even the bartender was staring up at the screen. The sound was muted, but the images needed no explanation.

Cedar Branch in the moment of its destruction.

The fact that the video had been taken from almost fifty miles away didn't lessen the power of the image. And despite the fact that they'd seen it repeatedly since they'd left Mia's ranch, it still made the hair on the back of Nick's neck prickle.

Mia stood frozen, her eyes widening in pain. He reached for her, his fingers closing around her elbow. "I'm sorry," she whispered, her eyes still glued to the screen. "It's just so hard."

"I know, sweetheart, but you've got to try and focus. The best thing we can do for your friends is find answers."

She nodded and wrenched her gaze from the TV.

"You see him?" Nick scanned the bar for signs of the old man, but the patrons all seemed too young.

"Over there." Mia nodded toward the far corner. A tall man in a cowboy hat emerged from the shadows, his weather-beaten face breaking into a smile.

"Little Mia Kearney," he said, holding out a sun-wrinkled hand. "It's been a long time."

"It's good to see you," Mia said, clasping the old man's hand.

"I'm glad to know you're all right." Ellis's relief was palpable. "I can't believe any of this. It's like one of them sci-fi movies my grandson is always watching. I should have called, but it's been hard to think clearly. Hell, it's been hard to do much of anything except stare at the TV." He tilted his head toward the screen, a local newscaster thankfully replacing the video images.

"Well, I'm here now," Mia said, her smile reassuring as Nick ordered a round of beers. "And you can see that I'm fine."

"Damn lucky you weren't there." The old rancher shook his head, his expression somber. "Leo always used to talk about how much time you spent in that studio."

Mia shot a look in Nick's direction, and he shook his head. No need to share the whole truth.

Ellis frowned, anger sparking in his pale blue eyes. "I may be old, son, but I'm not stupid. Why don't we sit down, Mia, and you can tell me what it is he wants you to keep quiet about. I take it you *were* in town when it happened?"

Mia shot another look in Nick's direction, then shrugged and slid into the booth. "Yeah. I was in my studio."

"But they're saying everyone died." Ellis slid into the seat across from Mia.

"They're lying," Nick said, trying to ignore the warmth of Mia's leg against his.

"And you know this because you were there, too?" Ellis frowned, his expression hardening.

"No." Mia shook her head. "I told you on the phone. Nick's with the government. He's been helping me."

"Sounds like the government is up to their ass in this," the older man said, eyeing Nick speculatively. "Are you sure you can trust him?"

"I wasn't sure at first. But I am now. He's risking his career to help me."

"I suppose if you trust him, that's good enough for me." Ellis's eyes didn't quite support the statement, but he definitely seemed less suspicious. "What can I do to help?"

"We're trying to get information about an environmental group that may have set up shop somewhere near Cedar Branch."

"Not sure I'm following." The barman arrived carrying a tray with three beers, and Ellis waited until he'd moved out of earshot before continuing. "I thought the accident had something to do with a missile. Accidental detonation of a warhead. Don't see what that's got to do with the environment."

Nick took a sip of beer, the liquid cold against the back of his throat. "We think there may be a connection."

"You think it was the work of terrorists?" The old man leaned forward, his expression quizzical.

"We're not sure what happened, Ellis," Mia said. "But something about all of it isn't ringing true. And we thought maybe by talking to you we'd get a picture of what it seemed like from the outside."

"A mighty big blast. I haven't seen anything like that since Antwerp. 'Course, we weren't using nukes."

"Ellis landed at Normandy," Mia told Nick by way of explanation.

"Hell of a fight, that one. But at least there were rules

of engagement. Sometimes we fought dirty, but we still had honor. Now—" Ellis waved his beer in the air "—hell, you can't tell the enemies from allies. Sad state."

"The blast," Nick said, to bring the old man back to topic. "Can you describe it?"

"Which one?"

Nick frowned, exchanging looks with Mia. "There was more than one?"

"Well, not exactly. But seems to me there were two events." He waited a moment, gathering his thoughts, and then leaned forward, his grizzled face stark in the neon light. "First one was hardly worth noting. In fact, probably would have written it off altogether if it hadn't been for the explosion that afternoon."

"So what happened?"

"There was a noise—like a car backfiring. Only bigger because I could hear it even with the mountains—or hell, maybe it was because of the mountains. Point is, it came from the other side—somewhere near Cedar Branch. Anyway, I heard the noise and suddenly everything in the distance seemed sort of fuzzy. Like looking through dirty binoculars. Didn't last long. And afterward, I wasn't even certain I'd seen it." He stopped to sip his beer.

"Where were you?"

"Back side of the ranch. We were branding calves."

"So there were other witnesses?"

"Just me and my foreman."

"Jake Mancuso, right?" Mia asked.

Ellis tipped his head in agreement. "We been together longer than I was married to Bernadette. Anyway, it all happened real fast. Jake didn't even see the mist. He was facing the wrong way. By the time he turned around it was gone."

"But he heard the sound."

"Yup. Said it was probably a rig over on the highway or maybe a shotgun. I figured maybe he was right. Until the blast that afternoon."

"The nuke?" Nick studied the old man, trying to ascertain if his observations could be trusted.

"I can see and hear well as most and better than some," Ellis said with a scowl.

"We know that," Mia assured him. "We're just trying to put all the facts together."

"If you ask me there were definitely two events. But not together. Second one didn't come for maybe four or five hours. Could have even been longer. We weren't watching the clock. But I do know it was getting on toward evening. We were fixin' to call it a day, and then suddenly there was a burst of sound. This one more expansive than the one before. No question that it was an explosion. A bad one at that."

"You're sure it was that late in the day?" Mia asked with a frown.

"Positive. Why?"

"My last memory is from that morning. I just assumed the explosion was early."

"Nope. Definitely late afternoon. Maybe your mind's playing tricks. An event that devastating affects a man in all kinds of ways. I saw it a lot in France. They have a name for it now. Traumatic stress or something like that. Anyway, point is you can't trust your memories."

"Post-traumatic stress disorder," Nick said, remembering the diagnosis well. When Katie died they'd tried to write off his anger with that explanation. But they'd been wrong.

"That's it," Ellis said with a nod. "Anyway, I'm positive it was in the afternoon."

"Maybe I am blocking it. I certainly don't remember anyone rescuing me." She stared down at her hands, her grief obvious.

The old man reached across to cover her hand with his. "They were good people, Mia, but not one of them would begrudge your surviving."

"I know," she whispered. "But it still feels unfair."

"Nothing ever feels fair, darlin'." Ellis shook his head and continued to hold her hand. There was something in his comfort that went deeper than any Nick had been able to offer. A commonality of place and time. This was their tragedy. As much the old man's as it was Mia's. Their community had been attacked. By accident or design, the result was the same.

"The actual blast," Nick said, pulling the conversation back to less emotional ground. "There was still nothing visual?"

"Nothing to confirm it was a nuke." Ellis released Mia's hand. "Mountains were still in the way, but the sucker stirred up a hell of a cloud of dust. And there was wind. Sharp and strong with the smell of war. Ain't no other way to explain it. I knew whatever it was, it was bad. Of course by then the news was all over it. Never did explain the fuzzy air though. But I know what I saw. And there ain't no way it doesn't connect to the explosion somehow."

"But the first time there was nothing visual to suggest it really was an explosion."

"Anyone else mention seeing the mist?" Nick asked, trying to make sense of this newest piece of information.

"I don't get out much. Ya'll are the first people I've spoken to 'cept Jake since it happened. But there's been people askin' questions. Came by the house a couple days after the explosion. Wanted to know if I'd had any trouble with my livestock."

"Had you?"

"Yup." He grinned, his teeth yellowed, but very much his own. "Didn't tell them a damn thing, though. City folk." His bushy eyebrows rose with the pronouncement, which clearly was not meant as a compliment. "Come to think of it, they might have been your tree-huggers."

"They give you a name?" Nick said, finishing the last of his beer. More likely it was Davies and his cronies, but it didn't hurt to ask.

"Sorry, threw 'em out pretty much before they'd had a chance to park their asses. But I recollect it had something to do with a ball." As information went it wasn't particularly helpful, but Nick got the sense that the old man was shooting straight.

"If you wouldn't talk to them," he asked, "why are you telling me?"

"Because you're with Mia. And she doesn't suffer fools. Gets that from her grandfather." He sat back with the look of a man who was right about people more often than not.

"What about the livestock, Ellis," Mia said, ignoring the undercurrent between the two men. "You said they were affected. How?"

"Ones we were working on were fine. Haven't seen any signs that they were hurt at all, but I had about thirty head up in the high meadow. They're dead."

"All of them?" Mia's raised brows echoed Nick's confusion.

"Every blasted one. Figured it was radiation. But the doc didn't agree."

"You had a vet look at them?"

"Damn straight. Did an autopsy on one of 'em. Figured if it was the radiation I had grounds to sue."

"Only it wasn't?"

"Nope. Not according to Doc Loring. Seen a lot of cattle die. Hell, it happens. But I've never seen anything like this."

"What do you mean?" Nick asked.

"Put it this way—they didn't go easily."

"Will Doc Loring talk to us?"

"If I tell him it's okay." The rancher's smile was quick, a wicked gleam sparkling in his eyes.

"It's important, Ellis," Mia said, this time reaching out to cover his hand with hers.

He sobered immediately. "I know it is." He transferred his attention to Nick. "You want to tell me why you're asking all these questions?"

"Not too much to tell, unfortunately. Let's just say we think there may have been something else going on in Cedar Branch."

"Something beyond the accident."

"It's looking that way. We're just trying to gather information and see what we can put together."

"But nothing sanctioned." The old man was definitely hitting on all cylinders.

"No." Nick shook his head. "Right now Mia's well-being is what I'm most concerned with."

The old man nodded, his gaze approving. "Then you're all right with me. I'll call Doc Loring."

"And you won't tell anyone we were here?" Mia asked.

"You know us old farts, Mia." Ellis's smile was reflected in his eyes. "We can't remember a goddamned thing."

CALEB LORING specialized in large animals, primarily of the bovine type. Which meant that his office was more for clinical lab work than anything else. After all, people weren't all that likely to bring their cattle in for a checkup.

Fortunately, the vet had been in when Ellis called, and he'd agreed to meet with Nick and Mia immediately.

"So Ellis said that you're interested in his dead cattle."

Mia nodded, trying to size the man up. If she'd had to call it she'd guess he was somewhere between twenty-five and thirty. He'd grown up in the area, according to Ellis, but was only just back after a couple of years away. "Yeah, I live in the valley and I've got some dead cattle, too. Ellis thought there might be a connection."

They'd decided not to tell Loring anything more than necessary, including the fact that Mia had been in Cedar Branch. The fewer people who knew what they were after the better. Davies and his men weren't stupid, and sooner or later they'd figure out what Nick and Mia were up to. If Loring didn't know anything, then he wouldn't have anything to tell. It was as simple as that.

"You want me to autopsy your stock?" The vet leaned back against a table, his eyes narrowed as he studied them both.

"No." Mia shook her head. "I'm sure with everything that's happened, you've got more important things to do."

"The phone's been ringing pretty much nonstop. Stock outnumbers people in this county something like a hundred to one. Everyone is trying not to panic. The newscasters all assure us that there's no danger. But I gotta admit, I can't seem to stop watching the weather map, waiting for it to show a cloud of radiation heading this way."

"My understanding is that the radiation dissipated almost at impact," Nick said, his tone matter-of-fact. "Besides, the mountains would have insulated you from additional fallout."

"You sound certain," Loring said.

"I have it on good authority."

The vet nodded, a faint smile tipping the corner of his mouth. "Sorry. It's just not every day we deal with fallout. You know?"

"Totally understandable," Mia said. "I've been doing exactly the same thing." Which, of course, was not exactly true, but Loring had no way of knowing it. "Look, Ellis just told me that you might could help shed some light on what happened to his livestock."

"Brewster said it wasn't radiation," Nick added.

"No. There were traces of radiation in the cow I autopsied, but not enough to cause death. In fact, based on what I've read about the accident, the amount of radiation present wasn't even up to the level you'd expect, given the location of Ellis's stock in relation to ground zero."

"Do you have a theory?" Nick asked.

"Not one that makes any kind of sense. The cattle all died around the same time. Almost instantaneously, if my conclusions are right. And they died from some sort of massive cardiopulmonary event."

"Can you give us a little more detail?" Mia asked. "Ellis said that they didn't go easily."

"Well, this is strictly based on observation. I've never had to deal with anything like this before. But when a cow is sick, she'll behave in a fairly predictable manner. Droopy ears, loss of appetite, head down, diarrhea. All of which takes a little time to manifest."

"Ellis said he was working on the back half ranch. So there wouldn't have been anyone to notice the changes," Mia said, leaning against a refrigeration unit covered with piles of paper. Housekeeping apparently wasn't high on Loring's list of priorities.

"Except that he'd been up there the day before, and there was no sign of any sickness. That's why he thought it was the radiation."

"But the radiation level was too low," Nick finished for him. "You said something about it not jiving with what you'd have expected from the explosion."

"Well, I'm hardly an expert. But I did a little research, and given the pasture's location, the cattle should have shown a higher level of radiation. Nothing lethal. But at least enough to make them sick."

"So could the radiation combined with something else have killed them? Maybe their immune systems were already compromised," Mia said.

"I considered that. But they were current on vaccinations and Ellis has always been careful about his stock. Besides, all this happened too fast. I've never seen anything like it. The cattle just dropped in their tracks. Almost as if they'd lost all muscle control. Cattle will lie down with their legs tucked beneath them. But they don't lie on their sides. This looked as if someone had come in with an oversize bowling ball and literally bowled them over."

"What about other livestock in the area?" Nick asked. "You said there'd been a lot of calls."

"Ellis's cattle were closer than anything else on this side

of the mountain. But Ely Jackson called to say that he'd lost chickens. The whole coop. He's supposed to be bringing one in for an autopsy. Willie Owens lost a couple of horses. He didn't want an autopsy, but I was out there, and at least visually the symptoms seem to be the same. There are others I haven't had time to follow up with. Do you see a similarity with your livestock?"

Mia pretended to consider the question. "Well, it's not exactly the same, but there are definite parallels. Of course, my cattle were farther away from the blast."

"So it's not just something with Ellis," Nick said, pulling the conversation away from her fictitious stock. "And none of it is consistent with radiation sickness. Did the autopsy tell you anything else?"

"Beyond the radiation, it confirmed cardio arrest and pulmonary paralysis. For anything more specific, I'd have to have more equipment and probably a hell of a lot more experience, frankly. I sent tissue samples to Texas A&M. They have one of the best labs in the country. Unfortunately, they're not noted for speed."

"Did you tell anyone else any of this? Besides the university, I mean."

"No. But there was someone here asking about it. Said he was with some environmental group—like you, he was trying to work out exactly what had happened. Offered to buy the carcasses if I knew of any. A settlement of sorts, he said."

"But you didn't believe him."

"Except for college and vet school, Mr. Price, I've lived here my whole life. And to put it nicely, we don't cotton to strangers. Especially ones that want to buy up dead animals." And even the ones in the company of a native, if the man's scowl was any indication. "Anyway, I told him I hadn't seen anything unusual."

"Did the man say who he was with?" Mia asked, the sound of her voice easing the tension a bit.

"Yeah, bio something. Hang on a minute," he said, "I wrote it down." He rifled through the papers on his desk, finally locating a scrap of paper. "Biosphere. That's the company he said he was with."

"I'm guessing it was the same guy who came to Ellis's. He said he thought the company name had something to do with a ball."

"Yeah. Ellis mentioned they'd been to his place, too." Loring handed the piece of paper to Mia.

"I don't suppose you kept any tissue," Nick said, keeping his expression purposefully blank.

"What if I did?" the vet said, his eyes skeptical.

"Then I could get it to people I know. People who could probably get results in a matter of hours. It might go a long way toward helping explain what the hell really happened here."

Loring frowned, clearly uncertain what to do.

"Look, Caleb," Mia said, her use of the vet's first name intentional, "this is really important. We're starting to believe that this whole thing is bigger than just a military accident."

Silence reigned for a moment as Loring considered her words. Then, with a brief nod, he walked over to the refrigeration unit. Mia moved aside to allow him access, shooting Nick a look of triumph. The veterinarian reached inside and produced a sealed vial. "Hell, I'd trust Ellis Brewster with my life. If he says you're good people, then that's good enough for me. I took multiple samples. Guess I can spare one."

"Thanks," Nick said, taking the vial. "You won't be sorry."

"Let me give you a copy of the autopsy report, as well. Your lab will need it." The vet pulled some papers from the stack on the refrigeration unit offering them to Mia.

"We'll put it to good use, I promise," Mia said, taking the report.

"You know, I think I believe you," Loring said, his expression lightening. "Or if not you per se, then Ellis. And he's obviously convinced that you can help."

"If I can't," she said, glancing over at Nick, "I certainly have friends who can."

Loring held her gaze for a moment, clearly turning something over in his mind. Nick opened his mouth to ask, but Mia shook her head ever so slightly.

"Caleb," she said, "I've lived hereabouts my whole life. My grandfather's father drove our first herd of cattle up here when Idaho was empty territory. The kind of place a man could build a life. If someone is trying to destroy what people like Ellis Brewster and my grandfather have worked so hard to create, then we need to do everything we can to stop it."

The vet sighed, and then reached over for another piece of paper.

"You'd better have this, too, then," he said. "I didn't want to release it in case Ellis decided to go through with his lawsuit. But since you're his friend, I reckon you ought to know." The vet paused, his somber gaze including them both. "Based on core temperatures I took, and the radiation level present, I can say without doubt that Ellis's cattle were already dead when the missile exploded in Cedar Branch."

CHAPTER SEVENTEEN

"Okay, so what does all this mean? When I try to put it together nothing fits," Mia said with a sigh. They were back at the no-tell motel, Dr. Loring's reports spread out on the table in front of them.

"I'm not sure I'm any clearer about it than you are. But at least if we piece together Ellis's story with Loring's we've got two unique incidents," Nick said. "The mist that Ellis saw, and the actual explosion of the missile."

"But it's possible the mist was something Ellis imagined. I mean, he's not all that young."

"Except that he also mentioned a secondary noise."

"Yeah," Mia said. "But even Ellis agrees it could be explained by a hunter or a backfire or something."

"But you're forgetting about the cattle." Nick stood up to check out the front window. Everything was peaceful, but he couldn't help feeling that the other shoe had yet to drop.

"No. I'm not," she said, shaking her head. "I'm just having trouble fitting them into the puzzle. We know for certain that they didn't die from radiation poisoning. And if Loring is to be believed, they were dead before the missile detonated. Which leaves what? A catastrophic mist that killed thirty head of cattle?"

"I don't know what it was. But I don't think we can

ignore it. We know it affected a coop of chickens and some horses, too. And that's just what we heard from one source. If we had the time to investigate, I suspect we'd find that there were other deaths, as well."

"So you're thinking that the blast that destroyed Cedar Branch was preceded by something else? Something equally deadly?"

"I don't know," he said, turning to face her. "I'm just trying to make the facts fit."

"I just wish we had something more concrete."

"We have the sample." He glanced at the cooler by the sink. The tissue section was inside, safely on ice, but Nick knew it was important to get it analyzed as soon as possible. Only trouble was he no longer had access to the resources of Homeland Security, and Matt still wasn't answering his e-mails.

"And no one to send it to," Mia said, echoing his thoughts.

"We'll find someone. Worst case, we can head to Pocatello. Someone at the university will be able to analyze it for us. Although to do that we'll risk exposure."

"Maybe we should just end this now. Go public with what we know. Once we've told the press, won't that make it harder for Davies and his cohorts to get away with silencing us?"

"If I thought that'd work, believe me, I'd have opted for that from the beginning," Nick said, running a hand through his hair. "But Davies and his team wouldn't have been called in to cleanse the situation if they weren't acting on behalf of someone really powerful."

"Senator Tucker." Mia nodded her agreement.

"It's possible. But it could be bigger than that. Tucker's connection with the CIA is an old one. It's been years since he was secretary of defense. The organization has changed. And I'm not aware of him having a direct line to the current administration, and through them, S&C."

"Yeah, but even with a different party in power, he's bound to still have contacts. You don't accomplish all that he's accomplished without making some powerful connections along the way."

"I agree, which means that we can't discount the possibility that Tucker is behind things. But he's not the only one who could pull something like this off. So the point is that any information we take to the press now is no more than speculation. And judging from Matt's warnings, I suspect whoever is behind this will be more than ready to counter anything we say. They'll paint me a traitor, and play up your ties to your mother's affiliations."

Mia frowned, opening her mouth to argue, but he waved her silent.

"I'm not attacking you or your mother. I'm stating a fact. Even though you had nothing to do with what happened in Cedar Branch, I'm absolutely certain that they can spin it to make it look like you did."

"Did you just say that you believe I'm innocent?" She blinked, tears glistening in her eyes.

"Do you think last night could have happened if I didn't believe in you?"

"I don't know. I guess I just figured it was heat of the moment…" She trailed off, clearly struggling to find words.

He reached out to brush his fingers against her cheek. "I've seen a hell of a lot in my life, Mia. Things that most people can't even imagine. In the beginning, the ugliness was tempered by the fact that I was certain I could tell the good guys from the bad guys. But the truth is that they all look alike. Sometimes the people you trust most are the worst liars. So with a couple of exceptions, I don't trust anyone."

"But you just said you believed me."

"I do."

"So that makes me one of the exceptions?" she asked, her eyes still bright with unshed tears.

"Yeah, I guess it does." He'd already said too much, the emotions more than he wanted to deal with. He didn't want to care. It was as simple as that. Unfortunately, life didn't always give you a choice. "Look, the important thing is that we're in this together. For as long as it takes. All right?"

She nodded, wiping the tears away. "I'm sorry. I'm usually stronger than this. I didn't mean to go all weepy on you. It's just been a tough week."

"Now's there's an understatement," he said with a smile, grateful that they were back on safer ground.

"Anyway," she said, squaring her shoulders, "going public is out."

"Yeah, at least until we have something more than speculation. Which means we hold on to the sample until I get hold of Matt."

"And if you can't?" she asked, chewing on the side of her lip.

"Then we'll go to Pocatello." He reached out to squeeze her hand. "But don't give up on Matt. You were right, there's no way he'd allow himself to be compromised. He's too smart for that. And in the meantime, we need to find out more about Biosphere."

She nodded, turning to the laptop in front of her. "I used a couple of search engines, but nothing is listed that seems to fit. It's a fairly common term thanks to the geodesic domes in Arizona. But they're no longer in operation. In fact, according to several of the citations I found, the land they occupy is scheduled for redevelopment. There are also several foundations listed. All of them centering on some unique ecosystem or other. None of them located in the Northwest. There's a band named Biosphere, and several sites defining the term. But that's about it. I was just about to try running the search using the words *Biosphere* and *Kresky*."

"Makes sense. Maybe you should try associating the term with Tucker, and for that matter Hatcher, too. Everything we have points to their involvement as well as Kresky's."

"It's worth a shot."

He pulled a chair up next to hers, perching on the edge so he could see the screen. The first two entries in the search engine proved to be dead ends. Some professor named Walter Kresky had been associated with the original biosphere experiments, but there was nothing to suggest that he was connected in any way to Jameson Kresky or Kresky International.

From there the association between the words *Kresky* and *Biosphere* dissolved into spurious connections of the name and the term, eventually dwindling down to single citations that referenced only one of them.

"Okay, so we'll try the senators," Mia said, typing in first Hatcher and then Tucker and then both men together. There were no links between either of them and the word *Biosphere*.

"Great," Nick said, rising restlessly to walk across the room toward the window. "So far we're batting zero. What do you suggest we do now?"

"Stay patient?" Mia suggested.

"Not my strong point. I'm a burst-in-with-a-loaded-gun kind of guy. Never been too good at digging through haystacks in search of needles. Even important ones."

"Right," she said with a laugh. "You'd just blow up the whole haystack."

"Got it in one." Despite the severity of the situation, he grinned.

"So go call Matt again and let me get to work. I can't accomplish a thing with you stomping around in here."

"Fine." He shrugged, already heading for the door. "I'll be right outside if you need me."

The air was cool despite the season, no doubt a product of the earlier rain showers. The parking lot was almost empty, a green pickup and a white Mercedes the only other occupants. He stopped, alarm bells ringing. Someone who could afford a Mercedes didn't seem the right kind of person to stay in a roadside motel.

Moving cautiously, hand on the butt of his gun, he walked over to the car, glancing through the front side window. A map lay across the leather seat, along with a pacifier and a green polka-dotted bear. The carseat in the back was decked out with multicolored plastic circles and squares.

Clearly not Davies.

He shook his head at his own overly suspicious mind and walked back toward their rooms, dialing Matt's number.

He'd stopped trying his friend's work number, certain that by now there were listening ears, but his cell was supposed to be secure. The phone connected, the hollow ring at the other end signaling that Matt still wasn't answering. Nick had already started to disengage when he heard the click of the line picking up.

"Hello?" a male voice on the other end asked. "Who's calling, please?"

Nick had no idea who the voice belonged to, but he was certain it wasn't Matt. He hit End, and then scrolled over to the outgoing-call list to double-check the number. He'd dialed correctly. Which meant one of two things: either Matt had turned on him, or something had happened to his friend.

And Matt definitely hadn't screwed him over.

Closing the phone with a snap, Nick fought to control his thoughts. No point in jumping to conclusions. Just because someone had the phone didn't mean they had Matt. He considered calling Gordon or one of the other agents he worked with at Homeland Security, but abandoned the idea. Gordon wouldn't want to turn him in, but he would. And the honest truth was there really wasn't anyone else he could be sure of.

He'd just have to wait for Matt to contact him.

He turned to go back into the motel room, stopping when he noticed that the Mercedes was gone. He'd been so busy trying to reach Matt, he hadn't been paying attention.

It didn't mean anything, really, except that his internal radar wasn't working up to par. Too much on his mind, maybe. Or maybe he was letting himself get distracted by a certain long-legged blonde.

It paid to keep your mind on business. He'd learned that lesson all too well. Distractions of any kind could be the difference between life and death. He gave the parking lot a second sweep, noting the arrival of an old Pontiac, the kind his grandmother used to drive. He hadn't gone to her funeral. He'd wanted to. But his mother wouldn't allow it. Of course, he could have defied her, but truth was, his grandmother was dead. And despite everyone's wishful thinking, when you were gone, you were gone.

So he'd figured it was better to give his mother the distance she required.

Hell of a life.

He stepped back into the motel room, his eyes lingering on the soft curve of Mia's shoulders, almost buried beneath the tumble of her hair.

"Did you get hold of Matt?" she asked without looking up from the computer, completely oblivious to the tenor of his thoughts.

"No."

She swung around to face him. "But there's more, right?"

"Yeah," he said, sitting down on the end of the bed. "Someone else answered."

"Did you recognize the voice?"

He shook his head. "No idea who it was. But there's no way Matt would let someone else answer that phone. Not if he had any say in the matter. It's supposed to be protected."

"Like that one?" She glanced pointedly at the cell phone in his hand.

"I've had it in my possession the whole time. There's no way Davies or anyone else could have messed with it. Besides, Matt isn't being tracked through his phone, he's just not answering it."

"And you think it means he's been compromised." For a woman who wasn't supposed to understand the ins and outs of an operative's life, she was a pretty quick study.

"I don't want to believe it's possible. But it wasn't Matt on the phone, so the story kind of tells itself."

"It could have been stolen. Or maybe he just left it behind. If someone is out to get him, he'd hit the road, right? That's what you'd do, anyway."

He smiled despite the tone of the conversation. "Yeah, that's what I'd do. Only difference is that Matt hasn't been out in the field in a while."

"Maybe you just need to have a little faith."

"Easier said than done, but you're right. He'll contact me when he can." He leaned forward so he could see the computer screen. "Any luck with the search?"

"Actually, I was just coming to get you. I'm not sure that this means anything, but I dug around a little and came up with a tax record from Montana. It lists a company called Biosphere. They're classified as a nonprofit research organization—which doesn't really tell us a lot." She tilted the laptop so that he could see better. "In fact, I probably would have ignored it altogether, except the taxpayer ID rang a bell."

Nick read the number and shook his head. "Seems pretty obscure to stir a memory."

"I've always had a head for numbers. Had a teacher tell me once it was connected to my creativity. Never really believed her, but who knows?" She shrugged. "Anyway, the interesting thing is that the number is the same as one that Kresky uses. Not for his main business, mind you, but for a research arm I found connected with weapons development."

"Another nonprofit?"

"At least as far as the federal government is concerned."

"So have you been able to come up with any additional information on the group in Montana?"

"Nothing definitive. There's no Web site. And we already know that Kresky isn't making the association overly public. But the tax record provides an address. It's a post office box, but it's still a lead. The box is in Bozeman. And I'm betting that'll mean the operation, whatever it is, is somewhere in southwest Montana. Especially if we're right and they had some kind of offshoot in Cedar Branch. Anyway, it's a starting place at least."

"It would fit with our theory that the transportation route was changed to cover the real facts. If Kresky was developing some new kind of nuclear warhead for the government, he'd have to keep it secret. There's still an international moratorium on new development. And considering the president's stance on other countries curtailing nuclear activity, it'd be crucial to keep something like that under wraps."

"Which would mean diverting funds from a camouflaged source like the amendment we found."

"Exactly. Kresky would want to keep it separated from his bread-and-butter operations. So with a little help from Hatcher and Tucker's amendment, he arranged to keep the real purpose of the money hidden."

"Enter Biosphere," Mia said. "A research facility for environmental studies, if the amendment is to be believed."

"It's a decent cover, considering Idaho's nuclear history."

"But then something goes wrong. The new weapon explodes. And takes out Cedar Branch with it." She stumbled over the last bit, and he restrained himself from reaching out to her. He knew about grief well enough to know that it was easily triggered, especially when someone was offering sympathy. She paused for a moment, sequestering her pain, then with a slow intake of breath, looked up to meet his gaze.

"It would explain the need for a cover-up. The senators certainly wouldn't want to risk exposing the work they were endorsing behind the scenes."

"Neither would Kresky," she added, clearly in control

of her emotions again. "But even if all that's true, it doesn't fit our timeline. There's still the dead cattle, the mist Ellis saw, and the fact that the last thing I remember clearly is working in my studio—feeling guilty about not eating my breakfast."

"Well, the only real lead we have for any of this is Bio-sphere," Nick said. "And since their post office box is in Bozeman, that seems as good a place as any to start."

CHAPTER EIGHTEEN

BOZEMAN, MONTANA, HAD the small-town feel of many of the little communities that dotted the Northwest, but unlike many of its counterparts, Bozeman was still flourishing. Originally founded as a way station for gold-fevered miners, the town had managed to survive throughout the years, establishing a university and turning its attention to tourism.

Mia had always liked the feel of the place, mountains rising up around it, purples and blues mixing with the cool green of pines and aspen. She'd even considered coming to college here. Her grandfather had been delighted with the idea, preferring she stay close to home, but her mother had wanted more for her daughter. And in the end, she'd prevailed, packing Mia off to California.

Not that any of that mattered now.

"This looks like the place," Nick said, pulling her back to the present. He pointed to an awning across the street proclaiming the name Mail Mart. It'd taken about half an hour to run down the physical address of the mail box, but computers were wonderful things, and now here they were.

"You think they'll tell us who owns the box?"

"Not without a little persuasion." He patted his jacket

pocket, the edges of the folded money inside visible evidence of their intended methodology.

"Thank God my grandfather believed in ready cash," she said. "Without it we'd have been shit out of luck."

"Nah." Nick grinned. "We'd have figured out a way. But this'll make it a hell of a lot easier." He checked for cars and then, grabbing her hand, headed across the street. The gesture was a natural one. Probably not even something he realized he'd done. But she liked it just the same. There was a rightness there that in ordinary circumstances would have left her feeling hopeful. But there was nothing ordinary about their relationship.

Nothing at all.

The door opened with a little jingle and Nick dropped her hand, heading for the back of the store. An older man straightened from the newspaper he was reading. "Can I help you?" His smile was friendly.

Mia's eyes dropped to the newsprint. The headlines had finally moved on to something else, but the second lead was still about Cedar Branch.

"Damn shame," the man said, nodding at the paper. "You folks from around here?" The words were banal, but his gaze grew watchful.

"No." Mia shook her head. "We're just trying to track down some information."

"You're not with the press?" His brows drew together as he considered her. "Apparently, the bomb that went off in Cedar Branch was headin' for Malmstrom. Them news boys is all over this part of Montana. Even here. Been driving locals crazy."

"I swear, we're not with the press," Mia said, holding up her hands in supplication. They'd agreed on a story and now it was up to her to make it seem plausible. "It's about our sister. Her husband's really a piece of work. He beat her." She looked down at her hands, feigning emotion.

"It's okay, Lainey," Nick said, reaching out to squeeze her hand. "I'm sure the gentleman understands."

Actually, said gentleman was looking kind of relieved. Mia sniffled and brushed away a couple of nonexistent tears. "I just hate having to talk about it," she said, keeping her gaze fixed on the counter.

"I know," he said, "but we need to explain things so that Lewis here can understand why we need his help."

She looked up with what she hoped was a weak smile, confirming from the man's name tag that his name was indeed Lewis. "It's just that Cathy's been through so much. Amos damn near killed her the last time. But she managed to get out. Even filed for divorce. But now he's threatening her again."

"I'm afraid I don't know anyone named Amos." The man tilted his head quizzically.

"You're misunderstanding," Nick said. "Amos has been sending my sister letters. Really nasty ones. And we've managed to trace them to a post office box here. But we don't have anything to prove it."

"What we need," Mia said, lifting her gaze to meet the clerk's, "is evidence. It's the only way we can get the police involved." She reached into her pocket and produced a torn piece of envelope. "This is the box number. All I need from you is confirmation that Amos is renting the box. We think he's living near Gallatin."

The man started to shake his head, but Nick placed a hand on the counter, three Ben Franklins peeking out between his fingers. The clerk swallowed. "I'm really not allowed to release this kind of information."

"I know," Mia said, "and if it weren't really important we wouldn't ask." She leaned over a little, her arms compressing her breasts, the cleavage providing added incentive. "But Cathy can't take much more. She's even been talking suicide. We need to stop this before something really bad happens. And right now you're the only one who can help."

Lewis hesitated for a couple seconds, then slid his hand over the money, pocketing it. "Hang on a minute." He took the torn envelope and walked over to a filing cabinet in the corner. He rifled through the files, finally producing one. He flipped it open and ran his finger down a sheet of paper, stopping about halfway down. "No one named Amos listed here. And the address isn't in Gallatin."

"Can I see it for myself?" Mia asked, glancing over at Nick, who shook his head and shrugged. "Maybe it's an alias, or maybe there's more there than you're seeing."

"Nope. It's pretty damn clear you've got the wrong box. Sorry I couldn't be of more help."

Nick shrugged and then flipped out a couple more hundreds. "This help change your mind?"

"Don't suppose it'd hurt for you to have a quick look," Lewis said. "Besides, I hate the idea of any woman being hurt. Especially if your sister's as pretty as you are." He palmed the money and slid the file forward. "Hope it helps."

Mia glanced down at the papers, smiling as she read what was written on the application. "I'm sure it will, Lewis. Thanks."

Nick took her elbow and the two of them walked through the front door before the man had a chance to change his mind. "I take it you got an address."

"Yeah," she nodded, buoyed by their success. "Looks like Biosphere is located just outside of Virginia City. But that's not the good part." She opened the car door, her gaze meeting his across the hood. "The contact listed for the box is Paul Brennon. We were right. Kresky's behind Biosphere."

THE PINES ON EITHER SIDE of the road cast dark shadows as evening slipped silently into night. It was too late to head to Virginia City. They needed to formulate a plan first. But Nick didn't like the idea of staying in Bozeman. If Lewis had been bought, he could be again, and even though they hadn't seen any evidence that Davies had found them, it was better not to take chances. They were headed toward Gardiner, a tiny ranching town on the Montana border.

"You're sure there'll be somewhere to stay?" he asked, shooting a sideways look at Mia, who was studying a map.

"Positive. When I worked in the park, Gardiner was the go-to place. It had some really great bars. And one of them was across from Pine Trails."

"Where do they come up with these names?" He slowed the car as they came over the top of a hill. They were cutting through Yellowstone National Park on an almost empty road, circling around to enter Gardiner from the south.

"No idea," she said with a smile. "But it's just what we need. The middle of nowhere with no direct road connecting to Virginia City. Davies will never find us."

"Don't make the mistake of underestimating the man, Mia. I don't like him, but that doesn't mean I don't respect his abilities."

"I wasn't. I just would like to believe that for the moment we've lost our escort. Makes me a little less jumpy, you know?"

He reached across the seat to squeeze her shoulder. "You're doing great. You're the one who got Lewis to talk, and now you're providing a hideaway. Not to mention uncovering Biosphere in the first place."

"Well, I kinda think that if I hadn't been there, you'd have managed just fine. Especially where Lewis was concerned. I don't think he'd have been able to stand up to any serious attempts to persuade him."

A spatter of rain hit the windshield, and Nick started the wipers, then flicked on the headlights. "Looks like the storm's back."

"Could just be a shower," Mia said, glancing down at the map. "It isn't much farther."

Behind them another car crested the hill, the lights dipping downward with the car, giving Nick a quick view of an old Pontiac. "Damn it. I was too busy watching the Mercedes."

"What?" Mia said, twisting to look behind her.

"I've seen that car. In the parking lot of the motel. But I was more concerned about the Mercedes parked near our rooms. It seemed out of place. I should have checked out the Pontiac."

"You think Davies is behind us?"

"Yeah," Nick said, cursing himself for his mistake. As if to support the fact, the car behind them sped up, its headlights looming through the rain.

"So what do we do?"

"Try and outrun him," Nick said, pushing the gas pedal to the floor. The little car lurched as the engine engaged, then shot forward. "Get the gun."

Mia opened the glove compartment and pulled out the Sig-Sauer. "Do you want me to shoot?"

"Only if he pulls within range. No sense in wasting bullets."

She nodded and cracked the window, the wind cold as it whistled through the opening. The road curved to the left, a sharp incline accompanied by yellow arrowed signs pointing the way. He yanked the wheel, the Toyota screeching in protest. The Pontiac was closing fast, the old shell hiding what appeared to be a powerful engine.

A bullet slammed into the Toyota's rear window.

"Shit," Nick said.

Mia lowered the window all the way, rain whipping into the car. "I'm going to return fire."

"This isn't the rifle range, Mia. We've already established that those guys are shooting to kill."

"So am I," she said, moving to lean out the window, the report of the gun muffled by the wind. She dropped back into the seat just as the car behind them swerved, momentarily losing traction.

"Good shot," Nick said, risking a sideways glance to be certain she was okay. Her face was ashen, but her shoulders were set with determination. Her grandfather would have been proud.

"Not good enough," she said, popping back out the window. She got off another round, the Pontiac swerving again, this time returning fire. The bullets shot out the rear lights and splintered the rearview mirror just seconds after Mia slid back to safety.

"Don't shoot again, it's too dangerous."

She nodded, turning to watch the Pontiac through the rear window. "I can almost read the license plate."

Nick recognized the significance of her words and pushed the little Toyota to its limits, but the park road was climbing now, and the four-cylinder engine just wasn't up to the task. "Next time we're going for a Ferrari."

"Works for me," she said, still staring at the car behind them. "As long as there *is* a next time."

"No problem. We've come through worse." Unfortunately, they only had one gun, and in a moving car, it had questionable range. So he'd have to gain the upper hand some other way.

The Toyota puttered forward, surging a bit when the road flattened out. "If we can just make the other side of the incline we should be able to pick up some speed."

"Only problem is that Davies will be able to do the same," Nick said, shaking his head.

"Yeah, but we should still have the advantage. The Toyota may not have much power, but it's got great maneuverability and its size and shape will make it more stable than the bigger car on the downhill side. He'll have to slow a little if only to make certain he's got traction."

"Not bad for a country girl." He shot her what he hoped was a confident smile and floored the little car. The peak of the hill was coming fast. He could see the signs identifying degree of incline as they streaked past.

Suddenly the Pontiac surged forward, bullets smashing into their rear bumper and trunk.

"Looks like they've realized we'll be gaining an advantage," Mia said, slipping back into her seat belt as a second volley of bullets slammed into the car. The Toyota lurched left and then skidded right.

"They got the back tires," Nick said, fighting for control as the car shimmied into a full-fledged spin. "Hang on," he yelled as they crashed through a guardrail over the edge of a cliff. For a moment they were suspended, and then the vehicle flipped on its side, crashing down the rocky incline. They rolled once more and slammed into the bottom of the ravine.

After all the noise, the silence was deafening, even the rain quieter here amid the thick copse of pine trees. "Mia?" Nick called. "You all right?" He struggled to push away the deflated air bag.

"I'm here," she said, her voice weak as she emerged from behind her air bag. Blood spilled down her head, and his stomach lurched in response.

"You're bleeding."

She lifted her fingers to her head, seeming surprised to see the blood smeared across her hand. "It doesn't hurt." Her words came slowly, and he felt a moment's panic as he reached over to check her pulse. "I'm fine. It's just a cut," she said, shaking him off, sounding more like herself. "We've got to get out of here."

He nodded, automatically reaching down to free himself from his seat belt.

"Nick." Mia's voice had gone soft again, accompanied by a tremor of panic. "I think I'm stuck."

The car was lodged on its side, the passenger door bowed inward. In addition, the front of the Toyota had been shoved forward in the impact, the glove compartment bent downward, trapping her knees. But it was the sparking wires and the smell of gasoline that worried him.

"Hang on, sweetheart," he said, fighting against his own fear. "Let me see what I can do."

"Get the sample first," she said, shooting a glance over her shoulder at the cooler. It had tipped on its side, but, re-markably, had stayed closed. He hesitated, the smell of gas growing stronger. "Nick," she urged, "we need the sample."

All he cared about was Mia. But he knew she was right. Forcing himself to clear his emotions, he nodded and reached behind him, pushing off the lid of the cooler and securing the vial.

"What about Davies?" Mia asked, her gaze moving over his shoulder to the window.

"Hasn't been time. We took the fast way down the hillside, remember? It'll take them a lot longer."

Her smile was weak, but he felt better seeing it. "Can you move your legs?"

She nodded. "I think if you can get the seat belt off, I can manage to wriggle out."

"Okay," he replied, reaching for the buckle. It was jammed, the metal bent. "I don't think the buckle is going to release. We'll have to try another way." Twisting so that he had access to his pocket, he produced a Swiss army knife.

"Always prepared," she said, the undernote of panic back. "That's my kind of guy. But I think you better hurry." She nodded to the orange glow of a fire backlighting a plume of smoke curling over the hood of the car.

He sawed at the seat belt, but the little knife wasn't intended to cut reinforced nylon. Progress was slow, the smell of gasoline growing stronger by the second.

"Nick," Mia said, her voice steeling. "You've got to get out now. There's no point in both of us getting killed."

"Sorry, I'm not letting you go noble on me now, princess. Remember we agreed that we're in this together." He gritted his teeth, sawing harder. No fucking way was he going to lose her.

"We weren't talking about being blown up in a car. If I'd known that I might not have signed on." Her attempt at humor touched him in a way nothing else could have, and he prayed for strength, more determined than ever to sever the damn seat belt.

"Almost there," he whispered. "Just hang on."

"I'm not going anywhere," she said, cutting a sideways glance at the fire now openly lapping over the end of the hood. "It's now or never, Nick."

As if coaxed by her words, the knife cut through the last bit of the nylon. Scrambling up to brace himself against the center armrest, he grabbed her under the shoulders. "On three, you push, I'll pull."

She nodded, and he counted down. "One, two, three…"

He yanked her forward, her body sliding clear of the mangled door and glove box. Without taking the time to assess her injuries, he pushed the door open, twisting again to use his feet to push it upward. Then, holding it with his left arm, he climbed out, pulling her behind him.

They jumped to the ground, rolling clear of the wreckage into the trees just as the car exploded. Yellow flames shot up into the night sky, a wave of heat washing over them in the fire's wake.

"You okay?" he asked, his hands moving over her body, searching for injury.

"I'm fine. But we've lost the gun. And the computer."

"Considering that we almost lost a hell of a lot more than that, I think we'll manage. But we've got to get out of here. The explosion might slow Davies down for a minute or so, but you can be sure he'll want confirmation of our deaths."

She nodded, pushing to her feet. He followed suit and, taking her hand, moved farther into the shelter of the forest. Behind them a second explosion rocked the night, this one followed by the smatter of gunfire.

"Looks like they're here," Mia said, reaching up to wipe blood from her eye.

"No. The sound's wrong. It's coming from somewhere higher up."

"Maybe they're just testing the waters," she said, shielding her eyes to try and see beyond the burning Toyota. Shots sounded again, this time followed by an answering volley.

"Someone's shooting at them."

"How can you be sure?" She frowned up at him, her face white in the glare from the fire.

"Listen," he said, holding his finger to his lips.

Shots rang out again, this time closer. After about a three-second delay the second gunman answered, the sound clearly different from the first. It was tempting to run, but they were in the middle of a national forest, and with the second shooter on the road, there was no way to double back. Better to wait and see how things played out.

"Keep low," he whispered, pulling her down between a blue spruce and a clump of bushes.

A man stepped into the light of the still-burning fire, pointing an automatic rifle up the hill. He fired once and then moved toward the bushes where they were hiding, apparently intent on finding cover of his own.

Nick tensed in preparation to run, his hand closing over Mia's. She nodded and they started to move, but just as they emerged from the bushes, another shot rang out, this one dropping the man by the car.

Silence filled the night, the smell of burning rubber permeating the air.

Nick signaled for Mia to wait. She shook her head but kept quiet, and he motioned her down again. Her eyes narrowed in disagreement, but she dropped back behind the bushes. Moving slowly, he edged around the car, working his way over to the downed man. He reached for a pulse, gratified to find none.

Grabbing the rifle, he inched forward, listening for the sound of the second gunman. It was tempting to think that the cavalry had come to the rescue, but it was far more likely that Davies had more than one team of hunters. Or Davies's bosses did.

A rock rattled as it tumbled down the incline. Nick ducked down, training the rifle in the direction of the sound.

The fire behind him suddenly shot upward again, apparently finding a last bit of gasoline to consume. The momentary burst of light illuminated the man on the hill. Nick leveled the rifle, his finger pressing the trigger, then his mind telegraphed recognition.

"Jesus, Matt," he growled, lowering the gun as his friend stepped into the clearing. "I almost blew you away."

"Not exactly the warmest of welcomes for the guy who just saved your ass."

"I had things under control."

"Yeah," Matt said, "and I've been sleeping with Angelina Jolie."

"Lucky you." Nick grinned.

"I told you he'd be all right," Mia said, appearing at his elbow.

"And I told you to stay put," he snapped, sounding more irritated than he'd meant to.

"I'm guessing you're the lady of the hour," Matt said with a laugh, holding out his hand. "Not exactly the most normal of situations, but I'm glad to finally meet you."

Nick watched as they solemnly shook hands, the fire

behind them reminding him that they weren't out of danger yet. "We should get out of here. Someone's bound to report the fire."

"Shouldn't we do something about him?" Mia asked, shuddering as she tipped her head toward the dead man.

"We could toss him into the fire," Nick said, considering the options. "Make it look like he was driving the car. You recognize him?"

"No, probably just a flunky of Davies." Matt shook his head. "But the guy up top is another matter altogether."

"So spill it," Nick said with a frown.

"You're not going to like it." Matt shrugged. "Casey Gall."

"Son of a bitch. That puts a whole new light on your abilities."

"Hang on a minute," Mia said, holding up a hand. "Who the hell is Casey Gall?"

"A contract assassin. He works for the CIA more often than not, but truth is he's not too picky about *who* he works for. Or who he takes out, for that matter."

"Don't think he gives a shit about much of anything anymore." Matt tipped his head toward the top of the hill. "Not that I'm sorry about it."

"But the fact that he was in the game at all ups the ante." Nick ran a hand through his hair, eyeing the wreckage and the other man.

"I don't understand," Mia said, her brows drawing together in confusion.

"If Davies called in Gall," Matt answered with a grimace, "then he's pretty fucking serious about taking you and Nick out of the equation."

CHAPTER NINETEEN

"WELL, YOUR TIMING WAS pretty fucking amazing," Nick said, pulling up to sit on the kitchen counter.

They'd managed to rent a cabin on the northern edge of the park, about fifteen miles from Gardiner. Basically, hiding in plain sight. Nick and Matt had arranged the crash scene so that the incinerated remains of Gall and his partner would be found inside the car. It wouldn't hold up under close scrutiny, of course, but it would buy them enough time to figure out their next move.

Mia was surprised at how calm she felt. After all, she'd almost died in a car crash, seen a man killed point-blank, been willing to kill another herself and helped Nick and Matt clean up the resulting mess. She should have been horrified, but the only thing she could think of was how glad she was that she and Nick were both alive.

"I was just following your trail of bread crumbs," Matt said. He was sitting on a bar stool at the counter, nursing a cup of coffee. "Our system worked like a charm. Although keeping up with your vehicle changes wasn't easy. You could have told me what you were driving."

"What? And take away all the fun?" Nick grinned at his friend. "So why didn't you just try to e-mail?"

"I couldn't risk it." Matt shook his head. "I was being

monitored. The only way to be certain I was safe was to drop off the grid altogether."

"You were wise. I tried to reach you on your secure phone, but someone else answered."

"Any idea who?" Matt frowned.

"No. I hung up immediately. I couldn't take a chance on them tracing the call."

"Probably someone from S&C. Caught them poking around my house—that's when I decided it was time to disappear. Left everything behind but my computer."

"Was it Gall?" Mia asked, handing Nick a second cup of coffee.

"No. Just a lackey—not even a full operative. But I figured the big guns would follow. Why do you ask?"

"Just wondering how Gall found us. I mean, your system is supposed to be infallible, and as you said, we've switched cars and generally outmaneuvered Davies on all counts. So he shouldn't have found us."

"My guess is Lewis gave us away." Nick took a sip of coffee and then set it on the counter. "I should have anticipated that he might."

"Lewis?" Matt asked.

"A clerk at a Bozeman mail store. He helped us ID Kresky's hidden company. But I should have known there was a possibility someone would think to monitor the place." He shot a look at Mia. "I've been a little distracted. Anyway, at least for the moment, we've got some breathing room. So besides S&C sniffing at your garbage, what else has been happening at division?"

"There were a lot of closed-door meetings between Norton and Ricks. Some of which I got snippets of, but nothing concrete. Mainly they were talking about you."

"And my supposed defection to the other side?"

Mia recognized a note of cynicism in Nick's voice. Not that she blamed him. She was becoming pretty darn cynical herself. "The problem is," she said, "there isn't another side. Unless you count the victims." She leaned back against the counter with a sigh, comforted when he reached out to cover her hand with his.

"So did you learn anything new?" Nick asked, turning his attention back to Matt.

"Nothing earth-shattering. Ricks is definitely orchestrating your takedown, but I got the feeling he was acting off of what he believed was solid information."

"So you don't think he's involved in this?"

Mia sipped her coffee, watching the two men. They were nothing alike, and yet there was a certain similarity in the way they carried themselves. A constant vigilance, as if they never truly relaxed. Matt's grin was easy, where Nick's smile was rare. And Nick's friend had that boy-next-door quality that made you instantly feel as if you'd known him forever.

But underneath all of that, she could see the steel in his eyes, the look of a man who had seen more than his fair share of ugliness. Nick wore his anger close to the surface, whereas Matt kept his camouflaged in jovial banter. But it was there nevertheless.

And whether because of that mutual background or something else, there was a definite bond between the two of them. Something she envied. She'd never really had a best friend. Her life had been too chaotic, and she'd never stayed in one place long enough to put in the time that kind of friendship demanded.

"I don't know anything for certain," Matt was saying,

"but my guess is that Ricks and Norton are being yanked around like the rest of us."

"Which leaves us pretty much nowhere," Mia said, pulling her attention back to the conversation at hand.

"That's not completely true. You've got a lot of evidence here. It's just a matter of putting it in the right order." Matt held out his cup and she refilled it. "So the real question is what could have happened on the morning of August 6th that killed Ellis Brewster's cattle, rendered you unconscious and started a chain reaction that ended with a nuclear blast that wiped out the town of Cedar Branch."

"Separate events with causal connection," Nick said, nodding his agreement. "But what the hell are we talking about then?"

"I don't know." Matt shrugged. "I'm just throwing out ideas."

"Well, if there were two unique events, that might explain why I didn't show any signs of exposure to radiation," Mia suggested.

"Yeah, but the cattle were exposed. The radiation just wasn't enough to kill them. Nick said you were in a bomb shelter. Maybe it protected you," Matt said.

"My grandfather built it right after World War II," Mia protested. "I think it's a stretch to believe that it would have protected me completely."

"Okay, so what about the mask?" Nick asked. "Maybe that contributed as well."

"The mask?" Matt asked, frowning.

"I use it when I work with toxic chemicals."

"Nick said you were an artist."

"I am. I've been working with etching techniques. For

metal. And the solvents involved can be poisonous if too much is inhaled. So most of the time I wear a mask."

"So together maybe they were enough."

"Or maybe she was never exposed to radiation at all," Nick said.

Mia's heart sank. "I thought you said you believed me."

"I do. That's not what I'm getting at. Your memory stops at sometime around ten in the morning, right?"

"Approximately." She nodded, trying to follow his train of thought.

"And that coincides with the first event Ellis talked about and the approximate time of death for the cattle as established by Dr. Loring."

"Except that I'm not dead."

"Doesn't matter. It puts your part of the story squarely in line with the first event." Nick frowned as he tried to order his thoughts. "So maybe you were part of the plan all along."

Mia opened her mouth, but Matt cut her off. "You think that they wanted Mia to survive. So if push came to shove they'd have someone to blame."

"But that would mean that they had to know the weapon was going to detonate," Mia protested.

"Which would mean it wasn't an accident." Nick's expression was grim.

Horror ripped through her, robbing her of breath, the idea making her sick to her stomach.

"It could have been a deliberate test," Matt suggested. "That would explain a lot of things."

"But not the dead cattle," Mia insisted, trying to push away the thought that her friends had been intentionally sacrificed.

"Maybe that really is a spurious connection," Nick said. "Or maybe the vet was wrong. He did say he'd never dealt with anything like this before."

"And you said he was young," Matt offered.

"So what? Now you think the livestock did die of radiation poisoning?" Her head was spinning from all the possibilities.

"The truth is we don't know anything for certain. Except that there definitely was a nuclear explosion in Cedar Branch, and that Kresky International as well as Senator Tucker and possibly Senator Hatcher were involved."

"But we have the sample," Mia said. "And if we can get it analyzed we'll know for certain what happened to the cattle. And maybe have a clearer picture of how their deaths tie into the explosion."

"*If* they tie in," Matt added. "I've got an old friend in Laramie. A pathologist. We went to school together. In another life I wanted to be a doctor. I think I can get her to run the tests we need."

"Good," Nick said. "That'll leave Mia and me free to check out Kresky's so-called research arm. The only way we're going to be able to move any of this beyond speculation is to find out what Kresky's been up to.

"If his company really is developing some new kind of nuclear weapon and that development resulted in the explosion that took out Cedar Branch—accidental or otherwise—we need solid proof. And the only way we're going to get that is to obtain documentation from Biosphere. And to do *that* we're going to have to find a way to get inside."

THE STORM HAD BLOWN OUT, the velvety sky sprinkled with diamond-bright stars. Mia sat on the upstairs balcony, letting the cool night breeze soothe her battered soul. If she lived through this, she'd have to start over. Make a new life. And, truthfully, the idea terrified her.

But there was something inherently comforting in the idea that despite man's inhumanity, the world just kept on turning. Sunrise and sunset continuing without so much as a by-your-leave. It was humbling if nothing else.

For most of her life, she'd listened to her grandfather and her mother rail against the horrors of nuclear fallout. They'd fought against reactors, test sites, missile silos, the works. And here she sat, the sole survivor of what would no doubt be remembered as one of the worst nuclear accidents in U.S. history. Only instead of trying to deal with her grief, she was running for her life. Scrambling to find answers that looked to be more horrifying than anything she could possibly have imagined.

And yet here she sat, drinking in the beauty of the night sky, the dark blue of the mountains framing a brilliant canvas of contrasting light and shadow. The Milky Way, the North Star, the Big Dipper—the same stars that had entranced mankind for countless generations, leaving hope that maybe there was something bigger out there. Something better.

"You should be sleeping." The sound of Nick's voice rasped against her nerve endings and she shivered, anticipation knotting inside her.

"I know. But I can't. Just too many things to think about, I guess," she said with a sigh.

"There was nothing on the news about the accident. My guess is Davies found Gall and his partner before anyone else did."

"Which means he's out there somewhere, looking for

us." She shivered, wrapping her arms around her waist. "Did you and Matt come up with a plan for tomorrow?"

"Not really. Matt did his best, but even with his computer skills, you can't create something out of nothing. He even tapped Kresky's computers, but there was nothing linking to Biosphere. If we hadn't seen the address I'd be tempted to say it doesn't exist."

"So what do we do?"

"Recon," he said, moving to lean against the balcony railing. "It's the only way we're going to get the lay of the land. Hopefully, we'll be able to formulate a plan for access once we've had a chance to see the place and study the comings and goings. If we're really lucky, maybe an opportunity will present itself."

"And if it doesn't?" she asked.

"Then we'll just have to make our own. You up for that?"

"If it helps to nail Tucker and Kresky, I'm up for anything." She stood, walking to stand beside him, still looking out at the night. "It's so peaceful here, it's kind of hard to believe we're caught up in something so heinous."

"Maybe that's why we have the stars. To remind us that we're not the be-all and end-all we think we are."

"I was just thinking the same thing," she said, closing her hands around the railing as she looked up at the sky. "When I was little my mom and I used to lie on the grass, and she'd name the constellations. Then she'd tell me the stories about each one. Cassiopeia hanging upside down on her throne. Andromeda chained to the rocks. Orion, who walked on water. It's really just his belt." She pointed to the sky, tracing the constellation. "It starts with Mintaka on the right. See?"

"They're beautiful," he said, but he wasn't looking at the stars.

Mia swallowed, anticipation blossoming into full-fledged desire. She'd promised herself she wouldn't do this again, but the mind and the body weren't always in accord. "Where's Matt?" she asked, her voice coming out on a sigh.

He smiled, reaching out to capture a strand of her hair, twining it around his finger. "He's asleep. Or at least safely ensconced in the bedroom downstairs. So I guess it's just you and me."

She swallowed, cognizant thought disappearing as pheromones flooded her body, heat spreading outward from somewhere deep inside. Her eyes locked with his, her heart beating staccato against her ribs. "We…we really shouldn't…" She fought for sanity, for words, but he shook his head, pressing his finger against her lips.

"Hush," he whispered. "The time for talking is over." A slow, sensual smile curved across his face and her breathing quickened, every nerve ending in her body firing at once. She shuddered with heat, then shivered with cold as he pulled her closer, his hand warm against the small of her back, his breath mingling with hers.

They stood for a moment, staring into each other's eyes, and then with a sigh she swayed forward, tipping her head back, offering herself to him. She needed his touch now more than she needed to breathe.

He dipped his head, his mouth slanting over hers, the kiss slow and sweet, building in intensity. Passion coiled tight, begging for release. She pressed against him, reveling in the hard strength of his body as he trailed kisses down her neck, caressing her ear with his tongue, sending a delicious warmth spiraling through her.

God, she wanted him—wanted him with a mounting urgency that negated all common sense. She fought for breath, whimpering with need as his hand slid inside her shirt, cupping her breast, kneading the tender flesh.

With a groan he pulled back, eyes dark with passion, his breath almost as ragged as hers. "Mia, I—"

She smiled, raising her hand to touch his face, tracing the line of his jaw, the curve of his lips. "No talking. Remember?"

He held her gaze for a moment, looking for something she wasn't certain she could provide. But then he pulled her back into his arms, his mouth claiming hers again, his kiss an echo of things to come, his tongue thrusting possessively, robbing her of all rational thought.

She ran her hands along the hard muscles of his back and shoulders, then slipped her fingers inside his shirt to the smooth skin of chest. She'd touched him before. Slept with him before. But somehow here in the starlight it felt different. Maybe it was the situation. Maybe it was the man. Maybe it would all disappear with daylight.

But here, now, this was what she wanted.

She framed his face with her hands, kissing his eyes, then his nose, his ears and finally his mouth. Then slowly, as if she were savoring a gift, she undid the buttons of his shirt, sliding it off his shoulders and down his arms.

He reached for her, but she stepped back with a little smile and pulled her T-shirt over her head, her nipples beading in the cool night breeze. Running her hands slowly down her own body, she unzipped her pants and slid out of them, finally standing before him wearing nothing but starlight.

Sucking in a breath, he closed the distance between

them, accepting what she was offering, his hot breath sending ripples of sensation coursing through her. His hands were warm against her skin as he caressed her shoulders and arms. Then he found her breasts, cupping them, his thumbs moving in slow, delicious circles.

Her nipples tightened in anticipation of the heat building between her thighs. She arched into him, wanting more, but he lifted her into his arms and carried her to the bedroom. The moon had risen, the silvery sliver kissing the room with ghostly light.

Nick bent his head to kiss her as he laid her against the cool cotton of the sheets. After removing the rest of his clothes he joined her on the bed, pulling her into his lap so that her legs straddled his, his penis pressing against the soft curls between her thighs.

She threw back her head, moving rhythmically, rubbing against him, the friction and heat feeding the desire stretching taut between them. His fingers circled her nipples, alternately stroking and pulling, the combination threatening to send her over the edge.

With a moan, she arched her back, closing her eyes. His mouth closed around her breast, sucking and nipping as she writhed against him, her fingers threaded through his hair. With her nipple still held between his teeth, he slipped inside her, his thumb caressing while his fingers began to move, thrusting and stroking, teasing her, building the fire.

She shuddered, every nerve in her body craving release, but he moved again, easing her backward, until her head rested against the pillow. She rose in protest, but he only shook his head, reaching down to cup her bottom, bending his head to kiss the inside of her thigh.

Closing her eyes, she gave in to his ministrations, shivering as he tightened his hold, keeping her captive. His mouth caressed the sensitive folds of skin, then parted them to flick lightly against her heated center. She arched upward as his tongue thrust deep, then deeper still, his hands hard against her hips. In and out, over and over, his tongue driving her higher, until she was floating in a sea of sensation—buoyed with each stroke, each touch.

Then, just when she was certain that there could be nothing better, nothing more, he lifted his head, moving to pull her back into his lap. With his hands braced on both sides of her, he lifted her up and then slid her downward, impaling her with his heat.

She gasped as new and better sensations curled through her, leaving trails of quickly spreading fire. She placed her hands on his shoulders and began to move, sliding up and down, feeling him within her. She threw back her head, feeling his mouth on her breast. Up, down, up, down, the rhythm was intoxicating. Spirals of ecstasy began to whirl through her brain, enticing her to move faster, urging her to take him deeper—deeper.

There would be no turning back.

He was asking for parts of her she'd never shared with anyone, and she knew she was going to give in to him willingly. There was a rightness about this. A connection between them that couldn't be denied.

Then there was nothing but the feel of him moving inside her and the pounding need for release. She reached for it, twining her fingers with his, sensation blotting out every other thought—until the heat inside her exploded into tangible joy, shudders shaking her body as she slowly drifted back, satiated beyond anything she could ever have imagined, content in the moment and the warmth of his body still joined with hers.

NICK CRADLED MIA'S BODY against his, feeling the rise and fall of her breathing, the soft silk of her hair splayed across his chest. Nothing in his life had prepared him for the emotions she brought out in him.

He wanted to protect her, to care for her, and most of all he wanted to possess her. It was a basic need, certainly—man wanting woman. But this was something more, something unexpected, and it scared the hell out of him.

"That was amazing," Mia whispered, her voice still colored by passion. She pressed closer against him, little spasms of release still rippling through her. He felt his body respond, already wanting her again.

She recognized the movement and shifted, the motion taking him deeper, making him harder. Then she moved again, slowly sliding up and down. Her eyes darkening with renewed passion.

With a groan, he drove into her, his hands finding her hips, establishing a rhythm. She was so hot, so wet, and she took him so willingly. He leaned back, eyes closed, as they moved even faster.

His mouth found hers and his tongue thrust into her, wanting to feel her, to taste her. She met him eagerly, sparring with him, their kiss building in intensity as they continued to move, until there was nothing but passion— white-hot passion.

Consciously he slowed down, trying to hold on to his control, wanting it to be as good for her as he knew it was going to be for him. But Mia was having none of it, grasping him with impatient hands, urging him to go faster, meeting each of his thrusts with her own. Giving and taking until nothing mattered but the two of them bound together, moving faster and faster, until everything was colored with their ecstasy.

And in that moment he was certain he had found something precious, something he'd never find again. They'd crossed some sort of bridge, reaching the other side not as two people but as one.

He knew that the magic would end with the morning. Knew that reality held threats they might never overcome. But in the space of this moment, holding Mia close against his heart, Nick felt like he'd come home.

CHAPTER TWENTY

"YOU'RE NOT SLEEPING," Nick said, propping himself up on one elbow.

"Too much on my mind, I guess." Mia shifted the pillows so that she could see him better. "Actually, I was thinking about you."

He waited, watching, the stillness between them making her hesitate. On the one hand, she'd never felt so connected to another person, but on the other she had no idea who he was—not really.

"I was thinking about your sister."

"What about her?" His tone was neutral, but even in the dark she could feel the tension.

"Nothing, really," she said, rolling onto her side. "It's just that I was thinking about the computer and all the pictures of her. I should have made you get that instead of the sample. They were all you had left. And now they're gone. I'm sorry."

"It wasn't your fault. And besides, it doesn't matter. Not really."

"Why?" Mia resisted the urge to reach for him, instinctively realizing it would be the wrong thing to do.

"Because I have no right to remember." He rolled onto his back and stared up at the ceiling, his skin stretched tight over his jaw, his anger almost a palpable thing. "I killed her. I killed my sister."

"There's got to be more to it than that." She sat up, clutching a pillow, searching for the right words. "I don't know the circumstances but I do know that you'd never willingly hurt someone you love."

"Maybe not, but that doesn't absolve a person of guilt."

The pain in his eyes made her wish she had the power to wave it away, but of course she couldn't do that. All she could do was listen. And there was clearly more to the story. That much she was certain of. "Was she younger than you?"

"By five and a half minutes," he said, the words so low she almost missed them.

"Katie was your twin?" Mia felt her stomach lurch, the need to reach out to him almost unbearable.

"Yes." The word hung between them, taking on a life of its own.

"Tell me about her," Mia said, holding her breath, knowing that if he was ever going to trust her, this had to be the first step. Minutes dragged by, the plaintive wail of a train slicing through the silence, its melancholy tone a fitting backdrop for her question.

"It's hard to sum a person up with words. But I guess you'd call Katie a free spirit. She never met a stranger, and she was totally fearless. I don't think anything scared her. I remember once on a school trip to Mystic we toured a nineteenth-century whaler. It had been restored right down to the rigging.

"Anyway, we'd all gathered on the port side to watch the 'dead horse' ceremony. And before the horse had even been strung up on the yardarm, Katie had managed to scale the rigging up to the crow's nest." He smiled in the darkness, his teeth white against the night. "Mrs. Yarbrough was furious. Not to mention the museum personnel."

"What happened?" Mia asked, answering his smile.

"Nothing dire. Katie could talk her way out of anything. They read her the riot act, she solemnly promised not to do it again, and that was that. In fact, she wound up doing an internship there after college. She was a marine archeologist. Never did understand her fascination with things buried under the sea."

"But you were still a lot alike. You're not exactly immune to taking risks yourself."

"Yes, but the difference is that I'd have figured out all the odds beforehand, weighed the alternatives and then made a calculated choice. Katie simply saw the rigging and thought it would be fun. She never worried about things like logistics." He sighed, the sound heavy in the darkness.

"I used to wish I had a twin. Someone who understood me better than anyone else. You know, a secret language, mental telepathy—I don't know, just something magical."

His laugh was harsh. "That's all a load of crock. There was no twin magic. Just two people who happened to share a predominance of genes. I mean, we were close. It would have been impossible not to love Katie. She was that kind of person. But there was nothing extraordinary about our relationship. If there had been, maybe I would have known—" he clenched a fist and closed his eyes "—hell, maybe I could have saved her."

"I didn't mean to dredge up old memories." She laid her hand on his, grateful when he didn't pull away. "It's just that I know Katie's death haunts you. And you said it yourself—in a very limited sort of way I understand. I've lost people I love, too."

"And blamed yourself," he said, rolling onto his side. "But in your case, it truly wasn't your fault. Nothing you could have done would have saved them."

"So what happened to Katie?" she asked, still not certain he'd answer.

"One of those right place, wrong time stories," he said flatly. "Katie had been doing some work in the Black Sea. A sunken Phoenician ship. I was with Special Forces then—stationed in the Middle East, on the Pakistani border. We were between missions, and scheduled for some R & R. So I arranged to meet Katie in Egypt. She wanted to rendezvous in Dahab."

"I've heard of it. Wasn't there a recent bombing? I remember hearing about it on the news. Islamic terrorists, right?"

He nodded. "Twenty-three people were killed. But of course that hadn't happened yet. Katie picked the place because she was already scheduled to meet with some colleagues on a dig near the Red Sea. It was convenient for me, so I agreed. I knew there was a risk, but like I told you before, once Katie had made up her mind there was no arguing. Besides, if there was trouble, I figured I could handle it." Bitterness colored his voice as he pulled away from her, turning onto his back again.

For a moment he was silent, simply staring up at the shadows shifting across the ceiling, and she wondered if she'd pushed too far, unleashed something that was better left alone. "I'm sorry. You don't have to—" she began, but he cut her off with a shake of his head.

"I want to tell you," he said, still not making eye

contact. "It's just not an easy thing to talk about. Even after all this time."

"But it's better—you said that it gets better," she said, seeking reassurance for herself as much as for him.

"I said you could sequester it. And yes, that makes it easier to deal with day to day. But you never forget. Which is a double-edged sword, I suppose. You want to keep the memory but not the accompanying pain. And unfortunately, the two can't be separated."

She nodded, fighting to keep her own memories contained. This time it was Nick who reached out for her, and she closed her hand around his, amazed at how much could be conveyed with a simple touch. She lifted her eyes to meet his, waiting, knowing that he needed to tell her the rest of the story as much as she needed to hear it.

"We arranged to meet at a small café. The kind of place teeming with tourists. Katie was a sucker for kitsch. Anyway, she was already in Egypt, but I'd only flown in the morning before. So I still had to make my way to Dahab. I should have rented a car, but I ran into some buddies in Cairo, and one thing led to another and I wound up catching a ride with them."

"So you were late?"

"Yes. But I called her." He paused for a moment, his face clouding with regret. "She wasn't even pissed. Said she'd expected the call, and that I was always off on some wild tangent or another. We arranged to meet the next day. Same place."

"But something happened," Mia prompted, still holding his hand.

"I got there on time, give or take a few minutes. The café was on a square. There was a market in the center, one of those open-air affairs. I had to make my way through it to get to the café. There were a bunch of kids. Americans in green T-shirts—not more than fifteen or sixteen. I remember a couple of girls giggling over a naked statue. Everything seemed exaggerated somehow. The sounds, the smells, all of it.

"I should have known that something was off. But I didn't. I was too busy thinking about the mission we'd be undertaking when I got back. I pushed through a stall with some kind of textiles—silk maybe, I can still smell them, grassy and sweet. It was hot, too. The sun blinding against the white canopies of the market.

"I stepped into the street, and I could see Katie sitting at a table on the other side, in front of the café. A couple of the kids from the tour were at the next table, and she was smiling at them, laughing at something they'd said. The tablecloths were blue. I never really notice color, but those tablecloths are burned into my brain right along with the kids in their green T-shirts. Katie had a camera with her. The old-fashioned kind with a huge lens. It belonged to my father. I remember being pissed off when my mother gave it to her. It's weird what sticks in your head.

"I lifted a hand, thinking that I'd managed to be late yet again, but she just smiled and waved back. I took a step forward, rehearsing my apology, and then all hell broke loose. One minute the café was there, and the next it disappeared into a cloud of dust and debris.

"I ran across the street, into the fray, but it was too late. Katie was gone. Sucked into the bowels of the rubble of fallen masonry. We never found her body. And believe me, I looked. I spent hours digging through the debris, calling her name, praying that I'd been mistaken, that the woman who'd waved wasn't my sister."

"But it was," Mia whispered, tears in her eyes.

"Yeah. In the space of a heartbeat some asshole destroyed the one person I truly loved. If there is something to twins being special, it'd have to be the fact that Katie was everything that was good. She was funny and bright, and always ready with a smile. Sounds trite, I know, but it's the truth. I was the one with problems. The one who could never quite find his way. She gave me a safe place. Someone I could trust with anything. And the one time she needed me, the one time I could have been the one to help her—I fucked it up. If I hadn't spent the previous night drinking until dawn, I'd have made our earlier meeting and she'd be alive right now instead of lying in splintered pieces beneath a plaza in Dahab."

"Maybe." Mia laced her fingers with his, her heart breaking. "But for all you know, the guy with the bomb was delayed, as well. Maybe he'd have been there the day before if he hadn't overslept. Or maybe his girlfriend called to say she was lunching at the café. Life is full of little things that add up to the big ones. And saying that a tragedy could have been avoided 'if only' is like saying that you can control fate. You can't, Nick, no matter how much you might like to think you can. Katie was in the wrong place at the wrong time. But there wasn't anything you could have done to stop it."

"I haven't told you the rest of the story." There was something in his eyes that stole her breath away. Something bitter and ruthless, a hard edge that probably served as protection. Armor against all that he'd seen and done.

She swallowed her fear, reminding herself that this was Nick. *Her* Nick. And she needed to hear him out. "So tell me."

"My mother flew out, of course, as determined as I was to find Katie, to believe that by some miracle she'd survived. But after three days of searching and bullying the Egyptian government, we were finally forced to accept that Katie was gone. That no amount of digging was going to produce my sister. Alive or otherwise.

"But accepting her death didn't mean I'd given up the idea of vengeance. Fifteen people died in that explosion, ten of them American—six of them just kids. I was determined to find the people responsible for the bomb and make them pay for what they'd done. My mother wanted me to stop. Wanted me to let well enough alone. She'd lost one child, she didn't want to lose the other. But if Katie was stubborn, I'm the classic definition of pigheaded, and I blew off Mom's entreaties and started making inquiries on my own.

"I had an advantage, of course. In my work with Special Forces, I'd made a lot of contacts. Some affiliated with our government, some not. Anyway, it wasn't hard to identify the organization that was responsible for the bombing. The bomber was dead, of course. A suicide mission. But the rest of the cell was still active, and it didn't take long to track them down." He laughed, but there was no humor in the sound.

"So what happened—when you found them, I mean?"

"That's where everything goes really screwy. I'd made my plans. Even enlisted the aid of a couple of friends. The cell was located near a town called Taba on the Israeli border near Lebanon. Everything was set. Our intel solid. But before we had a chance to execute the plan, someone tipped them off. We tried to regroup, but we kept encountering roadblocks. Eventually, my friends gave up. Went back to their units. I resigned my commission, still determined to run Katie's killers to ground.

"It ate at me like a cancer, invading every part of my being, until I was only living for revenge. My mother threatened to disown me if I didn't stop, but I didn't care. All I wanted was to destroy the people who'd killed Katie. But every time I got close, the bastards slipped away. Always one step ahead of me.

"And then, just when I thought it was hopeless, I got a lead. A meeting set up by one of the cell leaders. A murderous son of a bitch called Nassor Masud. I figured if I could get to him, I'd be able to find the others. So I set up surveillance and waited for the meeting to come down."

Mia clutched the pillow, her heart twisting at the sight of his pain.

"Nassor arrived on schedule. But after all the time I'd spent searching for him, it was almost anticlimactic. I took aim, ready to blow him to oblivion, but then his contact entered the room. I thought I'd lost my mind, even rechecked the scope to be certain of what I was seeing. But I hadn't made a mistake. The man meeting with my sister's killer was Charles Davies."

"What the hell was he doing in Egypt?"

"Working a source. And apparently warning him about me."

"Masud."

"Right. And I would have shot them both on sight, but one of Davies's cronies found me first. He convinced me that it was in my best interest to come with him for a little visit. It was all very cloak-and-dagger. But I didn't have a choice. They whisked me off to a safe house, where I was instructed to let it go."

"Which of course you didn't," she insisted, speaking before she had time to think better of it.

His smile was brief, but genuine. "No. In fact, I pushed harder, but Masud and his men had managed to drop off the grid again. But despite repeated warnings, I kept digging. And then I hit pay dirt. Masud's new location. He was in Lebanon. And it didn't take me long to run him to ground."

"So you killed him." She should have been shocked. Hell, a week ago she would have been. But things had changed—and this was Nick.

"Yes, but not before he told me that the CIA had known about the bombing in advance. Hell, some of my superior officers even knew about it. And they did nothing to stop me from going. Not one goddamned thing. Masud's cooperation was worth more to all of them than the lives of the innocents killed in Dahab. More than the life of my sister."

"My God," Mia whispered, his words robbing her of coherent speech.

"Ironic, isn't it? The people I believed in—hell, the people I trusted the most—knew I was at risk, that my sister was a risk, and the bastards didn't raise a finger to stop us."

"Was there fallout? From killing Masud?"

"Let's just say I was persona non grata for a while. But I still had friends. Some of them in high places. And they made sure that Davies's efforts to brand me as a traitor came to nothing. It was written off as post-traumatic stress disorder."

"That's what you were referring to when we talked with Ellis."

He nodded. "I'd already resigned, but they wanted me to come in. To get treatment. Partially as cover, but probably also because they knew that Masud's colleagues were still out there."

"And they didn't want you hunting."

"Exactly. So I went underground, operating below the radar until I managed to find them all."

"And did it help?" she asked, struggling to process it all.

"No. Katie was still dead. But I don't regret any of it."

"What about Davies?"

"His actions were sanctioned by the government. There was nothing I could do to change that. I wanted to kill him, believe me. He was as much responsible as the men who planned the bombing. Only there was no way I could touch him. Not without declaring war on my own country. But I wasn't going to work for them again.

"So I stayed underground, worked black ops. There are a lot of countries out there willing to hire men with Special Forces training. And I really didn't give a damn about what the ultimate goals were. I just wanted to keep pushing the edge. I figured as long as I kept moving, the pain couldn't catch up with me."

Mia nodded, the tears flowing freely now. She knew how that felt. The ghosts of her friends hovering just beyond the perimeter of every waking minute.

He reached over to brush her cheek. "I'm not so sure I'm worth crying for, Mia, but I cherish the sentiment behind the tears."

"But you came back," she said, fighting to pull her emotions back into control. "You work for Homeland Security. Or you did before you met me. Why?"

"9/11."

The words spoke for themselves. And Mia nodded her understanding.

"Gordon was my LT from my Special Forces days. He tracked me down and asked me to come on board to help. If it had been espionage I wouldn't have been interested. But I saw it as a chance to work to keep innocents safe— to protect them from suffering like Katie did. Every time I manage to subvert a terrorist plot, I feel like I'm making amends for not being there for my sister."

"But it wasn't your fault. No matter what your mother believes."

"She blamed me at first. Hell, maybe she still does, but the driving force for her anger is that I deserted her. That I was too lost in my own anger and pain to see how much she was hurting. And she's right. I did let her down."

"But it's never too late," Mia said. "Not if she loves you. Not if you love her."

"I don't know," he said with a shake of his head, reaching out to cup her face with his hand. "But somehow when I'm with you, I feel like anything is possible."

THE SHADOWS LIFTED with the coming dawn, the room washed in a pale orange glow. Mia rolled over, sighing in her sleep as she nestled against him, trying to avoid the light. Nick smiled, amazed that something so mundane could bring such joy. Clearly, he'd lost his mind, but it was too damn late to do anything about it now, because he'd also lost his heart.

He struggled with the idea for a moment, a part of him wanting to reject the notion, another part knowing it was too late. She fit him in a way no other woman could. Her courage, her heart, her amazing resilience. He'd fallen hard and fast, with no idea what the hell he was supposed to do next. He didn't lead the kind of life that allowed for permanent attachment. And until now he'd never considered that a disadvantage. But suddenly, he found himself wishing for the normalcy he'd always made fun of. The whole kids-house-suburbs thing taking on a new slant when Mia was part of the picture.

Not that they were guaranteed a happy ending. So far they'd managed to elude Davies and his henchmen, but the closer they got to the truth, the higher the risk of being caught. And Nick had no illusions as to what would happen then.

Whatever Tucker and Hatcher were trying to cover up, it had the power to end their careers. Which meant that everybody in their way was expendable.

Mia murmured something, fighting against her dreams, and he tightened his arms around her, wishing there was a way to spirit her away from all of this. To keep her safe. But Kresky's reach was considerable, and the only way they were going to come out of this alive was to find the truth and make it public.

Which meant Nick had to stay vigilant.

He stroked her hair, watching as the remaining shadows withdrew from the bedroom, the sun cresting the horizon to bring a new day. When it mattered most, he'd let Katie down, but he wasn't going to let it happen again. He'd been given a second chance with Mia, and no one—not Kresky, not Tucker, not even Davies—was going to stop him from protecting the woman he loved.

It was as simple as that.

CHAPTER TWENTY-ONE

"DEFINITELY MORE protection here," Nick said, panning the horizon with his binoculars.

Biosphere consisted of a smattering of buildings nestled into the rolling scrub of the Montana prairie. There was an electric fence surrounding the compound, and a checkpoint at the entrance that looked far more serious than the abandoned one they'd encountered at Kresky's Nevada plant.

"Is it going to be a problem?" Mia asked, lowering her field glasses.

"We'll figure out a way in. But it's going to take more time than I'd like," he said with a frown. Time was something they simply didn't have. Davies might have lost their scent for the moment but he'd find it again. Which meant they had to keep moving. Press the advantages they did have. "What concerns me the most is the guard at the entrance."

As if aware of the conversation, the man in question moved out into the road, bending to say something to the driver of a red Civic waiting for approval to enter the complex. "He's packing some serious heat."

Mia lifted her glasses again, zeroing in on the machine gun resting on the man's thigh. "M16?"

"No." He shook his head, frowning. "Uzi. Although they're equally deadly."

"Well, if we're right about Kresky using Biosphere to cover the development of some new kind of nuclear weapon, then the added security makes sense. Except that we've been assuming the plant was in Cedar Branch."

"If they really are developing something big, they'd have redundant systems," Nick said, still watching the guy at the gate. "Maybe not for production, but definitely for research. Which means that if we're lucky there'll be records here that should be able to shed some light on what really happened in Cedar Branch. But first we have to figure out a way to get inside."

He shifted his attention from the gate to the compound as a whole, searching for a weak link. Something that would give them access with minimum risk of discovery. The main building sat at the foot of a large hill. A stand of trees flanked the right side of the structure and a small parking lot ran the length of the left side.

A second, smaller building was across from the first, the parking lot stretched between them. Like its counterpart, it had an institutional feel, the architecture spare, with little thought to physical appeal.

There were no visible windows in the main building, but he could only see two sides from this vantage point. The second building had one large window in the front, but it was covered with a metal grill. The entire compound was inconspicuous, seeming to fade into the surrounding gray-green hills. A third building sat at the gate, presumably for the man with the Uzi.

There were a couple of additional outbuildings, but none seemed to be occupied. The Honda had been granted clearance and was currently following the drive that led to the parking lot. It moved slowly, a small cloud of dust following in its wake.

"Not many people on the premises," Mia said, frowning into her field glasses. "You think that's normal?"

"No," Nick said with a shake of his head. "I think it's just early. Look, there's another car coming in." He nodded toward the front gate and a second car waiting to be admitted. Behind it, a large truck waited its turn. "Maybe we should try to get a little closer."

Mia nodded, pushing to her feet to follow him.

Using mainly rocks and the occasional rise of the surrounding hills, they managed to make their way to an outcropping of rock a couple hundred yards from the main entrance. Nick dropped down on his stomach, inching forward until he had a clear view of the compound below. From this vantage point he could make out more detail. The name on the side of the truck, even the license plate on the car at the gate.

"Do you know what ASI stands for?" Mia asked, sliding in beside him.

"Yeah, I recognize the logo. American Shredding. They're an on-site document disposal company based out of L.A. We've used them before."

"They seem to be a little far afield." She lifted her field glasses, watching the truck below.

"No," he said. "They've got regional offices. Basically, they cover most of this side of the country. What really worries me is the fact that they're here at all."

"Because it means Kresky is covering his tracks?"

"It seems likely. Although it's also conceivable that this is just scheduled maintenance. A lot of companies have services once or twice a week. And Kresky was paranoid long before we got into the picture."

"Still, if he's destroying evidence, we're screwed."

"All the more reason to figure out a way to get inside." He watched as the guard raised the barricade arm and waved both the car and the truck through. "I'm going to try to get a little closer," he said, pushing to his feet. "I haven't seen any perimeter patrols, which means there's probably electronic surveillance, and I want to get a look at it. See what we're up against."

"I'll come with you."

"No," he said. "I want you to stay here. No point in both of us being at risk. All right?"

"Yeah, okay." She didn't sound happy about the prospect, but at least she'd agreed to stay put.

"You've got the gun, right?" he asked, his mind already moving to the task ahead.

She nodded.

"Don't be afraid to use it."

"I won't," she said, her smile faint but genuine. "Someone's got to watch your back."

"Can't think of anyone I'd rather have on point. I'll be back in a flash." He reached out to caress her cheek, then moved into the open, crouching so that he wouldn't be seen.

The incline was tricky going, loose rocks threatening to give his presence away. Fortunately, there was a small line of cars now, and the guard was busy checking people through the gate.

Nick tightened his hold on Gall's rifle and moved quickly down the hill, using scrub for cover. At the bottom he veered to the right, away from the road, ducking down behind a boulder. The fence was about twenty yards dead ahead, electrified and topped with barbed wire. Just inside, mounted on a wooden pole, was a security camera.

It moved rhythmically from left to right and then back again, no doubt sending a signal to a security center somewhere in the compound. Similar poles, complete with cameras, lined the visible perimeter, each placed about fifty feet from the next.

With the proper equipment he could probably disable the thing—at least long enough to get inside—but there was still the possibility of being picked up by the overlapping arc of the adjacent cameras. And the matter of the electric fence. They'd simply have to find a more direct way to access the compound.

He turned to go, his eyes automatically moving to the rise shielding Mia. He couldn't see her, but he could feel her presence as surely as if she'd stood up and waved. He hated the fact that she was here. That she was part of this. But he knew she'd never agree to stay on the sidelines.

The only way she was ever going to be able to live with what had happened was to understand why, and if possible to see that the people responsible paid for what they'd done. He knew exactly how she felt.

And he intended to help her any way that he could.

Safely out of range of the cameras, he started to make his way back up the hill, stopping occasionally to check the gate behind him. The steady trickle of cars had slowed, the parking lot at the far end of the complex about half-full now. Whatever they decided to do, it was clearly not going to happen when the place was full of employees.

Better to regroup, see what Matt had gotten from the pathologist, and then formulate a new plan.

He was almost halfway up the hill when something—

a sound, or maybe just instinct—made him stop. He swiveled around, scanning for something out of place. But everything seemed the same as before. He'd almost convinced himself that he was imagining things when something metallic flashed in the sunlight just ahead of him.

He hit the dirt as a bullet whizzed past his face, followed by a second. His only cognizant thought was to lead the shooter away from Mia, so he scrambled back the way he'd come, using rocks for cover.

Another shot sounded, this one from higher up the hill, and he reversed course again, this time tearing up the incline with no concern for finding cover. Something sharp bit into his shoulder and he stumbled, but regained his footing in time to get a shot off in the direction of his adversary.

Waves of pain radiated down his arm, but he clenched his teeth, determined to make it to the top—to Mia. Directly ahead a flash of yellow alerted him to movement, and he hit the ground before the bullet could find its mark. He crawled forward on hands and knees, ignoring the metallic smell of his own blood.

Then he heard Mia scream and sprang to his feet, rage propelling him forward. With gun blazing he burst into the little clearing where he'd left her, the empty ground mocking him. Broken wildflowers marked the place where they'd lain, watching the compound below. But there was no one here now.

He spun around, searching for signs of which way she'd gone. Dropping down, he crawled forward again, his eyes trained on the compound below. A black Lexus was parked by the road just outside the gate. He lifted his glasses, focusing on the license plate, already certain of what he'd find.

OBD-7Y2. Davies.

Two men emerged from the scrub, a struggling Mia held firmly between them.

He stifled a curse. At least she was alive.

The passenger door opened and Davies emerged, his face pinched as he shouted an order. The two men pushed Mia into the rear seat and Davies followed, slamming the door behind him. The gunmen turned back toward the hillside as the car moved away, heading down the road toward the highway.

Behind him, a twig snapped, and Nick rolled to his knees, firing in the direction of the sound. A man emerged from behind a group of rocks, returning fire, his shot going wild as he stumbled to his knees, blood spouting from the base of his neck.

Nick circled slowly around until he reached the man, eyes sweeping the area for signs that he had company.

Nothing moved. He reached down to feel for a pulse and then, satisfied that there was none, he grabbed the man's gun, still searching for signs of more gunmen. The breeze ruffled through the long grass—the hillside silent.

Instinct screamed for him to go after Mia. To try and waylay the car. But it was an impossible task. And he knew it. His strength was waning, and he was certain that Davies's men were on their way to make sure their colleague had finished his job.

As if to underscore the thought, all hell broke loose as another volley of bullets ripped through the clearing, the spray of rocks sending him running in the opposite direction. Dropping down behind a boulder, he took aim and waited, his patience rewarded when one of Davies's men shifted slightly, a silent shadow moving against the rocks.

Nick squeezed the trigger, the man falling face forward onto the ground.

Two down.

As tempting as it was to wait and pick off the other man, Nick knew there'd soon be reinforcements. Better to get the hell out while he had the chance. He wasn't any use to Mia dead.

Since Davies had managed to take her alive, there was no doubt where he'd be taking her. To Waters. But once the doctor was through with her… Nick clenched a fist, his stomach roiling. The S&C facility near Cedar Branch had marked the beginning of their journey—and if Davies had his way, it would mark the end, as well.

But then, Davies had always made the mistake of underestimating Nick's determination when it came to someone he loved.

"WELCOME BACK, Ms. Kearney." Dr. Waters's face swam into view as Mia woozily opened her eyes.

"You drugged me." The words were garbled, the effort to speak clearly almost more than she could handle.

"It was just a sedative. Apparently you weren't all that cooperative in the car. The injection was intended to immobilize you. What you're feeling now are the aftereffects." He hovered over her, his eyes reflecting nothing but professional concern, but she could hear the anger in his voice.

"Nick?" She pushed the word out, her heart pounding as she waited for his response.

"Mr. Price is dead."

"You're lying." Her stomach clenched, bile rising in her throat. It was like reliving the same dream over and over. Everything coming full circle. It had only been a few days since Nick had stood where Waters was, claiming that her friends were all dead. She'd thought he was lying, too. "He can't be dead," she whispered, struggling to remember.

She'd heard gunshots, and then someone had grabbed her. She'd screamed Nick's name as they'd dragged her struggling down the hill. Then Davies had stabbed her with the hypodermic and everything had gone black.

"Believe me, Ms. Kearney, I have no reason to lie. Nicholas Price is dead."

It wasn't true. It couldn't be. She choked on a sob. They'd only just found each other. Fate couldn't possibly be that cruel.

Waters reached out to take her pulse but she shook him off. "Don't touch me," she said, trying to sit up, the combination of medication and restraints making the task more difficult. Her left wrist was handcuffed to the bed railing, but her right arm was free. She swung at Waters, but he anticipated the move, catching her hand in his.

"If you insist on fighting, I'll have to up the sedative," the doctor said, nodding toward the bag of intravenous fluid. "It's your choice."

Mia sucked in a breath, fighting for composure. "I want to see his body." It was a bluff. The last thing she wanted to do was face the reality that Nick might be dead. But if they refused to let her see him, then maybe there was still hope.

"It's not here," Waters said, reaching again to take her pulse. Her skin crawled at his touch, but she forced herself not to pull away. "It was disposed of in Montana."

"But someone will ask questions."

"Who?" He looked up at her with genuine interest.

"Your family are all dead. And Mr. Price has been branded a traitor. Believe me, no one will mourn his passing."

"He's not dead. If he were, I'd know it. I'd feel it here." She hit her chest with her fist, tears filling her eyes, her body rebelling against the thought that she could have lost him. There was still so much left to say.

"Believe what you like," he said with a shrug, releasing her arm to write something on her chart. "It won't alter the truth."

Tears slid down her cheeks, but she ignored them, letting her anger take the lead. Dead or alive, Nick wasn't here now. Which meant she had to maintain control. It was her only chance. "How long are you going to keep me here?"

"Until we solve the puzzle. You're an anomaly, Ms. Kearney, and it's important that we understand why." Waters looked up from the chart, his face devoid of emotion. "That's why I fought to bring you here. They wanted you dead, too. But I convinced them that you'd be more valuable to us alive."

"So, what? You want me to thank you?" Bitterness filled her voice, coloring her words.

"Under the circumstances, I hardly think that's necessary."

Mia fought the urge to take another swing at him. Better to bide her time. To at least appear to cooperate. "You said that they wanted to kill me. Who exactly is *they?*"

"I'm not at liberty to say."

"Is it Kresky?" she asked, pushing for a reaction.

To the doctor's credit, his composure was almost absolute, but his fingers tightened on his pen, his knuckles going white. She'd hit a nerve.

"I'm right, aren't I? Kresky's behind all of this. He and Senator Tucker."

"I think you're asking the wrong person," Charles Davies answered, stepping the room. Unlike Dr. Waters, he made no effort to hide his animosity.

"She's only just woken up," Waters said, his tone defensive. "I was checking her vitals before I called you."

"No need to apologize, James," Davies said with a tight smile. "I just thought it might be a good idea if Mia and I had a little chat."

"I have nothing to say to you." She was hardly in a position to fight him, but it made her feel better to at least maintain the facade.

He took a step toward her, his eyes narrowing. "You caused us quite a bit of trouble, Ms. Kearney." Something about the way he said her name made her shiver, and she scooted back as much as the handcuff would allow. "So why don't you make this easy on yourself and tell me what you think you know about what happened in Cedar Branch."

"I know that you're up to your neck in it."

"That's overstating the obvious, don't you think? What I want to know is who else you think is involved. You mentioned Kresky."

She sorted through the details, trying to decide how much to share. Enough to make him believe she was cooperating, but not enough to tip her hand; what little she had was best kept secret for now. "I know that Kresky International was in charge of transporting the weapon that detonated in Cedar Branch."

Davies studied her, eyes narrowed. "What about Senator Tucker? You mentioned him, too. What makes you think he was involved?"

She met his gaze, keeping hers steady. "I only know that he approved the change in the transportation route. I figured as Nevada's senior senator, it was standard operating procedure. Besides, as a dedicated hawk, he's been advocating for Kresky for years." She bit her lip, hoping she'd provided the right amount of truth mixed with speculation.

Silence stretched as he weighed her words, searching her face for signs that she was lying. Mia worked to keep her expression neutral, positive now that she'd been right to keep her real suspicions to herself. Waters had said *they'd* wanted her dead. And Mia was certain that Davies was a big part of "they." All he needed was an excuse.

"And you have evidence to back you up?"

"What I've got, you've got." She rattled the chain of the handcuff to underscore her words. "Look, it's all pretty intuitive stuff. My town gets blown to hell. You all tell me it was a horrible accident. Once I managed to get out of here, it was fairly simple to work out the chain of events. The government gets antsy. Kresky wants to please the hand that feeds him. So the delivery schedule for the reworked B61-11 was changed. The reroute approved by Senator Tucker. The rest of the disaster is public knowledge."

"So you believe Kresky is to blame?"

"Yes. I do. And I think he used his connections to get people like you to help him cover it up." There was so much more to the story, but she wasn't about to let him know how much she knew. Her perceived ignorance was the only thing keeping her alive. It wouldn't work once Waters had his answers, but for now it bought her precious time.

"So who else knows about this? You have to have told someone."

"There was no one to tell." Her anger resurfaced, her thoughts turning to Nick. "You saw to that. Thanks to your lies, Nick's own people turned on him."

"Not all of them. Matt Young, for example."

"Who?" she asked, keeping her gaze level, trying to control her riotous thoughts. If Davies knew about Matt, then he knew she was lying. Of course, it could also just be a fishing expedition. Matt was Nick's friend, so the questions could simply be routine. "As far as I know Nick never contacted anyone."

"I don't believe you." He moved closer, a small smile playing at the corners of his mouth. "I can make you tell me."

"There's nothing to tell. And besides, I don't think Dr. Waters would want you to damage his specimen." She shot a look at the doctor, who was still scribbling on the chart. "That's what this whole thing has been about, after all. Making certain that you have control of the sole survivor."

"There's more at stake than you can possibly imagine," Davies said.

"All for the greater good, right?" Mia taunted him, clenching her fist and imagining what it would feel like to connect with his nose. "Like in Egypt."

Davies frowned, then tilted his head to study her. "Price told you about that?"

"Yes. About Katie, Masud—all of it."

"Did he happen to tell you he committed treason? Interfering with operations that ultimately would have given us the information necessary to destroy some of the biggest terrorist cells in the Middle East? And now he's doing it again. Once a traitor, always a traitor."

"If anyone is a traitor, it's you. First with American citizens in Egypt, and then in Cedar Branch. The deaths of my friends are on your head, Davies. Not Nick's."

"As you said, it's all about the greater good." He paused for a moment, eyes narrowed as he studied her. "And while I admire your spunk, things will go much better for you if you cooperate."

"And if I don't, what will you do to me? Kill me? You're going to do that anyway."

His expression hardened. "There are lots of ways to die, Ms. Kearney. Some of them more painful than others." He waited a moment, and she steeled herself, not willing to let him see her fear. "So why don't you tell me what you were doing at Biosphere."

A shiver worked cold fingers down her spine. If he was mentioning Biosphere by name, the idea that they were planning to kill her moved from *if* to *when*. "I don't know what you're talking about."

"The compound in Montana. Please don't insult me by pretending you don't remember."

"I didn't know its name. I'm not even sure of its purpose. We just knew that it was linked to Kresky. A research arm of some kind. We thought maybe there was something there to tie into the accident. Something that would clearly explain why the route was changed." She fumbled for logic. Something that fit into her story. "Originally the transport was routed very near Virginia City. It just seemed more than a coincidence that Kresky would have a facility nearby."

"How did you know about the facility in the first place?"

She swallowed, struggling to maintain her composure. "We found it at the plant in Wildwood. Tax records." It was more or less the truth. Just skipping a few key details along the way.

"I don't think I believe you." Davies took a step closer, the movement meant to intimidate.

"Well, I don't really care what you think," she said, lifting her chin in defiance.

Davies's hand connected with her cheek, the blow leaving her dizzy, pain radiating through her jaw. "Where is Matt Young?"

For a moment the non sequitur threw her, but she wasn't Leo Kearney's granddaughter for nothing. Squaring her shoulders, she glared up at Davies, her anger reaching out to his. "I don't know."

He hit her again, white lightning slicing through her head.

"Leave it for now," Waters said, his voice seeming to come from somewhere far away. "Can't you see she's still weak from the sedative? I don't want to take any chances. Right now, the answers her body can give us are far more important than the location of some renegade Homeland Security agent."

The doctor reached over to turn a knob on the tubing running into her arm, and everything seemed to slow down—molasses on velvet.

"Make no mistake," Davies whispered, leaning over her, his breath hot against her skin. "Waters may have given you a reprieve, but this isn't over."

Mia closed her eyes, unable to fight the drug any longer. But as she slipped down into the darkness, she smiled. Davies was the one who'd made the mistake. When he'd talked about Nick being a traitor, he'd done it in present tense.

Davies's renegade Homeland Security agent wasn't

Matt; he was looking for Nick. Waters had lied. Nick was alive. Which meant that Charles Davies had been right about one thing. It wasn't over—not by a long shot.

"DAMN IT, MATT. I don't have time for this." Nick glared at his friend, grimacing as the suture needle pierced his skin. "Mia needs me."

"Well, you're not going to be able to help her if you bleed to death," Matt said calmly, continuing to stitch the wound shut.

"Then hurry."

"I'm moving as fast as I can. And if you'll sit still, it'll go a hell of a lot faster."

Nick sucked in a breath, trying for some semblance of calm, but it wasn't easy. His brain just kept playing the same image over and over: Davies's men pushing Mia into the car. "I should never have left her alone."

"If you'd stayed with her, you'd probably be dead. I know that's not what you want to hear, but it's the truth. They wanted her back. And they wanted you out of the way. Almost managed to pull it off, too." Matt neatly tied off the thread and cut it, the stitches black against the angry red of the bullet wound.

"Well, they didn't, and now time is of the essence."

"Look, Nick, I get it. But going off half-cocked in a rage-induced haze isn't going to do anyone any good. They need her alive. You said it yourself. So that means we have a little time to make our plans and do it right. Okay?"

Nick nodded, angry at himself for losing control. But damn it all to hell, he'd never been so afraid. "They'll have taken her back to the facility where they first held her."

"But won't they know that's the first place you'll look?"

"Probably, but they also know I'm incapacitated. Which means I'm likely to make mistakes. So where better to take me on than their own turf? Besides, Davies is just arrogant enough to believe he can best me. Especially if I'm not operating at full capacity."

"I suppose that makes sense. Especially when you consider that the facility is protected by the radiation zone. That keeps them isolated and makes anything we try that much more likely to be discovered," Matt said, offering Nick a glass of water and a couple of pain relievers. "Sorry there's nothing stronger."

"This'll do." He popped the pills into his mouth and swallowed the water in one gulp. "If we're right about the B61-11, then most of the danger should be gone. That's the whole point of the weapon. But you're right, it'd be easy enough for Davies or whoever the hell he's working for to keep the area under quarantine. At least long enough to get the answers they need."

"We could always call for backup. Not everyone at Homeland Security buys the idea of you playing traitor."

"Yeah, but if any of this goes public, especially unsubstantiated, it'll force Davies's hand. He'll have to kill Mia, if for no other reason than to be certain we come off as liars. Maybe it would bring things out in the open, but I'm not willing to sacrifice Mia for the fucking greater good."

"Hey," Matt said, holding up a hand in apology, "I wasn't suggesting an interview with CNN. I just think it could be a good idea to make sure someone knows what we've stumbled on to. Otherwise, worst case, if we're too late to free Mia, or if Davies does manage to take us out, no one will ever know what really happened in Cedar Branch."

"But *we* don't even know what happened. At least not for certain. Did your friend have a chance to examine the bovine tissue?"

"Only enough to verify that the vet was right," he said, winding a bandage around Nick's injured arm. "Basically, the animals suffered a massive cardiac event combined with respiratory failure. Unfortunately, there are myriad possible causes—everything from poison to some kind of ninja virus. The only thing she could say for certain was that they weren't killed by radiation. In fact, she agreed that they were dead before they were exposed. She's running additional tests to identify what caused the cardiac arrest."

"Will she keep what she finds to herself?" Nick asked, flexing his arm to test the bandage. "We can't take chances on a leak. Not until we've gotten Mia back."

"Diane's totally trustworthy. I told you, I've known her since college. We met in biochem. Wound up as lab partners, actually. Which meant we spent an excessive amount of time in the lab—running experiments of a more personal nature. The point being that we have history. She's not going to tell anyone anything."

"So how long do you think it will be before we have answers?"

"Maybe tonight, but most likely not until tomorrow morning. She's going to e-mail the results. So as soon as she has them, we'll have them. Unfortunately, I don't think we can afford to wait."

"I agree. I'm not sure what Waters is looking for. But I do know what will happen once he's found it."

"So what do you remember about the facility?"

"It's pretty straightforward. The building is one-story, constructed primarily out of concrete. There are a minimum number of windows, maybe six total, and those that do exist are located near the roofline, like you'd see in a bunker or a cellar.

"There are only two doors in. One at the front of the building and another on the northeast side. The latter is a fire door. It releases from the inside. The front door is metal, no windows, and if I remember correctly it's an electronic lock. I should have paid more attention." He stood up, taking a couple of tentative steps.

"What about outside security?"

"There's a guard at the gate. He's the bastard who planted the bug. And a barbed wire fence around the perimeter. There's a possibility they've made modifications, but to be honest, we've kept them pretty busy since Mia got out."

"She used the back door, right?"

"Yeah," he said, reaching for a piece of paper to sketch a layout of the building. "It leads to the main hallway, which bisects the whole place." He marked the two hallways on the map. "The front door faces south." He marked an X at the south end of the main hallway, and another to indicate the location of the second door. "There are two other corridors, here and here." He sketched one leading off to the right, near the front door, and a second one leading off to the left. "Mia's room was in the left-side hallway. About here." He marked another X on the map.

"Were there any windows in her room?" Matt asked, studying the makeshift drawing.

"No. It was completely enclosed. We'll have to access it from the inside."

"So our best bet is the back door. Unless they have managed to modify it."

"More likely they've just increased personnel. It would accomplish the same thing, with a lot less hassle."

"Which means all we have to do is neutralize them. I'll take that over security devices anyday. Besides," Matt said, "we can always play one against the other. Make them think we're coming through the door, and then while they're outside chasing shadows, we come in through a window. The key is to keep them off balance."

"It might work. But we're going to need supplies."

"That's something I know I can handle. Why don't you try and get some rest, and I'll round up what we need."

Nick started to object, then abandoned the idea. He was bone tired, functioning on adrenaline alone, and the only way he was going to help Mia was to gather as much strength as possible. He had to believe that nothing was going to happen in the next couple of hours. Because if he was wrong about that, then nothing they did would matter—Mia was already dead.

CHAPTER TWENTY-TWO

"SOMETHING'S DEFINITELY going on down there." Nick twisted the lens on his field glasses, watching the commotion below.

Davies's facility was lit up like a baseball field, men scurrying around with boxes, papers and even the odd piece of medical equipment. Some of the stuff was being loaded into a truck just inside the front gate, but the bulk of it was being thrown into a large pile in the center of the compound. A second pile next to it was covered with a canvas tarp.

"Looks to me like they're packing up to go," Matt said, shifting to a more comfortable stance. They were crouched just above the facility, behind a stand of pines, the soft fragrance of the conifers filling the night air.

"Puts a hell of a kink in our plans." Nick sighed, his beleaguered brain scrambling for new ideas. "Do you see any sign of Mia?"

"No. But she's got to be here. You were right when you said that if they'd wanted her dead, they'd have killed her in Montana. She's still alive, Nick."

"Yeah, but how the hell are we going to get to her?"

"Might be a matter of waiting for the right moment," Matt said, pointing to a blue sedan coming down the gravel road leading to the facility. The car slowed as it approached the gate, then pulled to a stop at the edge of the yard just beyond the truck.

Two men in uniform emerged from the car and headed toward the building, their weapons visible even from this distance.

"What the hell are Special Forces doing here?" Matt lowered his glasses, his eyes reflecting his surprise.

"We've said all along that there had to be a connection somewhere up the chain of command. If Kresky really is developing a new weapon, he's got to have a buyer. It's just not the kind of thing someone does on spec. And with Tucker tied into it all somehow, that would seem to eliminate the international angle."

"Which leaves private or military," Matt said. "And judging from the men below, I'd hazard a guess and say military. You think the president could be in on this?"

"Anything's possible, but considering the current political climate, I'm betting his involvement is minimal. It'd be way too dangerous politically if something were to happen and his name was in any way attached."

"Like the damn thing blowing up and destroying a town?"

Nick nodded, anger rising. Politics had a way of negating everything. Double-edged diplomacy, where one hand was offered in agreement while the other schemed to make certain all eventualities were covered.

"So what do you want to do?" Matt asked, training his glasses on the men below.

"I want to storm the goddamn castle. But we're kind of outnumbered."

"At least we're well armed." Matt had managed to procure not only an additional rifle, but a couple of handguns and some extra ammo.

"I wouldn't mind a machine gun and maybe some nitro, but yeah, we can make do with what we've got."

"Hey, it's not what you've got, it's how you use it." Matt's smile faded as he considered their options. "I'm thinking we should assume the uniforms are here for Mia. It makes sense that if they're moving out, they'd want muscle to make sure she gets to wherever they're going without incident. So that leaves us with two options. We can either try and get her now, or we can play follow the leader and wait for an opportunity to strike."

"The logical choice would probably be to wait. But if we do that, there's the risk that the right chance won't present itself. We can't run the car off the road for fear of hurting Mia, and quite frankly, if we prove to be too much of a threat, there's a possibility they'll just take her out of the equation."

"So we opt for now," Matt said. This wasn't his fight. Hell, he really didn't even know Mia. But he was there just the same, no questions asked.

"All right then. We need a plan." The uniformed men had disappeared into the building, and the activity continued, with men scurrying back and forth between the growing pile of refuse, the building and the truck.

"Well, I've counted three men handling the removal. If they're armed, it's with small weapons, because there's nothing visual. As opposed to the men with the car."

"We know there's a man at the gate, and I'm certain he's armed. Which moves the number of hostiles to six. Three with visible arms, the others probably packing."

"Yes, but with their hands full they'll definitely be handicapped."

"Right. Beyond gate guy, there don't seem to be any additional guards. Although there could be someone else on duty, and there's no way to know who's inside. There's been no sign of either Davies or Waters, but my guess is the doctor is more likely to run for it than stay and fight."

"Not exactly the best of odds, but we've faced worse."

They hadn't actually, but Nick smiled, anyway. "Thanks for doing this."

"You know I never miss a party." Matt's answering grin was brief as he turned back to survey the scene below. "Is that the doctor?"

Nick lifted his glasses, adjusting them for a better view. Waters was standing in front of the building, speaking earnestly with one of the men carrying boxes. The man shot a look toward the canvas-covered pile and then nodded. Seemingly satisfied, Waters walked back into the building. "Yeah, that's him."

"How many people were on-site when you first arrived?" Matt asked.

"Besides Davies and Waters? A couple of nurses, a tech and maybe four armed guards. I wasn't there very long, so that's not a particularly scientific estimate."

"I suspect it's fairly accurate. And I'm guessing that considering they're liquidating assets, so to speak, there probably aren't a whole lot of nonessential staff on hand. Which means we've probably seen the worst."

"Never assume, my friend."

"Yeah, I know—makes an ass and all that. But I still say we've probably seen the worst, except maybe Davies."

"Well, it'd be dangerous to ignore the man, but in my opinion he's gotten a little too complacent. Otherwise I don't think for a minute that we'd have managed to survive as long as we have."

"You're discounting your abilities, as usual," Matt said, "but I hear what you're saying."

"The real point here," Nick said, lowering his glasses, "is that we're not prepared for a full-on frontal attack. Even assuming that some of the personnel down there aren't armed or would at least have trouble getting to their guns, we're still seriously outnumbered."

"So we divide and conquer."

"Great minds…" Nick said. "You think you can come up with a distraction? Something that will pull attention away from the building?"

"I can handle it, but you're going to have to move fast. There's no way I can hold them off for long. Where do you want me to hit?"

"I'm thinking the front gate. If nothing else, you'll be able to slow down their ability to follow us. At least by car. Which, assuming I'm successful, will be a decided advantage."

"Consider it done." Matt nodded. "How you planning to get in the building?"

"I'll improvise. Give me about ten minutes to get into place."

"All right. I'll need the extra ammo." He held out his hand for the box Nick was carrying.

"Don't blow it all in one place."

"Actually," Matt said with a grin, already heading around toward the front gate, "that's exactly what I intend to do."

MIA STRUGGLED TO PULL OUT of her drug-induced lethargy. Waters had removed the drip half an hour ago, but the sedative was still in her system. It was hard to know how much time had passed, and without a window she couldn't even tell the time of day.

She yanked her arm, sending the handcuff rattling against the bed railing. Even with her altered state, Waters didn't trust her not to try and escape. Wise man. She slid off the bed, wobbling on her feet a moment as she waited for her head to clear.

Something was going on. She could hear it even if she couldn't see it. Her door was closed, but she was guessing not locked. All she had to do was figure out a way to get out of the handcuff. She took a step forward, the cuff sliding along the bedrail beside her. At least she was capable of mobility.

She moved forward as far as the cuff would allow, but the door was still tantalizingly out of reach, the additional latitude only allowing access to the end of the bed. There was nothing in the room but the bed; even the monitors had been removed.

She pulled against the handcuff, feeling the skin on the back of her hand tear. But even if she stripped it to the bone she wasn't going to pull free. Cursing Waters, Davies and fate in general, she sat on the mattress, arm stretched behind her, trying to think of how to get rid of the blasted handcuff.

For a moment she considered giving in to the panic lurking at the edge of consciousness. She was so damn tired. She closed her eyes, drifting for a moment, fighting her emotions. And then, as clearly as if he'd been standing in front of her, she heard her grandfather.

"Mia, you can't beat them if you're not in the game."

Sucking in a breath, she pushed her fear aside. She wasn't about to let Davies win. There had to be something she could do to get free. Shifting back a little, she leaned down to study the underside of the bed. The springs were encased in heavy canvas, and even if she did manage to tear it open, she doubted she'd be able to manage the leverage to free a spring.

She'd already tried to liberate the railing, but it was firmly welded to the frame. Which left her absolutely nowhere. She straightened with a sigh, scraping her head on something in the process.

Muffling yet another curse, she bent down again, angrily trying to find the culprit—the bed crank. Leave it to Waters to cut corners on hospital equipment. She swallowed a laugh, knowing that it bordered on hysteria. Due in part, no doubt, to the chemically induced imbalance in her brain.

She shook her head, swatting at the handle. It flipped over once and then swung back and forth a couple of times before coming to a stop. Her synapses were definitely firing slowly, but they were firing. With grim determination she reached for the crank again, this time yanking with her free hand.

It didn't come off, but it did move a little. She shifted, twisting so she could brace one foot against the bed railing. Then, using her good arm, she yanked again, but again the handle refused to budge.

Tears of frustration filled her eyes as she tried to shake off the fog in her brain. There had to be a way to free the handle. If it wouldn't help her open the handcuff, at least it would provide a weapon of sorts. Something to tilt the balance of power at least a little in her direction.

She wiped at her eyes, angry at her own weakness, and tried again. Then suddenly, her brain caught up with the program, and she reached down, turning the crank counterclockwise. Five full turns and the handle was free.

It wasn't exactly lethal. Metal and plastic with a screw at the tip. But it made her feel powerful nevertheless. Taking action, any action, beat the hell out of meekly standing by awaiting her fate.

Sitting back on the edge of the bed, she picked at the lock of the handcuff with the tip of the handle without success. Banging it against the handcuff proved to be even more useless, and worse, it created noise. Holding her breath, waiting for Waters to descend, she palmed the crank and slid back into bed.

Footsteps neared and she tensed, her right hand gripping the handle, but almost as quickly the footsteps faded away. Certain that everything was quiet again, she sat up, using the handle again to try to jimmy the handcuff lock. A hairpin might have worked, but the screw at the end wasn't long enough or thin enough to do the job.

At least her head was clearing.

She closed her eyes, drawing in a slow breath, praying for strength, knowing that if a chance presented itself she had to be ready. Fortified, she stood up, the handle gripped at her side, screw outward. It might not be lethal, but she could sure as hell do a little damage. Hurried footsteps passed the door, someone yelling something. And then quiet descended, leaving her with hope. Whatever was going on, it seemed to have pulled people away from the door.

All she had to do was figure out a way to get free. Still holding the handle, she tugged at the bed, gratified when it inched forward. Five more tugs and she was exhausted, but she'd managed to move the bed so that the bottom half of it would be behind the door when it opened.

Climbing onto the middle, she knelt, waiting, handle at

the ready. She wasn't sure exactly what she hoped to accomplish, but it felt better to be doing something. And if nothing else, her new position would give her a momentary advantage.

She waited, breath held, but nothing happened. Minutes stretched to what felt like hours, and finally she sagged back, adrenaline leaving her spent.

Then she heard a quiet footstep, followed by another. The handle on the door turned ominously and she raised her hand, concentrating on the square of tile in front of the door. In one motion the door swung open and she slammed the handle downward, but the intruder twisted just in time, catching her arm before it could fully descend.

"Watch it, princess, a guy could lose an eye."

"Nick," she whispered, dropping the handle. He cupped her face in his hands, his kiss hard and full of promise. Then he gently pushed her back, his eyes hardening when he saw the bruises on her face.

"Did Davies do this?" he asked, his voice harsh with emotion.

"Yes. But it doesn't matter," she said, reaching out to touch him, to assure herself that he was real. "All that matters is that you're here."

"And that we've got to get out of here," he said, pulling them both back to the present and the situation at hand. "For the moment they're a little preoccupied. Matt blew up one of their trucks, but we don't have much time." His eyes moved to the handcuff on her wrist. "Looks like they've got you well and truly stuck."

"Guess Davies thought I might try and escape. Which was actually a good call, when you consider that I'm not really fond of the accommodations."

"Move as far away from the cuff as you can." He passed her his rifle and pulled out a handgun. "Keep the rifle pointed at the door."

"What are you going to do?" she asked, straightening her left arm and aiming the weapon with her right. "Nothing too drastic, I hope. I'm kind of attached to my hand."

"Just keep your eyes on the door, and trust me."

She nodded, her heart perfectly happy with the suggestion, her stomach not so certain.

The silencer on the gun hissed, accompanied by a somewhat more frightening ping. And then suddenly, the pressure from the handcuff was gone.

"Can you run?" Nick said, exchanging the handgun for the rifle.

"No problem." Adrenaline alone would carry her across the country and back.

"All right then. Let's get the hell out of here. And if anyone gets in your way, shoot to kill."

"Not gonna be a problem. I've played this scene before, and believe me, I'll take a gun over a chair leg anytime."

Nick smiled, then motioned her still and stepped around the door into the hallway. She held her breath as the seconds passed, and then he leaned in, signaling her to follow. The corridor was empty and they raced down it, slowing as they came to the T. Leading with the rifle, Nick rounded the corner and again motioned her to follow.

"Looks like everyone is outside, dealing with Matt's handiwork," he whispered. "I want you to head for the back door, and no matter what happens I want you to keep going. Agreed?"

She nodded, not certain she really meant it, but determined not to slow things down. The sooner they were out from under Davies's thumb the better. She veered right, delighted to see that the way was clear.

She'd only gone about halfway when the sound of gunfire drew her up short. Nick was still standing at the intersection, firing into the main hallway. She started to move in his direction, but froze as a man in uniform stepped out of an office, his attention on Nick's exposed back.

Without even stopping to think, she lifted the gun and fired, a crimson cauliflower blossoming on the man's back. Nick whirled around, getting off a second shot. The man fell, and Nick sprinted toward her. "I told you to keep going," he yelled as he grabbed her by the arm, propelling her forward.

"Fine, next time I'll let you die."

His grip tightened, but the lines around his mouth quirked every so slightly upward. "You're a real pain in the ass."

"Yeah," she countered, "but I'm *your* pain in the ass."

They burst through the door into the night air, the back of the building less brightly lit than the rest of the compound. The first thing that hit her was the acrid smell of the fire, the odor almost overpowering. Off to her left she could see a pile of papers, a canvas tarp and other bits and pieces of what looked like medical supplies. She even recognized one of the monitors that had been in her room.

"What the hell?" she asked, turning to Nick, her pace slowing.

"They're clearing out. My guess is they were getting ready to move you as well as whatever information they deemed crucial. The rest I assume they were planning to burn."

"Well, thanks to Matt they got a head start." She tilted

her head to the flames that were now rising above the front of the building, casting the structure into eerie relief.

They started forward again, only to draw up short when three men, all with guns, rushed around the corner. "Run," Nick said. "I'll be right behind you."

She sprinted toward the pile of rubbish, her heart pounding as she rounded the edge and ducked down behind the tarp. Nick had managed to take out one of the men, and bracing herself against the refuse, she managed to get off a shot of her own, her bullet slamming into the second man. He dropped to his knees, clutching his chest, as Nick's rifle took out the third man.

Mia dropped to the ground, waited a beat and then started to stand again, intent now on running for the barbed wire fence. But as she started to move, her gun caught on the edge of the tarp. As she worked to free it, the corner of the canvas flipped up, the wind yanking it free, lifting it into the air.

A scream rose and then died in her throat, the gun falling from lifeless fingers as her brain tried to process the horror of what she was seeing. The ground was littered with bodies, thrown haphazardly as if they'd fallen there, limbs askew, eyes open in surprise. Patrick, Nancy, Carson, Joe. They were all there. Betty lying across Wilson McCullough, her hand reaching out as if pleading for something, her salt-and-pepper hair a stark contrast to the cold hard ground.

Mia struggled against the bile rising in her throat, tears filling her eyes. In their hurry to empty the facility—to destroy the evidence—Davies's men had discarded the bodies, leaving them unburied. Abandoned. Exposed. The only sign of respect the flapping tarp. There was no question that they were dead, but still they called to her, their familiar faces twisted in anguish.

She struggled to breathe, her heart wrenching with an agony almost too great to be borne. Yet even as grief threatened to tear her apart, burning rage filled her. Fury at Davies and Waters and all of their colleagues. She scooped up the gun and started toward the front of the building— only to stop when she realized the fire had spread, the flames engulfing the piles of paper, crawling relentlessly toward her friends.

Acting on instinct, she ran into the fray, grabbing Patrick by the hands, struggling to pull him free of the fire. But she wasn't strong enough. She couldn't make him move.

"Mia, no." Nick's voice reached her, cutting through the haze of anger and grief. "He's past help now. There's nothing you can do. You have to let them go."

"I can't," she gasped, tightening her hold on Patrick's hands.

"Sweetheart, they're not here anymore. Whatever happened, they're long gone from this place. And I promise you, we'll find a way to make Davies and the others pay. But to do that we have to get out of here. Now."

As quickly as it had come, the rage retreated, leaving her drained, unsteady on her feet. Matt appeared from out of nowhere, his eyes dark with worry.

"Cover us," Nick said, moving to swing her up into his arms.

"No," she said, shaking off his hands, "I can do it myself. I have to do it myself." She turned for a last look, her soul aching as the fire leapt forward, feeding on everything in its path. Turning her back on the inferno, she forced herself to take one step and then another, the sound of gunfire behind her barely registering. Then Nick was there beside her, helping her over the barbed wire, the crisp night air clearing her head, if not her heart.

Together they ran through the brush, heading for the mountains, the funeral pyre behind them shooting sparks into the starry Idaho sky.

CHAPTER TWENTY-THREE

"GET IT WHILE IT'S HOT." Nick stepped into the cabin holding out bags from a local burger joint. They were back at the Gardiner rental, figuring they were as safe there as anywhere.

"I'm not really hungry," Mia said. She was sitting at the breakfast bar with an untouched cup of coffee. Remarkably, she was holding on to her composure, but the shredded napkin beside the cup reflected the reality of her emotional state, and Nick knew that eventually she'd have to let it out.

"Come on. You've got to eat something." He crossed over to the counter, setting down the sacks, careful to give her the distance she needed. He'd been where she was. Holding everything together by sheer force of will. And he knew that even the littlest thing could shatter her control.

It wasn't easy for him, either. He wanted to hold her. To swear that he'd keep her safe. But he knew it would be an empty promise. Mia needed to see this through. It was the only way she'd be able to survive the devastation. And that meant they'd have to go back to Biosphere. It was the only place where they'd be able to find answers.

"Where's Matt?" he asked, pulling plates down from the cabinet. The gesture seeming maddeningly mundane, given the circumstances.

"He's still in with his computer." She nodded toward the downstairs bedroom. "It's the only place he can get a signal." They were lucky to have it at all.

"So nothing from the pathologist yet?"

She shook her head. "How's your arm?"

He reached over to touch the bandage. "It's all right. Stitches held through the fighting, so I'm more or less good to go."

"They told me you were dead," she said, her eyes softening ever so slightly. "I didn't believe them."

He ached to pull her into his arms, but he'd have to settle for words. "I never should have left you."

"Then we'd both have been captured." Despite all that was weighing on her, she was absolving him, the idea humbling and enabling all at the same time. "Besides, you came to get me."

"Not before they had a chance to hurt you." He reached toward her bruised face, but forced himself to drop his hand. "I'm sorry, Mia. For all of it. I'm so goddamned sorry."

"You have nothing to apologize for."

"I didn't believe you. I thought you were a part of it."

"In the beginning, maybe. But even then you helped me. And when it really mattered, you took the risk, you accepted what I had to say. Besides, not even I expected to find something like—" She broke off, unable to voice the words. "You said there were no bodies."

"And that's what I believed. What everyone believed."

"So why did they lie?" She closed her eyes, clearly trying to push the images away, to replace them with older, better memories.

"I'm not sure. Maybe they wanted to run tests. Or maybe they didn't all die in the explosion."

"Oh, God…" She buried her face in her hands.

"Mia, I wish I could—" He broke off, his heart twisting, knowing there was nothing he could do to stop her pain.

"But that doesn't change the reality, does it?" She straightened, her expression grim, anger replacing agony. "So how many of Davies's men got away, do you think?"

"Waters for certain," he said, accepting the change of subject. "Maybe a couple of others, but we got most of them."

"Not Davies." She spat the last as if it were an expletive.

"He wasn't there, Mia. We'd have seen him otherwise."

"So he's still out there. Along with Kresky and the good senator." Her voice was calm, almost devoid of emotion, but she was gripping the cup with white-knuckled intensity. "I want them dead."

"I know. And believe me, given the chance, I'd like a shot at them, too. But it's not going to bring your friends back."

"Maybe not, but it'll be an eye for an eye. If that's possible."

Nick sighed, hating the bitterness coloring her voice. "I've been where you are, Mia. And I know the depth of your rage. But no amount of retribution is going to make you feel better. To do that, you've got to find a way to let it go. To move past all of this."

"Not until they're dead. Or at least until they've paid for what they've done." She lifted her face, her eyes dark with pain. "They've got to be stopped."

"More than you can possibly imagine," Matt said, walking in from the bedroom, his expression grim. "I just got the pathology report, along with Diane's findings. It's un-fucking-believable."

"What did you find?" Nick asked, swiveling around on the stool to face his friend.

"The cattle were poisoned. Diane couldn't identify the exact toxin. The closest thing she'd ever seen, chemically speaking, is a biotoxin called batrachotoxin."

"From dart frogs, right?" Mia asked.

"Yeah," Matt said, his expression quizzical. "How'd you know that?"

"She kinda has a knack for pulling out the odd useful tidbit," Nick said, repressing a smile.

"I spent a lot of time in Colombia when I was growing up. In fact, I used to play with the frogs."

"Had a death wish, did you?" Matt quipped. "*Phyllobates terribilis* has enough toxin in it to kill something like a hundred men."

"But only if you've got an open sore or a cut or something. Playing with them was sort of a rite of passage. The frogs are everywhere. There must be hundreds of species, and pretty much every color you can imagine. But from the time you're really little they tell you not to touch the gold ones. So of course that's exactly what you do."

"These are the same frogs whose poison is used for blow darts, right?" Nick asked.

Matt nodded. "The Chocó Indians use it. The frogs are indigenous in that part of Colombia."

"Was your grandmother Chocó?" Nick shot a look at Mia. The jungles of South America seemed miles away from the problems at hand, but he'd seen more spurious connections prove anything but accidental.

"Emberá Chocó. A village near Mutata in the Murindo rain forest. My grandfather still hunted with a blowgun. Although he also worked at a nearby banana plantation. Modern life is inescapable even when you live in the jungle."

"And you played with dart frogs," Matt repeated, sounding more amazed than anything else.

"I didn't dress them up and push them around in baby carriages, if that's what you're imagining. My cousins and I used to play frog roulette, if you will—daring each other to pick them up. At first you're really scared. Hold the frog maybe all of two seconds and then wait to drop dead. But after you survive the first couple of encounters, you get braver. Hold them longer. They're actually pretty docile for something so deadly. So it became a game with my cousins to see who could hold them the longest. I usually won."

"No surprise there," Nick said, glad to see that at least some of her pain had receded in the wake of better memories. "But I still don't see the connection to Ellis's cattle. Last I checked there were no dart frogs in Idaho."

"I never said the poison *was* batrachotoxin, just that it was similar in structure," Matt said, setting the laptop on the breakfast bar. "Here's the structure of batrachotoxin." He hit a key and the screen filled with hexagons and pentagons, the linked molecules that together formed the toxin. "And this one is from the tissue sample." He opened another window, the two structures side by side. They were almost identical, but there were clear variations.

"So you think it's a modified form of batrachotoxin." Nick shifted so that he could better see the computer screen.

"I think it's possible. It's already been successfully synthesized in an effort to understand its possible pharmacological applications. Batrachotoxin works by increasing the permeability of the outer membrane of nerve and muscle cells to sodium ions. This in turn blocks nerve signals, leaving muscles in a permanent state of contraction.

Parkinson's disease works in a similar way, as does Alzheimer's."

"So by working with synthetic batrachotoxin they're hoping to find relief for people suffering from those kinds of diseases."

"Exactly."

"But there have been efforts to synthesize it for more nefarious reasons, right?" Nick asked. "I seem to remember something about a lab they uncovered after Kabul fell in 2001."

"Good memory," Matt said. "They found notes indicating that al-Qaeda had been playing around with all kinds of nasties. And batrachotoxin topped the list. But no one has ever believed the poison could be used in any kind of mass application. It's rare, and thanks to the Colombian drug cartels, the frogs aren't easy to access."

"But if they have successfully synthesized it, wouldn't that take care of the problem with obtaining it?" Mia asked.

"Theoretically, I guess. But there are still major problems. It's not absorbed through unbroken skin and it can't be inhaled. It has limited toxicity when taken orally. And even if the structure was altered so that delivery of toxicity through absorption or inhalation was possible, it would still need to be aerosolized."

"A little water or a weak alcohol solution would take care of that. I've done similar kinds of things with my work on etching," Mia said.

"Still, we're talking major chemical modification. Which would take a hell of a lot of money."

"But it is technically possible," Nick said. "And I can see the attraction. Batrachotoxin is the deadliest poison on earth. A thousand times more deadly than cyanide. Up to now its only application has been on the end of a dart. But if they have found a way to modify it so that it could be administered in mass, it would be one hell of a weapon."

"And Kresky's got a lot of money." Matt closed the computer, the click underscoring his words. "Not to mention the diverted government funding."

"Oh, my God, you're saying the people in Cedar Branch were killed by some sort of mutated batrachotoxin?" Mia's words came out on a whisper, her hand rising to her throat.

"It fits the facts and timeline," Nick said.

"Which means what?" Matt asked. "The nuclear explosion was a cover-up?"

"It seems possible, and you've got to admit an ERW is as good a way as any to eradicate signs of some other catastrophe."

"And call a hell of a lot of attention to it at the same time."

"But Kresky was all set to take the heat. Apparently he owed Tucker. And if Mia hadn't managed to escape, there's a good chance they would have gotten away with it. Her survival was the only thing that threw a kink in the works."

"Which begs the big question of the day," Mia said. "How did I survive? My grandfather's bomb shelter was never intended to protect from something like this."

"I can think of a couple of possibilities," Matt said. "First off, there would have been some kind of filtering involved in your grandfather's shelter. It may have been intended to screen out radiation, but it still would have provided a certain amount of protection against any airborne danger. In addition to that, you said you were wearing a mask. And masks have been used successfully to protect against sarin and other chemical toxins for years."

"But the truth is I don't remember if I was wearing my mask or not. And even if I was, it wasn't industrial strength or anything. It was serious protection against the fumes from the chemicals I was working with, but it's not like I had to go to some kind of survival store to get it."

"It's still a possibility," Nick said. "And when you combine the shelter with the mask, you're gaining double protection. So even if both of them were flawed, one might compensate for the other and you could still wind up being protected."

"There's a second option, too," Matt said. "It's purely conjecture. Hell, it'd take a mountain of study to prove. But there's a possibility that your heritage saved you."

"I'm not following," Mia said with a frown.

"*Phyllobates terribilis* doesn't produce the batracho-toxin. It's been a longtime puzzle. One that's still being debated. But what seems to be happening is that the frog's diet is actually what's providing the batrachotoxin. Certain ants and beetles prevalent in that part of the Amazon carry the poison. It's actually been theorized that they in turn may be ingesting the toxin, as well—from certain plants in the rain forest. Anyway, the point is that the frog is ingesting the poison, but isn't affected by it. In fact, its body actually uses it for defense, secreting it to stop his enemies."

"Which is all interesting, but how does it relate to me?" Mia asked.

"Bear with me, I'm getting there. What researchers have found is that the receptor molecule in the frogs doesn't bind with the batrachotoxin. So it can be excreted without harming the amphibians. The theory is that it's se-lective adaptation. That the frogs' cells have modified over time so that they can adapt to their environment."

"And live with the poison," Mia said, her expression thoughtful. "So you think that because I share genes with people indigenous to the area, I might have developed an immunity to the poison, too?"

"It's possible. Frogs aren't the only creatures to selectively adapt. And at least to my knowledge, there haven't been any extensive studies of the Chocó people. It's always been assumed that they weren't harmed by the poison because they cook the meat they eat. Or because the small amount contained in the meat killed with poison darts is metabolized. But it seems equally possible that over time at least some of the people might have developed the same kind of defense the frogs did."

"But I'm not full-blooded Chocó," Mia protested.

"Doesn't matter. Genes are passed on through dominance. So if your grandmother passed it on to your father, then in all likelihood you'd have it, as well."

"Well, that would explain why Waters was practically salivating over the idea of studying Mia," Nick said, fighting his own anger. The idea of them using her like that was almost beyond contemplation. "And why they would have been willing to risk keeping her alive, even though it posed a significant threat to their cover-up."

"It probably frustrated the hell out of them," Matt said. "I mean, here they believe they've developed the perfect weapon, but when push comes to shove and it's tested, one of their subjects refuses to die." He flinched as the words came out of his mouth. "Sorry, I didn't mean to sound so insensitive."

"It's all right," Mia said. "It all makes sense in a horrifying kind of way. But it doesn't explain why I passed out."

"Again, there are any number of reasons that could

explain it. It could have been a lack of oxygen. The toxin's release certainly would have altered the air composition significantly."

"Or it could have been the chemicals you were working with," Nick continued. "You said yourself that you're not sure whether you used your mask, so maybe it was a chemical combination—the neurotoxin and something else you were working with."

"You could have tripped and hit your head. Or maybe Davies's men gave you something to make you forget."

"A drug?" Mia's eyes reflected her confusion.

"It's possible." Matt shrugged. "Such things certainly exist. Or, quite frankly, there's also a chance that you were awake the whole time but simply blocked it all out."

Mia shook her head, rejecting the notion.

"Sweetheart, it's possible," Nick said, wishing he could erase her pain. "Remember Ellis talking about post-traumatic stress disorder?"

"Maybe you left the studio, saw your friends and…" Matt trailed off, looking uncomfortable.

"But if that was true, wouldn't I be able to remember now? I mean, everything is out in the open. I saw them all at the compound. They're dead. It can't get any worse. Why would my mind continue to shield me?"

Nick reached out, touching her shoulder, needing the contact probably more than she did. "Look, whatever the reason, maybe it's best that you don't remember. Some things are better forgotten."

"But if I could remember, it would make things easier." Her frustration was almost a palpable thing.

"You don't know that," Nick said, his gaze locking with

hers. "And besides, you can't force it, sweetheart. It'll come when it's ready."

"Or it may never come at all," Matt said, his expression apologetic. "If they drugged you, then whatever's gone is gone."

"I hate this."

Nick felt her muscles tense beneath his hand. "The point here is that your remembering isn't the only key to finding out what happened in Cedar Branch. We've got Kresky and Tucker and Biosphere. All we have to do is connect the dots. And if Tucker and Kresky did manage to create an altered form of the biotoxin, it goes a long way toward explaining why Tucker had to bury the funding."

"Yeah," Matt said. "Particularly when you consider the U.S. agreed to honor the '72 Biological and Toxin Convention and the '93 Chemical Weapons Convention. Both of which would prohibit the development of this kind of weapon."

"So you're saying they tested it on purpose? Held a lottery to see which town would be the guinea pig?" She was standing up now, the flush of anger staining her cheeks.

"It could have been an accident, but the end result was the same. If we're right and Biosphere was developing this thing near Cedar Branch, there was method involved in site selection."

"Who gives a damn about the country people?"

"Less population, less damage," Nick agreed, his expression somber.

"Well, it isn't right. Nobody should be subjected to that kind of risk without their consent. This is worse than anything my mother could have conceptualized when she was fighting to keep nuclear testing out of Idaho."

"You're preaching to the choir here. It's Tucker and his cohorts who need the civics lesson," Matt said.

"I know. It's just hard to stomach the fact that our government will go to war to protect the rights of people in some country halfway around the world, and at the same time sanction production of a weapon that puts its own citizens in danger."

"It's all about the greater good. And the always popular 'what you don't know about can't hurt you' theory."

"Except that it can," Mia said, her eyes shining with tears.

"Doesn't seem to matter," Matt said on a sigh. "They did it with the Manhattan Project. They did it with the development of the Minuteman system. And apparently they're doing it again now. "

"The operative question being exactly who *they* are." Nick leaned back, crossing his arms. "We know Kresky and Tucker are involved. And probably Hatcher. Then there's Davies. He's definitely dancing to someone's tune. The question is whether or not it stops at Tucker."

"The reality is that it's going to be tough to prove any of it. All we can say for certain is that the modified batrachotoxin appears to be what killed your friend's cattle," Matt said. "And thanks to my handiwork tonight, there won't be an opportunity for any further examination." He stared down at his hands, the room going silent, the weight of his words heavy on all three of them.

Nick opened his mouth to say something, to try and absolve his friend, but Mia beat him to it.

"What happened at the facility wasn't your fault, Matt. You didn't set them on fire. You set them free. There's no telling what Waters and his people had in mind for them. Certainly not burial. All Waters cared about was getting answers. Treating them like specimens. But he can't do that anymore. And that's because of you."

"It doesn't feel that way."

"I know," she said, reaching out to touch his hand. "Did you know I wanted to stay there? To pull the bodies out of the fire? Nick had to drag me away. But he was right. They were already dead. And what was important was getting out of there ourselves. Because as long as we're alive, they won't be forgotten.

"As long as we're living and breathing, there's a chance we can beat this thing. Find the proof we need to nail Tucker, Kresky and Davies and whoever else is involved. And right now that's all that matters."

NICK PACED BACK AND FORTH across the bedroom floor, debating the wisdom of opening the bathroom door. Mia had seemed better, there was no question about it. She'd been completely focused during their discussion, even adding insight. But it was totally possible to function on one level while falling apart on another.

He'd lived like that for longer than he cared to admit. But he also knew that no one could have helped him. He had to find his peace all on his own, and it had been a long time coming. Hell, it was still a balancing act, but he had gotten better.

If only he could hit fast-forward and spare Mia the pain. God, he hated feeling helpless. His whole life had been about taking action. And yet here he stood, waiting outside a bathroom, feeling completely out of control.

"Mia," he said, knocking on the door. "Are you okay in there?"

There was no reply. He reached for the doorknob and

then withdrew his hand. Maybe she couldn't hear him. Or maybe she just didn't want to. If he were honest, that was what scared him the most—that the fragile bridge they'd built between them had been washed away in the wake of everything that had happened.

When he'd arrived at the S&C facility, he hadn't been looking for someone to love. But he'd found her nevertheless, and the thought that circumstances beyond his control were conspiring to take her away was almost more than he could bear.

He couldn't stand it. Sucking in a fortifying breath, he flung open the door, to find her standing in front of the mirror, staring blankly at her naked reflection, tears glistening on her face.

"Mia? Sweetheart, are you all right?"

At first he thought she hadn't heard him, but then she turned, reaching out for him, her eyes brimming with tears. "Hold me," she whispered. "*Please.* I can't get them out of my head. I can't stop seeing them lying there. Please, Nick, help me."

He closed the space between them in seconds, his arms coming around her in a gentle embrace. "You're shivering. Have you had a shower?" he asked, rubbing his hands over her arms and shoulders, her skin clammy and cold beneath his fingers.

She shook her head, and he let go long enough to reach out and turn on the spigots, testing to make sure the water was warm enough.

"Come on," he urged. "We need to get you warmed up. It'll make you feel better."

She nodded, but made no effort to move away from him.

"Sweetheart, there's a possibility you're going into shock." He'd seen it before in people who'd gone through a hell of a lot less.

"Okay," she nodded, still shivering, "but only if you come, too." In other circumstances the line would have been a come-on, but he knew Mia just needed reassurance. To physically feel that she wasn't alone in all of this.

"All right. We'll do it together." He stripped off his clothes and then maneuvered them both into the shower stall. The water ran over them, pounding against their skin. She stood still in the circle of his arms, tilting her head up, letting the water stream down her face and throat.

Nick took the bar of soap and slowly, gently began to wash her. Starting with her shoulders and working down in soothing circles, until she was slippery with lather. Gritting his teeth, he tried not to think about what he was doing, what he was touching. He tried to ignore the single-minded part of his body already tightening with need.

Mia sighed with contentment as he slid his hands around her, soaping her breasts and her stomach, suds sliding down between her thighs. Her nipples hardened beneath his palms, and he swallowed a groan, pushing back his desire. This was about Mia. Her needs. Not his.

He ran his hand lower, his heart pounding so loudly he was certain she could hear it, hear the blood as it raced through his body, pooling in his groin. And then with a little moan, she leaned back against him, lifting her hands to stroke his face. Moving slowly against him, pushing closer into the curve of his body, the water forming a curtain around them.

Then slowly, she turned to him, her eyes clear as they met his. For the moment, at least, her grief had been vanquished. Her breath caught as she reached up to trace the bandage on his shoulder, her body trembling against his.

"I'm sorry," she whispered.

"Mia, believe me, you have nothing to be sorry for."

Steam from the shower swirled around them and he reached out to pull her closer, her soapy skin sliding against his, the sensation almost more than he could bear. He spread his hands across the small of her back, letting the heat from the water beat down on them, and then with a groan he bent his head, taking possession of her mouth.

She raised her arms, her breasts pressed against his chest, the friction of their bodies rubbing together intensified by the pulsing water. He tried to maintain rational thought, but his heart was beating in tandem with hers and he knew that, at least for this moment, all that mattered was the two of them.

With a sigh, he bent and took one of her breasts into his mouth, circling it with his tongue, feeling the nipple tighten with his touch. Holding her with one hand, he moved the other in slow circles down her abdomen. Sliding lower and then lower still, until he slipped one finger inside, her heat surrounding him. She cried out as his finger moved deeper, and he smiled, gently biting her nipple.

She arched back, eyes closed, offering herself. The steam and the water only heightening the pleasure of stroking her, loving her. And he felt himself harden until the throbbing of blood matched the beat of the water.

He shifted, bringing his lips back to hers, and pushed her against the wall of the shower, the tiles cool beneath his hands. He ached to bury himself inside her. The water was behind them now, a fine mist caressing them both.

Holding her steady with his body, he cupped his hands under her hips, lifting her up. With a moan, she twined her legs around him, the invitation more than he could bear. In a single motion he thrust himself inside her, the sweet hot suction sending him to the brink.

With driving need, he began to move faster, her rhythm matching his. She wrapped her arms around him, holding tightly as he held her pinned above the world, everything in him centered on the exquisite feel of her body surrounding him as he pounded deeper and deeper, until there was nothing left except the two of them locked together, spiraling toward release.

Then suddenly she cried his name and the world spun out of control, pleasure exploding through him with unbelievable strength. As the powerful contractions consumed him, he could feel her body shuddering around his, and knew that he'd found a contentment beyond anything he'd ever imagined.

Slowly, he let her go, her body sliding against his as together they sank to the floor of the shower. He pulled her into his lap, her head nestled against his shoulder, the shower's gentle rain washing them tenderly with fine fingers of mist.

For the moment, at least, they'd managed to hold the darkness at bay. But Nick knew better than most that shadows had a way of resurfacing just when you'd convinced yourself that they were gone for good.

CHAPTER TWENTY-FOUR

MIA STRUGGLED AGAINST the images rolling through her brain. She knew it was a dream, knew that all she had to do to escape was open her eyes. But the weight of her mind's fantasy was too heavy, the dream clutching at her, holding her back, trying to bury her with the sheer horror of its existence.

She fought, rising through layers of sleep, only to be pulled back again. And then suddenly, she was awake, gasping for breath, the remnants of the nightmare receding into the shadows. The room was still dark, the blue-black sky framed by the window indicating it was still the middle of the night. She reached for Nick, needing the comfort of his warmth and solidity.

But he wasn't there.

Panic surfaced again and she fought against it, sitting up and shaking her head to clear her thoughts. She was strong enough to handle this on her own. Whatever was happening between her and Nick, she mustn't allow herself to depend on him for everything. She'd learned a long time ago that the only person she could really trust was herself. And now wasn't the time to forget the lesson.

She got out of bed and slipped into her jeans, then grabbed a T-shirt from the end of the bed. It was only as the soft cotton slid over her head and shoulders that she realized it was Nick's, the simple smell of him making her body quiver with desire.

She breathed deeply and then wrapped her arms around her waist, remembering his gentle ministrations in the shower. He'd washed her and held her, and only at her invitation had things become decidedly more heated.

When, she wondered, had she allowed herself to fall in love with him? Was it the night he'd burst into the line shack, daring her to team up with him, despite their mutual distrust? Or the night they'd jumped from a rooftop and managed to escape in a delivery van? Or maybe it was the night they'd first made love, when she'd desperately needed his touch to help her heal.

So many moments, in so short a time. Yet there was no doubt in her mind. She loved Nick Price. Loved him with an intensity she wouldn't have believed was possible a week ago—hell, a lifetime ago.

Smiling to herself, she headed out to the hallway and down the stairs. If she'd learned anything at all in the past few days, it was that life had to be lived now, because tomorrow wasn't a guarantee. Who knew if she and Nick had a chance in the real world? Who knew if they'd even survive long enough to find out?

For the moment, he was here with her, and that all by itself was miracle enough for now. Like Scarlett O'Hara, she'd face tomorrow another day.

She stopped at the bottom of the stairs, suddenly feeling awkward, the momentary buoyancy she'd felt in the wake of admitting her true feelings evaporating with the reality of the scene before her. Matt was leaning over the coffee table, studying something on the computer. No doubt making plans to find proof of their suspicions and vindicate her friends.

"Where's Nick?" she asked, stepping into the room, blinking at the bright light.

"He's checking the perimeter. We've been taking turns."

"And everything's okay, right?" Fear surfaced. "No sign of Davies?"

Matt shook his head, his gaze comforting. "There's no one out there. Nick just wants to confirm the fact. In case you hadn't noticed, he's a little overprotective when it comes to you."

Mia frowned, not certain how to answer.

"Don't get me wrong, Mia. I think it's a good thing."

"Really?" She perched on the arm of the sofa, chewing absently on her fingernail.

"You're going to make yourself bleed," Matt observed.

She jerked her finger back, self-consciously fisting her hand to hide her ragged cuticles. "That's what my grandfather always said."

"At least it proves the perfect girl is far from... well—" he grinned "—perfect."

"Believe me, I'm anything but."

"None of us are." He shrugged. "But I've got to admit I like what I see. Which is why I feel like I need to warn you about Nick. I'm sensing that there's more between the two of you than just friendship."

Mia opened her mouth to deny the fact, then closed it again on a sigh. Matt could see the truth. It was written all over her face, and nothing she said was going to negate the fact. "So what are you trying to warn me about? Katie? I already know, Matt. He told me everything."

"Wow, that's some mojo you've got going. Nick hardly ever talks about Katie, not even with me."

"I can't even imagine what it must have been like. To watch his sister die…" She trailed off helplessly.

"Actually, Mia, I think you do know. You've been through a lot these past few days. I was there when you found your friends' bodies, remember? It doesn't get any worse than that."

"But it wasn't my sister."

"Families come in all shapes and sizes. I don't share blood with Nick, but I'd defend him with my life. Hell, I've done so on more than one occasion."

"And he'd do the same for you."

"Yeah, he would. And I just wanted to say that I think you're good for him. And when we get to the other side of this, maybe there'll be something there for the two of you to build on."

"I feel kind of like you're giving me permission."

Matt laughed. "I guess maybe I am. Hell of a lot of nerve, right?"

"No. I envy the friendship the two of you have. Even with all that I've had in my life—and there's been a lot— I've never had someone I could count on like that. Someone I could trust to that degree."

"Well, now you do." The simple words wound their way through her brain, and for the first time since the explosion in Cedar Branch, Mia felt hope. Real hope.

"Thank you," she whispered softly, her smile negating the tears.

"Well, before you get all maudlin on me, I should also tell you that if you hurt Nick, all the evolved genes in the world aren't going to save you from me. Got it?"

She nodded solemnly and then they both started to laugh.

"So, what?" Nick bellowed, striding into the room. "You making moves on my girl now?"

"Yeah, right—like she has eyes for anyone else."

"Just want to make sure you're keeping your hands to yourself," Nick said with a grin, coming to perch next to her on the arm of the sofa. "He's a notorious flirt."

"And exceedingly good at it, too," Mia quipped, feeling absurdly happy considering the severity of the situation.

"Everything's clear outside," Nick said. "No sign of Davies or any of his men."

"Well, that's a comfort," Mia said with a shiver, her good mood evaporating with the thought of Davies.

Nick frowned, reaching for her hand. "You okay?"

How could she possibly explain that everything was awful and wonderful all at the same time? She felt guilty for even entertaining the notion of being happy in the wake of her friends' deaths. But she also felt as if she were poised on the brink of something absolutely amazing. "I'm fine," she said. "I just couldn't sleep anymore."

Nick's gaze held more questions, but he didn't ask, and she was grateful for the reprieve. She'd just had a heart-to-heart with Matt. And even though it had been positive, she wasn't ready for round two. And certainly not in front of Matt.

"I was just about to fill Mia in on our plans to get into Biosphere," Matt said, pulling them both back to the matter at hand. "I managed to locate a local driving schedule for ASI. Looks like we're in luck. A truck is due at Biosphere at five-thirty this morning."

"The shredding company?" She remembered seeing the truck just before Davies had grabbed her. "I'm not sure I'm following."

"Security at Biosphere is bound to be at a premium. Especially thanks to Matt's handiwork at the S&C facility. Which means if we're going to get in, we've got to be creative."

"So we're going to pose as employees of ASI?" It wasn't a bad idea, but considering their timeframe it seemed a lot to put together, even with Nick and Matt's connections.

"No," Matt said, shaking his head. "We're just going to use the truck. It's a cabover 'straight truck' with a twenty-foot box." He turned the laptop so she could see it.

"Do I look like a trucker?" she asked. "Normalese, please?"

"Sorry," Matt said. "When I was a kid, I spent a summer with my uncle driving his rig. Basically it's a big truck, and the container's tall enough so that a couple of people riding on top aren't likely to be detected coming through the Biosphere gate. Even if Davies and crew are in megasearch mode."

"And exactly how are you all planning for us to get up there?" Mia asked. "I'm assuming there's not a ladder."

"That's where it gets interesting," Nick said. The two were grinning like a couple of testosterone-driven adolescents. "We're going to have to jump."

"Off what?" She already knew she wasn't going to like the answer.

"There's a low overpass on 287 just past the exit for Biosphere. The access road goes under it before curving around onto the county road traveling south." Matt hit a key and the screen changed to the image of a map. "The bridge is just over fourteen feet, which means it's really only a step down."

"Onto a moving vehicle." Mia frowned. "Won't they hear us?"

"Not likely. Cabs these days are pretty soundproof. And the box is a completely separate unit. Combined with road noise and probably the radio, the driver won't hear a thing."

"Assuming we don't wind up as roadkill." The two of them had obviously lost their minds.

"Well, we are going to tip the odds in our favor a bit. A contact of ours is going to pace the truck, and when he gets to the exit, he'll pull in front of the driver and slow him down. My guess is that the guy will be so pissed he wouldn't notice if an elephant landed on the back of the rig."

"Don't you think it's risky getting someone else involved?" she asked.

"Matt didn't tell him anything specific. Just that we needed the truck slowed down."

"But won't he feel obligated to report in?"

"No. He's not exactly playing on our team," Matt said. "He's more of switch-hitter. So there's really no one for him to report to. And the truth is the whole plan is risky. But it's our best chance."

"So you really think we can do this?" Visions of her head going splat on the concrete weren't upping Mia's enthusiasm.

"I know we can," Nick said. "And frankly, Matt's right. We don't have much of a choice. You know as well as I do that they're going to be working overtime to cover their tracks. And since we know about the Montana facility, my guess is they'll do what's necessary to make sure it looks innocent."

"Oh, God," Mia said, her stomach sinking with the thought. "What if they've already done that? What if there's nothing left to find?"

"There hasn't been time," Nick assured her. "Besides,

we know that there's an ASI truck scheduled to be at Bio-sphere in a couple of hours, which means there's still something to be destroyed."

"And in addition to that, we're the only real threat to concealing the truth," Matt said. "Which means that they're far more likely to be spending their time trying to find us than moving the facility."

"Exactly," Nick agreed. "So if we can get in, there's a good chance we'll find something."

"But won't they be expecting us? They know we can't do anything without proof. And the only way to get that is to break into the facility in Montana."

"Yeah, they'll be watching, but they were watching for Matt and me at the S&C facility, too, and look where that got them."

"Point taken," Mia said, holding up a hand in surrender. "I'm not trying to be a naysayer. I just want us to look before we leap, if you'll excuse the pun."

"That's one of the reasons the ASI truck plays so nicely into our plans," Matt said. "We're in and out before they have time to regroup. And at five-thirty in the morning, I don't think there'll be that many people on-site, which will play to our advantage, as well. Hell, Waters will barely have had time to call it in. Which means Davies will want to see the damage himself before mobilizing a new plan of action."

"Which begs the question as to where our illustrious enemy was during the raid," Nick said. "I didn't see any sign of him at all. Did he say anything to you that might have indicated where he was going?"

"No. He was more interested in intimidation." She reached up to touch the bruise on her face, then self-consciously dropped her hand again. The last thing she needed was to remind Nick of what Davies had done. He hated the man enough already.

"Well, I can promise you one thing," Nick said, anger flashing. "When I get hold of Davies, he'll wish he had never touched a hair on your head."

"Revenge is never what it's cracked up to be," she said. "You told me that. And you're right. All that's important here is to find proof of what happened in Cedar Branch and then make certain the people who're responsible pay. One way or the other, Davies will get his."

"So what exactly are we going to be looking for when we get inside?" Matt asked, as usual, steering them away from emotional minefields.

"There's no way to know for sure," Nick said, standing up to pace in front of the window. "But I'd think anything that documents our theory that a biochemical weapon was released in Cedar Branch."

"And we need to find evidence that conclusively connects Kresky and Tucker to the project," Mia said.

"Well, sitting here talking about it isn't going to accomplish anything," Nick said. "What we need to do is finalize our plans and get moving. We've got to be in place in less than two hours."

"There's one more thing we've got to talk about," Matt said. "I've been thinking about what happens if for some reason we fail. Either because we can't find anything or, worse yet, because Davies outmaneuvers us. We need a fallback position. Something that guarantees that if the worst happens, the information we do have gets into the hands of someone who'll take up the fight."

"You think we should tell Gordon." Nick's eyes narrowed as he considered the idea.

"I think he's the only one we know for certain we can trust. Ricks might have bought into the CIA's bullshit, but not Gordon."

"Gordon Armstrong is the one who convinced me to come work for Homeland Security," Nick said, by way of explanation.

"The lieutenant in Special Forces?" Mia asked.

"Yeah." He nodded. "He's the one."

"Look," Mia said with a sigh, "I know you both have history with this Gordon guy. But my experience so far with Homeland Security hasn't been all that great. They didn't even hesitate when they bought into the idea of Nick as a traitor. Basically, they bent over for the CIA. And since the CIA seems to be playing a major role in covering up the deaths of my friends, I'm not too keen on them, either, at the moment."

"All right," Matt said, "how about this? We don't send the information now. I can route it so that it isn't delivered until after we're safely inside Biosphere. It'll be too late to stop us, but at least that way there'll be someone with all the facts. Someone to take over if we don't come out of this alive."

"I'm with Matt, Mia. I think we can trust Gordon."

"I don't know, I—"

"Look," Matt said, closing the laptop and pushing to his feet, "it's my turn to check outside. So why don't I take care of that and you guys can decide what you want to do about notifying Gordon."

"He's a good guy," Mia said, watching as Matt walked out the door. "You're lucky to have a friend like that."

"We're both lucky," Nick said, coming to sit on the table in front of her. "If you're still uncomfortable about telling Gordon what we think happened in Cedar Branch, there is another way we can be certain that the information is safe."

"If you're thinking about asking me to sit this one out, I can tell you right now it's not going to happen."

"All I'm saying is that Matt and I are used to doing this kind of stuff."

"Well, I've had a crash course. Besides, this is my fight. If I hadn't survived the batrachotoxin, or whatever its new derivative is called, then you wouldn't be here at all. I'm not risking your life on something I'm not willing to do myself, Nick. It was my town they destroyed. My friends. And I'm going to see this through."

"I just don't want anything to happen to you," he said, taking her hands.

"And I don't want anything happening to you. But the only way I can put this behind me and start a life with you is to see it through to the finish." The minute the words were out, she wished them back. They hadn't made any promises. He hadn't even told her he how he felt about her, and here she was talking about the future. "I'm sorry. I shouldn't have—"

He cut her off, pressing a finger against her lips. "I want a future, too, Mia. With you, if you'll have me. I love you. And that means I have to let you follow your own path. Even if it scares the hell out of me. So we'll do this together. Okay?"

She nodded, tears pricking the back of her eyes. "Honest to God, it's not Davies that worries me. It's jumping off of that freaking bridge."

"Don't worry," he said with a smile. "If you get scared, I'll just push you off."

CHAPTER TWENTY-FIVE

THE DROP ONTO THE TRUCK would be only a couple feet. Not far at all. But the truck wasn't here, and all Mia could see was the drop from the overpass to the asphalt below. And it looked frighteningly lethal.

In theory the ASI truck would be moving more slowly, already on the access road, and hopefully preceded by Nick and Matt's contact driving well under the speed limit. But the guardrail was there for a reason. Jumpers weren't encouraged.

The gray skies and low-hanging clouds didn't help matters any, the chilly wind easily penetrating her cotton sweater.

"You ready?" Nick said, offering her a leg up to cross the railing. Matt was already on the other side.

"As I'll ever be." She stepped into his hand and was up and over in seconds. "How much longer do we have?"

"I've got Rodney in view now," Matt said, looking through his field glasses. "The ASI truck is about four meters behind. ETA about three minutes."

"Matt will go first, then you, then me," Nick said, joining them bridgeside. "There won't be much time. So there's no room for hesitation. Just step off and brace with your knees."

She nodded, not willing to waste energy on words.

"They're coming," Matt said, his muscles already tensing for the jump.

Mia waited, breath held, as Rodney's red Volvo came out from under the bridge.

"This is it," Nick whispered, his hand firmly in the small of her back. Matt leapt forward, and with a decided shove, Nick sent Mia following after.

For one second she was falling and then her feet connected with the roof of the truck's container. Matt grabbed her hand, helping her as she dropped down to lie flat on her stomach, the reassuring sound of Nick's landing signaling that they were all three safely in place.

The truck's horn bellowed, the driver no doubt cursing the Volvo. Nick crawled forward, his body half covering hers as they lay together in the center of the container's roof, Matt lying just in front of them.

The wind up top was less powerful than she'd expected, no worse, actually, than driving in a convertible. It had something do with pressure and velocity, but physics had never been her bailiwick, so she closed her eyes and let the air rush over her.

It seemed like only moments later that the truck began to slow down, Nick's hand on her arm signaling that they were approaching Biosphere's front gate.

She lifted her head, her heart pounding as the truck slowed.

"Just keep still," he whispered, lifting enough to produce his gun. "Everything's going to be fine."

Matt, who had his gun out as well, signaled for them to duck down, and Mia hugged the metal roof, thinking herself as small as possible. The truck lurched to a stop, the resulting silence almost deafening.

Mia could hear the driver and the man at the gate discussing the early hour and the impending rain. Nothing out of the ordinary. Nothing at all to indicate that either of them were aware the truck was carrying three passengers.

A few more minutes passed as the men exchanged banalities, and then the driver shifted into gear and the truck rumbled into the compound.

"So far so good," Nick whispered, shooting a thumbs-up in Matt's direction.

They drove past a parking lot, and Mia was relieved to see that there were only a couple of cars. She knew better than to underestimate Davies, but hopefully, time was still on their side.

The truck slowed as it approached the loading bay for the main building, gliding to a stop and then into reverse as the driver carefully backed the truck into the bay. A man in coveralls stood on the dock, directing the maneuver with hand motions.

"Slide closer to the front," Nick whispered. "If we can see him, there's a chance he can see us."

Mia inched forward, Nick moving in tandem at her side until they were level with Matt. Below them the truck door slammed.

"The driver will go with the guy on the dock to retrieve the bins that need to be shredded. My guess is the whole procedure will take about an hour. Which means we've got to be fast," Matt said, careful to keep his voice low.

Snippets of conversation reached them as the driver and the dock worker greeted each other, their voices receding as they left the dock.

"Let's move," Nick said, already scrambling for the back of the container.

The drop to the dock was minimal. Mia landed on her feet, pulling out the gun Nick had provided. "What next?"

"We case the place and try and find proof that Biosphere is in fact producing a new biochemical weapon. We've got about fifty minutes before we meet back here."

They moved over to the doorway, Matt covering their backs while Nick stepped into the hall to make sure everything was clear.

"We're good," he whispered, motioning them forward. Matt waited for Mia and then followed her into the hall.

The bay doors sat roughly in the middle of what appeared to be a perimeter hallway stretching off to the left and right. The walls were painted a generic shade of gray-blue, the dark blue industrial grade carpet only adding to the institutional feel. The hallway ran the length of the building, with three additional corridors branching off from it, one at each end and one bisecting the middle of the building.

"Any sign we've got someone watching?" Matt asked, his gaze tracing the line of the ceiling. "I don't see any security cameras."

"Me, either. Could be they're all external. I definitely saw them outside on the perimeter fencing."

"Well, we're in and the enemy isn't charging. Seems to me we might as well take a look around. And since we don't know exactly what we're looking for it might be better if we split up," Matt said. "Why don't we each take a hallway, and reconvene at the other end."

"You all right on your own?" Nick asked, his expression telling her exactly what he thought of the idea.

"I'll be fine," she said, with what she hoped was a confident smile. "Besides, if we're going to make our ride home, we need to use our time as efficiently as possible. I'll go left. You take the center and Matt can go right."

He stood for a minute, clearly considering putting a kibosh on the whole idea, then reached out to cup her chin. "Be careful. All right?"

She nodded, and with a last look, he headed down his corridor. Matt shot her a smile and a thumbs-up and went off to the right, stopping when he reached a closed office door.

Mia sucked in a breath and set off left. Knowing that Matt still had her back, more or less, she pushed open a door identical to the one on his side of the hallway. She waited a moment, then, leading with her gun, stepped into the room.

It was empty. Not so much as a paper clip on the floor. Unless Davies had a cleaning crew following him around, there was no way this space had been used by anyone anytime in the recent past. In fact, it looked more like an office furniture display. The kind found in one of those warehouse supply stores.

She stuck her head out of the office and, satisfied that the way was clear, stepped back into the corridor. Matt emerged from the second office, shaking his head with an exaggerated shrug that indicated that it was empty, too.

She signaled confirmation and then made her way to the left end of the hall. She glanced over her shoulder in time to see Matt disappearing around a corner. With a breath for fortification she edged into the new hallway paralleling the one Nick was searching.

Like the first, it was empty, with only a couple of doors opening off it on either side. A quick search revealed more empty offices. The same setup, the same furniture, as if one room had simply cloned another. A couple of them had phone lines, and one held a stack of blank notepads, but other than that, there was nothing to indicate that the offices had ever been occupied.

She'd seen the truck driver and the man on the dock walk into the building—which meant that unless they'd simply disappeared into space, they had to be here somewhere. And if she found them, she was fairly certain she'd find Biosphere—if there was anything left to find.

The last doorway was a little larger than the others, with windows on either side. She reached out to open the door, then dropped back, waiting for a noise or some other kind of signal that someone was inside. But the room remained quiet.

Counting silently to three, she swung into the opening, gun hand braced on her left arm. Scanning the room, she moved the weapon in an arc from right to left, lowering it only when she was certain that the office was unoccupied.

Here there was more sign of activity. A credenza with a blotter and a pencil holder sat directly in front of her. Behind that was a desk with a computer. A stack of papers lay in a basket on the corner of the credenza. She picked one up, and a shiver ran down her spine as she read the letterhead.

Biosphere.

She skimmed the document, but was disappointed to find that it contained nothing more than a report on the ecological status of the mining area near Virginia City, an accompanying map documenting where mines still existed, and what kinds of dangers they presented to the surrounding habitats.

The rest of the pile yielded more of the same: environmental impact studies and results of testing on the various ecosystems in the area. She put the papers back into the wire basket, trying to contain her disappointment. If these were to be believed, Biosphere was in fact an environmental organization tasked with studying the impact of mining on the area's flora and fauna.

It didn't make sense. Why all the security if there was nothing to hide?

She turned on the computer, scanning the room for possible danger as she waited for the machine to boot up. There was a second door in the back of the room, making her wonder if this was some kind of reception area. Or a secretary's cubicle.

The computer's boot-up melody rang loudly through the office and she jumped, diving for the mouse to mute the volume. The same green logo featured on the letterhead filled the screen: a spinning globe with the word *Biosphere* flashing beneath it.

She clicked on the program files, quickly sorting through the various directories until she came to one labeled *documents*. She moved the mouse to open the directory, surprised when she wasn't prompted for a password. She opened the first document and found a report similar to the one she'd found in the basket. A second and third file revealed much the same. Reports, budgets, everything to indicate that Biosphere was exactly what it was billed to be.

She perused a couple more documents, and was just moving back to the main directory list when a noise from behind the door at the back of the room sent her heart skidding into overdrive.

Ducking down behind the desk, she reached up to turn the computer off, risking a quick look in the direction of the noise. The doorknob was turning, the door squeaking ever so slightly as it started to swing open. Dropping back into a crouch, silently fingering her gun, she tried to figure out the best way to escape.

The desk protected her from the intruder's view, but the credenza behind her blocked her escape back to the hallway. In order to reach it, she'd have to stand up. And that would put her directly in the line of sight of the person who'd entered the office.

She waited, listening intently for some sign as to the intruder's location, but the carpet effectively muffled his footsteps. A crack between the edge of the desk front and carpet allowed a minimal view of the area right in front of the desk.

She squeezed more tightly into the knee hole, her blood pressure ratcheting up another notch when her foot hit the side of the desk, the noise seeming abnormally loud in the quiet room.

Lifting the gun, she readied herself for confrontation, shifting so that she could more easily dive from underneath the desk.

A shoe appeared in her peripheral vision and she tightened her hold on the gun.

"Move one more inch and I'll shoot." Nick's voice was followed by his jean-clad legs as he stepped into the space between the credenza and the desk.

"It's me," she said, her voice rising two octaves.

"Shit, Mia," Nick said, reaching down to drag her out from under the desk. "I damn near shot you."

"Well, it would have been a double murder," she said, waving her gun at him. "What the hell are you doing in here? You're supposed to be in the other hallway."

"The offices connect."

She released a breath she hadn't realized she'd been

holding, resisting the urge to throw herself into his arms. "I thought you were one of Davies's people."

"Yeah, well, we were on the same wavelength." He reached out to tuck a strand of hair behind her ear, his touch intimate, his eyes saying things he couldn't tell her with words. Then he pulled back, his mind clearly returning to the task at hand. "So what have you got here?" he asked, motioning to the computer and desk.

"Papers and files supporting the fact that Biosphere is an environmental company geared toward investigating industrial impact on specific ecosystems. In this case, the old mines around Virginia City. The rest of the offices I checked were empty. Almost as though they'd never been used."

"It was pretty much the same thing in my corridor," Nick said. "A couple of empty offices and a supply closet. Lots of Biosphere letterhead. And the office connecting to this one has the same kind of information as what you found here. There's even a file cabinet full of impact studies. Groundwater, deforestation, geological readings, that kind of thing."

The door behind them inched open and Nick spun around, pushing Mia behind him as he leveled his gun.

"Hey," Matt said, stepping into the room. "No shooting. I'm with the good guys."

Nick relaxed, lowering his gun. "I seem destined to take you two out."

"Hey, you're the one with the happy trigger finger," Matt said, holding up his hands in mock surrender. "You all finding the same Biosphere—We're Saving the World—bullshit?"

"In here," Mia said, motioning to the computer behind her. "But the rest of the offices I checked were empty except for furniture."

"Same here," Matt said, "Except for across the hall." He jerked a finger toward the door behind them, "There's a mirror setup to this one. A two-office suite complete with maps and bound environmental impact studies as thick as my arm."

"So what does it all mean?" she asked, fighting frustration. "That we did all this for nothing? That Biosphere is legit?"

"No way," Nick said. "This is all too pat. The empty offices, the conveniently staged files. None of it feels real."

"So you think it's a setup?" Mia asked, her eyes shooting to the doorway.

"Not for us, if that's what you're thinking," Matt said. "My guess is it's for any kind of prying eyes. People who have to come and go for various reasons—vendors, or the like. They see all this and they don't ask questions. If we were here during business hours there'd probably be real live pseudo employees, too."

"It's pretty darn elaborate for a cover," Mia said with a frown, looking at the topographical map on the wall, complete with flags marking mines, and colored circles identifying unique ecosystems.

"Well, the reality is not exactly something they want the locals talking about. So the charade is necessary. Besides, if all of this is real, then where are the dock worker and the guy from ASI? They've got to be here somewhere. And if we can find them, I'm betting we'll find the real Biosphere."

"Maybe they're in one of the outbuildings," Matt suggested.

"It's possible, although paper is heavy, so you'd think our driver would want to park as close as possible to the bins containing the stuff to be shredded. It just doesn't make sense for him to leave the truck here and then haul things from another building."

"Hang on," Matt whispered, pointing to the door behind the credenza. "There's someone out there." Nick and Matt moved to the walls flanking the windows on either side of the door, and Mia hit the ground again, this time between the desk and the credenza.

From her vantage point she could see the bottom of the window to the left of the door. A rhythmic squeak grew louder as whoever was walking down the corridor approached. Mia held her breath as the noise stopped just outside the door, the wheels of a dolly appearing in the window.

The silence stretched thin, and then the squeaking began again, the dolly disappearing as it was pushed on down the hall.

"That was the guy from ASI," Nick said, motioning her up from the floor.

"No sign of the dock man, though." Matt lowered his gun and blew out a breath.

"Probably more than one container of paper to be shredded. My guess is he'll shred this round and then come back for the next."

"But where the hell did he come from?" Mia asked, daring a peek down the hall, the ASI uniform clearly visible as the man rounded the corner.

"That's what I'd like to know," Nick said, frowning. "You guys didn't see anything but empty offices, right?"

"Except for the one across the hall," Matt confirmed, "and it's just like this one. A door on the central corridor and one leading to the outside corridor, with a connecting door in between."

"Well, he had to come from somewhere." Mia leaned back against the desk with a sigh. "And if we don't figure it out soon, we're going to be dodging company." She glanced at her watch, confirming that time was slipping by.

"There's nothing to do but search again," Nick said. "Only this time I think maybe we'd better stick together."

Matt was nodding in agreement when the squeaking wheels signaled the shredder's return. He passed the office door again and rounded the corner. On Nick's signal, the three of them shifted to the other office, waiting to hear what direction the squeaking wheels went.

The noise grew louder as he approached the corner, and then, just as Mia was certain he was going to turn into the central hallway, the sound stopped. They waited for a minute and then another one, the silence holding.

Matt turned to Nick with a shake of his head. "Where did he go?"

Nick frowned, cracking open the outer office door. Leading with his gun, he took a step into the hallway and then stepped back into the office. "There's no one out there."

"But there has to be," Mia said. "We all heard him. Hell, we all saw him. He can't have just disappeared."

"Maybe he went into one of the offices?" Matt suggested without any real conviction.

"The noise stopped just as he reached the center corridor," Mia said. "So maybe we should check that office."

"It's not an office. It's the supply closet I was telling you about…." Nick trailed off with a frown, moving back out into the hallway, Mia and Matt following in his wake. He yanked the door open. Shelves lined the back wall, each of them filled with office supplies: printer ink, reams of unused paper, envelopes, boxes of letterhead. The bottom two shelves were divided into cubbies containing boxes of paper clips, pens, staples and tape. The same accoutrements found in any office.

But something about it felt off. Mia pushed past the men to stand in the doorway, trying to figure out what it was that bothered her. She picked up a box of staples, the label indicating it had been purchased from one of the big chains. The reams of paper bore the same mark. She put them back and reached up for a box of letterhead. It was the same as what she'd seen in the office.

There was nothing here that seemed out of place, but it still felt wrong.

"Well, he obviously didn't come in here," Matt said. "Maybe we should search the rest of the corridor again."

"Wait," Mia said, holding up a hand. "Something isn't right here." She scanned the closet again, letting her artist's eyes move from top to bottom and then back again. And then suddenly she saw it. "The depth isn't right."

Nick had moved to stand beside her. "I'm not sure what you mean."

"Look at the top shelf at either corner. I'm thinking it's about two and a half feet from the front of the shelf to the back of the wall."

Matt moved up behind them, both men looking up at the shelving.

"It's deeper than the rest. See?" She pointed to the third and fourth one. "The back of the other shelves is about a foot and a half closer than the top one."

"Which means there's space behind the lower shelves," Nick said, clearly following her train of thought.

"But that doesn't make sense," Matt said, frowning. "Unless…"

"Exactly." Mia nodded, reaching up to feel along the crevice running the length of the left side between adjacent walls. The seam between the two was solid until she reached the third shelf. "There's an indentation here." She pressed downward, a sharp click and then a mechanical whirring accompanying the motion.

A panel in the right-hand wall popped open, the shelving sliding silently into the resulting gap to reveal the polished metal door of an elevator.

Mia took a step back, her heart in her throat. "I think we just found the real Biosphere."

CHAPTER TWENTY-SIX

"So what do we do now?" Matt asked.

Nick moved around Mia, scanning the newly revealed door and wall. To the left was a call button, situated above a magnetic panel that most likely worked to automatically open the shelving when the elevator arrived at the top. To the right was a second button, next to a short expanse of wall abutting the corner. Centered above the button was a keypad, a light shining red at the bottom.

"Obviously, we've got to go down there," Mia said. "Except that there's no way to know if there'll be someone in the elevator when we press the call button."

"So we wait for the ASI guy to come back and *then* we go down."

Nick tapped on the wood paneling next to the elevator, the hollow reverberation confirming his suspicions. He hit the button on the right, but nothing happened, the red light blinking in protest.

"You think there's something behind the panel?" Mia asked.

"Yeah, I think it's possible." Beside him, the elevator door vibrated a warning, the motion accompanied by the low-pitched whine of the elevator ascending.

"Looks like we're out of time," Matt said, already moving out the door.

"Wait," Mia said, pointing at the keypad. "The light's green."

"Must have granted access from below." Nick pushed the right-hand button again. This time the wall panel slid silently in behind the shelving, revealing a set of stairs leading downward. "Let's get out of here."

"Not to be a pain," Matt said, glancing at his watch, "but if we go down there, we could be kissing our ride out of here goodbye. If that's the guy from ASI—" he nodded toward the elevator door "—I'm betting this is the last trip."

"Then we'll just have to find another way out," Nick said, looking to Mia for confirmation.

"We've come this far," she said with a nod. "Matt?"

"Hey, I'm just along for the ride, but if we're planning on staying of our own volition, I suggest we hurry. The elevator's almost here." The humming grew louder, accompanied by the screech of the moving box, the noise only serving to underscore Matt's pronouncement.

"Let's do it, then."

Guns drawn, they stepped over the threshold, the panel automatically sliding shut behind them, the dim glow of the stairwell lighting beckoning them forward. "I'll go first," Nick said, starting down the stairs, keeping his back to the wall, Mia and Matt following behind.

The stairs were steeper than normal grade, cement risers clearly designed for maximum functionality with little thought for comfort. They turned twice, the landings merely serving the purpose of marking the depth of descent. There were no exit doors except the one at the top, and conceivably the one at the bottom.

As they descended, the light dimmed. Nick raised a hand to signal stop and stepped off the last riser to edge toward the windowed door. The hallway on the other side appeared to be empty, and he pulled the door open, nodding to Matt.

With almost a single motion, Nick swung out into the hall, Matt mirroring his movements so that they wound up back-to-back, their guns pointing in opposite directions. The hallway was windowed on one side, the opaque glass allowing light, but obscuring the view. "We're clear," Matt said, and Mia stepped out of the stairwell to join them.

"What now?" she asked.

"We try to find something that confirms our suspicions," Matt replied.

"I don't like the feel of this," Nick said, turning in a circle, searching for any signs that they were being watched. "It's too quiet down here."

"Could be that Davies has already been here," Matt offered. "Maybe he secured the area and called in ASI to deal with the remnants. We know they were trying to destroy evidence at the S&C facility. Maybe they started here first."

"Yeah, it's possible. But I just can't shake the feeling that this has all been too damn easy."

"Look, the sooner we see if there's anything to find, the sooner we can get the hell out of here." Mia moved past him to the single door that opened off the corridor.

Nick moved to flank Mia on the right, with Matt on her left. "Okay," Nick said, "Go slowly, and lead with your gun."

She nodded and, bracing her gun, swung into the room. Nick followed, with Matt staying at the door to make sure there were no surprise visitors. Everything remained quiet, the soft glow from electronics and lab lamps casting a greenish wash across the room.

"This place is huge." Mia walked to the center of the room, turning so that she could take in the entire expanse.

The space was open, divided only by workstations, some of them partitioned off with the same opaque glass that adorned the windowed walls dividing the room and the hall. Computers mixed in with microscopes, centrifuges and a variety of machinery Nick couldn't identify, but he had no doubt that it was in fact a lab. The far left wall had only one door, possibly leading to a smaller lab.

Across the room on the right side another door opened off of the central lab. The rest of the right-hand wall was covered with filing cabinets, the metal containers flanking the windowed lab to the right and the left, extending almost to the back of the room.

"So where do we start?" Mia's tone was hushed, as though they'd entered some kind of sanctuary. Perhaps in many ways that's exactly what they'd done. If nothing else, the lab was a shrine to man's inhumanity, his ability to rationalize even the most egregious of sins for the sake of what he believed was the greater good.

"Seems like the files and computers are the best bet. Why don't I take the files, since I'm not nearly as good on the computer as the two of you," Nick said. "Everyone stay alert."

Mia sat down at a computer near the center of the room, Matt choosing one closer to the front. Nick headed over to the file cabinets after rechecking the front hall for signs of activity. He stopped at Mia's cubicle, her face tinted green in the plasma glow of the computer. "Finding anything?"

"Nothing yet. I haven't managed to get past their password protection, but I will," she said without looking up from the computer, clearly engrossed. She'd laid her gun on the desk next to her, and he marveled at how normal it seemed, wondering how the hell she'd managed to move so effortlessly from art to espionage in just a matter of days.

Once again, he fought the urge to pick her up and carry her away from all of this. Somewhere safe. Somewhere far away from biotoxins and Davies and the memories of Cedar Branch. But she'd been right when she'd said that the only way they could move forward was to find closure for the past. Cedar Branch, Katie's death—all of it.

"Don't get so lost in cyberspace that you forget to keep watch."

She smiled absently. "No worries. I've got it covered."

With a quick nod, he moved on to the files. The sooner they found something, the sooner they'd be out of here and free of Davies and his bosses.

The filing cabinets were arranged in three distinct groups. The first contained scientific test results, some of them dating back almost ten years. Clearly, the research here had been going on for quite some time. Which synced with their theory that the newer facility in Cedar Branch had been for production, not research and development. It was clear that part of the mission had been accomplished here.

He skimmed files, trying to understand what he was reading, but the technical jargon was too difficult to decipher. The pages contained in the files consisted primarily of chemical equations and diagrams. There were charts and what appeared to be three separate trials or experiments. And although there was a chemical representation of batrachotoxin, there was nothing here to indicate definitively, to a layman, anyway, that they'd been working to manufacture the toxin.

The second group of filing cabinets was no more helpful than the first. The files here contained personnel information, time sheets, equipment requisitions and quality control reports. Again, there were hints that seemed to back their assumptions, but nothing concrete. Nothing that would finger any of the key players and certainly nothing to identify who ultimately was responsible for the project.

The last group of filing cabinets was topped by a series of gray binders. And it was here that Nick finally found something that might lead to confirmation of their theories. The binders contained research data not only on batrachotoxin, but on the frogs themselves. There were studies of the amphibians' genetic makeup, the chemical and biological connection between the frogs and the poison they emitted.

A woman in Madagascar had evidently discovered a similar toxin in the feathers of birds, and a study in Papua New Guinea had confirmed her theory that the larger animals, be they frogs or birds, had ingested the poison and through genetic adaptation had managed to create internal systems that allowed them to excrete the toxin without damage to themselves.

There were also articles on the chemical structure of batrachotoxin and its lack of antidote. Key passages highlighted, with notes in the margins, indicated that the reader or readers had been the same as those who'd authored the scientific reports and diagrams in the first group of files.

He replaced the last of the binders and opened a file drawer, reading through the titles. It started innocently enough with *Batrachotoxin*, the file revealing notations on toxicity, symptomology and diagnostics on time of death, based on the amount of toxin delivered. The test subjects ranged from mice to monkeys.

The second file was labeled *A-1*. The pages within it were almost exactly the same as those for batrachotoxin. Except the chemical diagram had clearly been modified, the notations within the file indicating that there had been success in dissolving the new toxin in alcohol to create an aerosol.

The next was labeled *A-2*, the next *A-3*, the *A* files terminating at *A-9*. From there the files switched to *B-1*, the chemical combination again slightly modified to create a newer, more potent version.

The files continued, drawer after drawer, letter by letter with ascending numbers—each manila folder holding documentation of increased success with newly synthesized versions of batrachotoxin. From a toxin with limited range and no ability to permeate skin beyond a direct puncture, the scientists had modified and restructured it until they wound up with *K-19*.

The last file.

According to the documentation, the final version had a toxicity increased tenfold from its parent, batrachotoxin, with the added benefits of aerosolisation capable of entering the human body through skin absorption and/or inhalation. It differed from the previous K versions in that it killed in minutes, and thanks to further chemical manipulation, dissipated in less than an hour, leaving the area safe for immediate occupation.

K-19 was the perfect weapon. It destroyed human life, not infrastructure, allowing an army to hit an enemy fortification or town, eliminate the opposition and occupy or confiscate the remaining buildings, tanks or weapons without fear of being exposed to the toxin themselves.

"You found it." Mia's voice pulled him from his contemplations. "K-19." She nodded toward the file he held. "It's documented on their computers, too. There are even 3D models showing the effect at varying ranges. And I found production notes as well. I'm printing them now. They were definitely manufacturing the stuff."

"Near Cedar Branch," Matt said, joining them, a piece of paper in his hand. "I found a budget for construction of the facility."

Nick took the document, scanning the page, while Mia read over his shoulder.

"Look at the bottom paragraphs," Matt said, his tone grim. "Where it says 'contingencies.'"

Nick read the words, then forced himself to read them again, just to be certain.

"My God," Mia whispered. "Intellectually, I knew it was true, but in my heart I wanted to be wrong."

Outlined in the last few paragraphs were security procedures for the new plant, including a list of adverse conditions that could potentially occur, a summary of the corresponding action that would be taken and a reference to numbered reports containing the actual plan.

The last one was titled *Contamination:*

Although all efforts have been made to secure the production of K-19, should accidental release result in contamination of the local population, measures will be taken to assure that, once autopsied, all casualties are destroyed, and the area cleansed using measures laid out in Report 7862, Appendix XV-8. Any additional action must be cleared through assigned security personnel or the CIA's S&C.

"They killed them," Mia said, her voice trembling with the effort to hang on to her emotions. "And they blew up the town to cover their mistake."

"At least we have verification," Matt offered, his face tight with anger.

"We've got proof that Kresky was involved, and through the memo, indirect confirmation that Davies was part of things, but there's still nothing here to tie it to Tucker," Nick said, fighting his own rage. It was hard to swallow the idea that Americans had died on American soil because some bastard decided to take nature in his own hands for the supposed benefit of the nation.

"So we keep looking," Mia said, her hands clenched. "I want to nail these bastards—all of them."

"We've got enough. We need to get out while we can." Matt looked to Nick for agreement.

"Matt's right. We've been here too long already."

"Just give me five more minutes with the computer. Please." She waited, watching them both.

Matt nodded first, and Nick had just opened his mouth to concur when the glass partition next to him shattered, a second round slamming into a file cabinet, the metal screeching in protest.

"Get down," Nick yelled, grabbing his gun, scrambling back over broken glass, trying to assess which direction the bullets had come from.

Matt popped up from behind a computer console a row or so away, firing toward the door. Answering volleys blew out the computer, but Matt had already scrambled out of range and Nick's vision.

Pinned for the moment, he waited to move, searching for Mia and some sign that she was still okay. Finally he saw her, behind him to the left, crawling along the floor, using the furniture for cover.

She lifted her gaze, her eyes meeting his. "My gun," she mouthed, pointing toward the center of the room.

He nodded, then popped up from the desk, shooting in the direction of the earlier shots, giving her cover. He dropped back, releasing a breath when he saw that she'd made it as far as the large lab table flanking the computer console.

He crawled forward, listening for anything that might give away the location of the intruders. The room was quiet. Then off to his left, at the corner of his peripheral vision, he saw a shadow shift across the front windows of the lab. Moving on instinct alone, he dove free of cover, firing at the window, shards of glass raining down into the room.

The shadow materialized, and he recognized Davies. Enraged, he rose up to shoot again, but before he could get the shot, a second gunman fired from somewhere just inside the front door. The bullet slammed into Nick's injured shoulder, the pain stunning him for a moment.

Matt materialized on the other side of the aisle created by the tables, firing over the top of one of the glass partitions, the distraction working long enough for Nick to pull back behind the comparative safety of a large metal desk.

Fighting to regain control, he managed to rip a strip from the bottom of his shirt. Using his teeth and good hand, he tied it around the upper part of his arm. The cloth immediately turned crimson, the improvised tourniquet only partially stanching the blood.

Shots rang out again, this time in the direction Mia had disappeared. He staggered to his feet, his head spinning with the effort, but he managed to fire in the direction the shots had emanated from.

"Hang on," Matt mouthed, popping up to fire again, another glass panel shattering on the far side of the room. He dashed across the distance between them, managing somehow to avoid the flying bullets. He slid down beside Nick. "How bad is it?"

"Not good. It might have nicked an artery. I can't tell, but there's a lot of blood."

Matt was already pulling off his T-shirt, ripping it neatly in two. Moving with a skill acquired on the battlefield, he quickly bound the wound again, his field dressing far superior to the one Nick had attempted.

"We need to get you out of here," Matt said.

"No. I can hold my own." Nick fought another wave of dizziness. "You've got to find Mia. I'll keep you covered."

"Any idea where she's gone?"

As if in answer, gunfire rang out again, this time coming from somewhere toward the back of the room. "Sounds like she found her gun," Nick said, grimacing as he shifted position. "Go get her. Then we'll get out of here."

"You sure you're going to be okay?" Matt hesitated, clearly not happy to be leaving him on his own.

"I'm fine. Just go." Nick pushed up to his knees, firing as a second shadow detached from the wall. The man turned and fired, the shot going wide. Nick fired again, this time sending the other man crashing back through the remaining glass partition.

He turned to look behind him, searching for signs of Mia or Matt.

Another round of gunfire erupted from somewhere off

to his left. Moving with grim determination, he crawled closer to the third gunman.

Ahead of him against the white of the far wall, he saw Mia stand up, saw her turn in his direction—the gunman's direction.

"Mia," he yelled, adrenaline pulling him to his feet. "Get down."

CHAPTER TWENTY-SEVEN

MIA HIT THE FLOOR, crawling backward through an open door behind her, the image of Nick covered in blood burned on her brain. Gunfire echoed through the main room, coming from two directions at once. Which meant that at least Nick and Matt were still alive.

Every instinct inside her was screaming for her to run to Nick, but she knew the gunmen would have the door covered. They'd seen her go in, which meant that they'd be waiting for her to come out. Or worse still, they'd come in to get her. She needed to be ready.

Inching deeper into the room, keeping her back to the wall, she searched the shadows for another way out. The room was cluttered. A table, a desk and a couple of book-shelves. She could see the shadows of other objects, but in the half-light she couldn't quite make out what they were.

Across from her on the far wall, she could see the glimmer of what looked to be a mirror. Careful to stay out of range of the gunmen, she shifted so that she had a better view, the reflection disappearing with her movement. It was a window, not a mirror, and the window was part of a door.

A second way out.

To reach it she'd have to cross the line of sight, but it seemed worth the risk if the doorway led to the hallway outside. She moved deeper into the room, crouching beside a desk.

Three quick steps and she'd be across the swath of light made by the open door. It was possible that this far in the gunman wouldn't be able to see her or even detect the motion. Taking a deep breath, she pushed off the ground to her feet and dashed across the open floor, almost upsetting a stack of cages in the process, the mice inside frantically scurrying, no doubt as startled as she was.

At least she wasn't completely alone.

A shadow filled the doorway, bullets strafing the cages, the mice now squeaking in protest. Mia dove for cover behind a bookcase, waiting and listening, her heart pounding in her throat.

"Miss Kearney?" a voice called. "I know you're in here."

She pressed against the hardwood back of the shelving, trying to identify the voice. But although it seemed vaguely familiar, it didn't evoke a name.

"Your friends are dead," the voice continued.

Her stomach dropped, but she maintained control. No matter what, Nick would want her to keep fighting.

"You might as well come out. It'll go easier for you if you do."

Like hell.

She popped up, firing a round. Stunned when the gun clicked harmlessly, the chamber empty. Matt had the extra ammo, which meant she was shit out of luck. But she'd be damned if she was going to go down easily.

"No bullets?" the voice asked, his tone taunting. "I'm afraid that means it's time to give up."

She couldn't see him, but his shadow stretched across the floor just to her right. She pushed lightly on the bookshelf, delighted to feel it give. Now all she had to do was wait.

"Come on, Mia," the gunman said, taking a step closer, his shoes clicking against the tile floor. "Don't make this harder than it has to be. I don't want to hurt you."

The shadow shifted until it disappeared, blocked by the shelving. Summoning all of her strength, Mia counted silently to three and pushed. The bookshelf teetered for a moment and then went crashing down, the man cursing as it caught him full in the chest, dragging him to the floor.

Not waiting to see the extent of the damage, she shot across the room to the second door, yanking it open, sliding through, and slamming it behind her. She turned to run, dismayed to find that it wasn't a hallway after all. Instead she was in a small lab of some kind. A table sat in the center, with what looked to be an empty aquarium on top.

On closer examination it proved to be a cage of some kind. Mouse feces littering the bottom. It was hooked to a large machine, gauges and dials with LED readouts shining red and green in the half-shadows of the room. A canister sat on the opposite side, the burnished metal lit up like a Christmas tree with the reflected colors of the machinery around it.

Turning back to the door, she searched for a lock, but there was nothing but the knob. Risking a quick glance through the window, she saw her assailant push the bookshelf aside and reach for his gun.

Moving on adrenaline and instinct, she grabbed the canister, testing its weight, satisfied that it was hefty enough to give the guy a hell of a headache. A face appeared in the window, dark and angry. Mia moved to the wall beside the door, raising the canister, ready to strike.

The door slammed open, the man springing into the room, leading with his gun. Mia swung downward with the canister, the blow landing on his shoulder, just missing his head. His fingers closed around her wrist as he yanked her from her position against the wall.

Still holding the canister, she swung again, this time connecting with his gut. He bent over with a gasp and she ran for the door, but he was faster, grabbing her arm and slinging her against the far wall. Her head slammed against wallboard and she lost her balance, slipping to the floor, the canister landing in her lap.

"You've caused me a lot of trouble," the man said.

"Good." She blinked to clear her vision, recognition finally kicking in. He looked older than the photograph she'd seen. His dark hair was dotted with gray, the creases around his mouth and eyes signaling that he'd clearly seen the other side of sixty. In all honesty he didn't look the part of murderous thug—except for the lethal Walther PPK in his hand. "My life hasn't exactly been a picnic, either, Senator Tucker."

His mouth twitched as he contained a smile. "I wondered if you'd recognize me."

"You look older than the pictures I saw." She shrugged. "But the likeness is there."

"How very astute of you. But then you've proven to be very good at ferreting out information, haven't you?"

"I had a little help."

"From Nicholas Price." He said the name as if it were a curse. "Didn't really do you much good, though, did it? Considering I'm the one with the gun. You know, if you'd just stayed in our facility none of this would have happened."

"If I'd stayed in your facility, I'd be dead." She glared up at him, her brain scrambling to find a way out.

"Which would have made my life a lot simpler. As it is, you've cost the American people one hell of a lot."

"How do you figure that?"

"K-19 has the power to bring our enemies to their knees. And thanks to you and your friends, the program has been set back at least a year."

"After what you did to the people of Cedar Branch, the program should be disbanded!" Her hand closed around the canister, the cold metal comforting.

"*I* didn't do anything. And my colleagues certainly didn't release K-19 on purpose. It was a tragic mistake in calculation—a blown valve that resulted in the explosion that released the toxin."

"With horrifying results. Innocent people were killed, an entire town was destroyed."

"Cedar Branch wasn't a town. It was a bump in the road. A café, a feed store and gas station."

"Owned by human beings. People who didn't deserve to be guinea pigs."

"They were sacrificed for the greater good. If America is going to survive we have to play hardball. And that means we have to have an arsenal capable of annihilating the enemy. It was true in 1945 when Little Boy was dropped on Hiroshima. And it will be true again when K-19 is used to defeat the Arab extremists who dare to threaten the greatest nation on earth. Their isolated acts of aggression are akin to poking a sleeping tiger, Miss Kearney. Sooner or later the animal will awaken, and with a wave of its massive paw, destroy its tormentors."

"Might over right?" She shifted slightly, trying to gauge the best angle for smashing the canister into his shins.

"Might *is* right," he said. "It's been that way for centuries. The strongest always win. And K-19 is my contribution to American supremacy."

"Yours and Kresky's."

"Kresky is nothing more than a means to an end. I needed a front, and Kresky's research arm had already been working with toxins. The scientists were in place. All they needed was the proper inducement."

"Enter Davies."

"You've done your homework." A tiny smile curled at the corner of his mouth, his eyes remaining cold and hard. "Let's just say that Charles Davies and I agree on a number of things. And I find his *connections* to be infinitely valuable when it comes to getting things done. Without him I wouldn't have found you and your cohorts, would I?"

"Who else is involved?" she asked, playing for time. "Hatcher?"

"Only as far as his greed carried him. He wanted to look good for his constituents, and I made that possible. He got his amendment, and I diverted the funding to creating K-19.

"Surely there had to be someone above you. Someone with the power to orchestrate all of this."

"I'm afraid you're underestimating me, my dear. I've spent the whole of my adult life in public service. Made a lot of interesting friends along the way. So you can believe me when I say that there was no need to involve anyone higher up."

"But then how would K-19 have made it into our arsenal? That was the whole point, right?"

"You're speaking past tense," he said, eyes narrowing. "K-19 is anything but. Even with your interference. Unlike your tree-hugging family, the military will be delighted to have a weapon like K-19. It's just a matter of making sure the right people are approached with the idea. And since the research and testing has been accomplished, all that remains is to sell it."

"With a tidy profit going to you."

"I'm not in this for the money, Miss Kearney. K-19 is my triumph. A contribution that will assure my place in history. Think of me as a patriot's patriot. I risked everything to develop this weapon, and I'll be damned if I'm going to let a little slip of a thing like you take it away from me."

"What happens now?" she asked.

"My men finish up out there and then you and I take a little ride."

"So why don't you just shoot me here. Get it over with." She shifted her weight, maintaining her hold on the canister.

"Believe me, if Davies had his way, that's exactly what would happen. But Dr. Waters still believes that understanding why you lived could be a great benefit to our project. Imagine how useful it would be to have an antidote."

"Seems to me like that would only defeat the purpose," she taunted. "I mean, what's the point of having the world's deadliest weapon if there's an antidote?"

"It would mean protection for Americans deploying the weapon. It would also help protect the home front. We're not the only ones working with batrachotoxin. Certain terrorist groups have been working with it for years. We're just trying to even the playing field."

"No. You're trying to eliminate it."

"I don't see a problem with that—do you?" His smile was hollow.

"I guess it depends on how you look at it. There are those who believe that arms races of any kind only lead to increased hostilities."

"Those are the same people who live with their heads in the sand, pretending that the world's problems can be solved with diplomacy and discussion. Unfortunately, history has taught us that when cultures clash, diplomacy rarely wins the day."

"So we develop weapons that will completely destroy the other culture?"

"Better them than us," he said, glancing toward the door with a frown.

"Looking for someone?" she asked.

"Davies should have been here by now." The senator's frown deepened, and his hand tightened on the gun.

"I suspect he might have run into a little trouble." Mia shrugged, using the motion to slide the canister more securely onto her lap.

"I told you, your friends are dead."

"You have a lot of faith in Davies." There was no way she was letting his insinuations dig into her brain. Nick had to be alive. She wouldn't allow herself to consider any other possibility.

"I have faith in numbers. My men outnumber yours— it's as simple as that."

"Nothing is ever really simple, Senator Tucker. If I've learned anything over the past few days, it's that the deeper you look beneath the surface, the more distorted reality becomes."

"Stand up," he ordered, motioning with the Walther.

She rose to her knees, bending forward with her body to obscure his view of the canister. This might be her only chance. Sliding one foot to the floor, she pushed off, rising to her feet, and slammed the canister into his knees.

Tucker's eyes widened in surprise, and he stumbled backward, struggling to maintain his footing. For a moment she thought he'd fall, but then he managed to right himself, anger marring his features. Leveling the gun, he pointed and shot.

There was no time to react.

And there was no pain.

Mia dropped back to the floor, watching as Tucker touched his chest and then frowned down at his bloody fingers. Matt stood in the doorway, his gun leveled on the senator. But it wasn't necessary. The man collapsed to his knees, then fell backward, his surprise still reflected in his eyes.

"Are you all right?" Matt asked, rushing over to pull her to her feet.

"I'm fine," she said, still reeling from the turn of events. She was alive. Tucker was dead. "Where's Nick?"

"He's in the lab. He's been shot again. Same shoulder."

"Oh, my God. Is he okay?"

"He's fine. For the moment just not as ambulatory as I am."

"You shouldn't have left him." Mia frowned, still watching Tucker, not completely convinced that the danger was over.

"Believe me, I didn't have much of a choice. He ordered me to come and get you. I'm not even going to think about what might have happened if I hadn't found you in time."

"Well, you did find me," Mia said. "And I'm grate—" Her words were cut off by the report of a gun.

"Hit the ground," Matt yelled, swiveling to fire in the direction of the sound.

Charles Davies pivoted in the doorway, managing to dodge the bullet. His aim proved more accurate with his second shot. Matt was thrown backward, crashing into the table, then sliding to the floor. Blood poured from a wound at his temple, and Mia started toward him, her only thought to stanch the flow.

"Stay where you are," Davies ordered.

"But he's hurt," she protested.

"That was the general idea." Davies walked over to Tucker, bending to retrieve the Walther. He checked for a pulse, his expression impassive, and then moved on to Matt, careful to keep his gun pointed at Mia.

"Is Matt dead?" she asked, not certain that she wanted to hear the answer.

"No. But he will be soon enough." Davies shrugged. "So all that's left to decide is what I'm going to do with you."

"What about Nick?" The words came of their own volition, her heart twisting as she faced the possibility that he was dead. Hysteria rose in her throat, but she fought against it. If she was going to survive she had to keep her wits about her. Nick would expect that. No matter what the situation.

"Let's just say he's finally out of the game."

"And that's all this is for you, isn't it?" She leaned back against the wall, noticing the canister lying next to her on the floor. "A game. At least Tucker, no matter how misguided, believed he was doing something for his country. *You.* You're nothing more than a hired gun."

"That's not true. At least not completely. I believe in

what the senator was trying to accomplish. K-19 will give us the upper hand we need. Since the cold war our power has been eroding."

"You're talking about the CIA."

"Principally, but the same holds true for all the military-industrial complex. We've been so preoccupied with making sure we do the right thing that we've lost sight of what really matters. Survival of the fittest."

"And you think this new weapon gives the United States the upper hand."

"I know it does. And the man who delivers it will be heralded a savior."

"But that was Tucker's role."

"It was, but now he's dead. So the task falls to me."

"You won't get away with this. You said it yourself—Senator Tucker is dead. Someone is bound to ask questions." For the first time she noticed the lettering on the side of the metal cylinder.

K-19.

She'd been casually throwing around a bottle of death.

"And even if you can explain that away somehow," she continued, working to calm her breathing, "you don't think we were foolish enough to come here on our own, do you? Nick notified his superiors." Actually he hadn't. Matt had sent a time-delayed e-mail—but when it arrived it would be too late. "They'll follow up on us if we don't surface," she said, trying to keep him talking, her gaze shooting between Davies and the canister.

A triggerlike apparatus at the top of the cylinder was meant to hook into the tubing attached to the cage, the glass box a death trap. The adjacent machine was for measuring the vital statistics of the mice trapped inside.

"By superiors, I presume you're speaking of Gordon Armstrong?" Davies laughed. "Amos Ricks will quash any inquiry he might initiate. After all, Nick Price is a traitor. And I can prove it."

"It's all lies."

"Ah, but lies, like everything else in this world, are subject to interpretation. If I twist the story just a little, the truth will actually support the lie."

"You're talking in circles," Mia said, her mind churning. All she needed was a distraction, something to get him to look away.

"Hardly." He shifted, his stance menacing. "All I have to do is bring to light the unfortunate evidence that Price fell for you, hook, line and sinker. And since you were behind the disastrous explosion in Cedar Branch, the poor boy turned to the dark side, so to speak. And when Tucker found you both, along with Nick's misguided sidekick, he confronted you with proof of what you'd done, and you killed him."

"And what? Just disappeared?"

"Unfortunately, no. It seems that although I arrived at the scene too late to save the senator, I did manage to take the three of you out—saving the proverbial day."

"But what about all of this?" She waved a hand at the lab. "How will you explain it?"

"Come on, use your imagination, Ms. Kearney. Nothing happened *here*. I'm in charge of one of the most clandestine divisions of the CIA—all I have to do is move the bodies to a neutral place. Nevada, maybe. You spent enough time chasing around the state."

"But the evidence won't support the facts."

"I'm disappointed. I thought you were smarter than that. Believe me, it's no effort at all to manufacture the necessary corroboration. Most of it was already in motion, anyway. A fail-safe procedure once you escaped. All I have to do is tie up loose ends, and when I'm finished, you'll be blamed for one of the most heinous incidents in American history—and K-19 will continue its production schedule as if nothing at all had happened."

"So why am I still standing here?"

"Protection. I need to get out of here, and just in case one of your boys has any life left in him, or maybe had the chance to call for reinforcements, I figure I can use a get-out-of-jail-free card."

"Me."

"Yes. For some reason you seem to inspire a ridiculous amount of loyalty."

It was a hell of a lot more than loyalty. And it went both ways, but she wasn't going to think about that. The only chance she had was to keep thoughts of Nick and Matt out of her mind. She'd deal with reality, whatever it might be, if she managed to get out of here alive.

From over by the table, Matt groaned, his eyes fluttering open for a second and then closing again. Davies turned toward the sound, shifting on instinct, his gun moving toward the perceived threat.

Mia grabbed the canister, her finger closing on the trigger. Davies swung back, leveling the gun.

"I wouldn't do that," Mia said, holding the canister in front of her, the stenciled label facing Davies. "One little squeeze and it'll all be over."

He flinched, but didn't move the gun. "You're bluffing."

"If you want to take that bet, go right ahead. But think about the bodies you found in Cedar Branch. They didn't go easily."

"You can't be sure you'll live through it again."

"I'd say the odds are pretty good. See, there's a really good chance that somewhere in my distant past, the genetic code was altered. A slight modification that allowed my ancestors to survive exposure to batrachotoxin."

"Put the canister down."

"Or what? You'll shoot me? Not going to happen. See, this canister is rigged for the test chamber over there. When it's attached, the trigger's pulled in—like this." She held up the container and tightened her fingers.

Davies blanched.

"No worries. In order for the K-19 to be released into the cage, the trigger has to be released again. When it's used in conjunction with the cage—" she nodded toward the glass box "—the machine next to it signals the release. But in my case all I have to do is let go. And if you shoot me, well, I'll have no choice but to release the trigger. Muscle reflex." She waved the canister at him, and he took a step back.

"What about Young? He's still alive. You let that thing go, he dies along with me."

"You said it yourself. He's already dying." She had no intention of killing Matt, but Davies couldn't know that for sure. "Give me your gun." She held out her free hand.

"No fucking way," he said, shifting so that his right hand was braced by the left, the gun pointing directly at her heart.

"Then I guess we're stuck here. My grandfather would have called this a Mexican standoff," Mia said with a shrug. "Me, I figure I've got the winning hand. So I'm willing to wait."

NICK PULLED HIMSELF to his feet, shaking off the haze still hovering in his head. Intellectually, he was aware of the fact that his body was going into shock, reacting to the loss of blood, but he couldn't allow nature to hold sway. Not when Mia needed him.

He glanced at his watch, trying to figure out how long he'd been passed out, but the face was shattered, the minute hand bent. Still, he couldn't believe he'd been out too long. The lab was quiet.

Bending to retrieve his gun, he moved forward, stepping over a body as he made his way toward the left side of the room and the doorway where he'd last seen Mia. A second body lay slumped over a lab table. Adding in the man shot in the hall, that was a total of three. All told, Nick had identified four shooters, possibly five. Which meant that Davies was still out there, conceivably with backup.

Keeping low, he worked his way across the room, fighting the pain in his shoulder and left arm. He'd been through worse and lived to tell about it, and he wasn't about to give in now. Turning, he scanned the lab for signs of life. Nothing moved. Back against the wall, he slid forward until he was beside the open door. He waited a beat, then spun into the doorway, gun at the ready.

But the room was empty, shadows obscuring full view.

Edging farther inside, he turned slowly in a circle, searching for some sign that Mia or Matt had been this way. He'd just spotted the open doorway when he heard voices.

Mia. And Davies.

Stepping around a fallen bookcase, he moved next to the door, his back to the wall, trying to assess the situation.

"Give me the gun and this will all be over," Mia was saying, her voice calm and strong.

"Like hell," Davies growled in response. And Nick smiled. If he had to place a bet, he'd take Mia every time. Survival ran in her genes.

Inching forward, he risked detection for a quick view of the second room. Mia had her back to him, holding something in her hands. Davies was facing the door, his gun pointed at Mia. Matt lay against the foot of a table, eyes closed, but Nick was pretty sure he was breathing. A second man was sprawled on the floor near Mia's feet.

Nick pulled back, trying to formulate a plan. Any attempt to enter the room would end with Mia caught in the cross-fire. And Davies would see him before he could manage to get her out of the way. He looked around the room, search-ing for something that might give him the advantage.

"Maybe I should just release the K-19," Mia said. Nick edged closer to the door, heart pounding as the meaning of her words hit home. "End this thing now."

"You'll kill me," Davies said, "but you'll also kill Young. And quite possibly your boyfriend out there."

"You said Nick was dead." Nick could hear the hesita-tion in her voice. The hope.

"I said he looked like he was out of the game. Not exactly the same thing. There's no way to know for sure. So why don't you give me the canister and we'll call it a day."

Nick closed his eyes for a minute, willing her to feel his presence. To know that he was alive. That he was going to figure out how to save her. It was a Hail Mary attempt. Hell, he didn't even believe in things like that. But desperate times…

"Not going to happen," Mia said, the hesitation gone. "Sooner or later someone is bound to come down here. We'll just wait."

Nick sent a silent prayer heavenward. Now all he had to do was figure out how to get into the room. He leaned against the wall, fighting a wave of dizziness. Tipping his head back, he sucked in air, fighting for control, the pain swelling and then retreating. His vision cleared, and he frowned up at the white ceiling tiles above his head. They covered the entire ceiling except for one place near the center of the room. The tile there was different from the others.

Vented.

Walking back across the room to the desk, he climbed on top of it, moving slowly to avoid making any noise. Reaching up, he popped the rectangular vent out of the bracket, the gaping hole above confirming his expectations. A ventilation shaft.

Stowing his gun at the small of his back, he pulled himself upward and into the shaft, ignoring the spiking pain in his shoulder. Crawling forward, he moved along the metal tunnel until he reached the vent that led down to the next room.

It was different from the first one, a Plexiglas plate lining the opening. Rubber insulation surrounded the plate, an electrical locking mechanism located along the right side. The room below was a containment lab, and the Plexiglas was part of a seal that could be activated when toxins were in use.

Fortunately, the lock was open, and it took only a few minutes to remove the insulation and pry the Plexiglas from the vent. Setting it aside, Nick lay on his stomach to peer through the slats in the vent. Davies was standing a couple feet away, back turned, with Mia in front of him, clutching a metal canister. The K-19.

Sliding across the vent, Nick managed to turn around

in the narrow space so that he was facing the same direction as Davies. Holding his breath, he lifted the vent upward, laying it on the floor of the shaft across from him. Below him, Davies didn't budge, his weapon still pointed at Mia.

But Mia had seen the vent move, her eyes widening just slightly as he'd removed the tile. Leaning down into the opening, he risked dipping his head into the room long enough for Mia to see him, her chin tipping upward in recognition.

Pulling on all his remaining strength, Nick reached for the far side of the vent and swung down into the room, his feet connecting with Davies's head. The man stumbled forward, the gun flying out of his hand.

Nick dropped to the ground, covering the distance between them in a matter of seconds. The other man swung around, clearly confused, and Nick slammed a fist into the side of his head, reaching back with his other hand for his gun.

Davies fell to one knee, pulled a Walther and then rolled to his feet, firing. Nick dodged the bullet, centering his gun, but before he could shoot, Mia, with a look of supreme satisfaction, beaned Davies with the K-19 canister.

The man hit the floor, but managed to maintain his balance, shifting to point the gun at Mia. Working on adrenaline and instinct, Nick fired, his bullet hitting the mark. Davies dropped to the floor, his lifeless eyes staring at the open vent above him.

"Oh, God, Nick…"

He spun around, his heart in his throat. He'd thought that Davies's shot had gone wide, but Mia's voice held a note of sheer terror. His gaze raked over her, looking for some sign that she'd been shot, but instead her eyes were glued to the canister she held in front of her.

"I'm sorry," she whispered, lifting her eyes to meet his. "I let go of the trigger when I swung at Davies."

If he'd ever doubted the fact that she loved him, there was no way to doubt it now. Her face was ashen, her lips drawn tight with fear, her eyes beseeching him to forgive her.

He stared down at the tank and reflexively held his breath, knowing that it was already too late. "It's okay," he said, finding words at last.

She shook her head, tears filling her eyes. "I love you. I would never ever…" She trailed off, her gaze falling back to the open cylinder.

"I know, sweetheart. I know. " He crossed the room and she dropped the tank, falling into his arms. They sank to the ground, Mia's breathing coming in gasps. "I love you," Nick whispered, stroking her hair. "I love you."

Silence surrounded them, minutes ticking by, and then behind them something moved.

Nick grabbed his gun, swinging around, ready to face whatever new threat awaited. But instead of an enemy, it was Matt. He was propped against the lab table, holding the canister, his shirt streaked with blood.

"If you're waiting to die, it's not going to happen. At least not today." His friend held up the canister. "Look at the gauge. It's empty. The goddamn thing was empty."

Mia reached out and touched the tank, then burst into hysterical laughter. "I threatened Davies with nothing more than an empty tank? Oh, my God, I thought I'd killed us all." Tears streamed down her cheeks as she cupped Nick's face in her hands. "You're okay. You're okay," she repeated, as if trying to convince herself it was true.

For a moment they stood, gazes locked, as if they were memorizing each other's faces. And then he crushed her to him, his mouth on hers, reveling in the feel of her body against his—warm and alive.

"Um, guys?" Matt said, clearing his throat for emphasis. "Wounded friend here?"

Mia pulled away, rushing to Matt's side, while Nick checked the bodies. Davies was dead. He bent to retrieve the Walther and then rolled the second man over, not particularly surprised that it was Tucker. The senator had almost succeeded in creating a weapon that would have changed the face of the world, but in the end the monster had destroyed the master.

"How you doing?" Nick asked Matt, turning his back on Tucker.

"Better now that I know the tank was empty. Thought for a minute there our number was up," his friend said. "Nice of you to show. You almost missed the party."

"I got a little tied up." He shrugged. "But there was no need to worry. Mia had everything under control."

"What can I say," she said, coming over to nestle again in the warmth of his arms. "I learned from the best."

Matt struggled to his feet, using a cloth to blot the blood from his forehead. "Seems like now might be a good time to call Gordon? Someone has to clean up this mess."

Nick nodded as he pulled Mia closer into his embrace, content for the moment just to feel her breathing, the world suddenly seeming full of endless possibility.

EPILOGUE

Seven months later

THE DAY WAS GRAY and blustery, traces of snow filling the crevices and hollows of the still-blackened ground that had served as a funeral pyre. The press were clustered around the monument, the names of each of the casualties at Cedar Branch preserved forever in brass and bronze— a permanent reminder of man's innate ability to twist reality to fit his own warped view.

Mia stood back from the crowd, watching as the governor dedicated her artwork to the memory of her friends, Nick's arm warm around her shoulders. Matt stood to one side, Ellis Brewster on the other, both of them ready to ward off overly eager photographers and newshounds.

It seemed that although she'd lost one family, she'd gained another. The tenacity of life nowhere more evident than at this moment here in Cedar Branch.

"Your grandfather would have been proud of you," Ellis said, his craggy face lighting with a smile. "Your momma, too."

Mia nodded, tears welling.

The metal sculpture soared upward like a flame, the camera lights giving it an otherworldly glow. At first, she'd declined the invitation to create the memorial, her loss too fresh, the pain too overwhelming. But Nick had been right—with a little time and distance she'd come to realize it was an important part of her healing, each curve and line a loving testament to the people she'd lost.

The days following the shootout at Biosphere had been overwhelming. Interrogations and debriefings, medical probing and genetic testing. Government officials and civilians alike fascinated by her seemingly miraculous survival. Nick had been with her every step, bullying and cajoling their way through the minefield that had become her life. As yet, there was nothing conclusive. Perhaps there never would be. But at least her part in the story was over. Today marking the final chapter. The last word.

Davies and Tucker were dead. Walter Hatcher was in jail, awaiting trial. Jameson Kresky had fled to Africa, but his days of freedom were numbered, extradition proceedings already begun. The facility in Montana had been destroyed, along with the remaining supply of K-19.

The government had turned on itself, investigations and hearings probing to uncover anyone else who had been a part of Tucker's conspiracy. S&C had been disbanded, CIA Director Harry Norton disgraced and unemployed. Amos Ricks had fared better, still heading Homeland Security—but he owed his reprieve to Nick, Matt and their boss, Gordon Armstrong.

Nick's name had been cleared. And he and Matt had been reinstated at Homeland Security. But although Matt had reclaimed his position, Nick had declined, agreeing instead to act as a consultant, using his expertise to advise other agents as they worked to stem the tide of terrorism threatening the United States.

Perhaps most importantly, Nick and his mother were working to bridge the gulf between them. It wouldn't be an easy road, but the end result would be well worth the effort. Family was everything, and somewhere up there, Mia knew Katie was smiling.

The governor finished his speech, the crowd breaking into respectful applause. Mia fought back her tears. The physical wounds had healed. The nightmares receded. But she'd never forget. Here on this hallowed ground, her friends had breathed their last breaths, said their last words, and passed on from this world to the next.

Patrick and Nancy. Joe and Betty. Wilson and Carson. The residents of Cedar Branch.

"They'd be happy for you," Nick said, his arm tightening around her.

"I know." She nodded, touching the gold wedding band on her finger. Out of all the evil—all the pain—something wonderful had been born. It didn't change the reality of what had happened. Nothing could do that. But she was wise enough to recognize just how precious the gift was.

"I love you, Mia," Nick said, his fingers lacing with hers.

"I love you, too," she whispered, her eyes on the distant gray of the mountains, a ring of spruce and pine serving as sentries—watching over the remnants of what had once been Cedar Branch. And there, in a bank of ice and snow, a single yellow crocus spread its golden petals—a brave new beginning built on the ashes of the past.

REQUEST YOUR
FREE BOOKS!

2 FREE NOVELS
FROM THE ROMANCE/SUSPENSE
COLLECTION PLUS 2 FREE GIFTS!

YES! Please send me 2 FREE novels from the Romance/Suspense Collection and my 2 FREE gifts. After receiving them, if I don't wish to receive any more books, I can return the shipping statement marked "cancel." If I don't cancel, I will receive 4 brand-new novels every month and be billed just $5.49 per book in the U.S., or $5.99 per book in Canada, plus 25¢ shipping and handling per book plus applicable taxes, if any*. That's a savings of at least 20% off the cover price! I understand that accepting the 2 free books and gifts places me under no obligation to buy anything. I can always return a shipment and cancel at any time. Even if I never buy another book from the Reader Service, the two free books and gifts are mine to keep forever.

185 MDN EF5Y   385 MDN EF6C

Name _____ (PLEASE PRINT) _____

Address _____ Apt. # _____

City _____ State/Prov. _____ Zip/Postal Code _____

Signature (if under 18, a parent or guardian must sign)

Mail to **The Reader Service:**
IN U.S.A.: P.O. Box 1867, Buffalo, NY 14240-1867
IN CANADA: P.O. Box 609, Fort Erie, Ontario L2A 5X3

Not valid to current subscribers to the Romance Collection,
the Suspense Collection or the Romance/Suspense Collection.

Want to try two free books from another line?
Call 1-800-873-8635 or visit www.morefreebooks.com.

* Terms and prices subject to change without notice. NY residents add applicable sales tax. Canadian residents will be charged applicable provincial taxes and GST. This offer is limited to one order per household. All orders subject to approval. Credit or debit balances in a customer's account(s) may be offset by any other outstanding balance owed by or to the customer. Please allow 4 to 6 weeks for delivery.

Your Privacy: Harlequin is committed to protecting your privacy. Our Privacy Policy is available online at www.eHarlequin.com or upon request from the Reader Service. From time to time we make our lists of customers available to reputable firms who may have a product or service of interest to you. If you would prefer we not share your name and address, please check here. ☐

BOB07

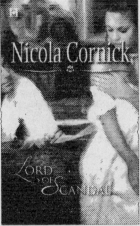

DEE DAVIS

77163	EYE OF THE STORM	__ $5.99 U.S.	__ $6.99 CAN.
77060	EXPOSURE	__ $5.99 U.S.	__ $6.99 CAN.
77048	ENIGMA	__ $5.99 U.S.	__ $6.99 CAN.
77036	ENDGAME	__ $6.50 U.S.	__ $7.99 CAN.

(limited quantities available)

TOTAL AMOUNT	$ _____
POSTAGE & HANDLING	$ _____
($1.00 FOR 1 BOOK, 50¢ for each additional)	
APPLICABLE TAXES*	$ _____
TOTAL PAYABLE	$ _____

(check or money order—please do not send cash)

To order, complete this form and send it, along with a check or money order for the total above, payable to HQN Books, to: **In the U.S.:** 3010 Walden Avenue, P.O. Box 9077, Buffalo, NY 14269-9077; **In Canada:** P.O. Box 636, Fort Erie, Ontario, L2A 5X3.

Name: _____
Address: _____ City: _____
State/Prov.: _____ Zip/Postal Code: _____
Account Number (if applicable): _____

075 CSAS

*New York residents remit applicable sales taxes.
*Canadian residents remit applicable GST and provincial taxes.

HQN™

We *are* romance™

www.HQNBooks.com

PHDD0607BL